STEPHANIE

THE CHOSEN UNION

The Fount Book 3

Syafant Press

Syafant Press

New York, New York

Copyright © 2020 Stephanie Fazio.

All rights reserved. No part of this book may be reproduced in any form or by any electronic or mechanical means including information storage and retrieval systems, without permission in writing from the author. The only exception is by a reviewer who may quote short excerpts in a review.

Cover designed by Keith Tarrier

This book is a work of fiction. Names, characters, places, and incidents either are the product of the author's imagination or are used fictionally, and any resemblance to actual persons, living or dead, business establishments, events, or locales is entirely coincidental.

Stephanie Fazio

Visit www.StephanieFazio.com

Printed in the United States of America
First Printing: May 2020

Library of Congress Control Number: 2020905330

ISBN 978-1-951572-03-7

To my readers

PROLOGUE

*B*REAKING NEWS. *Aircraft carrier sunk off the Gulf of Mexico.*
 *Alien attack! Residents fear for their lives as blue lightning and tidal waves pummel Corpus Christi.

*Exclusive interview with Texas farmers who fought the aliens, coming up after this commercial break.

*US Navy mobilized to strike back.

*Watch out, aliens. You messed with Texas.

The reporter adjusted her microphone and did a quick check to ensure her makeup wasn't melting in the brutal Texas heat. There was a slight tremor in her hand as she reviewed her notes once more. She nodded to her cameraman.

"Good evening," she began. "Right now, we're following reports of an alien invasion.

"It happened just after six in the evening, local time here in Texas. The situation is still developing, but we already have reports of at least twenty deaths."

The reporter took a breath as the camera shifted to a young woman with badly-bleached curls and a neon swimsuit cover.

"I'm here with Emma Parks, who was on a nearby party cruise for her sister's bachelorette party. Emma, can you tell us what you saw?"

"It was nuts." Emma bent down until her lips almost brushed the mic. "It was, like, a really nice day, but then we saw tons of lightning. I don't know where it came from.

"Then, the waves got huge. Like *huge*. There were all these people jumping off that giant military boat and swimming. And then the boat just sunk. I've never seen anything more terrifying." She widened her eyes for the camera. And then she popped her gum.

"Wow, thanks for that, Emma." The reporter walked to the end of the pier, where a still-dripping wet soldier was huddled under an emergency foil blanket.

"Next, we'll hear from Petty Officer Jonathan Zuke, who managed to escape the sinking aircraft carrier and swim to shore. Petty Officer Zuke, can you tell us what you experienced?"

Zuke cleared his throat. "Yes, ma'am. I was doin' ship preservation on the hanger deck when those…people showed up." He shivered, making the foil blanket crinkle. "I ain't never seen nothin' like it before. They looked like humans, but they had weapons that…glowed blue. And they just moved so fast." He swallowed, his eyes darting around. "I saw one of 'em disappear into thin air…like magic."

He blinked several times, like he was doubting his own sanity. He cast another glance over at the frothing water, which was all that remained of the aircraft carrier.

Sirens wailed and helicopters buzzed.

"Petty Officer Zuke, have you ever heard of an aircraft carrier sinking like this?"

"No, ma'am." The man shook his head slowly. "A ship that big should never have sunk."

At that moment, the farmer who had been waiting for his turn to be interviewed stepped in front of the camera.

"It was goddamn alien magic, that's what it was!" he yelled.

Wincing at the curse, the reporter turned her attention on the farmer.

"We're hearing from—"

"I tried to tell ya'll," the farmer drawled, plucking the toothpick out of his mouth and pointing it at the camera. "I fought the aliens myself. They can't be killed by reg'lar guns, and they're gonna take over. We gotta fight. We gotta kill 'em before they kill us. We gotta save 'merica!"

"Rescue crews are on the scene now," the reporter cut in. "We hope to have a casualty report soon. In the meantime, authorities are asking locals to stay indoors while they search for survivors and answers.

"Now, we'll hear from some extraterrestrial linguists who are standing by to find out what the aliens want."

Already, all of the major news networks were gathering expert witnesses to try to explain the inexplicable.

Mechanical engineers had diagrams and blueprints that proved how an aircraft carrier shouldn't be able to sink so quickly. Meteorologists were discussing the impossible weather patterns in the area immediately surrounding the aircraft carrier. Scientists were brought on air to debate the possibility of a solar flare or other natural phenomenon that might provide insight into these strange occurrences.

Psychiatrists and grief counselors were on standby for the witnesses and survivors.

Alien enthusiasts were already crowding the pier. They held signs that said, "Come in Peace" and "Welcome to Earth."

The surrounding roads were clogged with vehicles going and coming. Homeland Security elevated the country's terrorist alert level to red.

By the day's end, all of the speculation, terror, and excitement boiled down to a single, irrefutable fact. Aliens were real. And they had come to Earth.

CHAPTER 1

ADDY

Addy was choking on blood and tears. The coppery tang mixed with salty wetness. The air was warm, but she felt so cold. Crushed seashells bit into her knees as the water lapped at her soaked sneakers.

She hardly noticed.

She looked down at the blackened flesh over Tol's heart. Smoke was still wisping up from the sticky mess of melted fabric, burnt skin, and blood.

So much blood.

Addy couldn't understand how he was the one with that hideous wound, when it felt like her insides were the ones being shredded. It was like someone had reached inside her and ripped out her heart.

Her sobs tore through the quiet.

"Tol." His name croaked out of her. Her throat felt like it was lined with jagged glass.

He was still inhumanly beautiful, despite his wounds. There was a gash across his forehead and his lip was split.

She touched his cheek, leaving behind two streaks of fresh blood. Addy had been gripping her shears so tightly they'd cut into her flesh.

"My Tol."

Why did you do it? she wanted to scream at him.

She knew the answer. The Supernal had been about to kill her. Tol had taken the blow that was meant for her. He'd done it because he loved her the same way she loved him.

Some part of her mind was aware of the helicopter landing nearby. It sent sand spraying all around her. She was aware of the deafening roar of the rotor. She heard her friends' voices and cries as they surrounded her.

Addy didn't look at them. Their words were a meaningless drone. All she saw was Tol.

She lay her head down on him...carefully, like she was afraid of making his wounds worse.

It didn't matter now. Nothing mattered anymore. Tol was gone.

Surrounded by the sickly scent of charred flesh and fresh blood, Addy wept.

Wait.

Addy's breath caught as she felt a faint tremor beneath her cheek. A few seconds later, she saw a barely-visible flutter at his throat.

Tol was alive.

"He's breathing!" she screeched in a voice that was unrecognizable. She didn't look away from Tol. "Nira, Gerth, someone!"

Nira fell to her knees beside Addy and started ripping Tol's shirt away. She brushed her fingers down the skin on either side of his gaping wound. Tol didn't shiver or flinch. He didn't react at all.

Nira reached for Tol's wrist and felt for a pulse.

"See?!" Addy demanded, clutching Nira's arm and giving the other girl a shake. "He's alive. You just have to do something. Bandage him...or...." *Something.*

"Ads, no one could survive that."

Addy felt Fred's hands on her shoulders. She heard the apology in his voice. She ignored him.

"You're a doctor," Addy begged Nira. "He's still breathing. There has to be something you can do."

"I—" Nira looked down at Tol. "The only explanation that makes sense is that Tol's connection to Olivia must be keeping him alive."

"If that's true, then what does he need to heal?" Addy asked Nira.

Her mind was racing. Tol was alive, and that meant all she had to do was keep him that way.

A tear slid down Nira's face, but Addy wasn't interested in grieving anymore. All she cared about now were solutions.

"The wound was created with the Supernal's magic," Nira whispered. "So Source might be able to heal him. Maybe."

Addy turned from side to side. Gerth was crouching beside her. His chest heaved from his silent sobs.

"Source," Addy commanded. "Who has some?"

It had gotten dark out some time ago, but their Hazes illuminated the despair on everyone's faces. Nira, Gerth, and Jaxon shook their heads.

"Here." A vial—Erikir's—was tossed through the air.

Addy caught it one-handed, unstopped the vial, and poured the entirety of its contents between Tol's lips. Nira tipped Tol's head up, making sure none of the precious liquid escaped.

Everyone went silent as they watched the liquid pass down Tol's throat. One second passed. Two. Three.

Tol's Haze flickered back to life. It was dim, but it was there. Addy knew she wasn't imagining the way the wound over his heart closed up just a little.

A ragged cry escaped from Addy.

"It's working," Nira breathed.

"More," Addy shouted, holding out a hand behind her without tearing her eyes away from Tol.

When no vial was placed on her palm, she looked around. The expressions on her friends' faces told her everything she needed to know. There was no more Source.

Jaxon didn't have a necklace, and Fred wouldn't have one. Erikir's was lying beside her in the sand, empty. Gerth and Nira....

Addy looked at their vials. They were mostly empty, but they hadn't been filled with Source. The red stain from Addy's own blood coated the clear walls of the vial.

Her blood.

Addy dug the point of her garden shears into the smooth skin at her wrist.

"Ads, what the hell are you doin'?" Fred gasped.

"I have Source in my blood." *And Tol can have it all.*

"You can't." Gerth's voice was as raw as her own. "Even if it worked, you'd contaminate him. He wouldn't be able to blood marry you or anyone else."

"Like I care about that now," Addy snarled.

"You can't," Gerth said again, his gaze fixed on Addy as tears slid down his cheeks. "Once Tol is…gone…Erikir will be the Chosen prince. He'll be able to do the blood marriage." Gerth scrubbed a hand across his red eyes. "But if Tol ingests your blood and lives, no one will be able to fulfill the Celestial's pronouncement. Our people will be doomed."

Addy didn't care. This was Tol's life.

Blood welled to the surface of her wrist.

Gerth grabbed her arm.

"Don't," he said, his voice hollow. "This is the only way to save our people."

"By letting him die?" Addy's voice cracked.

Gerth's tears were falling faster, but he nodded. "Tol wouldn't trade his life for everyone else's immortality."

Addy knew Gerth was right. Tol might have been willing to do almost anything for a future with her, but he wouldn't be willing to sacrifice his people's lives. He cared deeply about them and saw it as his responsibility to save them. If she took away his people's future, he'd never forgive her.

And yet, the thought of spending eternity without Tol was too horrible to even consider. She had barely wrapped her mind around her own immortality, but the thought of living it without Tol was unbearable.

Her shoulders shook with the emotions she couldn't contain. She tipped her head back and screamed.

"Let him go," Gerth choked. "We have to let him go."

He's right, her brain said.

Her heart rebelled.

"I can't."

Addy cared about Tol's people, but compared to his life, they were nothing.

She wrenched her wrist out of Gerth's grip and held it over Tol's lips.

"No." Nira shoved Addy. The blood gathering on Addy's wrist dripped onto the sand. "My aunts' lives depend on the blood marriage. All of our people are depending on the blood marriage."

"Tol wouldn't want this," Gerth whispered.

He and Tol were as much like brothers as Addy and Livy were sisters. She knew his heart was breaking just like hers.

"Do it, Addy." The words came from Erikir. He was behind her, and she turned to him for the first time. His eyes were red, and tears were tracking through the dirt streaked across his face.

Horror washed over Addy anew when she caught sight of her twin in Erikir's arms. Addy had been so focused on Tol, she hadn't even thought about Livy.

Livy looked so small in Erikir's arms. Her face was drained of color. Her Haze was dim, but it was there. Addy could see the tiny flutter of her eyelashes.

Addy turned her attention back to Tol. For her, there simply wasn't a choice. This was the man Addy loved most in the world—in any world. She would sacrifice anything for him. Even if it meant the deaths of hundreds. Even if Tol would never forgive her.

"Addy, no," Gerth begged.

"Don't try to stop me," Addy told Gerth in a savage voice. She spared Nira a glance. "Same for you."

She blocked out Gerth's hoarse shouts and Nira's shrieking curses. Fred wrapped his arms around Nira, holding her as she reached out to claw at Addy with her long nails. Jaxon hauled Gerth back as he continued to plead with her.

Calming the tremor in her hand, Addy gouged a deeper hole in her skin. Then, she lowered her wrist to Tol's lips.

CHAPTER 2

TOL

*G*ods, *he hurt.*

Tol's throat was raw. His chest was on fire. His body spasmed as he coughed.

"Tol?"

He blinked against the light of her Haze. Her sunset hair hung like a curtain as she knelt over him. Her green eyes were full of pain and fear. She looked haunted.

"Addy." It came out as a whisper.

The moment he spoke her name, all of his memories came rushing back.

He remembered fighting the Forsaken on the aircraft carrier's deck. He remembered the ball of magic he and Olivia had been creating to end the Supernal. He remembered abandoning their weapon when he realized the Supernal was about to kill Addy.

The blue lightning bolt. Falling over the edge of the ship. Blackness.

The sun had been setting before. Now, it was completely dark. Tol had no idea how much time had passed.

"How am I alive?"

Addy was crying. Her whole body shook as she covered her face with her hands.

"I'm sorry," she sobbed. "Tol, I had to. I'm sorry."

Seeing her in so much agony gutted him. All that mattered was fixing whatever it was that was tearing her apart. He could get his answers later.

"It's okay." He reached up, wincing at how the motion made his chest feel like it was being torn open. He brushed his fingers across her cheek. "Everything's going to be okay."

He had no idea what kind of miracle had kept the Supernal's magic—and his fall from the top deck of the aircraft carrier—from killing him. He wouldn't question it now, though. He was alive, and he had Addy. They'd sort everything else out. Together.

He felt his chest knitting back together. The pain was still there, but it was bearable. When he glanced down, he saw his bloody and burnt shirt had been torn down the center. There was an ugly zig-zagging wound over his heart, but it wasn't as bad as it should have been. He winced at the memory of that lightning bolt entering his flesh.

How was he alive?

He wasn't just alive. The pain was seeping out of his wound, and the heavy fog was lifting from his mind.

"Addy." Tol reached for her.

"I'm so sorry," she said again. Her whole body was convulsing with the force of her crying. Tol had never seen her like this.

"Don't be sorry," he told his beautiful, blood-spattered warrior goddess. "Kiss me."

The whole world spun, but somehow, he managed to sit up. He leaned heavily on his prosthesis, which was as mangled and broken as the rest of him. The fingers were melted and warped.

His parents wouldn't be pleased.

"Mate."

Tol felt a grin split his battered face at the sound of Gerth's voice.

"I'm alright," he said. But when he met Gerth's eyes, they were as full of misery as Addy's.

Something about all of this wasn't right. Tol's brain was too muddled to make sense of it, but as he looked from Addy to Gerth to Nira, he knew something terrible had happened.

"What's wrong?" he asked, his whole body tensing.

No one answered. He studied Addy more carefully.

"You're hurt," he said, reaching for her. The fingers of her left hand were crooked and swollen. Fresh blood was streaming down her forearm.

She flinched away from him.

"I had to," Addy said. She had stopped crying, but she had a faraway look that was somehow worse. She looked empty.

"Someone tell me what in the two hells is going on," Tol ordered.

Jaxon was the one who finally spoke. "You were going to die, so Addy used her blood to bring you back to life."

Tol blinked. He let the words rattle around in his skull for several seconds. He let their meaning settle in.

He looked at the gash on Addy's forearm. He wiped a hand over his lips and stared down at his fingers. They were red with blood. *Addy's blood.*

A cold knot of dread settled in the pit of his stomach. He forgot about the fiery pain in his chest. He forgot about his other wounds.

Tol stared at Addy as horror gripped his chest.

He'd drunk her blood, and that meant he couldn't blood marry. He wouldn't be able to do his part to save the Chosen. So long as he lived, his people would die.

"How could you?"

Addy wrapped her arms around herself. "I couldn't lose you," she whispered.

"No." Tol shook his head as the impossible truth sunk in.

Giving his life for Addy was one thing. But letting the rest of his people die because of his love for her? No.

She'd betrayed him. She'd done it out of love, but she'd put him in an impossible position.

No, not impossible.

There was still a way for Tol to salvage this disaster.

The thought of taking his own life had him fighting down a surge of nausea. He hadn't thought twice about taking a death blow meant for Addy. But slashing open his own veins and watching his life drain out into the sand....

Could he do it?

He had to.

"Give me those." Tol held out his hand for the only weapon in sight—Addy's shears.

Addy's eyes bulged when she understood what he meant to do. She scrambled back, but he wrapped an arm around her, drawing her to him. She didn't resist his hold, but she kept her hands fisted around her shears.

"I love you," she cried, burying her face against his neck. "Please don't do this."

A thickness filled Tol's throat.

"I love you, too," he told her.

Gods, it was the truth. He wanted to spend an eternity loving her.

That was when he remembered.

"Olivia," he said, as yet another horrible truth came rushing back to him.

The bullet heading for Erikir…Olivia stopping time…Olivia using the Celestial's magic to push the bullet off course.

Olivia choosing to become the Celestial's Fount. For eternity.

Tol swallowed. Then, he met Addy's heartbroken gaze.

"Your sister chose to keep the Celestial's powers to save Erikir's life. Even if you hadn't…done what you did…we would never be together."

The look on Addy's face mirrored his despair.

They all turned to look at Olivia. She was still unconscious, but her lips were moving as she twitched restlessly in whatever dream held her in its grasp. Her face was white as a sheet.

"When I'm gone, Erikir will be the heir to the Chosen throne," Tol said. He kept his eyes fixed on the ground so he wouldn't have to see Addy's expression. "He and Olivia will be able to have the blood marriage and save our people." He forced himself to meet Addy's stare. "But to do that, I need to be dead."

"Please," Addy whispered.

"Don't do this," Erikir told him. "We'll figure something out."

Tol barely spared his cousin a glance. He wasn't interested in prolonging the inevitable.

"Tol." Gerth's voice broke.

When Tol looked at him, he saw the truth reflected on Gerth's face. If there was any other option, Gerth would have thought of it. The tears he saw in his best mate's eyes confirmed what Tol already knew. The only path forward for his people began with Tol's death.

They both turned to Jaxon, who held out one of his half-moon blades in offering to Tol.

Addy lunged for the weapon, but Tol was closer to Jaxon.

"I will Influence you," Tol warned her before she could grab the weapon.

"I need you," Addy gasped. "I can't live without you."

"You can." Tol's voice broke. His strength was failing him, and if he didn't do this soon, he'd lose his nerve.

"You know me." He ducked his head until she met his gaze. "You know I can't live like this. Not when it means the rest of my people will die."

"We'll figure something out," Addy said. "We'll—"

"There is nothing else." He pulled her closer. "I made my choice, and I'm not sorry for it. I'm glad I got time to say goodbye."

He pressed his lips to hers, keeping the weapon behind him where she wouldn't be able to take it. She tasted like blood and tears.

He broke the kiss.

"Look away," he whispered.

His hand shook only a little as he raised the half-moon blade. In one quick move, he slashed it across his throat.

CHAPTER 3

OLIVIA

Addy's scream ripped through the quiet, shocking Olivia into wakefulness.

Her twin was hurt. Olivia had to help her. Except, when she tried to move, a heavy grogginess fought to drag her back down into oblivion.

As Olivia's body lay in unconsciousness, her mind had been filled with the Celestial's voice. She didn't know how much time had passed.

Olivia felt wrong. No, not wrong…she felt like something was missing.

"Olivia."

She opened her eyes to see Erikir. It was his arms cradling her, his warmth surrounding her.

"Gods," he said on a ragged sigh. "You're alright. I was so worried—"

Addy screamed again. The sound was filled with such agony that Olivia thought her own heart would break.

Too weak to stand, Olivia freed herself from Erikir's arms and crawled to her sister. She didn't care how pathetic it looked. All she cared about was that her twin was suffering.

She got to Addy just as Tol was pushing himself upright. He was kneeling on the sand and holding one of Jaxon's blades in his right hand. Blood dripped from the sharpened edge of the blade and disappeared into the sand. A muffled cry escaped Olivia's lips when her eyes found the source of the blood. There was a long slash across Tol's neck.

As she watched in dumbstruck panic, the skin around his wound sealed back together.

Was she hallucinating? Was all of this some vision instead of reality?

"What the hells?" Tol's voice was raspy and thin.

With a jolt, Olivia understood the emptiness she hadn't been able to pinpoint before. Tol was no longer in her head. She couldn't hear his thoughts or sense his emotions.

"Oh gods." Nira covered her face with her hands as an anguished sound tore through her.

"You're still alive." Gerth reached out a tentative hand toward Tol before pulling it back. "You're alive."

Addy, who had her arms wrapped around her torso like she was trying to warm herself, seemed beyond words.

"How is this possible?" Tol demanded.

"Addy's blood," Gerth said in a hoarse voice. "It's stronger than pure Source. That, combined with your strength as the Chosen prince, must be why you can't..." he trailed off.

...die.

Olivia heard the unspoken word in her mind. More thoughts filled her head. They were coming from Gerth and Nira, whose emotions were a whirlwind of grief and terror.

...can't blood marry the Fount if he's contaminated with Addy's blood.

...if Tol can't die, the rest of our people will.

Their thoughts struck Olivia with the force of a physical blow. She remembered the choice she'd made. She recalled how, in her moment of greatest need, she'd kept the Celestial's powers to save Erikir's life rather than transfer them to Addy. That meant that she could never relinquish her role as the Fount, and that she would need to blood marry the Chosen prince in order to save his people.

Not his people, she reminded herself. *Her people.*

The Chosen were hers now, because she was the Fount. The Chosen were hers to protect. They were hers to save.

She had felt a strange protectiveness over the Chosen growing inside her over the past weeks. Now that she had fully embraced the Celestial's powers, those feelings were stronger than ever before.

"I have to die." A cornered wild animal look filled Tol's eyes. "It's the only way."

Tol glanced down at the wound in his chest, the one that should have killed him. It looked painful rather than life-threatening.

"What do I do?" he whispered. For some reason, Tol's panicked gaze found Olivia's.

Olivia felt tears burn her throat.

The vision she'd seen over and over for the last few weeks, of Addy sobbing on a shore, was playing out before her. Olivia had done everything she could to give Addy and Tol the happiness they deserved. In the end, none of it had mattered. Olivia had chosen to become the Fount for eternity.

"Maybe there's another way," Olivia said, almost to herself.

"Haven't you done enough?" Addy snapped, her green eyes blazing with anger and betrayal. "If you hadn't wasted your magic on the weasel," she glared daggers at Erikir before turning back to Olivia, "we wouldn't be in this position right now."

Olivia flinched back. Her sister had never spoken to her that way before. Addy had never before looked at Olivia with something like loathing.

Olivia wanted to shrink into an invisible ball. *I'm sorry, I'm sorry, I'm sorry!* she wanted to chant. There was no point in apologizing for something she couldn't undo—wouldn't undo, even if she could.

Her stomach turned over.

She couldn't stand that she had caused the broken look on her sister's face. And yet, she'd made the only decision she could make.

There had to be some way to fix this.

Olivia forced herself to meet Addy's challenging stare. "If we talk to the Celestial, maybe—"

"We don't have time for more guesswork," Tol said, his voice heavy with defeat. "Our people are out of time."

THE CHOSEN UNION

"We may not need to guess," Olivia said, her confidence rising as her strength returned.

She closed her eyes and let her consciousness sink back into the place it had been a few minutes ago.

Before, she never would have been able to reach out across worlds and connect with another mind. But everything was different now. She was no longer the timid, cautious girl who retreated to quiet corners with a book. She was the savior of the Chosen race. She wouldn't fail them.

As soon as she needed her magic, it was there. The rippling, colorful strands organized themselves in her mind. A narrow beam of light took shape in the distance.

Celestial? she thought.

Fount.

A surge of strength went through her at the sound of the Celestial's voice. It was like a kind of homecoming. Something inside Olivia sighed in relief.

We were just wondering....

Minutes later, she opened her eyes.

"Livy?" Addy asked. She was clutching her garden shears with so much force her fingers had gone white.

Olivia looked at Tol, whose gaze was boring into her.

"There might be a way for you to..." Olivia paused, trying to bring the Celestial's exact words to the surface, "purify your blood."

She didn't say what was achingly obvious to all of them. The Celestial hadn't been clear on the price Tol would need to pay to remove all traces of Addy from his blood. Whatever it was, it might very well destroy him.

Olivia continued, "The Celestial said if this is what you want, you have to go to Vitaquias and bargain directly with the gods."

It sounded like such a pathetic offering.

Why couldn't my life have been the price needed for Addy and Tol's happiness?

Olivia forced out the rest of the words, even though they felt like hot coals burrowing into her chest. "The Celestial said that if you can convince the gods to purge your blood, then you'll be able to blood marry...me."

For several seconds, no one spoke.

"I'm sorry, Olivia," Tol said roughly. Disgust twisted his mouth, and even though Olivia knew it wasn't revulsion at her, it made her want to shrink away from him. "I know you don't want this any more than I do."

Olivia let out a jagged sigh. "It's the price we have to pay for saving our people, right?" She forced a brave expression on her face.

Tol didn't look at her when he asked, "If I can...purge my blood, will you agree to bind yourself to me?"

Olivia had to resist the absurd impulse to laugh. She'd never imagined what it would feel like to be proposed to, but if she had, she wouldn't have pictured this. Tol looked like he'd rather die than be with her.

"Yes," she said simply, because there was nothing else to say.

"I have to do this," Tol told Addy. There was apology and desperation in his voice. "I vowed to save my people, and I couldn't live with myself if I failed them."

"Let me come to Vitaquias with you," Addy said in a whisper.

Tol shook his head. "It'll only make things harder, in the end."

Olivia's heart twisted.

She glanced at Erikir. The anger he usually hid behind was nowhere to be seen. He looked like he was going to be sick.

Whatever she'd had with Erikir no longer mattered. Just as Tol was distancing himself from Addy, Olivia needed to accept the consequences of her decision. She couldn't let herself think about what might have been between her and Erikir if she'd been free to love whomever she chose.

All at once, Olivia's thoughts slid away. Everything around her disappeared.

"Liv?" Fred called from somewhere far away. "Your eyes are turning silver...."

She felt the black veil being pulled over her sight. And then she was inside a vision.

She had never been to London, but she recognized Big Ben and Westminster Abbey. Both were on fire.

People were running through the streets, choking on ash and smoke as they tried to outpace the flames. Some of them managed to escape onto side streets that were spared from the fire's path. Others weren't so lucky.

THE CHOSEN UNION

The fire ravishing the city wasn't a natural one. The flames were blue.

Olivia could feel their heat filling the air. The hoses being used to fight the flames were useless. When the fire caught on one of the firemen's suits, it burned right through the fabric.

Olivia heard the man's screams as clear as if she were standing right beside him. The flames ate away at his protective gear until his skin was on fire. The blue flames licked at his skin, devouring his body. His shriek turned spine-chilling as the fire ravaged his vocal cords.

Olivia could barely stand to look, but she couldn't turn away. She was rooted in place as the jets of water pummeling the flames went right through the fire without lessening its impact.

Another shout turned her attention away from the fireman for only a second. By the time she turned back, there was nothing more than a pile of smoking ashes where a man had once stood.

Olivia threw herself into the fray, trying to help…trying to save. But she wasn't really there, and her reaching hands passed through the people as if she herself was smoke.

"Run!" she cried, even though they already were, and no one could hear her, anyway.

Laughter rang through the air. The sound was familiar and raised the hairs on the back of Olivia's neck. The Supernal, as tall as some of the buildings he had set aflame, hovered over the city. His entire body pulsed with the same blue glow as the fire that was devouring London. Balls of fire appeared on his palms. He threw them down at the people below, chuckling when the bursts of fire exploded and turned people—entire families—into smoking corpses.

Olivia stumbled out of the vision on a gasp.

"Are you alright?" Erikir's steady hold on her was all that kept her on her feet. She could still feel the flames' heat on her skin.

"What did you see?" Jaxon asked as he replaced his blade in the scabbard across his back.

"London," she managed, her throat still thick with the memory of ashes. "It was burning."

Her heart was pounding a fearsome rhythm. There was something she needed to understand about this vision…something beyond the horrendous images she'd seen.

"When?" Gerth demanded. "How much time do we have?"

Her stomach dropped out. She realized what it was that had bothered her so much about this vision.

When she had a vision of the future, the image had a kind of fuzziness around the edges. The one she'd just had was perfectly clear.

That meant everything she'd seen had already happened.

CHAPTER 4

TOL

Tol was numb. He didn't know which fact was harder to accept…that he couldn't die, or that because of him, the rest of his people would.

He needed to go to Vitaquias. He needed to do whatever the gods commanded of him so he could save his people.

"London first," Gerth told him.

Before Tol could protest, Gerth continued, "There might be survivors we can help. Vitaquias can come after."

Tol wanted to send the rest of them to London without him, but he knew his best mate was right. He had failed to take down the Supernal when he had the chance. Now, the mortals were paying the price for his failure.

So, he nodded to Addy. She closed her left hand into a fist to activate the magic in her ring. She winced in pain, and that was when Tol remembered her fingers were broken.

"Nira," he said, gesturing at Addy's hand.

"I don't know what you expect me to do without any supplies," Nira said, but she had already taken Addy's hand and started inspecting her fingers.

"This will hurt," Nira said. Without warning, she took Addy's index finger and forced it back into alignment.

Addy gasped.

Without thinking, Tol wrapped his arm around Addy from behind. He puts his lips to her ear, murmuring nonsense to keep her attention on him rather than what Nira was doing. He tightened his hold just as an audible pop came from Addy's middle finger.

When Nira took hold of Addy's ring finger, Addy turned her head so her lips grazed Tol's neck. He leaned into her because it was impossible not to.

"This one's bad," Nira said, her voice devoid of its usual sulkiness.

"Just do it," Addy said through gritted teeth.

"On three," Nira said. "One, two—"

Tol kissed Addy. Hard.

He felt the shock of her pain through his whole body, but she didn't pull away. She kissed him back.

"Fred, give me a piece of your shirt," Nira said from somewhere far away. "I need to make a splint."

When Tol forced himself to let Addy go, he couldn't look at her. He was sick at the thought that, after everything they'd done to try to be together, it had all been a waste.

Destiny was a real bitch, Tol decided.

As soon as Addy's fingers were as mended as they could be, her ring began to glow. Smoky tendrils whipped out and began to swirl together into a portal. The wind picked up.

Sand spiraled around them, scraping against the zig-zagging gash on Tol's chest and the various other cuts on his body.

"Go," Addy yelled, raising her voice to be heard over the rushing wind.

Tol waited for the others to be absorbed into the portal. When he and Addy were the only ones left, he put a hand on her arm to keep her from stepping into the portal. The swirling sapphire light slowed, and the portal disappeared. The wind calmed and the sand settle back down.

"Addy," he began, having no idea what he even wanted to say.

"I know," she said, reaching up to press a kiss to his cheek. "It's okay." She let out a short, bitter laugh. "I mean, it's obviously not okay. You're going to marry my sister."

"Addy—"

She put up a hand. "You're alive. As long as that's true, everything will be okay."

Tol didn't want okay. He wanted forever with Addy. But there was no point in talking about something they would never have. So instead, he wrapped his arm around her waist. Gods knew it might be the last time he ever got to touch her.

With a shuddering breath, Addy re-opened the portal. Together, they were sucked into the rush of magical energy.

Before Tol could take a breath or gather his thoughts, he was spit out onto a paved street. His chest burned.

There were grunts and *watch it's* and *ouch's* as they tried to untangle themselves.

Fred grabbed onto Nira as he tried to stand on wobbly legs. He said, "Traveling that way always makes my insides feel like scrambled eggs."

Nira pointed one of her long nails in his face.

"If you puke on me again, you'll really know what it feels like to have your insides scrambled."

"I didn't puke *on* you." Fred scowled. "Just near you."

"Keep your voices down," Jaxon ordered.

It had been late night in the States, but here, a pale dawn was creeping up over the horizon.

Tol got to his feet and turned in a slow circle.

"Holy shite," Gerth murmured.

Horror clawed its way up Tol's throat as he took in the ruin.

London was burning. Blue flames and black smoke engulfed everything. Addy's portal had deposited them in Westminster, where a burned-out Big Ben was still smoking.

Tol felt like he was standing inside a furnace. His hair was plastered to his face as sweat rolled down his temples. The reek of burning filled his nose and made his lungs feel like they were on fire, too.

The iconic Palace of Westminster's Victoria Tower was destroyed. Massive chunks of stone were littered all over the road. One enormous block had crushed a car unlucky enough to be in its path. Tol could see blood splattered across the windshield.

Screams and ash particles filled the air. Mortals abandoned their cars and raced down the road on foot.

Everything was madness.

"They're coming!" a woman in a torn and smoldering business suit shrieked as she sprinted past.

Forsaken, their glowing blue weapons clutched in their hands, were close behind.

"Spread out," Addy ordered. She was as calm and poised as the mortals were frantic. She tossed back her hair as she raised her garden shears.

Warrior goddess, Tol thought. He felt a sharp pang that had nothing to do with the wound in his chest.

Jaxon had his half-moon blades at the ready, while Fred was holding a Forsaken knife he must have found on the aircraft carrier. Gerth and Nira's lips were red from Addy's blood, which filled their vials. Erikir didn't have Source or Addy's blood, but he was holding Olivia's hand. His Haze was bright enough that he must have somehow been sharing her magic.

Olivia's Haze was the brightest of them all. Her eyes glowed silver. Tol could feel the power of her magic, even though he could no longer feel her.

Tol reached for his vial, before remembering he didn't have it anymore. And then he realized he didn't need Source, because Addy's blood was filling his body. He tested its strength and hurled a tendril of Influence at the Forsaken running toward them.

"Look at me," he ordered the soldiers.

Two of the Forsaken caught his eye and went still.

Good enough.

Their small group spread out as the Forsaken sprinted down the road.

"Careful, Tol," Gerth warned. "We don't know how far the protection of Addy's blood will go."

Tol nodded. He might not have been able to kill himself, but it was possible one of the Forsaken would find a way to end Tol's short streak of invincibility.

Now that purging his blood was an option, he much preferred it to beheading.

"Tol, watch out!" someone called.

He looked up just in time to see a Forsaken man raise a double-bladed axe to cut him down.

Tol reached for the man's mind, but he was out of time. The glowing blue weapon was already descending. In a desperate move he had no expectation of working, Tol reached up and grasped the axe's handle.

No Chosen could ever hope to match one of the Forsaken's physical strength, and yet, Tol stopped the axe's descent with one hand. The man's tree trunk-thick arms trembled as he fought against Tol.

No matter how much the Forsaken man struggled, Tol's one-handed grip on the weapon was enough to hold it off.

Instead of using pure Influence, Tol gave himself over to the unfamiliar feeling inside him that was guiding his hands. Tol closed his right hand into a fist. He drove it into the warrior.

The blow sent the Forsaken man flying backward. The soldier hit a wrought-iron fence with so much force that he blasted straight through it. He crashed into the stone building behind the fence and didn't move.

What the bloody hells?

Tol looked at his fist, like it would provide some explanation for what had just happened.

Out of the corner of his eye, he caught a flash of copper-red—Addy's hair.

Of course. Her blood must somehow be interacting with his innate Chosen abilities to make him inhumanly strong. *Forsaken* strong.

Gerth would lose his mind when Tol told him what he could do.

Nearby shouting caught Tol's attention. A double-decker bus was stuck between two abandoned cars. People inside the bus were crying out for help as they pounded on the windows. Some of them were filming the bedlam with their cell phones. They were all looking up.

Tol followed the direction of their gazes in time to see a ball of blue flame plummet through the air.

Tol started for the bus, but an iron grip yanked him back.

Jaxon, his face streaked with someone else's blood, said, "There's nothing we can do."

They both watched in muted horror as blue flames engulfed the bus. The fire didn't incinerate the people immediately. It took agonizing seconds for them to die, which to Tol felt like hours. The mortals' cries filled his mind until he thought he'd go mad.

When the fire receded, all that was left were blackened skeletons and the bus's metal husk.

Tol's knees wobbled.

"This is my fault," Jaxon whispered. He was staring at the ruin with a stricken expression on his face.

Tol tried to speak, but the words wouldn't come.

"I was the stone's keeper," Jaxon continued. "If I'd kept it away from the Supernal, he wouldn't have been able to do any of this."

Tol was intimately acquainted with the guilt that was eating Jaxon alive. He let out a shaky breath.

"This isn't on you," Tol said. "You did everything you could to prevent this."

Rage built inside Tol as he stared at his ruined city and the fleeing mortals. He looked around for his bloody and battered friends. He had just enough time to assure himself that the others were unhurt—albeit exhausted—before an enormous shadow blocked out the sun overhead.

Tol looked up and into the face of the Supernal.

The Supernal must have been ten feet tall, although it was hard to be sure with the way he was hovering above the ground. He was even bigger and more muscled than he'd been when they battled him on the aircraft carrier.

The Supernal's Haze was a harsh blue. The light flickered and danced around him, looking more like the blue flames devouring the city than actual Haze. His golden-blonde hair reached his shoulders and was several shades darker than his pale skin. His eyes, impossible to hold for more than a second, were jagged black irises surrounded by blinding gold.

All Tol could think about as he stared up at the Supernal was that this…thing…was Addy's father.

Addy, who was pulling her garden shears out of a Forsaken, turned. Her Haze transformed from its usual gold to a blue as bright as the Supernal's.

Her eyes flashed gold for an instant as she turned the full force of her loathing on the creature hovering overhead.

She strode over to Tol, blood dripping from the blades of her shears.

Tol stood at Addy's right, while Gerth and Jaxon took up a position on her left. The rest of their group was busy elsewhere with the Forsaken.

"I thought I killed you," the Supernal boomed, his reptilian eyes fixating on Tol.

"Yeah, well, it didn't stick," Tol replied.

"Your Haze," Addy murmured.

Tol looked down at himself. He gaped at the sight of his Haze, which had taken on a bluish tinge.

"That's new," Gerth murmured.

"I can feel my magic within you," the Supernal said, his mouth twisting in disgust. "How is this possible?"

"I gave him my blood."

Addy, looking tiny and fearless as she faced the Supernal, laced her fingers through Tol's as she stared up at the being.

"You gave the gods' blood to a Chosen?" he snarled.

"I think it's a little late for dating advice," Addy replied dryly.

Tol snickered at that.

Shivers of blue electricity danced along the Supernal's skin. Tol could hear the crackle of magic, feel the heat of it pulsing in the air between them.

The Supernal held out his palm. A ball of blue flames erupted and, before Tol could react, the Supernal hurled it at him.

It came as fast as the lightning bolt had. There was no time to do anything except watch as the fire blasted toward him…and then stopped.

The fireball hit an invisible barrier directly in front of Tol. Particles of magic that Tol could feel rather than see gathered around the fireball, held it in place, and then sent it shooting back at the Supernal.

What in the two hells?

The Supernal let out a furious shriek. He flicked his hand, and the blue embers disappeared in a puff of harmless smoke. He created another fireball.

Again, the invisible wall appeared in front of Tol, shielding him from the attack. He was aware of the others ducking behind him, but his gaze was fixed on the Supernal as the being hurled one ball of fire after another at him. Each one came up against the transparent shield and bounced back.

A searing heat across Tol's chest drew his attention down to his torn shirt. His wound, which had been in desperate need of stitches only a few minutes ago, was completely healed. A jagged white scar was all that remained of the deadly injury.

"It's Addy," Gerth said, his voice somewhere between scared and excited by the new discovery. "She's got godly power in her blood, and you've got royal Chosen blood." He gave Tol a humorless smile. "Kind of like a watered-down version of a blood marriage."

Tol craned his neck to stare up at the Supernal. "Guess you should have been a bit more thorough about killing me," he said.

Blue flames poured out from the Supernal's very being.

"Leave the mortals alone," Jaxon called up to the Supernal in a strong voice.

"*You*," the Supernal sneered, his whole face contorting in disgust as he pinned Jaxon with his inhuman stare. "You tried to keep me from my power."

The Supernal lowered himself to the street. Tol moved in front of their small group in case the Supernal attacked.

"You are nothing," the Supernal continued, his golden eyes boring into Jaxon. "You are godless and without a people. You are the true Forsaken."

Tol glanced to the side and saw Jaxon's face pale.

"He's with us," Gerth said, at the same time Addy said, "Don't listen to him, Jaxon."

Tol had had enough of the Supernal. He tried Influencing the creature, but he couldn't get a hold on the Supernal's consciousness. He also didn't have the strength to attack the Supernal physically.

Tol was out of breath from his wasted efforts. The Supernal couldn't attack him, but it was obvious he couldn't harm the Supernal, either.

"What are you doing here?" Tol demanded, stepping closer to the Supernal. "What do you want?"

The Supernal's lip twitched in a mocking kind of humor.

"I have been powerless for two-thousand years." Another blood-freezing scowl at Jaxon. "My people have been weakened and ignored. Now, we will take this world for our own. The mortals will serve my people. And I will be worshipped as a god."

"Why London?" Gerth asked carefully.

Tol saw the look on his mate's face. Gerth already knew the answer and wished he was wrong.

"The mortals in this city were just an afterthought." The Supernal's irritation turned to an amused smirk. "I'm here to destroy the Chosen."

CHAPTER 5

ERIKIR

Erikir fought within touching distance of Olivia. Unlike the past, when he'd given her his strength, now Olivia was feeding her magical energy into him. He'd used the last of his Source to help Tol, but touching Olivia was like being connected to a continuous well of Source. She was so damn powerful.

But so were the Forsaken.

Erikir had been on almost every one of the Forsaken raids since he was sixteen. Over the last five years, he'd gotten to know the way they fought.

These Forsaken weren't like the ones he'd faced before. They were faster, stronger, and more resistant to Influence. And then there were their weapons.

The Forsaken weren't just wielding weapons. They *were* weapons.

One of the warriors flicked his wrist. A blue arrowhead shot out of his skin. Erikir grabbed Olivia and pulled her out of the way, just as two more arrowheads flew from the man's wrist.

Another warrior opened her mouth. Instead of making a sound, dozens of tiny blades poured out of her mouth.

Erikir threw himself to the ground in a graceless heap to avoid being impaled. Unlike his newly-invincible cousin, Erikir could die. He'd be damned if a bunch of saliva-drenched blades would be his undoing.

The exhaustion that came with using a great deal of Influence was dragging at Erikir, but he didn't relent in his attacks. Olivia was still fighting, and he wasn't going to leave her side.

When he'd thought Olivia was dying, it had broken something inside him. He's never understood Tol's willingness to sacrifice everything for Addy. Now, he did.

"Pay attention, weasel!" Nira snapped.

Weasel. It was the name Addy had given him, and Nira had immediately adopted.

Erikir gave Nira a death glare. His attention went involuntarily to Olivia to see whether she'd heard the insult.

Forget about her, he told himself furiously. Even without the other complications, he'd given up any chance he might have had with Olivia when he betrayed her trust. He'd made an arrangement with General Bloodsong that had almost gotten Tol killed.

Erikir would never forget the look on Olivia's face when he told her what he'd done.

"We need to help these people," Fred said, mopping at the sweat streaming down his face.

The city streets were the emptiest Erikir had ever seen them. Most of the city's population had fled or already been killed. Only a handful remained.

Fred continued, "They're panickin', and some of them are runnin' right to the Forsaken."

"That's Darwinism," Nira said with a toss of her long hair. "If they're too stupid to save their own hides, then—"

At the look Fred gave her, she wilted. Erikir had never seen Nira listen to anyone except Tol.

"They matter," Fred said in a quiet voice. "That's why we're here, ain't it?"

Two Forsaken were herding a group of mortals toward a burning building. Any who fell behind were impaled on the warriors' blades. The rest were steps away from being incinerated.

"Take care of the Forsaken," Erikir told the others, already running for the building. "I'll deal with the mortals."

By the time Erikir reached them, the Forsaken were stumbling back from the mortals, their eyes glazes over from the effect of Influence. Erikir used what was left of his strength to exert a subtle hold on the mortals' minds. He stopped them in their tracks.

"Come away from that building," he ordered them.

His Influence wobbled, and the mortals' terrified eyes flicked from the fire to the Forsaken who had dropped their weapons and were backing away.

Slowly, the mortals did as they were told. Sweat streamed down all of their faces from the heat of the flames. It was so hot Erikir was struggling to draw in a breath, but he didn't let up until the mortals were safely away from the burning building and the Forsaken.

"Come on," he told them, unsure of how much longer his Influence would hold. He needed to get them somewhere out of the Forsaken's sight until Addy could portal them outside the city.

He gestured them onto a side street that was free of fire. He directed the group to hide behind a pile of stone rubble.

"Wait here," he ordered them, catching each of their gazes.

"They're going to destroy the world," a woman said in a toneless voice.

"We're not going to let them," Erikir replied. He took the woman's hand and squeezed, more to enhance the strength of his Influence than to comfort her with his touch.

"Are you…like them?" the woman asked, her glazed-over eyes holding his.

"I'm one of the good guys," Erikir said, wincing internally. He wasn't exactly sure what he was, but *one of the good guys* seemed overly generous.

"Is he really God?" a man in the group asked Erikir, his voice breaking on that word.

"Er, no," Erikir said. "He's just very powerful."

"Some people are saying he's the Devil. They say Hell has gotten too full, and so he's come to claim Earth."

"I understand you're scared," Erikir said in what he meant to be a soothing voice, but which came out scratchy because of all the smoke in the air. "Right now, I need you to hide here until we come back from you. Can you do that?"

Erikir felt relief at the mortals' jerky nods. Saving a group of thirty seemed like nothing compared to the thousands who had been slaughtered, but it was something.

Erikir was almost surprised at himself for caring. A few months ago, he would have ignored the helpless mortals altogether. He would have said he cared for no one except his own people. But that had been before Olivia…before she'd shown him understanding and compassion…before she'd shown him kindness.

"You can't save them all, Magnantius," a voice taunted.

Erikir's blood froze in his veins. He knew that voice. It was one he never wanted to hear again.

He turned to face the Forsaken general. Lezha Bloodsong. The woman who had murdered his father and so many of his people.

She was wearing a crisp military uniform that bore no hint of the battle they'd fought on the aircraft carrier hours earlier. She reminded Erikir of the Madam Tussaud's version of Addy. She was stiff, perfect, and unreal. The only emotions she displayed were the ones she wanted the world to see. Her red hair was pulled into a neat bun, without a strand out of place. There wasn't a fleck of blood or ash anywhere on her.

"You," Erikir began.

Liar. Murderer.

Erikir hurled Influence at her.

A searing pain lanced through his skull. His knees buckled, and he barely managed to stay standing.

The general's eyes remained clear of Influence. The ruby stone on her index finger flashed.

That's when he remembered. The general's ring—which contained a piece of the Supernal, just as Addy's ring contained a piece of the Celestial—protected the general from Influence.

Fear pulsed through Erikir. He hated himself for it. He hated how tight a hold this woman had over him. He hated that he was powerless against her.

Where were Jaxon and Addy? Of all of them, they were the only ones who had the right kind of power to face this enemy.

The thought soured Erikir's stomach. He had vowed to himself he would take down this woman. He'd had a chance before and failed. It looked like he was about to fail again today.

The general lifted up her arm. A glowing blue spear appeared in her hand, which had been empty a moment before.

Erikir tensed.

The general smiled. It was a cold, calculated kind of smile that reminded Erikir that the general held all of the power and he had none. She raised her spear.

"General Bloodsong."

The Supernal's voice filled the air, even though he was somewhere out of sight. Erikir took several steps away from the sound before he stopped himself.

"Leave the Chosen alive, since you will be needing slaves to do your bidding in the days to come."

Even though Erikir couldn't see the look on the Supernal's face, he could hear the being's smug satisfaction.

"Kill the weakling mortal children," the Supernal continued. "They are useless to me."

At that moment, the sound of shoes slapping against the pavement drew Erikir's attention to the street behind him.

A group of kids, covered in soot and ranging in age from about five to twelve, were darting out from behind an overturned car. One of the older children was carrying a younger one on his back.

"No," Erikir began, reaching for Influence again, even though he knew it was useless. A crippling wave of nausea surged into his throat.

If Erikir hadn't been staring right at the general, he would have missed the flash of emotion across her face. It was only there for a second, but Erikir saw it. There was hesitation and disgust.

She didn't want to obey the Supernal.

"My Lord," the general said, carefully. "Perhaps, it would be better if we—"

"Are you challenging me, Lezha?"

There was a hint of amusement in the Supernal's voice.

"Of course not, My Lord. I merely—"

"Because you know what will happen if you challenge me. We have a deal, general. Never forget that the fate of your people rests in my hands."

For a few seconds, Erikir wondered if the general would refuse to carry out the order. Then, with a small shake of her head, she turned and aimed her spear.

Erikir tried to knock the spear out of her hand. He was too slow.

Erikir shouted a desperate warning at the kids, even though he knew it was useless. He was powerless to do anything but watch as the spear swerved around an abandoned car, cut through every one of the scattering children, and delivered itself back into the general's waiting hand. Blood dripped off the spear's head and splashed onto the pavement.

The general sagged a little before straightening.

Rage built in Erikir's chest until he thought he might explode.

"You monster!" Erikir threw himself at her, his fingers curling like claws. He wanted to tear her apart. He wanted to ruin her.

The general's green eyes glimmered with contrived satisfaction as she shoved him back with one hand. "Perhaps I am a monster." She shrugged. "But you should be wary of throwing accusations at me. You and I have far more in common than you might think."

"I have nothing in common with you," Erikir snarled, realizing too late that he should have stayed silent rather than taking the bait.

The general *hmmed*. "You are willing to pay any price to ensure your people's survival. You were even willing to trade your own cousin's life."

She arched an eyebrow at him as Erikir felt shame heat his cheeks.

"The difference between you and me," she continued before Erikir could find his voice, "is that my people know what I've done for them." She looked down at Erikir like he was barely worthy of notice. "You've spent so long in your cousin's shadow, your people have forgotten your existence."

All of the air was ripped out of Erikir's lungs. It was like the general had looked into the core of his very being. He had no defense against the truth of her words. He felt cracked open and exposed.

"Your father was strong, you know," the general continued, watching Erikir for his reaction.

"Don't you dare talk about my father." Erikir hated the way his voice broke.

"It must be a curse to look so much like him and have nothing to show for your noble bloodline."

She gave Erikir a bored look before raising her spear. She turned toward the alley where Erikir had hidden the rest of the mortals.

Before she could release her weapon, she crumpled to the ground. Fred stood behind her with a bloody rock in his hand.

"I'm sick of hearin' you talk," Fred told the unconscious general.

A snarling, animal-like sound pulled itself free from Erikir's throat. He went to grab the spear and end the woman before she could wake up and torment him again. But when he reached for the spear lying on the pavement, the weapon leaped into the air.

It hovered over the general's prone form, keeping itself just out of reach.

Before he could try to think of what to do, Erikir caught sight of Addy, followed by the rest of their group. They were sprinting down the road. The Supernal strode down the pavement behind them, taunting them.

The Supernal was massive, and Erikir felt the grip of fear renew its hold over him.

"Open a portal," Gerth gasped out to Addy. "We need to get the hells out of here."

"And the mortals," Erikir said, pointing in the direction of the alley. "I told them—"

The Supernal lowered himself to the ground and faced their group.

The Supernal's skin, hair, and eyes radiated with pure magical energy. For as huge as he was, he was perfectly proportioned. His arms were

THE CHOSEN UNION

corded with muscle. He looked like he'd stepped out of some painting of the Greek gods...if the gods were tinged with other-worldly, blue light.

"Go Addy," Tol said. "Get everyone out of here. I'll keep him busy."

The Supernal's laughter was like thunder.

"My own daughter, taking orders from one of the Chosen." He glared down at Addy, who seemed pinned in place by the Supernal's golden eyes. "You reek of your desperation to be one of them."

Addy's face was even paler than usual.

Erikir could sense Tol's wrath as his cousin grabbed Addy's left hand and raised it up. The blue-black stones on her ring glittered in the light of their combined Hazes.

"Addy is wearing the Celestial's ring," Tol called out, his voice full of a power Erikir's would never command. "She is as much a part of our people as I am."

"If you were one of them," the Supernal said, directing all of his attention on Addy, "then I wouldn't be able to do this."

Addy gasped. She stared down at her left hand, which was covered in hideous bruises and wrapped with Nira's makeshift splint. She pulled away the shreds of cloth holding her mangled fingers together. As they all watched, the bruises and swelling disappeared. Her twisted joints shifted back into alignment.

Her hand was as good as new.

"I will defeat you," Addy called up to the Supernal, her eyes gleaming with furious tears. "I won't just banish you like the Celestial did. I'm going to kill you."

"You may have my power in your veins, but you are no threat to me." Another thunderous, mocking laugh. "Why do you think I healed you? Why do you think I'm going to let you and your little friends scurry away like gutter rats?" The Supernal answered his own question. "I think it'll be far more entertaining to let you live. That way, I'll be able to see the look on your faces when everything in this world—including you—belongs to me."

Erikir saw the loathing on Addy's face as she stared up at the Supernal. As much as Erikir disliked Addy, he couldn't help but respect the way she refused to cower or crumble under the weight of knowing this creature was her father.

Tol threw himself at the Supernal. And was promptly thrust back with a force great enough to send him sprawling on the pavement. It was like he'd come up against an invisible wall. Every time either of them tried to come closer to the other, a flare of blue light would appear and shove them apart.

"The mortals," Erikir told Addy, not knowing how long Tol's distraction would hold. "There." He pointed at the alley.

"There's no time!" Nira shouted.

"Olivia," Erikir began. "I need—"

"I've got you," Olivia said, knowing what he was thinking before he even needed to say it. She reached out to him.

Her small hand fit perfectly in his as their fingers interlocked. He felt her power punch through his blood, and then his Influence flared to life. Together, they used their combined magic to capture the mortals' minds, even from two streets away. Seconds later, the mortals emerged from the alley. Their soot-dirtied faces were serene, and they didn't so much as glance at the Supernal. They moved quickly as they converged around Addy.

The sapphire wisps of smoke were swirling out of the stones in Addy's ring. The wind kicked up as the lasso of magical energy swirled into an ever-widening circle.

While the Supernal and Tol struggled against each other, the rest of the Forsaken closed the distance between them.

Gerth, Jaxon, and Nira kept the Forsaken from reaching the portal, while Erikir and Olivia guided the mortals closer. Erikir could feel their fear in the deepest recesses of their minds, but it was overshadowed by the Influence he and Olivia were exerting. Without blinking, all thirty of the mortals allowed themselves to be swallowed into the portal.

Erikir had no idea where Addy was sending the mortals, but it didn't matter. As long as they got away from here, they'd have a chance.

When the last mortal disappeared, the light of the portal winked out. The Forsaken flung their weapons and reached out for the mortals who had disappeared into Addy's portal.

They were too late. The portal was closed, and the mortals were gone.

Erikir felt a rush of relief and triumph, which transformed almost as quickly. The Forsaken turned their attention on them.

Gerth and Nira's vials were empty. Fred still had his knife, but it wouldn't do much good against a dozen Forsaken. Erikir was utterly spent, and Olivia looked as drawn as he felt. Addy was trying to fight her way through a wall of Forsaken that separated her from the rest of his group.

Tol stumbled back as a wave of blue fire crashed against his invisible shield.

The Supernal bellowed at the Forsaken, "Restrain them."

This wasn't a fight they were going to win. They needed to get the hells out of here.

"Addy," Erikir yelled. "Portal. Now!"

CHAPTER 6

ADDY

Addy's left hand was no longer mangled and throbbing, but she almost wished it was. That way, she wouldn't have to remember how the Supernal had proved her Forsaken-ness by healing her.

Her Haze was no longer blue, at least, but she could still feel the Supernal's strength coursing through her. His power called to her.

Addy loathed it.

Now that she was no longer distracted by the portal's weightlessness, all of her failures and hopelessness crashed back over her like a tidal wave. She couldn't breathe from the crushing weight of it all…and the fact that Nira was sprawled on top of her.

"Get off," she ordered, irked that somehow, despite everything they'd been through, Nira's cloying perfume had survived.

"Why did you bring us back here?" Erikir asked, getting to his feet and looking at Aunt Meredith's farmhouse at the end of the long driveway.

Truth be told, it had been the first place that had come to mind when the mortals clambered into the portal. In the chaos, it hadn't occurred to Addy that she actually had to send them somewhere. If she'd had more time to think things through, she would have picked a more sensible location.

But Hell would freeze over before she admitted that to Weasel.

"And why are we on the road instead of at the house?" he continued.

Again, if Addy had been thinking more clearly, she would have portaled them onto Aunt Meredith's front lawn. But she'd been more focused on her deranged parents. So, here they were, a quarter of a mile from their destination.

"I'm so sorry," Addy told Erikir, her voice dripping with sarcasm. "Why don't you go ahead and put your ideal location in the suggestion box? You'll find it straight up your—"

"Addy," Livy said in a quiet, plaintive voice.

Addy couldn't look at her twin. She loved Livy with all of her heart, but she was angry with her sister in a way she never had been before. Livy had saved Erikir's life, and because of that, Addy had lost her only chance to be with Tol.

She understood that Livy couldn't hurt a fly, but Erikir was the reason why they had all ended up on that aircraft carrier in the first place. Everything that had happened after was his fault. The fact that Addy and Tol no longer had a future together was because of him.

It took all of her self-control not to wring his sorry neck.

She gave Erikir a glare, hiding behind a mask of anger so the others wouldn't see the truth. That she was broken.

"No, bringing everyone here was good thinking," Gerth said. "The Supernal will hit the big cities first. The mortals will be safe here for a little while, anyway."

Addy wanted to kiss him. Right now, she was feeling short on allies.

"We need to get to the manor," Tol said, his expression tight with fear and desperation. "We have to get everyone the hells out of there before the Forsaken get to them."

"Nobody panic," Gerth said, raising a hand and giving Tol a warning look. "Now, here's what's going to happen."

He pointed at Addy and Jaxon. "The two of you are going to the manor, since you're the best equipped to deal with the Forsaken if they show up." To Addy, he said, "Tol's parents will listen to you. Just tell them what's going on and that you need to get all of our people out of there."

Gerth gave Jaxon a stern look. "There's no point in engaging the Forsaken, since the Supernal can just bring them back to life. Your priority is to portal everyone out."

Jaxon gave Gerth a terse nod.

"I'll go with Ads," Fred piped up.

Addy felt another flash of warmth for her best friend. Even with all the craziness of the past months, Fred had stuck by her side.

"No," Gerth said. "I need you, Livy, Erikir, and Nira to stay here and deal with this." He pointed at the group of mortals, who had congregated on Aunt Meredith's front lawn.

"They're going to need some explanations."

More like therapy, Addy thought but didn't say out loud.

Addy and the others weren't close enough to see the mortals' faces, but she could only imagine how they were feeling right about now.

"And I suppose you think you're coming to Vitaquias with me?" Tol asked Gerth heavily.

"Handsome *and* intelligent." Gerth pinched Tol's cheek. Tol swatted at him.

"Go with Addy and Jaxon," Tol told Gerth. "They might need backup at the manor."

Gerth shook his head. "Addy saved your mum's life. No one's going to mess with her."

Tol opened up his mouth to protest.

"Save it, Tol," Gerth told him. "I'm coming with you, and that's that."

Sighing, Tol nodded.

"Just the two of you?" Addy asked, hearing her voice crack with the worry she was barely containing.

"Addy."

Tol's black velvet voice sent tingles through her. Clearly, her body hadn't gotten the memo that she wasn't allowed to react to him that way anymore.

Addy didn't understand how she could feel so much pain and still be alive. Her heart was shattered.

She let Tol take her elbow and lead her away from the others.

"I'm not sure if you remember," she said, letting the ire in her voice drown out the hurt and worry, "but the last time we were all on Vitaquias, we barely made it out alive. I already had to watch you die once—" She looked away, unable to control the emotions that were clawing their way through her insides.

"Hey." Tol brushed his fingers along her cheek.

Addy jerked back. Hurt flashed across Tol's face.

Addy bit down on her lower lip to check the tears that burned in her eyes. Letting them fall wouldn't change anything.

Tol was going to Vitaquias to *purge her blood* from his body. He was going to blood marry Livy.

"Before I go," Tol said, "I need to tell you something."

"Please, don't," she whispered. "It'll only make this harder."

Tol's expression softened.

"Gods, Addy." Tol's voice broke. "I wish it didn't have to be like this. If there'd been any other way—"

"I know." Addy cleared her throat, which had become almost too tight to draw in air. "I want your people to survive, too."

Tol winced. It hadn't escaped him that Addy had said *your* people instead of *ours*.

It was time for both of them to stop pretending. Addy was Forsaken. And she and Tol were never going to be together.

"Here." She started to pull the beautiful ring off her newly-healed finger.

"No." He put a hand over hers to stop her. "Please." He looked away. Addy could tell he was having as much trouble controlling his emotions as she was.

"The blood marriage will change me," Tol said, his mouth twisting in bitterness. "I'll be devoted to her. Consumed with her." He held Addy with an intense gaze. "But I'll never love her. Not like I love you. Because my heart is already yours."

She didn't resist his touch when he reached up to wipe away the tears she couldn't hold back any longer. She leaned into him. She couldn't help it.

"I want you and Livy to be happy," she managed.

It was the truth. Nothing would ever change the fact that they were the two people she loved most.

Tol moved his hand to cup the back of her neck. "I want you to know there will always be a place for you among the Chosen."

Addy choked back a bitter laugh.

"Let's not start lying to each other now."

"What can I do to make this easier for you?" Tol asked. There was so much anguish in his voice that it threatened to rip her to pieces.

Even though he was suffering as much as she was, he was more worried about how she'd cope with his loss than he was about himself.

Let me come with you to Vitaquias, she wanted to say. *Let me pretend for one more day that I'm yours and you're mine.*

"Just stay alive," she told him. "Come back in one piece. That's my only non-negotiable."

She took a steadying breath and stepped back so his heat and intoxicating spicy scent were no longer filling her senses.

She saw his whole body shudder, but then, he nodded.

"I'll get your people away from the manor," Addy said. "Just make sure you and Gerth stay safe."

She turned away before she broke down.

When she hurried to catch up with the others, the pitying looks on their faces were more than she could take.

"Addy, I'm so sorry," Livy began, but Addy cut her off with a look.

Some logical part inside Addy knew that Livy's life was being ruined right alongside hers and Tol's. But she couldn't have this conversation right now. If she let her sister comfort her, she'd fall apart.

"Are we going to make moves, or are we just going to stand around here reliving our failures?" Addy demanded.

Gerth recovered first. "Right. How about that portal, then?"

"How are you guys gonna get back from Vitaquias without Ads?" Fred asked.

Addy's lips parted. She hadn't even considered that.

"I can do it," Livy said. "Find the Celestial and tell her whenever you're ready to come back. Just make sure you're standing in the same place we were the first time we landed on Vitaquias. I'll open up the portal here and bring you back."

"You can do that?" Addy asked.

Livy nodded. "I don't see why not. I can telepathically connect with the Celestial, and I control the portal between here and the site of the original Crossing." She gave Addy a tentative smile. "Of course, I'm not as useful as you, since I can only control this particular portal. You can go anywhere."

Addy knew her sister was trying to make her feel better, but she couldn't muster a smile in return. Addy wasn't sure she'd ever have the strength to smile again.

"Hey," Fred began, squinting into the pre-dawn light. "Does it look like there are too many people on Meredith's front lawn?"

Fred was right. Even in the bad lighting, she could see there were way more than thirty people.

Addy doubted her aunt was having a party she hadn't bothered mentioning before.

"We've got a more important problem," Nira announced, holding out her phone. The screen was cracked, but the video playing was still visible.

They all crowded around to see as she turned up the volume.

Addy's stomach dropped as the post-apocalyptic version of London they'd just left appeared on the screen. The Supernal moved into the frame, with the general and a few other Forsaken standing on either side of them. Hatred filled Addy until she could hardly breathe.

"Mortals of Earth," the Supernal said, his voice crackling out of the phone's speaker. "Rumors and partial truths have abounded for the last day, and I'm here to set the record straight." He gave the camera a dazzling smile.

"What a scum bucket," Nira said.

Addy shushed her.

"As you have seen," the Supernal continued, "we are blessed with otherworldly powers. Your armies and weapons will have no effect on us." His gaze pierced the camera, and it was almost as though he was looking straight at Addy. "I do not say this as a threat or to frighten you—"

"Liar," Fred accused the phone.

"—I say it so you will all understand the situation and will be able to make an informed decision. I am a merciful god, after all."

Someone made a gagging sound.

"I'm giving the entire mortal world one week to make a decision. Either submit to my rule and become faithful servants—"

"Slaves, he means," Fred muttered.

Addy nodded. It was obvious that was exactly what he meant.

"—or I will obliterate each and every one of you," the Supernal said. "One week, mortals. Either submit, or what happened in London will be a mercy compared to what I do to the rest of your world."

The screen went dark.

Jaxon hurled one of his half-moon blades into the dirt with so much force the entire weapon was buried.

Addy had never seen him lose his temper before, but she knew exactly how he was feeling. They were so helpless…so useless.

Gerth put a hand on Jaxon's forearm and said something too quiet for Addy to hear. Jaxon gave him a short nod, even though his muscles were still tensed.

Addy ground her teeth. "We have to figure out how to kill him."

Jaxon looked at her, his gray eyes glittering with the same hatred that was spreading through her insides like poison.

"He gives our people strength, but the reverse is also true," Jaxon told her. "If you want to weaken him, then you need to give the Forsaken a reason to abandon him."

"Like what?" Addy asked. She didn't bother trying to argue that she wasn't one of his people.

Jaxon looked straight at her. "You have to become the leader we need."

CHAPTER 7

OLIVIA

Olivia's footsteps were heavy as she followed Erikir, Nira, and Fred up the driveway. Addy had already portaled Tol and Gerth to Vitaquias, and then she and Jaxon had gone to the Chosen manor. Olivia's mind was consumed with worrying about all of them, and wishing she'd had more time to apologize to Addy before they parted ways.

Olivia was still a little shell-shocked from everything that had happened, so as their bedraggled group reached the end of the driveway, she convinced herself she was hallucinating.

It was the only explanation for what she was witnessing.

"Are you guys seeing what I'm seeing?" Fred asked. He scruffed a hand through his already-wild hair as he stared straight ahead.

"I think I must have inhaled some nitrogen or something in the portal," Nira said. "Because it looks to me like there's an army of farmers on your aunt's front lawn."

Nira's words jolted Olivia back to reality. She wasn't hallucinating. There really were at least twenty farmers with guns raised and pointed. They were surrounding the Londoner refugees, who were soot-stained and cowering in the middle of the circle of farmers.

Even with all the other people crowded on the lawn, Olivia recognized Aunt Meredith. She stood in the midst of the refugees with a checkered dish towel thrown over her shoulder and her shotgun cocked.

Olivia started to run.

"Wait." Erikir grabbed her arm. "We can't just go barging over there."

"He's right," Nira said. "We can't afford to get you shot before the blood marriage."

If Addy hadn't already left with Jaxon, she'd say something biting and witty about Nira only caring about Olivia's use as the Fount. Since Addy wasn't with them, Olivia just ignored the other girl. They had more important issues to worry about than Nira's attitude.

Close to twenty guns were pointing at Aunt Meredith.

"Give up, witch," one of the farmers ordered.

He was speaking to Aunt Meredith.

"Let's just keep our heads on straight," Aunt Meredith called back, her grip never faltering on her weapon. "I'm not a witch, and I don't appreciate ya'll threatening my guests."

"We were comin' here to confront you about poor Tony's murder, and whattya know?" a different farmer shouted. "Thirty Brits just *fall outta the sky* onto your property."

"Now, you listen here," Aunt Meredith began, but the farmer didn't let her finish.

"How do you explain their appearance if you didn't *magic* them here?" he demanded.

"She isn't a witch," another called. "She's one of them goddamn aliens."

"Alien...witch...same difference."

"Careful. I heard if you shoot 'em, ten more'll grow outta their guts."

Aunt Meredith scoffed. "Even you aren't dim enough to believe everything you hear, Robertson."

"Shut yer mouth, witch!" the man yelled. "And the rest of you's," he waved his gun at the refugees, "put your hands in the air or we'll start shootin'!"

Olivia could sense that Nira and Erikir were too exhausted and Source-depleted to Influence anyone from this distance. Fred had his Forsaken knife, but that wouldn't do him much good against the farmers' guns.

This was up to her.

She turned her attention inward. She blocked out the Texas heat, the porch lights glinting off metal gun barrels, and her own growing fear.

Olivia felt the power build inside her until she was no longer flesh and bone, but a churning mass of magical energy. Her pulse sped up. She felt the familiar rush inside her, like she'd just downed the most intense energy drink of all time. Her mind cleared.

She turned her attention on the globes of light hovering over each of the mortals. She worked her magic around the luminescent spheres of their minds, weaving gentle suggestions. In seconds, she had all of the farmers standing placidly with their guns at their feet.

"Neat party trick," Nira said, not sounding the least bit impressed. "What do we do now?"

Olivia wasn't exactly sure. She could convince the farmers to go away, but they'd come back, and then what? She wouldn't hurt these people, despite the fact that they'd threatened Aunt Meredith. She could see their fear and uncertainty. Olivia couldn't fault them from wanting to protect their homes.

"I'm on it," Fred said.

He jogged the rest of the way to the farmers and began collecting their weapons. He unloaded and disassembled each gun, tossing the pieces in different directions. When he'd finished, he called, "Okay, let their minds go."

Olivia could sense Nira and Erikir were as hesitant and uncertain as she felt, but she trusted Fred.

"Hey, what's the idea?" one of the farmers demanded, shaking his head as the Influence slowly wore off.

"Listen to me," Fred called in a voice that was loud and full of an authority she'd never heard from her friend before. "I'm not an alien or nothin' like that. I'm a dairy farmer from upstate New York."

"You're one of us," said Robertson, the man who had called Aunt Meredith a witch before.

Fred nodded. "I'm here because I'm helpin' the…um…good aliens."

"There ain't no such thing!" a woman snarled. "And what the hell did you do with our guns?"

Aunt Meredith stalked up to the woman and thwapped her with the dish towel. "Don't interrupt," she told the farmer, before crossing her arms and nodding at Fred to continue.

"It's a trick," Robertson called. "They're getting' us to drop our guard so they can turn us into stone!"

Aunt Meredith barked out a laugh. "Robertson, in case you haven't noticed, my property is getting crowded. There just isn't room on this lawn for your stupidity."

Amazingly, the farmers quieted down enough to hear Fred's next words.

"There is such a thing as good aliens," he insisted. "I thought the same as you at first, but now I know the truth. They're from a different planet, but they're like us. We didn't even know they were here for the last eighteen years 'cause they acted just like us.

"It was only when the bad ones started trouble that we had problems."

The farmers' expressions ranged from frightened to combative, but their attention was fixated on Fred.

"Look, I know it ain't easy to have outsiders in our world," Fred continued. "And I know all this stuff is confusin' and strange, but I'm tellin' you that some of them are really tryin' to help us. But they can't defeat the…bad aliens…alone."

"So, what are you sayin'?" Robertson demanded.

"I'm sayin' they need our help," Fred replied.

His words were met with disbelieving scoffs.

"We've seen the news," a farmer said. "The aliens burned down all of London in five minutes. We can't go up against somethin' like that."

"Yeah, we can," Fred argued. "Think about it. There's only a few hundred of the bad aliens. They might be stronger than us, but there are more of us humans than there are of them. We can fight 'em."

"We're farmers, not soldiers," someone pointed out.

"Who's better to defend our world than farmers?" Fred challenged. "We're strong, smart, and we're not afraid of gettin' our hands dirty."

"But we don't know how to fight," someone else argued.

"I can teach you," Fred replied. "Me and the good aliens will turn you— ya'll—into the first bad alien-fighting army ever. Whatdya think?"

THE CHOSEN UNION

The farmers murmured to each other. Some of them looked perplexed. Others seemed intrigued. Olivia held her breath.

"I guess I'd rather fight than sit on my ass and wait for our farms to get torched," Robertson said.

"Yeah, I mean, who's gonna to save our world if we can't?" someone else said. "We're farmers. We've been keepin' people alive since the dawn of humanity."

Fred pointed at the Londoners, who were still huddled around Aunt Meredith, looking as frightened as they'd been before.

"You guys can help, too," Fred told them. "There's plenty of bad aliens to go around."

The refugees looked at each other.

"Those alien bastards killed my friend," one of the Londoners said. "I'll help you fight them."

"Me too."

"And me."

"We'll all fight 'em together," Robertson shouted.

Fred jumped up onto the picnic table. "For humanity!" he called.

"For 'merica!" the farmers chorused.

The farmers were cheering so loudly, the Londoners had no choice but to join in. Olivia even thought she heard someone yell, "God save the Queen!"

Olivia's arms were covered with goosebumps. Looking at this fearless group, she felt the beginnings of hope.

"Now," Fred said when everyone had finally quieted down, "the first thing we need to do is build a bunker. It's gotta be big enough to hold everyone and also be easy to defend against the Supernal."

"The what?" a farmer asked, scratching his head.

"The leader of the bad aliens," Fred clarified.

"Before you start digging up my yard," Aunt Meredith said, "there are people here who need medical attention." She gestured to the Londoners, who were still looking a little stunned.

"We ain't doctors," a farmer said, throwing an accusing look at the refugees.

"I am." Nira, hands on hips, marched across the lawn.

The circle of farmers broke apart and turned to gape at her.

"You, there." She pointed a manicured nail at one of the men, whose cheeks turned red at the attention. "Get these people some water. They were already dehydrated before Addy dumped them in Texas. You, you, and you," she pointed at three more farmers, "clean out every pharmacy you can get to. Bring me everything they've got for treating wounds and burns."

The men stuttered and gawked at Nira for several seconds. When she clapped her hands in their faces, they scurried off. They all wore a slightly dazed expression that had nothing to do with Influence.

"You know," one of the famers said, blinking in awe at Nira. "I always said some of the aliens were good folk."

He did something strange with his eyes, and Olivia thought he might be trying to wink.

"Maybe you and me could…."

Erikir snickered. Fred curled his hands into fists.

"Down, cowboy," Nira said. "There won't be a *you and me* on this world or any other."

Nira breezed past the farmers and went to the refugees. "Londoners who need medical attention, queue up," she ordered.

Since Fred and Nira seemed to have everything under control, Olivia skirted around the edge of the crowd until she reached Aunt Meredith.

"Oh, Livy!"

Olivia found herself swallowed up in her aunt's tight embrace.

"Good grief, you're covered in dried blood. Is it yours?"

Olivia met her aunt's wild-eyed stare. The battle on the aircraft carrier flashed through her mind.

"No," she said, trying to forget about everything that had happened in the last day. "It isn't mine."

"Where's your sister?" Aunt Meredith asked, her worry growing by the second.

Olivia swallowed. "Addy's fine."

Physically, at least.

Olivia pushed down the wave of guilt that threatened to pull her under.

"Addy had to go to Tol's house to get his people out," Olivia explained. She gave her aunt an uncertain look. "I think she's planning to bring all of his people here."

Aunt Meredith surveyed the disorganized chaos taking place on her lawn and chuckled. "Well then, I guess I better look into getting some porta potties. Tramping around my yard is one thing. Invading my personal throne is quite another." She wrapped an arm around Olivia's shoulders and started for the house.

"I'm so sorry about all of this," Olivia told her aunt.

"Never you mind." Aunt Meredith gave Olivia another squeeze. "I was just complaining about how I didn't have enough people to feed with you lot out saving the world." She wrinkled her nose. "But if these Brits think I'm about to start serving up fish and chips or whatever else they're used to, they've got another think coming. They'll be getting good ole Texas grub while they're staying with me."

Olivia had always admired her aunt, but she'd never known how unbreakable she was. It made Olivia feel stronger herself—more able to face down whatever crisis hit them next.

When they reached the porch, Aunt Meredith turned to give her a critical look. "You're sure that blood doesn't belong to anyone important?"

"I'm sure." Olivia gave her aunt a tired smile. "Just the bad aliens."

* * *

Even a shower and clean, blood-free clothes weren't enough to lift the pressure that had settled on Olivia's heart.

The Celestial's magic sparked inside her, begging to be used even though her body was exhausted.

Olivia could feel her power pulling her farther away from her old life, which seemed like a betrayal of her family's memory. She felt like she was clinging to thoughts about her parents and sisters the way she might try to hold onto a dream as sleep faded. She was afraid that, by accepting her role as the Fount, she would lose what little hold she still had on her family.

Not ready to be surrounded by all the people outside, Olivia went into her aunt's bedroom where she'd slept when they first arrived. On the nightstand, she found the copy of *Pride and Prejudice* Erikir had given her.

Olivia picked up the book and hugged it to her chest, comforted by its solidness and familiarity. She hated not knowing how her own story would end. She felt constantly unbalanced.

A knock came at the half-open door.

"Pumpkin, you doing alright?" Aunt Meredith asked.

Her aunt took one look at Olivia's face and came into the room, shutting the door behind her. She sat on the bed, patting the mattress for Olivia to join her.

"Talk to me, Sweet Livy," her aunt said, taking off her cowboy hat and setting it on the comforter next to her.

"I think—" Olivia began. She bit her lip until the tears that wanted to leak out stayed put. "I did something, and I don't think Addy will ever forgive me."

She remembered the way Tol had tried to fight her on the aircraft carrier when he realized what she was going to do. She heard his screams in her mind.

What have you done?

She thought about the way Addy had looked at her as she'd knelt next to Tol's bloody, broken body on the sand. She thought about the expression on her sister's face when she realized she'd never blood marry Tol.

"Now, you listen to me carefully, Livy Deerborn." Her aunt gave her a stern look. "There is no stronger bond than the bond of sisterhood." Her expression softened. "No matter what's happened, I promise you, Addy will forgive you. That's what being a sister is all about."

Aunt Meredith's brown eyes misted over.

"Your mom and I had our differences," Aunt Meredith said, staring at a framed photograph of the entire Deerborn family hanging on the wall. "We didn't always get along, and we certainly didn't always agree, but we always loved each other. That's what it means to be sisters."

A loud thud, followed by even louder curses, came from somewhere outside.

"Dang it all." Aunt Meredith got up and shoved her cowboy hat back on. "If all that racket puts the cows off their feed, I'm going to lose what's left of my marbles." She stalked out of the room, muttering to herself.

Olivia felt lighter than she had a few minutes ago. She told herself she had used up her allotted moping time for the day, and that it was time to make herself useful.

The front lawn was a hive of activity. Olivia barely recognized the place.

A medical tent had been erected under the giant oak tree's shade.

On the other side of the lawn, Fred was overseeing a massive digging project. Farmers with all kinds of construction equipment, and others with nothing more than shovels, were spread out. Some of the Londoners were bringing around pizza boxes to all the people spread out around the property.

A small whimper drew Olivia's attention to the side of the house. She caught sight of a girl sitting at the edge of the porch, her knees drawn up to her chest. Her jeans were soot-stained and there was dried blood on her ballet flats.

"Are you alright?" Olivia asked, approaching slowly so she didn't frighten the girl.

"That's a dumb question." The girl, who looked like she was about twelve or thirteen, glared at Olivia.

Other people might have been put off by the girl's attitude, but Olivia's younger sister Stacy had acted like an angsty teenager since she was about five.

"You're right," Olivia agreed. "That was a really dumb question."

Olivia sat down next to her.

"I don't know what I'm supposed to do," the girl said, all of her bravado fading away. "I'm...scared." Her chin wobbled.

"So am I," Olivia admitted. "But you survived the London attack. You're brave."

Olivia was rewarded with the girl's watery smile. The girl wiped her nose on her sleeve and nodded at the book in Olivia's lap.

"I love Jane Austen, too," she said.

"Oh." Before she could think too hard about what she was doing, Olivia handed the book over. "Take it."

"Really?" the girl started flipping through the pages. She sighed in a way that reminded Olivia of the way she felt whenever she returned to one of her treasured books.

Leaving the girl to her reading, Olivia got to her feet.

The new bond she felt to all of the Chosen told her Nira was in the medical tent. And Erikir—

Her heart lurched. He was on the other side of the lawn, but his attention was fixed wholly on her. The harsh expression in his eyes had softened, and the scowl that was always pulling his lips down was gone.

Olivia didn't know what she was supposed to think about Erikir. She didn't want to think about how her connection with him was different from what she felt toward the rest of the Chosen.

She didn't want to think about the softness of his lips or the way she fit perfectly into the cocoon of his arms.

He smiled at her. It was so small and fleeting she almost missed it. It was real and beautiful, though, and it was an expression she'd only ever seen him give to her. And she couldn't help but smile back.

CHAPTER 8

TOL

Tol and Gerth landed on the cold ground on Vitaquias.

"I think I'm getting used to traveling by portal," Gerth said, getting to his feet. His baggy shirt had come loose, and he haphazardly began stuffing it back into his pants. In typical Gerth fashion, he got distracted halfway through.

Tol's first reaction was relief that the world still existed. After the storm that had been raging the last time, he wasn't sure anything would still be standing. His relief evaporated as they crossed the stretch of barren land that brought them within sight of the castle ruins.

The castle, which had still been in some semblance of a building before, was now just rubble. The entire structure had been razed to the ground.

Tol's thoughts went immediately to his grandfather.

Wordlessly, he and Gerth broke into a run. They didn't slow until they burst through the doorless entrance at the top of the ridge.

"Walidir?" Tol called.

His only answer was the howling wind.

A tingling in his left shoulder made him forget about his grandfather and the reason why he was here. He yanked up his sleeve and unbuckled his prosthesis, letting it clatter onto the ground. He watched in awe as the gold particles of light and magic began to congregate around his shoulder. They splintered and then re-formed, buzzing around until they made the shape of a real, fully-functional arm.

This will soon be permanent.

The words filled Tol's mind, along with images of what else would be possible after he fulfilled his duty to his people and his world.

"Tolumus? Gerth?"

Tol's heart stuttered. He and Gerth exchanged a look, and then they ran in the direction of the voice.

"Grandfather!"

Tol's insides squeezed at the sight of the man, hobbling out from under a precarious wall of rock.

"You're alright." Tol went weak with relief at the sight of his grandfather.

Walidir had lost the youth he'd gained after drinking Addy's blood. His hair had turned back to white, and age spots covered his wrinkled forehead. But in spite of everything he'd been through, Tol's grandfather still had a regal bearing.

He was as stubborn as Gran.

"I'm very much alive." Walidir gave Tol and Gerth a toothy smile before clapping each of them on the back. "It's more than I can say for the rotcumbers, though."

It took Tol a few seconds to process his grandfather's words. He looked around and realized they were in the small garden his grandfather had so meticulously tended over the last eighteen years.

It was torn apart. A large sinkhole had pulled the entire center of the garden down. The wind had done its work on the rest of the rotcumbers. The hairy brown vegetables had been torn out by their roots. Their gelatinous guts were smeared across the muddy ground.

"What have you been eating?" Gerth asked, Tol's worry reflected on his face.

"Oh, I've been feasting," Walidir replied, still grinning. "My favorites are these delightful creations called *Cheez-Its*, but I'm also partial to the *Snickers*."

Tol and Gerth exchanged a mystified look.

"Our packs," Gerth said, snapping his fingers.

Tol followed the direction of his gaze to the huge backpacks propped against a pile of crumbled stone. Tol had forgotten about all the supplies they'd brought to Vitaquias and left during the chaos of the storm. Now, his gratitude for Gerth's planning knew no bounds.

Walidir frowned. "But leave those jellied worms out the next time." He shuddered a little. "They're a bit too realistic in shape and consistency for my taste."

Gerth laughed. The sound was so foreign in this hollow, dark place that it startled Tol. Walidir began to laugh, too. Tol looked at the two of them, guffawing and clutching at their stomachs, wondering if they'd gone mad. Then, deciding he didn't really care, he joined them.

They must have been a sight.

Walidir wiped a tear of mirth from his cheek and breathed out a contented sigh. When he glanced at Tol, his good humor transformed to confusion, and then to concern.

"Why are you boys here?" He glanced up at the brooding sky, which seemed to be readying itself for more unpleasant weather. "You haven't completed the blood marriage, surely?"

With those words, Tol's heart iced back over.

"The Celestial," Tol said, his urgent errand returning to him in a rush. "I need to talk to her." *And beg her to help me fix the disaster I created.*

"I'll be back as soon as I can," he added.

"Sure, Tol." Gerth gave him a patronizing smile. "Whatever you say, mate."

Tol scowled but didn't try to argue when Gerth and Walidir followed him out of the castle ruins.

"Gotta earn my keep as your Chief Strategist," Gerth replied with an easy smile.

"And I'm coming because you boys are far better company than the rotcumbers," Walidir said.

They slipped, caught each other, and sloshed their way down the hillside. At the bottom, the winds were quiet enough for them to hear each other without needing to shout. Gerth hurriedly filled Walidir in on what had happened since the last time they'd seen each other. When Gerth was finished, Tol braced himself for his grandfather's judgement. What he got was worse.

His grandfather looked at him with pity.

"I'm sorry," Walidir said. "I know what it is you've lost."

Tol just nodded, because he didn't trust himself to say anything.

"I know how much you loved her," Walidir continued, and then stopped, like he didn't have the words.

Loved...past tense. Like Addy was dead.

In a way, Tol supposed, she was. To him, at least.

Don't think about, he ordered himself. *Figure out how to save your people.*

That was all that mattered now.

Tol forced his feet forward until he was sinking into the muck of the oily Source puddle where they'd found the Celestial before.

Uncertainty took hold of him.

Last time, Olivia had been the one to summon the Celestial.

"You can probably summon her yourself," Gerth said, reading Tol's mind as usual.

Gerth was right. Tol wasn't the Fount, but he was the Chosen prince.

Feeling foolish and desperate at the same time, he cleared his throat.

"Celestial?" He waited for several seconds. "Olivia said you could help me. I need to figure out—"

"Why does my Chosen prince reek of the Forsaken?"

They all turned toward the whispery voice.

The Celestial hovered above them, illuminated in the brightness of Tol's Haze.

For a moment, Tol just stared at her. He didn't know how a ghost could look somehow more...ghostly. Only her eyes were the same. They were the same molten silver that Olivia's had become when she chose to be the Fount forever.

Gerth and Walidir sunk to their knees in front of the Celestial, but Tol stayed where he was. In as few words as he could manage, he explained the situation to the Celestial.

THE CHOSEN UNION

"Is there a way to fix this?" Tol asked when he was finished. "Is there a way for me to still complete the blood marriage and save our people?" He heard the heaviness in his own voice.

Tol held his breath as the Celestial stared at him.

Finally, she spoke.

"It is possible, in theory. In order to purge your body of the tainted blood," she gave Tol a look of disgust, "you would need to drain your body completely. Then, you would need to complete the blood marriage, filling your veins with the Fount's blood."

"You said *in theory*," Gerth said, looking up at the Celestial.

She held Tol's gaze as she answered. "Even with your strength, you could not survive the purge long enough to completely the blood marriage, unless the gods willed it."

"Then, how do we get them to *will it?*" Tol asked, his last vestiges of patience leaving him.

The Celestial pointed straight ahead, at the snow-capped mountain in the distance.

"The summit of that mountain is the closest point to the gods on all of Vitaquias. It is there that you will need to make your case and hope the gods see fit to grant your request."

They'll grant it, Tol thought savagely. *Because I'm not leaving until they do.*

Tol turned to Gerth and his grandfather. He knew he'd never be able to convince Gerth to stay behind, but Walidir didn't have the strength to climb a mountain.

"Don't even say it, Tolumus," his grandfather said. "I have climbed the gods' peak before, and I will do it again."

"You've climbed it before?" Gerth asked, interest lighting up his face.

"I may have sought out the gods a time or two between storms," Walidir replied with a good-natured shrug. He started toward the mountain, hunching his shoulders against the wind. "Shall we? I know all the best footholds."

The Celestial floated beside Tol, her image flickering in and out of sight.

"I don't suppose there's any other way?" Gerth asked the Celestial. "I mean, I know the Fount is set in stone, but is there any way for someone else to take over Tol's part of the blood marriage?"

The Celestial nodded slowly. "There is a way for another to fulfill the blood marriage with the Fount, but—"

Tol stopped walking.

"—the sacrifice is too great. Even the most desperate wouldn't be willing to pay such a price."

For several seconds, Tol was too stunned to speak.

"Try me," he said, his voice a deadly quiet.

The Celestial's silver eyes turned mournful. If she had been in a physical form, Tol might have grabbed her and shaken her. He was that impatient to hear what she had to say.

"You would have to convince the gods to separate you from everything that makes you the Fount's other half. Then, you could gift those powers to another, and then that person could blood marry the Fount."

"How does he give up his power?" Gerth asked, taking charge of the logistics of the conversation while Tol's mind reeled with the possibility.

"That is between him and the gods," the Celestial replied.

"Say that they let him do it," Gerth persisted. "What would happen?"

The Celestial turned to Tol.

"If you can convince the gods, and if this is truly what you wish for, then your magic will be torn from you." Before Tol could process the thought of losing his ability to Influence, the Celestial continued.

"You would become mortal. And you'd no longer be Chosen."

CHAPTER 9

ADDY

The portal spit Addy and Jaxon out onto the tree-lined drive that led to the Chosen manor. Every other time Addy had been here, she had felt the tranquil beauty of the place.

This time was different.

She and Jaxon stood in the epicenter of pandemonium. People poured out of the manor. Black cabs and limousines lined the driveway, and the drivers were hurriedly stuffing half-open suitcases into the trunks.

She had never before realized how many people lived inside the manor. She'd known from Tol that many of the scholars and his parents' advisors lived here along with the royal family, but everything was usually so organized, it was easy to forget how many people were on the property at any given moment.

"Are they always like this?" Jaxon asked, eyeing a man who was trying to carry a stack of books that was almost as tall as he was. Predictably, the stack faltered halfway down the front steps. The books scattered across the checkerboard-mowed lawn.

"They're never like this," Addy said, searching around for a familiar face.

She finally gave up and just tapped the nearest person on the shoulder. It was a harried man who was balancing an armful of what looked like old-fashioned hat boxes.

"What's happening?" Addy asked, stopping the man before he got into one of the cars.

"What do you think?" he asked over his shoulder. "The Forsaken are coming."

"I know. I'm here to get you all somewhere safe," Addy said, putting her hand on the car door to keep the man from slamming it in her face.

"Ha! You're the reason why we're stuck in this world in the first place. If it wasn't for you, we'd all be sitting pretty on Vitaquias."

Addy froze. It was true.

She looked at the chaos surrounding her with new eyes. This wasn't the Supernal's doing. It was hers.

If she'd been a stronger person, she would have done what Tol's parents had asked from the beginning. She would have disappeared from Tol's life. Instead, she'd tried to keep Tol for herself. And she'd lost him all the same.

Addy's chest started to constrict. She clutched at her throat.

"Breathe," Jaxon commanded.

There was no kindness in his voice, but it wasn't unkind, either. He put a hand on her back, and the solid pressure was both a comfort and a reminder. They were here to do a job. She'd promised Tol.

"Wait—" Addy began, but the man had already disappeared inside the car with all of his hat boxes.

"They're going to be sitting ducks on the road," Jaxon said, appraising the crowd. "Our people will be able to ambush them."

Our people. Because, once again, it was Addy and Addy's ilk who were responsible for the Chosen's misery.

"Addy."

This time, Jaxon's voice was sharper.

Right. "We have to find Tol's parents."

Addy and Jaxon wove through the people making a mass exodus from the manor. Everyone was so burdened down with suitcases, books, and priceless artwork that they didn't even notice Addy and Jaxon.

"It's a miracle the Chosen have survived this long," Jaxon muttered.

At this particular moment, Addy was inclined to agree.

"If Gerth was here, he'd have all these people walking through your portal in five seconds," Jaxon said.

When Addy glanced at him, she saw there was a softness to his gray eyes, which were usually all business.

Before she could respond, she recognized the royal family's cranky Chief of Staff hurrying out of the manor. The man had never quite taken to Addy. It probably had something to do with the fact that, the last time she'd shown up at the manor, she'd been covered in blood. Tol's people could be so picky.

"Henroix!" she called, waving her hand to get his attention.

The flustered man turned to Addy. He took one look at Jaxon, with his white-blonde hair, massive physique, and gray eyes, and screamed.

"Forsaken!"

Oh, wonderful.

"Hang on a second." Addy pushed Jaxon back from the people who were all reaching for their vials of Source. She kept her gaze averted just in case any of them decided to try to Influence her. "You know me. Tol sent us here."

"Why didn't he come himself, then?" someone demanded.

"Because he's busy," Addy snapped. "Where are the king and queen?"

"Adelyne?"

Addy went weak with relief at the sight of Tol's grandmother.

"Getyl!"

She hurried to the other woman, towing Jaxon along behind her.

"Where's Tolumus? What are you doing here?" Getyl stared up at Addy and Jaxon through the thick lenses of her spectacles, which were balanced precariously on the end of her nose.

"We'll tell you everything, but right now, we need to get all of you out of here," Addy said. "I can portal you somewhere you'll be safe until we figure out what to do about the Supernal."

Getyl tilted her head back to stare up at Jaxon.

"Who are you?" she asked.

"Jaxon, ma'am," he said, giving Addy an uncertain look before taking the hand Getyl held out to him. After a moment's hesitation, he raised her hand to his lips and kissed her arthritic knuckles.

"Tolumus does keep strange company these days," Getyl said, which Addy took as a sign of approval.

"We have to get going," Addy pressed. "The general and a hundred Forsaken are heading this way. It won't be long before they get here."

"The king and queen are…occupied," Getyl said. Her eyes darted back to the front steps, where an argument had broken out over a painting that two old women were trying to wrest from each other's hands. The painting tore down its center, and the women's loud wails were added to the other sounds of bedlam.

"They're doomed," Jaxon said under his breath.

"We need to talk to the king and queen right now," Addy told Getyl as firmly and politely as she could manage.

"Very well." Getyl sighed. "Come along."

Even with her cane, Getyl kept up a good clip as she led them into the manor. The inside was in shambles. Addy was grateful that Tol wasn't here to see the place. It looked like it had been ransacked.

The hallways were empty as Getyl led them to a part of the manor Addy had never visited before. When they reached a set of double doors, Getyl stopped.

"Wait here, please," she told Addy and Jaxon.

Getyl gave a soft rap on the door with her cane, opened it just enough to squeeze her small frame through, and then shut it in Addy and Jaxon's faces.

"They're not usually like this," Addy felt compelled to say.

"We're wasting time," was Jaxon's only response.

A gut-wrenching cry came from inside the room. Addy didn't hesitate. She had her garden shears out and ready. Jaxon was pulling his half-moon blades out of the sheath on his back. She threw open the doors and barged inside, with Jaxon on her heels.

They both froze.

The king and queen were sitting on either side of a hospital-style bed. The elderly woman lying beneath the blanket was hooked up to a myriad of IVs dripping fluids into her veins. A dozen other Chosen were standing around the room. Some of them were sobbing. Others had their heads bowed.

The woman who had cried out before was standing at the head of the dying woman's bed.

"What's going on?" Addy demanded.

"I think it's obvious," Jaxon whispered in her ear.

He was right. It had been a stupid question.

"This is your fault!" the woman standing at the head of the bed snarled at Addy.

Addy staggered back a step, unprepared for the venom in the other woman's glare.

"Her mother's Source is gone," Getyl explained in a quiet voice. "This is a very difficult time for her family."

"She's dying because of you!" the Chosen woman standing beside the bed howled. "You bewitched our prince. You deprived us of our salvation." She choked on a sob. "Forsaken whore."

For a second, Addy couldn't breathe. She'd never felt so much hatred directed at her in her entire life.

"Liniadius, you will not speak to my future granddaughter that way," Getyl said in an unyielding tone.

Future granddaughter. Those words were like claws digging into her chest. Getyl didn't know what Addy had done. None of the Chosen knew that Addy had further jeopardized their chances at immortality because of her selfish love for Tol.

"I can help."

The words burst out of Addy. She wrenched away from Jaxon as he put out a hand to stop her.

"Unless you've got a vial full of Source, there's shite you can do for my mother," Liniadius snarled.

"I have something better," Addy said.

She felt the distrustful, angry gazes track her every move as she crossed the room to the bed. She pricked her forearm with her garden shears.

"There's Source in my blood," she explained to the silent and tense crowd. "You'll see. Your mom's Haze will be stronger than it would be with normal Source."

Addy looked at Tol's parents for permission.

The king nodded, so she pressed her bleeding forearm to the dying woman's chapped lips.

The woman's skin, which had been garish and paper-thin, began to transform to a healthy bronze. Her Haze, which had been almost invisible before, brightened the room. Her white hair turned to thick black curls.

Addy winced as the old woman began to suck on her open cut.

"It's a miracle," Liniadius whispered.

"It's really not," Addy said, not wanting to take credit for something undeserved. "It's just that—"

She didn't have a chance to finish. Everyone except for Tol's family swarmed her.

They begged, pleaded, *demanded* some of her Source-filled blood for themselves.

Addy began backing away as they got closer and closer.

"Get away from her," Jaxon ordered. His half-moon blades shone in the light of everyone's Hazes as he put himself between Addy and the crowd clambering for her blood.

"Don't," she told him.

These were Tol's people. She wasn't about to attack them.

Jaxon ignored her.

"This is the future Forsaken general," Jaxon said in a cold, authoritative voice. "If you attack her, I will kill you."

"No," Addy protested.

"Run away, Forsaken scum," a Chosen man said to Jaxon, even though his ravenous gaze was fixed on Addy. "While you still can."

"Back off," the king ordered. "Give the girl and her guard some space."

Addy wanted to weep with relief. The king could stop this before it turned bloody—or, in the case of her arm—bloodier.

She waited for all of the Chosen to fall back. But they didn't so much as pause their advance.

Someone grabbed Addy's bloody arm with violent force. Jaxon's half-moon blades flashed. Someone's arm, cut off at the elbow, fell onto the oriental rug. Addy stared at the severed bone and bloody flesh. Screams filled the room.

"No!" Addy shouted. "Please!"

This was what Tol had feared. Addy hadn't understood at the time. She'd thought he was paranoid for wanting to keep the power of her blood a secret. Now, too late, she realized it wasn't paranoia at all.

These people were like a pack of starving wolves. Or vampires.

Some of them were even licking their lips in anticipation.

"Jaxon," Addy began, and then faltered.

Jaxon's piercing gray eyes were unfocused, his muscles relaxed. There was a heavy thud as his two blades hit the carpet. He made no move to pick them back up.

Oh no.

"Does this one have Source blood, too?" the woman whose hand was wrapped around Jaxon's unresisting wrist demanded.

"No, so let him go," Addy said, trying not to let her growing panic show.

"Stand down," the king thundered. "Back away from the Forsaken."

His subjects ignored him.

Addy's frantic gaze turned to the queen, who was shouting, too.

"This is the prince's fiancé. She saved my life. *Back away.*"

Addy knew it was useless, but she still wasn't willing give up. Tol was trusting her to protect his people. She couldn't let him down.

"The Forsaken are coming." She faltered, and then amended, "The Forsaken who mean you harm are coming. I need to get all of you out of here."

"We aren't going anywhere," said the woman in the bed, who was sitting up and looking as healthy as Addy. "Your blood is the weapon that will allow us to kill every one of those barbarians."

"Listen to me," Addy begged. "You have to—"

All of Addy's worries slid away. She held the fathomless stare of the Chosen woman sitting up in bed. Everything else around her disappeared. Only that woman mattered.

"Cut your other arm," the Chosen woman ordered. Her voice was beautiful, like a perfectly-tuned instrument.

Addy was only too happy to comply.

Addy used the sharp edge of one of her shears' blades to slice a line across her wrist. There was no pain, only joy at doing what she was told. She felt the wetness on her arm. She felt lips and teeth graze her flesh.

The whole experience was pleasant. The only part she didn't like was all the yelling. Tol's grandmother was banging her cane on the floor. The king and queen were tied up and gagged. Addy wasn't sure why the Chosen would do that to their monarchs, but she wasn't bothered by it. The woman whose eyes were locked on hers told her it wasn't a problem, and so it wasn't.

When Getyl was finally dragged out of the room, Addy was relieved. There was no longer anyone or anything to stop her from enjoying this delicious peace. She couldn't remember ever feeling this relaxed.

When her savior, as she'd come to think of the woman, came to stand beside her, Addy was filled with a wonderful sense of anticipation. She eagerly waited for her next command.

"Do the same to your other arm," the woman told her, giving Addy a smile that was so perfect she wanted to weep.

Addy didn't hesitate to do as she was told.

More people were in the room now, and they were all pushing and shoving to get near her. It didn't concern her. Her savior would make sure they all got their turn.

For some reason, words someone had spoken to her in the past came to her now. A tall woman who looked just like Addy but wore a military uniform had spoken them.

Tell me every one of the Chosen wouldn't bleed you dry if they knew what your blood contains.

The words were slippery, like oil in water, and they were gone as soon as Addy recalled them.

THE CHOSEN UNION

She felt someone rip her collar. Something sharp pierced her neck. She looked at her savior, who just smiled and nodded. Addy immediately relaxed, letting the woman's dark gaze comfort her as blood slid down her neck.

A soft smile played at her lips as Addy's vision went dark.

CHAPTER 10

ERIKIR

Erikir opened his eyes. He had been in a deep sleep, but it only took him a moment to understand what had woken him. A sharp, pink nail was jabbing into his chest.

"Nira, what the hells?" he grumbled.

"Get up, Weasel," she ordered.

"Piss off."

He turned over on the couch.

"I'm bloody tired of all these mortals," Nira complained, plopping down on the edge of the couch.

Erikir pulled the pillow over his head, but it did nothing to drown out the whine of Nira's voice.

"As soon as I heal them from one wound, they're back two seconds later with another one. These mortals are so... *fragile*."

Even in his barely-awake state, Erikir knew what was really bothering Nira. All of the Chosen knew about her two aunts, who were barely hanging on to life. He had seen that helpless look in Nira's eyes every time she was with them. He understood that look, because it spoke to a deep ache inside him.

Nira felt the same helplessness to save her aunts that he felt for all of the Chosen. It was a desperate need to protect them, and being completely unable to do so. It was infuriating.

THE CHOSEN UNION

It was the only thing he and Nira had in common. They built walls around their hearts so they wouldn't be destroyed by their utter helplessness…their uselessness.

He'd never say any of that out loud to Nira, of course. Even if he wanted to, she'd probably poke his eyes out with her glittery claws.

"Fred's dad will be here soon," Nira continued, "along with all of his farmer friends from Wherever-those-people-come-from, New York."

She sighed and tugged the blanket off Erikir so it was covering her. "Fred really thinks he's going to create a mortal army that can fight the Supernal, and I suppose it'll be up to me to make sure they don't get their mortal arses burned off."

"Do you have a reason for being here?" Erikir asked, lifting the pillow off his head to glare at her. "Aside from being a nuisance?"

"I do." She tossed her hair, letting it fall over her shoulder. "I thought you'd like to know the object of your desire is having a vision. She's doing that thing where she convulses on the floor."

Erikir was up so fast Nira went sprawling. He barely noticed.

He would have cursed her out for not telling him immediately, but that would only waste more time. He ran for the door.

It was late, but huge floodlights had been set up on the front lawn. The beams bathed everything in a harsh glow. He scanned the lawn until he found the small group, including Meredith and Fred, bent over a still form on the ground.

Olivia.

He shoved through the crowd and fell to his knees beside her. Meredith was holding Olivia's head to keep it from hitting the ground.

Olivia's magic flooded over Erikir. It wasn't the soft rush of power he got when he drank Source. This was raw and unharnessed. Unstable. Silver light was raging in her open, unseeing eyes.

Erikir gently wrapped his arms around Olivia's back and drew her to him. Her entire body radiated cold.

"Get a blanket," he said to no one in particular.

As soon as he pressed a hand to her ice-cold cheek, all sight and sound slipped away. Erikir was dragged down into a darkness so complete it was endless.

Just as he began to despair at ever finding his way out, a light appeared in the distance.

Erikir?

Olivia's voice, timid and hopeful, filled his mind.

I'm here, Olivia.

It's so cold, came her soft reply. *And I don't know how to find my way.*

Erikir followed the tug on his heart. When he reached her, they fell into each other's arms.

They clung to each other as the darkness transformed.

They were hovering over a bedroom with elegant furniture and large windows. There was a cradle in the corner, but it was empty.

Books were strewn across every available surface. The room smelled like paper and the leather bindings. The smell sent a sharp pang through Erikir that made him want to weep for no reason he could fathom. His attention was drawn away from the books at the sound of laughter.

There was a couple standing beside the bed. The woman held a baby in her arms, and the man held her. They were smiling at the child with such love that it made Erikir's heart stutter with a fierce longing he thought he'd banished long ago.

When the woman looked up, Erikir saw a face he knew more from portraits than from his own memory. The man looked away from the baby and stared straight at Erikir.

Father.

He'd known he looked like his father, but seeing the resemblance in washed-out portraits wasn't the same as this. There were slight variations, like the bone structures of their faces. His father's eyes were more hooded and his nose straighter. Other than that, they were nearly identical.

Erikir reached out a hand, but it passed right through his parents' locked arms without them reacting.

His parents continued to look at each other and the infant version of himself with open affection until the image began to blur out of focus.

THE CHOSEN UNION

Wait! Erikir shouted, trying to hold onto the vision.

The picture wavered and then clarified. Erikir was filled with relief, until he looked more closely. The scene had changed. It was blurred around the edges, and Erikir remembered Olivia saying that meant it was a vision of the future.

It was no longer Erikir's parents. It was him and Olivia. He recognized her long, curly hair even though her face was turned down. They stood in the same room, and they were wearing the king and queen's crowns on their heads. Olivia was holding a child...*their* child. Olivia tipped her head up toward his. There was so much love and happiness in her gaze that he couldn't breathe.

Then, the version of himself that wore the crown bent to kiss her. She rose up on her toes to reach him.

But no...that was wrong. He wasn't that tall—Olivia didn't need to reach so high to meet his lips.

The king turned his face, and revulsion stuttered through Erikir. He wasn't the one Olivia was smiling at. It wasn't his child in her arms. It was Tol's.

Erikir felt himself break.

The vision was swallowed up, but Erikir barely noticed. The smell of old books and unfamiliar flowers were replaced with cedar and Texas heat.

"Livy, Erikir, what happened?"

Meredith, crouched on the grass, looked at them with concern written into the lines of her face.

Erikir realized he was still clutching Olivia to him, probably hard enough to hurt. He let his arms drop and moved back.

"Are you alright?" he asked her. The monotone of his voice matched the deadness inside him.

"I'm sorry," she gasped, her eyes wide and her whole body shivering. "I don't know why those visions came to me."

Erikir had a sinking suspicion it was because he'd been touching her at the time. Those visions contained two possible versions of the future. One held his deepest desire, while the other displayed his deepest dread.

From the apprehension in her eyes, she knew it too. She'd witnessed something he never would have willingly shared.

Olivia was waiting for his anger. He could see it on her face.

It would be so much easier to hide behind anger. He'd done it all his life. But if he did that, it would hurt her.

Erikir would rather die a thousand deaths than cause Olivia an ounce of pain.

He let out a deep breath. "You didn't see anything you couldn't have guessed," he said, hating that they were surrounded by people. "It doesn't matter."

Olivia opened her mouth, but Erikir didn't want her comfort. He didn't want to think about what they'd just seen ever again.

The only one who would ever understand his bitterness was Addy, and she would sooner cut him into bite-sized pieces and feed him to the birds than offer him solace.

Olivia gave Fred a distracted smile as he tucked a blanket over her shoulders. She was chewing on her lip, and that meant there was something on her mind.

"Here, sweetums," Meredith said, handing mason jars full of lemonade to each of them. "You'll feel better once you get some sugar in you."

"Before that...vision," Olivia began, her eyes flicking to Erikir and then away again, "I saw something else. All the Chosen at the manor...they were fighting—" She cut herself off. She shivered a little, and Erikir had to stop himself from reaching over to fix the blanket so it covered more of her.

"I thought Red was bringing our people back here," Nira said, a hint of panic in her voice.

Olivia shook her head. "I didn't see Addy or Jaxon anywhere. And there weren't any Forsaken, either. There were only the Chosen." She pressed her fingers to her temple.

Erikir's own head was pulsing. He ground his teeth in an effort to distract himself from the ache.

"There was blood dripping from all of their mouths, but they didn't seem injured." Olivia's brow creased. "I know it sounds crazy."

"Do you think it was some kind of metaphor?" Erikir asked. He knew Olivia's visions weren't always literal.

"I don't think so, but I can't be sure."

"Look again," Nira ordered. "If they're in trouble, we have to know."

Erikir gave her an irritated look. The last thing Olivia needed right after she'd woken up from a vision was to be interrogated. Besides, it wasn't like there was anything they could do from here, anyway.

"The two of you look like you need to lie down," Olivia's aunt said, giving them a stern look. "Come on."

Before they could move, Erikir heard the thrum of engines. Headlights were bouncing down the driveway toward the house.

"It's my dad," Fred said excitedly. "And reinforcements."

"Oh great," Nira grumbled. "Because the one thing we were missing from this circus was more flannel and overalls."

"What's wrong with flannel and overalls?" Fred asked as the first taxi pulled up.

A man started to get out of the passenger door.

"Dad!" Fred shouted as he raced around to help the man, who was struggling to force his legs into a pair of braces.

Still feeling like a hammer was rattling around in his skull, Erikir got to his feet and offered Olivia his hand. She gave him a weak smile as she stood.

"Livy!" the man who was locked in a bear hug with Fred boomed. "There you are, my girl."

A huge smile warmed her face as she went to Fred's father. Erikir felt a flare of emotion at the easy way Olivia wrapped one arm around Fred's waist and the other around his father's. The way she smiled when Fred's father ruffled her hair made it clear these people had been in her life since she was a child.

Erikir didn't have that kind of easy affection with anyone.

He shrugged off the thought before it could dig its claws into his mind.

"Come." Meredith draped an arm over Erikir's shoulders. "I'll introduce you."

She steered him right into the group of farmers who were taking their turns giving Fred back-slapping hugs. To Erikir's amazement, the group made room for him and Meredith.

The farmers looked him straight in the eye, having no idea how much that simple gesture meant to him. Most of his own people avoided looking at him, since he was the spitting image of his father. Erikir was a walking reminder of everything the Chosen people had lost. Erikir's own uncle hadn't met his gaze in as long as he could remember.

"Steven." Meredith wrapped Fred's father in a warm embrace. "So glad you're here."

"'Course I came. I hear my son's leading an army. I'm gonna be his first lieutenant." Steven Brown looked at his son with pride.

"And here I was thinking I'd get that job," Nira said, pretending to pout.

Steven looked at Nira, and then at his son. His eyes bugged.

"Don't tell me *you're* Nira," he said.

"What kinds of rumors has Fred been spreading about me?" she asked, laying on the charm as she took Steven's hand and gave him a smile that was completely devoid of her usual snark.

"I didn't say nothin'," Fred mumbled.

The floodlights weren't doing Fred any favors. They exposed the deep blush that was spreading across his freckled face.

"All I know is you're much too lovely to deal with the likes of us," Steven told her.

"Dad, she's also a doctor," Fred said. "Why is everyone always talkin' about the way Nira looks?"

"Are you blind?" Steven countered. "Now, show me this bunker you're constructing and let your old man see if he can think of any improvements."

Meredith looped her arm through Erikir's as they all made their way across the lawn. Even with the remnants of his shared vision with Olivia and his worries about the Chosen haunting him, he felt a sense of belonging he'd never had before.

"What's going on in your neck of the woods?" Meredith asked Steven, who was moving slowly with the help of his braces and Fred's steady grip on his shoulder.

Steven's good-humored smile faded.

"It ain't good," he said. "Everyone's panickin'. People are tryin' to decide whether to join up with that blue devil or go into hidin'."

A small town in upstate New York would be safe for some time, since the Supernal would target the major cities first. But Erikir didn't doubt the Supernal would make good on his promise to enslave or kill every mortal on the planet. Unless they could find a way to stop him.

Steven's progress across the yard was slow and laborious. They kept needing to stop so the man could catch his breath. Erikir saw the way Fred's brow was creased in worry.

"You know, I might be able to help you manage your pain," Nira offered, indicating Steven's shaking hands.

"My son was right." He gave Nira a broad smile. "You are an angel."

"*Dad.*"

Nira turned away while Fred and his father continued to bicker good-naturedly.

"Better go insult someone," Erikir goaded Nira in a quiet voice. "Otherwise people might start getting the wrong idea about you."

"What would you know about people, Weasel?" she hissed back. She crossed her arms and gave him a look that would make a lesser man falter.

Fortunately, Erikir had always been immune to Nira's icy beauty.

"You should take some of your own advice," she continued with a meaningful look in Olivia's direction. Nira tapped Erikir's chest. "You better watch out, or your heart of ice is going to thaw."

Too late, he thought as Olivia's perfect lips turned up in a smile.

Before Erikir could deliver a biting retort, Nira was absorbed into a conversation with Fred and his father about compression gloves and pain-relieving skin gel. Meredith, Olivia, and Erikir left them to it and headed back to the house.

"What do you think, you two?" Meredith asked as they made their way to the porch. "Blueberry pancakes or banana?"

A prickle along Erikir's spine had him turning toward the road, where a long line of headlights was just becoming visible.

"More farmers?" he asked.

Olivia shook her head. "Everyone from Nowell already arrived with Fred's dad."

"And everyone I know is already here," Meredith said.

When the first vehicle came within view, Erikir saw it was a Hummer painted in army camo. All of his hopes for a peaceful night fled.

"Forsaken!" he shouted.

CHAPTER 11

TOL

The mountain was steeper than it had appeared from a distance. They had some climbing equipment, thanks to Gerth's foresight when he packed their bags for their last trip to Vitaquias. Walidir led them from handhold to foothold. Even so, it was slow going.

The air was so cold it burned Tol's lungs. He and Gerth had gone skiing in the Swiss Alps one winter, and he'd thought that was cold. It couldn't hold a candle to these temperatures.

Tol's Haze kept them all from freezing to death, but the whole experience was the exact opposite of pleasant. The fingers of his right hand were numb and bloody from gripping the rock. His left arm, made out of golden light and magic, was proving to be a far greater asset. It was stronger and didn't feel pain or cold like his right arm.

They reached a ledge wide enough for the three of them to sit just as the summit came into view. They sank down onto the frozen ground and rested their backs against the sheer rock. Walidir dug three squished Snickers bars out of his pocket and passed one to each of them. Tol had no appetite, but he took the candy to satisfy his grandfather. The Celestial hovered beside them. She didn't say anything, but Tol could feel her steady presence.

"I'm not going to try to give you any advice about what decision to make," Walidir said, breaking their silence. "But I will say that a blood marriage isn't the deepest bond two people can form, despite what everyone believes."

Tol's grandfather kicked his feet in the air over the ledge. He reminded Tol more of a child on a swing than a seven-hundred-year-old Chosen man sitting three-thousand feet off the ground.

"Your gran and I never blood married, and I challenge you to find two people with a stronger bond."

"Yeah, but you're forgetting one thing." Gerth pointed his half-eaten candy bar at Tol. "Tol would have to give up his powers and immortality to get his true love."

Walidir's expression grew solemn. "You must simply decide what you cannot live without."

Or who.

"You know," Walidir said, licking caramel from his lips, "you boys are humbling me."

Tol looked at his grandfather.

"I'm not sure how you can say that when I keep putting our people's immortality at risk," Tol said, unable to hide his bitterness.

"You're trying to make it right." Walidir waved a hand at the mountain and then up, toward the gods. "You have shown more bravery and determination than any of our people." He took another bite of his Snickers and chewed.

Tol had a sudden image of Gran, sipping from a cup of tea, as she imparted cryptic advice that inevitably led to some deep revelation. He almost laughed.

"My generation caused this." Walidir pointed his candy bar at the bruised sky surrounding them. "Our hunger for more caused us to lose everything, and we all paid the price."

A great weariness seemed to settle on his grandfather's shoulders, and for a moment, Walidir looked his age. Then, he straightened his spine and pinned Tol with a Gran-like stare.

"We call the Forsaken evil," he said, "but I believe the true evil was perpetuated by our own people's greed." He stared off into the darkness beyond the mountain.

"That just means we need to be better than our forebears," Gerth said, undaunted by the challenge. "But to do that, we'll have to make it off this mountain alive."

Gerth got to his feet. He punched his fist up in the air, imitating the comic book heroes they'd read about together as kids.

"In the immortal words of Stan Lee," Gerth began.

"Upward and onward to greater glory," Tol finished, returning his friend's grin.

✽ ✽ ✽

The last stretch of the climb was the most difficult.

They had almost reached the top when Tol heard a hoarse cry. Rock cracked apart and tumbled back down the sheer stone face. Tol's stomach lurched at the sight of Gerth, hanging one-handed from the mountain a few meters below. His legs were scrabbling for a foothold that wasn't there.

"Hold on!" Tol yelled.

He climbed down and to the side, hoping he'd be able to reach out a hand to steady Gerth.

Tol got down to the same level and was parallel to Gerth when all of the handholds disappeared. There was nothing between them except a solid sheet of rock covered with ice. Tol couldn't reach Gerth, and there was no way to get closer.

"Can you swing yourself this way?" Tol asked.

Gerth's face was white with fear. All of his effort was focused on holding on.

"Okay, scratch that," Tol said.

Tol wedged the fingers of his right hand as deep into its crevice as the rock would allow. He ignored the way his bones ground into bare rock.

Don't look down, he warned himself. *Don't look down. Don't—*

He glanced down. Instantly, he was overcome by vertigo.

He blinked until the mountain righted itself. Then, he let go of his precarious toe holds and swung himself to the side.

His left hand just managed to close around the fabric of Gerth's jacket.

If Gerth had been on his other side, his right hand wouldn't have been strong enough to support Gerth's weight. But his left arm was made from magic that came from the gods.

Tol managed to haul himself and Gerth back to a place where there were enough handholds for them to steady themselves.

"You okay?" Tol gasped. His whole body was trembling from the close call.

"You saved me," Gerth said in a shaky voice.

Tol let out a short laugh. "I wasn't aware there was another option."

Gerth's face went from relieved to furious in the span of a single heartbeat.

"You bloody idiot," Gerth shouted, his voice rising above the gale that was ripping his long hair from its messy ponytail. "You could have gotten yourself killed! You're our prince—"

"And you're my best mate." Tol took his left hand off the ledge to grab Gerth's arm. "My brother."

They managed an awkward hug while clinging to the side of the mountain.

"Boys, what gives?" Walidir called down from the mountain's summit. "You let an old man beat you to the top."

Tol exchanged a grin with Gerth before they finished their climb.

Tol was the last of their little group to haul himself onto the mountain's summit.

The air was thinner up here, but he wasn't out of breath. He wasn't tired from climbing. If anything, he felt stronger than ever.

Strangely, the weather was calmer up here. The dark purple clouds still hovered overhead, but everything was quiet. Beams of golden light cut through the darkness.

Tol felt a stillness come over him. All his fears and uncertainties washed away the moment he sensed them. *The gods.*

They had never been more than an abstraction in Tol's mind, but for the first time in his life, he actually felt their presence. They weren't high overhead where he'd always imagined them to be. They were all around

THE CHOSEN UNION

him. Tol's essence drew them, and he could feel the brush of their consciousnesses against his own. He could feel their power.

It was terrifying. Endless. Magnificent.

He could hear Walidir and Gerth talking behind him, but their words held no meaning. He let the power of Vitaquias, the power of the gods, engulf him.

Welcome home, Prince Tolumus. Future king of the Chosen. Most powerful of all our children.

Rightness shuddered through Tol.

Something wrapped around his ankle, drawing his attention away from everything that mattered. Irritated, he glanced down.

It took him a moment to recognize the insignificant immortal tugging on him.

Gerth, he remembered.

"You're bloody levitating," Gerth called up to him.

Tol shook his head, trying to clear it. That's when he noticed the Celestial hovering just off the side of the summit.

"What's happening to me?" he asked her.

Before she could answer, golden light congregated around a spot directly in front of Tol. As he watched, the golden light formed itself into a dagger. It was as real as Tol's left arm, and when he reached for it, he nicked his finger on the blade.

"The gods have decided that you must purge your blood and bind yourself to the Fount," the Celestial said.

Warm protection wrapped around Tol's mind. The gods were assuring him that they wouldn't permit him to die. They would protect his body until the Fount arrived to bring him back to life.

Revulsion stuttered through Tol. He didn't want Olivia's blood filling his veins. He didn't want her voice in his head.

Are you ready to accept our gifts? the gods asked. *We've waited for you for so long.*

The summit and purple clouds disappeared from Tol's view. He was now standing on the cliff overlooking the lake of Source. Instead of the ruined, dead world Vitaquias was now, everything had been restored. The sky was blue, the lake was clear and sparkling, and the castle was pristine marble.

He wore his father's crown—no, *his* crown—on his head. His people, newly-immortal, spoke his name in the same reverent way in which they prayed to the gods.

Tol and his queen ruled side by side, their combined magic an unstoppable force. They were each other's perfect balance. Tol was all raw power. She was empathy and justice and everything else that would give their people an eternity of prosperity.

Everything was perfect.

Except it wasn't. The woman sitting on the throne beside him had kind, brown eyes. For some reason, that seemed wrong to Tol.

As soon as the thought crossed his mind, the vision was swallowed up into darkness. Tol reached out a hand, trying to drag it back. Before he could grasp it, a new vision materialized.

Tol was standing in a bedroom. A gentle breeze blew through the open window, bringing the scent of flowers, ocean salt, and piña coladas.

Tol leaned down to kiss the woman in his arms.

Addy.

But as Tol watched, his appearance began to change. His black hair turned gray. His skin wrinkled, and his spine bent. He watched himself age a hundred years in the span of seconds.

Tol was transported to a cold, dank-smelling mausoleum. In the gloom, he could just make out the wooden coffin. It had been propped open to reveal a gray, lifeless body inside.

An uneasy feeling took hold of Tol. He was looking at his own corpse.

He saw how his life had been a mere blink compared to the eternity of darkness that stretched out before him. He saw Addy's pain as she lived on without him. He saw the other Chosen live on. He saw them forget his name. He saw himself become irrelevant to the world that continued to go on for centuries…millennia after he had perished.

Tol's throat began to close.

"Tolumus," a voice called from somewhere far away.

His grandfather, Tol thought with little interest. What did one immortal's voice matter compared to everything he was witnessing?

"Your gran contacted me. Something happened at the manor," Walidir's faraway voice continued. "Adelyne has been badly hurt."

Tol tore his mind out of the gods' grasp with a single, desperate yank.

He fell out of the air, where he'd been hovering. He felt the gods' anger stir. He didn't care.

"What happened?" he demanded, blinking through the golden beams of his Haze to focus on his grandfather.

"Our connection was snuffed out before I could learn more," Walidir said apologetically.

Tol's mind reeled. *Addy was hurt*. He had to get back to her.

"No," the Celestial's whispery voice said in his ear. "Bind yourself to the Fount…the one you were destined for from the beginning. Live the bright eternity the gods will gift you."

Tol turned to the Celestial.

"I'd rather have a single year with Addy than an eternity without her."

It was the only decision he'd ever make. Addy would be furious with him for sacrificing his immortality, but it couldn't be helped. Now that he had found her, he wasn't giving her up. Not if he could help it.

"You are willing to give up your magic and your immortality for her?" the Celestial asked, incredulous.

"Yes," he said simply.

"Then, you are no longer my Chosen one. I cannot protect you."

"I'm not asking you to," Tol said, feeling his irritation spike. "Tell me what to do so I can get off this gods-damned mountain."

"If your mind is stronger than your magic, then you will know what to do."

"If my mind is stronger than my magic…what in the two hells does that mean? Celestial?"

She was gone. Tol felt something in his left hand. When he looked down, he saw he was gripping a smooth obsidian stone. It looked just like the one that had contained the Supernal's powers.

All at once, he understood that he was supposed to drain the power from his body into this stone. It was just like what the Celestial had done two-thousand years ago when she'd stolen away the Supernal's power. Tol just didn't know how.

"Take it," he ordered the gods. "Take all of my power. Take my immortality."

He felt a wave of their wrath tear through him like fire. Before he collapsed, the agony was replaced with the seductive lap of power. But he wasn't drawn in a second time. He needed to get this over with so he could get back to Addy. She was all that mattered, and regardless of what enticements the gods offered, they wouldn't be enough.

He chose her. He'd always choose her.

Tol felt a strange pulling at his heart.

His magic, he realized. It had been a part of him all his life, and now, it was coming free.

The gods howled at him. The wind shrieked. The mountain rumbled in protest.

Tol grasped hold of his magic with mental fingers. He tried to yank it apart from himself, feeling the separation as though he were clawing off his own skin. Pain burned up his insides.

"Take it," he ordered the gods as he continued to tear his magic free. "Take it back!"

An earsplitting crack of thunder broke across the sky. Tol was scorning the gods' gifts, and the offense wouldn't go unpunished.

He didn't care.

Take it, take it, take it. He chanted the words as he ripped, clawed, and tore his magic away.

An inhuman scream poured from his throat. Some part of Tol knew he couldn't survive being separated from such a vital part of himself. The more essential part didn't care. Addy needed him, and the sooner he did what he'd come here to do, the sooner he could go to her.

Tol sunk to his knees. He felt the mountain tremble beneath him as the gods roared. Still, he pulled.

Tol retched and writhed, but he didn't stop.

You are worthless without your magic, the voices chorused.

Tol ignored them.

His power began to seep outside of himself. He saw it congregating in a bright, luminescent ball above his head. The golden glow grew in intensity as he drew more and more out of himself.

His vision was beginning to darken, but he forced himself to stay conscious.

Why? the gods thundered. *Why do you scorn our gifts?*

"I love my people," Tol managed, "but I love Addy more."

Erikir had been right. He was the wrong man to be king of the Chosen. The truth of it was never as clear as it was at this moment.

Tol drew the last vapors of magic from him. He may as well have torn out every one of his vital organs. He was alive…somehow…but he was a shell of the person he'd been.

He clutched the obsidian stone and held it up to the golden light hovering above his head. As soon as the two connected, Tol's magic was absorbed into the stone. The stone heated until it was a small inferno burning through his palm, but he didn't let go. He stayed still until every ounce of power had been pulled into the stone, which now glowed gold.

Then, even though Tol could barely think through the emptiness that was eating him alive, he felt a fire spread through his left arm. He looked down.

His arm was no longer gold. The particles of light were dying one by one. It looked like a terrible rot was spreading from his fingertips up his forearm, and then higher.

His shoulder burned with a ferocity he'd never known. He clenched his jaw until he thought it would break. The pain was inescapable.

Through watering eyes, he watched his left arm disintegrate. Tol felt the loss of each particle of light, because he knew it was the last time he would feel anything there. He knew the next time he came to Vitaquias, his arm wouldn't magically reappear. It was gone forever.

You're abandoning us a second time, the gods bellowed.

And then, everything went quiet.

Terror prickled at the back of Tol's neck. A dark shadow was moving toward them.

"Oh no," Gerth said.

That's putting things lightly, Tol thought.

He knew this shadow…the Nyxar. It was a being that had been released when the Source was drained from Vitaquias. It killed anyone in its path and grew stronger with each life it took.

The Nyxar was still far away on the horizon, but Tol could tell it was more lifelike than the last time he had encountered the creature. Its face looked like one giant, open pit of darkness. Swaths of shadow hung down from its body like a cloak. Its arms reached out as it crossed the wide expanse of sky. Its smoky fingers grasped…reached….

Tol could somehow sense that the gods were controlling the Nyxar, which was making steady progress toward the summit.

"Celestial, help us," Tol begged.

"I can slow it down, but I cannot stop it," a whisper came from somewhere nearby. "You have scorned the gods. They will kill you."

Not happening, Tol thought, gritting his teeth as the Nyxar came nearer. Not after everything they'd been through. Not after how hard he'd fought.

They had to get off this mountain before the Nyxar came and swallowed them. They had to get back to the portal so Olivia could get them out of here.

But Tol was barely strong enough to stand, let alone climb back down a mountain.

"Come on," Gerth said, ducking under Tol's right arm and bearing the brunt of his weight. "We've overstayed our welcome here."

Walidir came onto his other side. Tol forced his legs to help as the three of them began scrambling back down the mountain. Walidir and Gerth caged him, using their own strength to guide Tol's jellied legs from one foothold to the next. Without his magical left arm or his prosthesis, he was even more useless.

The Celestial was no longer beside them. When Tol looked, he saw her ghostly apparition tangling with the Nyxar.

THE CHOSEN UNION

The shadow tried to wrap around the Celestial and absorb her. The Celestial disappeared and rematerialized on the Nyxar's other side. She drew the shadow farther away, but Tol got the sense she wouldn't be able to hold the creature's attention for long.

"Faster," Gerth urged, his gaze straying to the Nyxar.

Try as he might, Tol couldn't make his limbs obey even the simplest command. They were barely halfway down the mountain, and it felt like his body had turned to stone.

"Tol. *Tol*," Gerth called.

Even though Gerth was right above Tol, his voice sounded like it was coming from far away.

The last of Tol's strength abandoned him.

He gave into the darkness. His eyes closed, and he knew nothing more.

CHAPTER 12

ADDY

Addy woke to the sound of muffled whispers. She blinked, bringing a dark and blurry shadow into focus. She couldn't tell if she was in a dark room or if it was her vision that was faulty.

"Addy? Can you hear me?"

Jaxon. She tried to say his name, but she was too weak to even manage that. He was doing something with her wrists that was making her raw skin sting even more. She wanted to tell him to cut it out and let her sleep.

"Adelyne," a different voice whispered. "Wake up, Adelyne."

"I'm tired," she muttered to the bossy woman.

Her eyelids could barely stay open. She just needed to—

The metallic smell of blood filled the air. *Her blood.*

She lurched into a sitting position, ignoring the way the room spun.

She'd been Influenced. She'd used her own shears to calmly slice her skin open so the Chosen—the people she had been trying to help—could drink from her like goddamn vampires.

She squinted at Tol's gran, who was waving her wrinkled hand in front of Addy's face.

"Good girl," Tol's gran said. "Now, can you stand up?"

That was a definite *no*. Before she could say anything, she felt herself lifted into Jaxon's arms.

"Follow me," Getyl whispered.

Addy heard the snick of a door opening, and then she felt cool, rain-scented air on her face. She tried to open her mouth to let the rain clear out the taste of blood, but her face was mashed into Jaxon's chest.

"I want Tol."

The words slipped out of her, even though she knew she was supposed to stay silent. She remembered why she'd come here and why Tol wasn't with her.

Was he okay?

Her heart gave a painful stutter.

"Hurry," Getyl was saying.

Addy didn't pay attention to where they were going. She was coming more awake, and at the same time, the numbing remnants of Influence were wearing off. She'd thought she was hurting before. Now, she could feel every place where her skin had been shredded. When Jaxon shifted her in his arms and she glanced down at herself, all she saw was the rusty color of dried blood. It covered her skin…her clothes…even the ends of her hair.

They'd cut holes in her shirt to have more access to bare skin. There were gashes, some shallow and others much deeper, on her shoulders and even the back of her neck.

The dark, angry beast inside Addy stirred.

She'd come here to help these people, and they'd bled her nearly to death. They would have killed her if it wasn't for Getyl and Jaxon. She would destroy them—

But no. These were Tol's people. She blinked against the harsh light as her brain tried to understand.

Tol's people had almost killed her.

"Put me down," she told Jaxon, slurring a little. "I have to—"

What? She didn't know.

It didn't matter. Jaxon and Getyl were arguing about something in quiet tones, and neither one of them was listening to her.

"Once she has her strength back, she can portal us out of here," Jaxon said.

Their plans turned to a dull drone in the back of her mind. A familiar buzzing sensation hovered at the edge of her consciousness.

"Forsaken," she gasped out as soon as her sluggish brain made the connection. "Forsaken are coming."

The solemn, unflappable Jaxon cursed.

"How close?" he demanded. "Which direction?"

Addy didn't know. She was too turned around herself. Everything was spinning.

"Put me down," she managed.

As soon as she was on her feet—supported by Jaxon—she felt a little better.

"A whole army's worth, and they're coming from—"

"I don't remember giving our feisty little blood bag permission to leave."

Getyl and Jaxon whipped around at the voice. Everything moved more slowly for Addy.

"Close your eyes," Getyl ordered Addy and Jaxon.

Before she did, she caught sight of the woman who was alive thanks to Addy.

Addy squeezed her eyes shut before the Chosen woman could think about trying to Influence her.

"Mabrynn, do you have any idea what my grandson is going to do to you when he sees Adelyne?"

Pebbles crunched under Getyl's feet as she moved in front of Addy and Jaxon, facing off against the other woman.

"Her blood is strong, Getyl. It lasts longer than Source. It will protect us until the blood marriage."

Through one slitted eye, Addy saw more of the Chosen, their mouths stained red with her blood, start to converge on them. Jaxon moved protectively in front of Addy, his half-moon blades raised as he readied himself to attack.

True panic set in when Addy realized she didn't have her garden shears. She remembered giving them to one of the Chosen when she was under Influence, and now she had no idea where they were.

Hazes flared around them. Getyl ordered the other Chosen back, but they were ignoring her. Soon, they'd be close enough to touch her and

Jaxon, and then their minds would be enslaved again. There was nothing they could do....

"Addy, get us out of here," Jaxon whispered.

She tried, but she couldn't stand on her own two feet, let alone awaken the magic in her ring.

You're not supposed to be my enemy, she wanted to shout at the bloodthirsty monsters.

"You're behaving worse than the barbarians," Getyl said in a shrill voice. "The king and queen ordered you to leave her alone. This is treason."

"At least we're alive," Mabrynn replied. Her lip curled, and Addy saw that the grooves between her teeth were stained red from Addy's blood. "At least we're strong enough to defend ourselves."

Mabrynn lifted her vial, displaying the ruby liquid filling it to the top.

A scream bubbled up from Addy's lips. She tried to launch herself at the mass of Chosen. She was beyond thoughts of Tol and promises she'd made. She would kill all of them for what they'd done to her. She'd—

Addy's world upended. Her head spun as her legs gave out. Jaxon grabbed her before she fell face-first.

"Get the girl inside," Mabrynn ordered. "Kill the other one."

"What should we do with the king's mother?" someone asked.

Addy didn't hear Mabrynn's answer. Jaxon pulled Addy against him as he backed away from the crowd that was about to swallow them up. They both kept their gazes locked on the ground to protect themselves from Influence.

The mob paused as sounds of terror filled the air. Addy felt a crackle in her veins. She met Jaxon's eyes.

"They're here."

As soon as the words left her mouth, Addy saw a flash of blue.

Then, chaos was upon them. The first warrior to burst through the trees didn't wait for the others before he began his attack. His flicked his right hand, and all of his fingers transformed into slender, wicked blades.

He swiped his hand in a blur of motion. Blood sprayed through the air, and two Chosen fell to the ground.

This was the vision Livy had described days ago, playing out before Addy's eyes. Jaxon shoved her behind him, his half-moon blades raised in a defensive pose, but he made no move to attack. He looked from the Forsaken to the Chosen, uncertainty in his gray eyes.

He didn't want to kill.

Addy could see the way he looked on all the bloodshed with a deep weariness. In that moment, he seemed so much older than his twenty years.

The Forsaken man with knife blades for fingers cut down three more Chosen before his movements went from graceful and lethal to stilted. He stared down at his knife fingers through unfocused eyes. Then, a lazy smile crossed his face.

A scream caught in Addy's throat as the man jabbed the blades of his index and middle fingers into each of his own eyeballs.

All around her, the Chosen and Forsaken were locked in combat. Weapons flew through the air and embedded themselves in the Chosen. Forsaken under Influence attacked each other and died on their own weapons.

Bodies were strewn across the lawn.

The Forsaken were stronger than ever before, but so were the Chosen. Their lips were stained red from Addy's own blood.

Addy didn't know what to do with herself. She didn't know who was friend or foe. More than likely, the only allies she had in this entire battle were Jaxon and Getyl, and they were just as unsure about what to do or who to fight as she was.

"What are your orders?" Jaxon asked Addy, his voice cold and inflectionless.

Addy started when he turned to her.

I have no idea, she wanted to shout at him. *I'm dizzy and useless without my shears.*

Before she had to come up with some kind of answer, another knowing shiver travel down her spine. She glanced to the side and locked gazes with her mother.

General Lezha Bloodsong yanked her glowing spear from a Chosen corpse. Her green eyes swept across Addy, narrowed, and then widened.

She flicked her spear at another of the Chosen without so much as glancing away from Addy. The general's body went through the motions of fighting, but her expression was frozen in horror.

Addy must look worse than she felt.

She didn't like seeing emotion from the emotionless general. She didn't like seeing the evidence that her mother cared.

Getyl lifted her cane off the ground and pointed it at the general like it was a weapon.

"Adelyne needs help, and you're going to get her out of here."

Addy wasn't sure if the general could even hear Getyl over the agonized screams and wet thuds of weapons carving into flesh.

The general let out a short, piercing whistle. A path opened up through the fighting. The Forsaken kept the space clear while Getyl hobbled through the mass of Chosen and Forsaken. Jaxon readjusted his blades so he could carry Addy.

The ruby stone in the general's ring flashed. The Chosen cried out as their Influence struck up against the invisible shield the ring created.

The rest of the Forsaken made a wall that separated Addy's group from the Chosen.

Because they're my people, Addy thought dimly, *and the Chosen are the enemy.*

The general led them to the front of the manor. Army jeeps parked nose-to-tail lined the entire driveway.

Without discussion, the general got into the driver's seat of the first jeep. Getyl took the passenger seat, and Jaxon helped Addy into the back. They had barely pulled their doors shut before the general was peeling out of the driveway.

"Where can we hide her that's nearby?" the general asked Getyl in a clipped voice. "I can't go far, or the Supernal will know I'm not where I should be."

"There's a nice little park tucked away just down the road," Getyl replied, pointing to the right at the end of the driveway. "We can let Addy recover there until she's strong enough to portal us out."

They were all silent as the jeep barreled down the road.

Jaxon sat rigid in his seat with his fists clenched around his blades. The last time they'd all been together, the general had tried to kill both Addy and Jaxon. Then again, the general had just rescued them from the people who, once upon a time, were going to be Addy's subjects.

Someone had a strange sense of humor.

The jeep ground to a halt in front of a stone fountain. Little purple flowers grew in neat clumps on either side of the carefully-groomed gravel path. A bubbling stream completed the picturesque little park.

It was difficult to remember that, less than a mile away, the Chosen and Forsaken were tearing each other apart.

Addy managed to get out of the car without help. Jaxon kept one hand curled around his blades as he helped her sit down on the lip of the fountain. The stone was cold, but it was a relief against her feverish skin.

The general followed Getyl, who kept turning around to glare at her.

Addy remembered how, the first time she'd met Tol's gran, Getyl had tried to kill Addy because she'd thought she was the general. Addy's mother had murdered Getyl's firstborn son—Erikir's father.

Now, even though the two women were enemies, they were working together to save her.

"You have a reprieve from me, soldier," the general told Jaxon without looking up from the first aid kit she was sifting through. "Thank you for helping my daughter."

Aside from a muscle that twitched in his jaw, Jaxon didn't react.

"And you have a reprieve from me," Getyl told the general, a little out of breath from her walk between the jeep and the fountain.

Addy's mother began squirting distilled water on her arms, making them sting. Addy's eyes watered.

"These wounds need stitches and a real doctor, but I'll put you together well enough to get wherever you're going." She pierced Addy with a hard stare. "I did warn you, didn't I?"

Tell me every one of the Chosen wouldn't bleed you dry if they knew what your blood contains.

The general used butterfly stitches to hold Addy's skin together.

"Why are you helping us?" Addy asked, biting the inside of her cheek as fresh blood trickled between the closures.

"For the same reason I spent eighteen years searching for you," the general replied. Her voice was full of unspent anger, but her touch was gentle as she continued to pinch, tape, and wrap Addy back together. "Because I'm your mother."

The general looked up. It was unsettlingly like Addy was looking into a mirror that displayed her face in twenty years. She glanced away, disturbed.

"They would have killed her, Walidir," Getyl said as she tapped her cane in agitation against the other side of the fountain. "…very weak…."

Addy's mother raised an eyebrow.

"She…communicates telepathically with her husband," Addy said as her only response. She didn't know how much the general knew about Vitaquias still existing, and she didn't want to give her mother any information she didn't already have. The general might have saved Addy's life, but she was still the enemy.

Wasn't she?

"Tell me how to defeat the Supernal," Addy blurted out.

The general's lip quirked up in a variation of Addy's sarcastic smile. It was disconcerting.

"You don't have the heart to become what it would take to defeat him."

Addy opened and closed her mouth. She thought about the ease with which she turned to violence and murder…her utter lack of regard for life as she wielded her garden shears….

Sometimes, she scared herself.

I'm the daughter of a rapist and a murderer, she reminded herself. The predisposition for becoming a monster was rooted deep inside her.

"Besides," the general continued. "Even if I held the answer to his defeat in the palm of my hand, I wouldn't share it with you."

"You don't approve of what the Supernal's doing to the mortal world," Addy accused, wrenching her arm out of her mother's hands.

The general's shoulders tensed. "Perhaps not," she conceded. "But he alone can give the Forsaken a world that belongs to us. On Vitaquias, the gods would have sooner watched us turn to smoke than give us an ounce of assistance against the Chosen. The Supernal has returned our people's full strength and given us something we never would have gotten from the gods on Vitaquias. For the first time in our existence, we won't be abandoned."

The cell phone hooked onto the general's belt buzzed.

After giving Addy a warning look, the general answered the call. She listened, and her pale face went even whiter.

"On my way," she said, before hanging up the phone.

To Addy, she said, "The Supernal is coming. You need to get out of here before he senses you. If he finds out I let you go—" a small shudder went through her.

"He'll never know," Addy said.

Addy hated that scared, uncertain look on the general's face.

Even though Addy had never done anything for her mother except try to kill her, the general was still trying to protect her.

"Watch your back, Bloodsong," Getyl said as the general strode back to her jeep. "The next time we meet, I won't be so gracious."

The general's lip twitched. "Same to you, Magnantius."

Addy's mother stopped in her tracks. She took something out of her back pocket and tossed it.

Jaxon reached up and caught it. He looked down, and his serious expression softened. He turned and opened his hand, revealing Addy's garden shears.

A smile cracked across Addy's lips.

"Thank you," Addy said, just as the jeep's engine roared to life.

She didn't think the general heard.

Addy didn't know what to make of everything that had happened. Since she'd discovered this world of Chosen and Forsaken, Addy had thought of the Chosen as good and the Forsaken as evil. After all, Tol was Chosen, and the ones who had killed her family were Forsaken.

Addy was coming to realize that things weren't that simple.

"You don't need to become evil like your father to be the leader our people need," Jaxon said as soon as the general had gone.

Addy didn't respond, because she didn't know what to say.

Now that she was feeling more awake, she focused on activating the magic in her ring.

"Back to the farmhouse?" Jaxon asked as the light from her ring began to form a portal.

"Not just yet," Addy replied. She looked at Getyl. "Tol sent me here for a reason, and I'm going to make sure we get whatever's left of your people out."

CHAPTER 13

OLIVIA

A panicked ripple went through the Londoners on the farm, who had barely escaped the last Forsaken attack.

"Farmers, assemble!" Fred called, rushing into the yard. "Everyone else, fall back."

Olivia could hear the rumble of the Hummers' engines. Their headlights bounced along the unpaved road that led to the farmhouse.

Olivia gulped down her panic, which was making her want to run around the yard like a headless chicken. She reached for her magic.

Olivia felt the tension inside her ease as her Haze flared brighter. There was a rightness, a kind of homecoming, that she got whenever she accessed her abilities. It was like something inside her had settled.

It made her feel powerful and, at the same time, reminded her of the price she was paying to access the magic: an eternity as the Fount. An eternity blood married to the man her sister loved. A world apart from the life that would have let her keep her family's memory alive.

The Forsaken parked their vehicles just outside the range of the floodlights. The doors opened with such synchronicity that it was almost mesmerizing. Olivia had to shake herself.

Everyone tensed. Olivia waited for blue weapons to come shooting out at all of them.

Instead, the Forsaken exited their vehicles with their hands raised high in the air to show they were unarmed.

Olivia exchanged a quick, puzzled look with Erikir.

Olivia counted more than sixty of the enemy, and not a single weapon among them.

They approached slowly.

A Forsaken man who must have been pushing eight feet in height called out to them in what Olivia thought was Russian.

"We're not going to hurt you," Erikir translated. "We don't wish to fight."

"Ask them why they're here," Olivia said, breathless with fear.

Erikir opened his mouth, but then the Forsaken spoke in heavily-accented English.

"Jaxon told us about the general's daughter some time ago," he said. "We are looking for her."

The Forsaken stopped advancing. The farmers clutched their weapons, even though they would be useless against the Forsaken. Olivia kept her magic flowing, just in case she needed to Influence all of the Forsaken at once.

"What do you want with my sister?" Olivia asked. In spite of the fear and uncertainty flooding her body, her voice came out strong.

"We are being hunted by our own people and seek refuge," the Forsaken replied.

Of all the things he might have said, these were the last words Olivia had expected.

"Why are they huntin' you?" Fred asked.

The man's gray eyes turned on Fred.

"We spared a group of mortals we were instructed to kill."

"And?" Nira asked, tapping her foot on the ground in impatience.

The Forsaken warrior gave her a bland look. "*And* if the general or Supernal discovers our whereabouts, we'll be executed."

For several moments, no one spoke.

"Why didn't you kill the mortals?" Olivia asked.

"We don't wish to see this world and its inhabitants perish."

"Why should we trust you?" Nira demanded, her voice full of her usual imperiousness.

"What other reason would we have for coming here?" the Forsaken replied.

It was a reasonable point.

"How do we know you haven't led the Supernal to us?" Erikir asked.

The Forsaken man made a show of looking around.

Olivia couldn't argue with that, either. If this was some kind of trap, the Forsaken would have already sprung it.

"What do you think?" Erikir asked Olivia in a low voice.

What did she think?

Her first reaction was to turn to Addy and ask her opinion, but Addy wasn't here. If she was, she'd tell Olivia to Influence them and find out what they were really doing on their aunt's property.

But if she did that, and it turned out the Forsaken were telling the truth, she'd lose their trust forever.

"We can help you," the same Forsaken man continued.

"How?" Fred asked, clutching a nail gun in one hand and a handmade crossbow in the other.

The warrior jutted his chin at the weapons in Fred's hands. "Those will not work against our kind." He reached his right hand above his head. Out of nowhere, a glowing blue axe materialized.

Olivia, Erikir, and Nira tensed. The farmers surged forward.

The Forsaken man put the axe on the ground and stepped back. "We can give you weapons and teach you how to fight," he said. "We can show you how to defend yourselves against the ones who would kill you without a thought."

"And in exchange?" Erikir asked, his voice guarded.

"Refuge," the man replied.

Olivia took a deep breath and silently prayed that she wasn't about to make a mistake that would get all of them killed.

"Jaxon has been an amazing friend to us," she told the group of Forsaken. "If you're anything like him, we'll be lucky to have you on our side."

She heard Nira scoff. She glanced at Erikir. His mouth was pressed in a tight line, but he gave her a short nod.

"I'll defer to whatever Addy and Jaxon decide when they get back," Olivia said, trying to channel her sister's confidence and feeling strange about speaking for all of them. "But until then, you're welcome to stay with us."

"Come on and grab a shovel, ya'll," Aunt Meredith said, waving the Forsaken over to the other side of the yard. "We're building a Supernal-proof bunker. Someone get the good aliens some pizza."

And, just like that, the Forsaken warriors started working alongside the mortals.

Before Olivia could begin to make sense of the strange sight, a burst of sapphire light appeared in the middle of the yard.

"Oh Lord, what now?" Aunt Meredith demanded, hands on hips as she stalked over.

Olivia hurried to follow her.

"It's the Chosen," she said, breathless with recognition and excitement.

Her people were here.

The lasso of blue light and magic whipped the warm Texas night into a frenzy. Olivia ran forward, too eager to see her twin to wait a second longer.

The Chosen began falling through the portal and onto the front lawn. Ten…twenty…fifty. They kept coming. Some of them were dry-heaving from the disorienting motion of the portal, while others cradled their heads like they had a splitting headache. Having experienced both of those effects from portal travel herself, Olivia commiserated with their discomfort.

"It'll pass in a little while," she promised, craning her neck for the sight of red hair.

Nira let out a small cry as she ran toward two frail, elderly women. Olivia could feel the worry pouring off Nira as she helped the women get to their feet. Olivia knew Nira's only family were her two aunts. Now that she saw the women, she understood why Nira was so afraid of losing them. Olivia's heart pulled at the wheezing sound one of the women made as she tried to suck in air. The other woman looked even more fragile.

"Aunt Starser," Erikir said, catching the Chosen queen as she fell through the portal. "What happened?"

Shock rippled through Olivia. Every other time she'd seen the queen, Tol's mother had been pristinely dressed without a fleck of dust or hair out of place. Now, she was mess. Her expensive Chanel jacket was torn, and there was a nasty gash on her cheek. There was also a rectangular red mark across her mouth that looked suspiciously like duct tape had been pressed there and then ripped away.

"Did the Forsaken do this?" Erikir demanded.

"No," the queen said, her voice hoarse. Then, she did something that shocked Olivia even more than her disheveled appearance. She began to cry.

"Where is my son?" the queen demanded, pushing away Erikir when he tried to comfort her. "I need to tell him…. We couldn't protect her. We tried, but—"

Olivia forgot about everything else when Jaxon spilled out of the portal. He was cradling Addy, who lay limp and unconscious against him.

"What happened?" Olivia cried, running to them.

"Stay away!" Getyl yelled, positioning herself in front of Jaxon and Addy, brandishing her cane at Olivia. When she adjusted her glasses, which were haphazardly perched at a diagonal across her face, she squinted at Olivia.

"Oh, it's you," Getyl said, lowering her cane. She motioned for Olivia to come closer before taking up her protective stance again. Olivia didn't stop to ask questions. All of her attention was on her sister.

She fell to her knees beside Jaxon, who was pushing Addy's hair back and feeling for her pulse.

Addy was covered in dried blood. There were long wounds down her forearms and peeking through her shredded shirt. The cuts were barely held together with bandages that pinched her bloodless skin together. Addy's face was white as a ghost.

Nira! Olivia screamed the name in her head. *I need you. Now!*

She didn't know if whatever connection she'd just accessed would work, but a few seconds later, Nira came running.

"I'm here," she said, breathless. "What happened?"

Olivia cradled her sister's freezing cold hand to her cheek, trying to warm it, as Nira started barking orders at the Farmers and Londoners who had crowded around.

"Addy!" Aunt Meredith shrieked, her voice high with the same panic pumping through Olivia's veins.

"Bottled water," Nira shouted at Aunt Meredith. "And get that saline solution from the medical tent." To Fred, who was also hovering nearby, she ordered, "I need my stitch kit and antibiotics."

She clapped her hands in his face. "Chop, chop."

Nira must have known it would be useless to order Olivia away. She wasn't going to leave her sister for a single second.

While Nira cleaned and dressed the wounds on Addy's arms, Olivia applied pressure to a long gash down Addy's calf. Jaxon held Addy to keep her from twitching or thrashing as Nira stitched her up. Even though she was unconscious, she was fighting them.

Every time Addy flinched, it made Olivia's heart stutter back to life. Addy was so pale, and there was so much blood....

Once Nira got to the stage where she was smearing antibiotic ointment over the fresh stitches and wrapping clean bandages around the wounds, Jaxon told them what had happened.

Olivia held her sister's limp, cold hand as Jaxon explained what the Chosen had done to Addy.

Olivia was shaking, she was so furious. Her people had hurt her twin. They would have killed her if it hadn't been for Jaxon and Getyl.

"What else does Addy need right now?" Olivia asked Nira, her voice oddly calm in contrast to the tempest raging inside her.

"Sleep," Nira said. She gave Jaxon an appraising look. "Same for you, Forsaken. You look like you could use it."

"I'll carry her," Fred said, frowning at the way Jaxon stumbled a little when he got to his feet. After a short hesitation, Jaxon nodded.

"I'll make sure she stays warm and safe," Aunt Meredith said, her lips white with her own barely-contained emotions. To Olivia, she said, "You deal with the fuckers who did this to her."

If Olivia had been more in her right mind, she would have been floored. Her aunt didn't swear. Ever.

Olivia wasn't feeling like herself at the moment, either. She usually ran from conflict.

Not this time.

When it came to this, none of the usual rules applied. The Chosen might be her people, but Addy was her family…her twin.

Olivia crossed the lawn to where the Chosen were crowded together. She dug deep into the well of magic inside her. It felt good to let it boil inside her.

Olivia felt her vision flicker between the mortal world and the mental plane as she tapped into the complete power that was now a part of her. When she spoke, it wasn't with her voice, but with the all-powerful cadence of the Celestial.

"You hurt my sister," she said in a voice that struck fear into the hearts of the Chosen.

She took no pleasure in causing them fear, but she didn't back away from it. These were her people to love and protect. But they were also hers to rule and guide. To hold accountable.

Olivia looked into the minds of the people standing before her. She saw their motivations and wishes. She watched the way they'd fed from Addy. She witnessed them fill their vials and their bodies, glutting themselves on Addy's blood. She saw the way their strength grew at Addy's expense, and how their desire for more increased with each drop of blood they took.

"You have let your greed consume you again," Olivia said in the same inhuman, ethereal voice. "This is why Vitaquias was destroyed eighteen years ago."

She allowed the Chosen to feel her anger. She let it slide from her mind and into theirs.

"Your prince and I will not rescue you, so that you may fall prey to your greed once again. You will be punished for reaching beyond the limits of your power."

The girl is Forsaken. She is lesser. She is nothing.

Olivia heard the thoughts of the Chosen woman who stood nearby, clutching a vial filled with Addy's blood.

Olivia had never been an intimidating figure, but she knew that her eyes had turned molten silver. She could feel her curls swirling around her face in a wind her own magic was generating. Her Haze was getting brighter and brighter, forcing the Chosen to shield their eyes.

Olivia used her magic to dig deep inside the minds and bodies of her people. There were cries of anguish, and some of the Chosen tried to pull their minds free. She tightened her hold.

She squeezed her left hand into a fist. All around her, blood-filled vials shattered. There were shocked cries as the material, which had been forged on Vitaquias and was supposed to be indestructible, turned to dust.

I am the Fount, Olivia thought.

She curled the fingers of her right hand, sensing for the foreign blood inside her people's bodies.

Terrified gasps surrounded her as Olivia caught hold of Addy's blood and began drawing it out of the Chosen. Their eyes filled with red liquid. They wept blood.

It poured from their eyes and ran down their cheeks. For some, it was only a few drops. For others, it kept coming and coming. It drenched their collars, and then their shirts. It splattered onto the ground. The impossible brightness of Olivia's Haze illuminated the little rivulets before they were swallowed up into the earth.

She kept going until every drop of Addy's blood was gone from their bodies. But she didn't stop there.

She drew from their gods-given strength, weakening them and drawing at their essence. Lines appeared on previously-flawless skin. White hairs sprang out amid the black.

Every one of the Chosen who had ingested Addy's blood aged. Olivia kept going until all of her people truly understood the magnitude of her power. She let them see that she could end all of their lives with a thought. Then, she stopped.

She left them, aged and alive. She pulled her Influence out of their minds until they had command over their bodies once again.

"I am the Fount," she said. The truth of her words echoed through the silent yard. "You have been shown justice and mercy today. Do not test my magnanimity again."

Olivia was still angry, but she was in control of her emotions and her magic. She felt something shift inside her. There was acceptance, as well as a kind of readiness. Olivia barely recognized herself.

She'd just taken control of hundreds of minds. She hadn't asked for permission or apologized. She'd done what was needed, and she had no regrets.

I am the Fount. The words were right and true.

For the first time, she didn't question her right to be the Fount. For the first time, she acknowledged that the Celestial hadn't made a mistake in choosing her. For the first time, she believed she was the right person to be the Chosen queen.

CHAPTER 14

OLIVIA

Something was bothering Erikir. Olivia had been noticing his turbulent emotions all day, and they were only growing darker by the hour.

Even though she could sense all of the Chosen to some degree, her connection with Erikir was different. She felt an immediate awareness whenever he was nearby. When he left, it seemed like he brought all the warmth with him.

It wasn't like what she felt when Nira or Gerth were around. It was something decidedly un-Fount-related…something she couldn't let herself examine too carefully.

After the visions she'd seen when he touched her, she'd been trying to give him space. But whatever was upsetting Erikir, she wasn't going to let him deal with it alone any longer. She made her way toward the bunker, where he'd been for the last several hours.

The farmers and Forsaken were working side-by-side to extend the bunker deeper underground. Already, there were long passageways and rooms that were in the process of being turned into finished living spaces. Olivia made her way deeper into the bunker, following the incessant tug on her heart as she searched for Erikir.

Everything smelled like fresh paint, fresh earth, and freshly-sawed wood. They were farm smells, and she breathed them in.

Olivia couldn't believe what they'd managed to create in only a few days. It gave her hope for the future of humanity, even though this temporary sense of safety was an illusion. They only had four more days before the Supernal annihilated the mortals. And they were no closer to having an answer to his defeat.

Her awareness of Erikir grew stronger when she reached a quiet section of the bunker. It was mostly finished and empty of construction equipment and people. There were no lights, but her Haze was bright enough to illuminate the path.

Olivia saw the gleam of Erikir's Haze seeping under a door at the far end of the bunker. She frowned.

Erikir slept in the house with the rest of their group. So, why was he here?

As if in answer, Olivia felt a sharp yank on her heart as Erikir's pain flooded her. She burst through the door, already thinking about whether it would be easier to get Erikir to Nira or Nira to Erikir.

She stopped just inside the room. Erikir was sitting on the dirt floor, his back propped against the wall. A thick book was open on his lap, the words on the spine in a language Olivia didn't recognize.

Erikir jumped a little at her sudden presence. His brow furrowed in confusion.

"Is something wrong?" he asked.

Yes, she wanted to say. *Tell me what it is.* But she'd already invaded Erikir's private thoughts more than either of them was comfortable with. So, instead, she blurted out, "Your hair is down."

She'd never seen it in anything except a tight braid. Now, it was loose and falling over his shoulders.

"Oh, right." Erikir started to gather his hair and braid it back.

"Stop," she said, her feet drawing closer. "I...like it this way."

It felt like a special intimacy to see him like this. It was also just plain sexy.

"I guess it's just one of the things our people clung to from the Old World," he said, looking uncomfortable. "But I know most mortals don't like it."

"I'm not most mortals," she said before thinking about what she was saying.

Erikir's lip twitched. "Truer words were never spoken."

Feeling more determined than flustered, she stepped farther into the room.

"What's bothering you?" she asked before she lost her nerve.

Olivia could almost see the way he closed himself off. He gave her a stony expression.

"Don't think that, just because of what you've seen, I'm granting you open access to my mind," he said, his voice taking on a harsh edge.

Weeks ago, she would have slunk out of the room with her tail between her legs. Now, she went and sat on the ground next to Erikir, close enough to feel the warmth radiating from his body.

Erikir's expression was guarded, but he leaned closer.

"Olivia," he said in a low voice.

He traced the shape of her lips with his finger.

"You're just trying to distract me so we don't have to talk," Olivia accused, breathless.

Erikir gave her a slow smile. With the lightest of touches, he drew a line down her throat with his index finger.

"It's working, isn't it?" he asked in that same seductive voice, his fingers curling under the hem of her shirt.

Yes.

Her heart began to thud against her ribcage. She wanted to raise her own hands to explore the sharp angles of his jaw and cheekbones, but he didn't give her a chance. He kissed her.

Her whole body came alive. She wanted to be closer. She wanted more.

Something wasn't right, though. For as close as they were at that moment, Erikir's muscles were tense and his mind was guarded.

It took all her willpower to break the kiss.

"No." She pulled free and scooted back until there was enough space between them for her to have a coherent thought. She knew they could easily lose themselves in their physical connection, and whatever had been bothering him would fade away. But she didn't want to. She wanted him to share his mind with her, which Erikir guarded more carefully than his body.

"Fine," Erikir said, his expression tightening as he turned back to his book. "Then, go away. I'm busy." As if to emphasize his point, he flipped the page.

"You weren't reading," she told him with a boldness she barely recognized.

"I wasn't?" Erikir raised an eyebrow at her.

"No." She crossed her arms. "You were brooding."

His eyes narrowed. Olivia tensed in readiness for his anger. She wasn't going to apologize for seeing into his mind. Not this time.

Erikir sighed and closed the book, turning the heat of his gaze on her.

"Today's the anniversary of my father's murder."

Olivia's lips parted, but no words came out.

"I—I'm so sorry," she finally managed.

Erikir stared past her at a spot on the wall. For a long moment, he was silent.

"It's not something the Chosen talk about," he said in a quiet voice. "All of our people have lost someone. Some have lost everyone."

Olivia didn't have words, so she took Erikir's hand. She wasn't sure he'd accept the comfort, but he curled his fingers around hers.

"We have so many dead, they all get lumped together," he said. "My mother was a hero at the Crossing. She saved dozens of lives before the Forsaken killed her, but I've never heard anyone say her name out loud."

Erikir stared down at their clasped hands as he rubbed his thumb over her knuckles.

"Sometimes it feels like my parents are just figments of my imagination. They were king and queen, and yet no one so much as mentions them. It's like they never lived."

Olivia's throat felt like it was coated with sandpaper.

"There are times when I just want to curl in a ball and cry for my family," she admitted. "Addy misses them as much as I do, but she's strong enough to do what she has to without letting grief get in the way."

Erikir tipped his head in thought. "Sometimes, I think it takes more courage to face the grief than to bury it."

"It's not courage for me," she told him. "I'm afraid if I don't hold onto their memory, I'll become so much a part of this new life that I'll have nothing left in common with them."

She laughed a little at herself.

"It's stupid to think I have anything in common with the dead, but—"

"No, I get it." Erikir squeezed her hand. He leaned closer until his lips were almost touching her ear. "Iseth et esleywn loraifil meiyn."

The language was wholly unfamiliar, but there was a lyrical quality to it that pulled at Olivia's heart.

"It's from the language of Vitaquias," Erikir said. "It means *Honor the dead with the richness of life*."

Olivia repeated the words, committing both them and their meaning to memory.

"Not bad," Erikir said with a small smile. "We'll have to work on your accent, though."

He brushed his lips over hers, so gently and with so much love behind the caress that it threatened to tear her apart then and there.

"We can't," she said, beginning to panic at how badly she wanted him to keep going.

Erikir pulled back just enough to look at her. "Because you don't want to, or because you're Tol's?"

Olivia bristled at that.

"I don't belong to Tol." *Not yet, anyway.* "Or to anyone else for that matter."

Erikir's brow smoothed out, and warmth filled his expression.

"Gods-damned right you don't."

He cradled her face with his hands. His eyes roved over her, like he was memorizing her.

"Why does it have to be like this?" she whispered, leaning into his touch.

"Olivia." He said her name in a way that made her whole body heat. "I wish—" He swallowed as his gaze dropped to her lips.

Me too. The words passed through her mind and across her heart before she could stop them.

Olivia thought of the vision she'd shared with Erikir. She saw the two of them staring down at their child. Before their shared happiness could settle into her bones, she remembered the way Erikir had transformed into Tol.

A shudder went through her at the reminder of the awful truth—that the best-case scenario ended with her blood married to Erikir's cousin. Addy's true love.

"I know it's my…our responsibility," Olivia said, "but how am I supposed to bind myself to him?"

Even saying the words made sickness roll through her. It sounded wrong. It felt even worse.

Erikir looked away from her, a muscle flexing in his jaw.

"You won't remember this," he said, staring at the dark corner of the room.

Olivia scoffed at that. "No matter what happens, I'll never forget about this."

Erikir turned back to look at her, his expression softening. "You won't have a choice," he told her quietly. "Once the bond is formed, it will consume you."

Panic snaked through Olivia's insides. She shook her head, rejecting the possibility.

"I don't want to forget."

As much as it would hurt, her few stolen moments with Erikir were memories she'd treasure for the rest of her life.

"Then, I'll remember for both of us." Erikir lifted their joined hands and pressed them to his chest. "With all of my heart."

CHAPTER 15

TOL

Tol collapsed on his hands and knees, retching. He felt like he'd been torn apart from the inside out. It had nothing to do with the portal, and everything to do with the fact that he was now a mere shell of what he'd been.

"Are you guys okay?"

Olivia crouched down in front of them.

"Thank you," he managed, his throat raw.

"We would have been done for if you hadn't brought us back," Gerth added. "Tol *really* pissed off the gods."

Gerth didn't look much better than Tol felt. His face was raw and blistered from frostbite, and his fingers were bloody from their climb back down the mountain.

Tol's memory of their descent was blurry at best. All he remembered was that, somehow, Gerth and Walidir had gotten all three of them down the mountain. Tol had been hovering on the edge of unconsciousness when Gerth told the Celestial to summon Olivia. He remembered Walidir running for the castle ruins, where he said he'd be protected from the Nyxar.

Gerth and the Celestial had fended off the Nyxar until the sky tore apart and the portal sucked them in.

Even after everything he'd already done, Gerth still had the strength to get to his feet and haul Tol up with him.

"I'm just glad the portal worked," Olivia said. "I was so worried."

"You were brilliant," Gerth assured her. "Got us out just before the Nyxar devoured us."

Olivia's eyes widened. Before she could ask any questions, Tol asked the only one that mattered.

"Is Addy alright?"

That one question, held in his head and heart, was the only thought that was keeping him conscious. His entire body was trying to shut down.

"She's fine," Olivia said quickly. "Sleeping."

Tol staggered under the weight of his relief.

"What happened?" he asked. "Gran said she was injured at the manor. Was it the Supernal?"

Olivia's face paled. "No, it wasn't—"

"Tolumus, where have you been?"

His mum, followed by his father and Gran, pushed through the throng of people to him. Jaxon and Nira were next.

Jaxon went to Gerth, while Nira grabbed Tol's wrist and started tracking his pulse.

"You're more dead than alive," she informed him.

Her words were terse, but there was real worry in her eyes.

"Where is your Haze?" his father demanded.

They all looked at him. Tol didn't know what to say…how to explain what he'd done. He hadn't even had time to wrap his own mind around it all.

"Give the boys some space," Gran ordered. "They'll tell us everything once they've had a chance to breathe." She looked past them, and with a surge of guilt, Tol realized she was looking for Walidir.

"I'm sorry," he rasped.

"Don't be," Gran said in her brusque way. "I can sense that he is alive and well. I'll see him soon enough."

Tol opened his mouth, but no more words would come.

"Tol, you need fluids," Nira said, trying to tug him over to a medical tent that hadn't been on the property the last time he'd been here. "And sleep. Your pulse is too slow. I need to—"

"Prince Tolumus," a voice called. It was echoed by more cries of his name.

Tol was seeing double, and he had to blink several times to bring the world into focus. Meredith's lawn was swarming with people. There were mortals, Forsaken, and Chosen.

It was the Chosen who were calling his name now. When he caught the jist of their pleas, his too-slow pulse sped up.

"Give us a display of power," they begged. "Tell us how you're going to defeat the Supernal."

Give us a reason to hope was what they meant.

"Stand tall," Gerth whispered to him.

He understood what his friend was telling him. He needed to play the part of the prince until he could give the Chosen a new source of hope. If he told them the truth now, they would panic.

Tol's mouth went dry. He stared out at the faces of his people and, for the first time in his life, had no idea how to address them.

"Tol battled the gods," Gerth said, coming to his rescue. "Give the man some time to rest. He'll astonish you with his extraordinary powers later."

Laughter. Relieved sighs.

It was enough to stave off the inevitable questions and demands for another show of his power.

"What would I do without you?" Tol asked Gerth when the Chosen had dispersed.

Gerth gave him a fleeting smile. "Letter of recommendation, perhaps?" He lowered his voice. "Now that you're not going to be king, I believe my Chief Strategist role just dried up."

Guilt twisted Tol's gut. When he made his bargain with the gods, he'd only been thinking about Addy and himself. But of course, his decisions affected so many more.

"Don't sweat it, mate," Gerth said, reading his expression.

"We'll figure it out," Tol promised. He knew how badly Gerth wanted to be in the thick of Chosen politics. Since they were kids, it had been their plan—king and strategist.

"Tolumus," his father said, his voice a warning growl.

"Later," Tol replied in the voice Gerth had always referred to as the *king* voice. He supposed he wouldn't be needing that anymore, since he was no longer going to be a king. He took a steadying breath.

"I need to talk to Olivia. Alone. And then I'm going to see Addy."

Everything else could be handled later.

"Tolumus," his mum began, but Gran herded his parents away. Tol gave her a grateful look.

"What do you need from me?" Gerth asked.

Tol shook his head. Gerth had almost died for him…not for the first time.

"Have Nira deal with your frostbite," he told Gerth. "Eat. Sleep."

There would be time to work out the rest afterward. Like how to tell his parents he was never going to be king. And figuring out how in the two hells Tol was supposed to contribute to a world full of magic when he no longer had any magic.

Jaxon slung Gerth's arm over his shoulder and helped him limp toward the medical tent. Nira, after giving Tol another worried look, followed them. Tol waited until everyone else was out of earshot, and he and Olivia were alone.

"You really don't look well," Olivia said as Tol focused on breathing and standing on his own two feet. She glanced at his left sleeve, which was empty of either a magical arm or a prosthesis.

Tol cursed himself. He'd left the mangled remains of his prosthesis in the castle ruins on Vitaquias, and the gods had made it abundantly clear that they would never magically restore his arm again.

Loss flooded through him before he quashed it.

Later, he told himself.

Because he was too exhausted for long-winded explanations, Tol took the stone from his pocket and dropped it onto Olivia's palm.

She flinched as the heated stone touched her skin, but she didn't drop it.

"It's my magic," he explained.

He saw Olivia's eyes go wide in understanding.

"How?" she asked, her gaze fixed on the golden stone.

Tol's mouth pulled in a sardonic smile. "Not easily."

"But—"

"It's yours," Tol said, interrupting her. "I mean, it's yours to give to whoever you want to blood marry. Whoever you want to share your throne."

All of the color left her face. She went to say something, but no sound came out. Tol gave her a knowing smile.

Olivia swallowed, but instead of crumpling under the weight of that new revelation, she stood taller.

"I'll just ask that you don't say anything about it to anyone until I've told Addy and my family." He grimaced at the thought of it. He wasn't looking forward to either of those conversations.

Olivia curled her fingers around the stone. "What did you have to sacrifice?" she asked in a whisper.

The look she gave him was full of sympathy. She understood the meaning of sacrifice better than anyone.

"Nothing I wasn't willing to pay."

Tol was anxious to go to Addy. Sleeping or not, he needed to see her to convince himself that she was alright. His grandfather had been so certain that something horrible had happened....

"Listen," he said. "I'm sorry I was such a prat to you before. It had nothing to do with you."

"I know," she said quickly. "And you don't have to apologize. I understand."

"The Celestial was right," Tol told her. "You're going to be a fantastic queen."

Olivia let out a shaky laugh before her expression turned serious. "On a related note, I did something that I need to tell you about. But before I do, I need you to give me your word that you won't kill anyone once I tell you."

Tol laughed, which made his battered body hurt. "I'm hardly in any condition to kill anyone," he pointed out.

"Well, that might change after you hear about what happened to Addy."

Tol's exhaustion vanished in an instant.

"Tell me."

* * *

Tol eased the bedroom door open. After talking with Olivia, he thought he'd been prepared. But when he saw Addy, corpse-still and with her arms covered in bandages, he had to steady himself against the wall.

His people had done this to her. He'd sent her to save them, and they had almost killed her.

He slid down to the floor before he passed out.

His people. His people.

Meredith, who had been sitting in a chair beside the bed, got up and came to crouch beside him.

"She's going to be just fine," she whispered. "Just needs a little R&R."

When Tol dragged his gaze off Addy, he saw the same fury that was devouring him reflected in Meredith's expression.

Influenced her…made her cut herself so they could drink her blood….

Olivia's words circled around and around in his mind. If there was anything left in his stomach, he'd be heaving it up.

Addy's eyes opened. Her stare was unfocused, but when she caught sight of him, her pupils dilated.

"Are you real?" she asked in a raspy voice. "I've been dreaming about you and wishing—"

"I'm real," he choked. "Oh gods, Addy."

He staggered to the bed and sank down on the floor beside her, too afraid of hurting her to touch her. He was aware of the door shutting, leaving the two of them alone.

"Tol." A tear slid down her cheek as she lifted a bandaged hand to his face.

"I did it, Addy," he said, his voice rough. "I'm yours."

Her eyes widened. "You…what?"

"I'm yours," he said again, leaning into her touch as her hand cupped his cheek. "If you still want me."

Before Tol could react or try to stop her, Addy threw herself at him. He had a moment of horror at seeing the bandages on her neck and around her chest. Then, he couldn't see anything except for her curtain of copper hair.

It took all of his concentration to lock her body against his before they both went crashing through the wall.

She was sobbing against his neck, saying *My Tol* over and over again.

"Addy, I'm filthy," he said, trying to peel himself away from her. He was afraid he'd infect her wounds. He should have showered before coming here, but he couldn't bear another second without seeing her.

"I love you," she gasped, holding onto him tighter when he tried to extricate himself. "Tol, I love you."

"I love you, too." He gave up trying to separate himself and held her back. "My Addy."

He buried his face in her piña colada-scented hair and breathed her in.

"But, I don't understand." Addy pulled back to look at him. "What about your people?"

He tensed. "My people can rot in the hells," he growled.

They had almost killed Addy, and he would never forget it.

"Tol." Addy's bandaged hands tangled in his shirt as she looked him up and down. "Where's your Haze?" Terror filled her green eyes as she continued to stare at him. "What did you do?"

Tol blew out a breath. "Can we sit down?" he asked.

Before he fell down. His adrenaline was fading, and he was having trouble supporting his own weight.

"Start talking," Addy ordered.

"I gave up my magic," Tol said, knowing Addy didn't want the truth dressed up. "Olivia can choose who she wants to blood marry, and then I'll officially abdicate the throne."

Addy sucked in a breath.

"So, you can't Influence?"

Tol's heart stuttered. Influence had been a part of his life…a part of him…since he was an infant. He couldn't wrap his head around the idea of living without it.

He'd be forever weak. Defenseless.

"That's right." His voice came out sounding thin.

"Do you regret it?" she asked quietly.

"No," he answered immediately. "Never."

A hesitant smile crossed her lips.

"So, that's it, then? We can be together?"

"We can't blood marry," he said carefully.

Emotions flitted across Addy's face too fast for Tol to interpret them.

"Whatever," Addy decided. "As long as I get to be with you forever."

"Um, well, about that—"

Addy's whole body went rigid. "What?" she demanded. "Tol, *what?*"

Tol took her bandaged hand carefully in his.

"I gave up my immortality." He spoke quietly, hoping it might soften the blow.

Addy looked at him, uncomprehending. Her lips moved as she repeated his words. She launched to her feet.

"What?!"

Tol reached for her, but she scrambled away from him.

"Undo it," Addy ordered. "Whatever you did. *Now.*"

She was hyperventilating. Tears streamed down her face.

"Addy, stop," Tol said. She was going to tear out her stitches. He reached up to brush her tears away with his thumb.

"You can't do this to me," Addy cried. "I won't let you."

"It's already done," he told her in a soothing tone.

"I can't survive for an eternity without you!" She gasped for air as she clutched at him.

"Adelyne Deerborn, look at me," he ordered her.

He waited.

"You are the strongest person I have ever met." He spoke slowly so she wouldn't miss a single word. "You're my warrior goddess. You can survive anything."

She was shaking her head back and forth as her tears continued to fall.

"I'd rather have a mortal lifetime with you than an eternity without you," Tol said. "If our positions were reversed, I think you'd say the same."

"And you'd be as furious with me as I am with you," she snapped.

She was right, but Tol didn't give her the satisfaction of hearing him say so. Their positions weren't reversed—thank the gods—and so he'd never have to live without her.

"What if I tell you I refuse to be with you if you're mortal?" Addy asked.

"Me being mortal is the *only* way we can be together," he pointed out.

"Then, I don't want to be with you." Her words were curt. She turned away from him.

A fiery pain went through his chest at the thought of Addy rejecting him, even though he understood she was doing it out of a desperate need to protect him.

"You should take your immortality back and spend a happy eternity with Livy," she said in that same toneless voice. "Because you aren't going to be with me. Not like this."

Tol took a deep breath. "You have the right to reject me, and I have the right to spend every day of the rest of my life trying to win you back." He forced an arrogant smile on his face. "Once I start really putting on the charm, you won't be able to hold out."

Addy wasn't in the mood.

"I wish we'd never met," she said, covering her face with her bandaged hands. "Then, you wouldn't have given up your life for me."

Tol's hurt passed in an instant. He understood all the unspoken fears behind her callous words.

"Yeah, and then I would have spent an eternity without ever knowing what it feels like to really live," he told her.

That got her attention.

"I never thought I would fall in love," he told her honestly. "I didn't know it was possible to feel like this, but now that I know, I wouldn't give it up for anything."

She let him put his arm around her. She leaned into him, pressing her face into his neck. He felt the wetness of her tears against his skin.

She lifted her head to look at him. The expression in her eyes stole his breath away.

"But where are we going to live? Your people—"

"They're not my people," Tol said, his voice tight. *Not after what they did to you.*

She tilted her head to the side, and their lips met. She kissed him fiercely, almost desperately.

"So, what happens now?" Addy asked, breathless, when they separated.

Tol felt a smile pull at his lips. "I still want to marry you, even if we can't do the blood part of it. If you're still in."

"Well, I want to keep the ring." Addy heaved a dramatic sigh. "So I guess I have to stay with you."

Tol grinned.

"You know what I realized?" He leaned against the headboard, pulling Addy into the crook of his arm.

"What's that?"

He looked at her. "We've never been out on a date."

A surprised laugh bubbled out of Addy.

"As soon as we've dealt with the Supernal and we have a free night without an impending disaster, I'm taking you out," Tol informed her.

"Hm, I'll have to check my calendar," Addy replied with a noncommittal shrug.

"You do that." He kissed the tip of her nose. "Just make sure you book me for the whole night."

CHAPTER 16

ADDY

It was still dark when Addy woke, cocooned by Tol's warmth. Her first thought was relief. The emotion was so strong tears sprang to her eyes.

His appearance hadn't just been some hallucination. He was okay, and they were going to be together....

That thought was followed by panic as everything he'd told her the night before came back in a rush.

She shifted so she could look at Tol.

She's grown so used to Tol's bright Haze that she barely recognized him without it. There were bruise-like circles under his eyes, and there was a hollowness to his face that hadn't been there before.

"What have you done?" she whispered.

Tol didn't stir.

She got out of bed and tiptoed to the wardrobe. She slipped into one of Tol's button-down shirts. The fabric was soft enough that it didn't rub against her bandages, and it smelled like Tol.

She closed the door softly behind her. It was early enough that everyone else should still be sleeping, but there was a light on in the living room. Gerth and Jaxon were sitting on one couch, talking quietly as they stared at a mass of papers spread out on the coffee table. On the other couch, Weasel was holding up a book in his left hand. His right hand was stroking something on his lap. At first, Addy thought maybe Aunt Meredith had gotten a cat, but as she came closer, she caught sight of a mass of brown curls.

Oh no, you didn't.

Addy's vision turned red. Livy was asleep with her head on a pillow on Weasel's lap. He was running his fingers through her hair like he had some right.

"You," she half-snarled, half-whispered.

The three guys looked at her.

"Addy, you're awake," Gerth said. "Looking a little rumpled, but all things considered—"

Addy didn't hear whatever else he said. She marched around to get in Erikir's face.

"Get your hands off my sister."

"What is your problem?" he whispered.

"Problem?" Addy scoffed. "My problem is that if I kill you right now, you'll bleed all over Livy's head."

Livy opened her eyes and blinked at them.

"Addy," she said, her voice groggy with sleep. "Are you okay? Do you need anything?"

"I do," Addy said, barely noticing when Gerth and Jaxon slunk out of the room. "I'd like to know why you're cozying up to this deceitful, double-crossing, son-of-a—"

"Addy," Livy said gently, like Addy was getting hysterical for no good reason. Like Livy wasn't letting Tol's would-be murderer touch her.

Livy turned to Erikir. "Can you give us some privacy?"

When he gave her a look full of concern, like he actually gave a shit about anyone besides himself, Addy had to clench her hands to keep from breaking his neck then and there.

By some tremendous force of will, Addy managed not to explode in the amount of time it took for Erikir to skedaddle.

"How are you feeling?" Livy asked, reaching to pull back one of Addy's sleeves to check her bandages.

Addy yanked her arm back. "That's not what I want to talk about right now," she whisper-shouted. If it wasn't for Tol asleep in the other room, she'd be just plain shouting.

"I wanted to tell you before," Livy said, her cheeks turning pink.

Addy's jaw hit the floor. If Livy was into sick jokes, then Addy would have assumed this to be one. But Livy didn't have that kind of cruelty in her. She was being serious.

"Have you forgotten that idiot is the reason why Tol almost died?" Addy demanded.

Livy always saw the best in everyone, but this was taking things too far.

"He realized he made a mistake," she said carefully, sensing that Addy was about to combust.

"No," Addy corrected. "A mistake is forgetting to lock the back door at night. What that weasel did is unforgivable."

"I'd like you to stop calling him that," Livy said patiently.

While Addy gaped at her sister, Livy continued.

"When we were on the aircraft carrier, Erikir was willing to give up his life to save Jaxon. I've forgiven him, and I wish you would, too."

"That's right, he did try and sacrifice himself for Jaxon." Addy turned the full force of her fury on her twin. "And you saved his useless life." She ignored Livy's wince. "If you hadn't done that, you could have made me the Fount, and then Tol wouldn't be about to die!"

Some part of Addy knew she was being unfair. The other part of her didn't care. The look of pity that crossed her twin's face made everything worse. Addy didn't want pity. She wanted a target for her pent-up rage.

"He's not about to die," Livy said, trying to take Addy's bandaged hand.

"He was supposed to have eternity. And now, because of what you did, he gave that up. He's—he's—"

Tears sprang to Livy's eyes. "Oh, Addy."

When Livy put her arms around Addy and pulled her down on the couch with her, Addy didn't resist.

"It's like, since you became the Fount, you're a different person," Addy said.

When Addy saw the hurt expression that crossed her sister's face, she wanted to take the words back.

"In a way, I guess I am a different person," Livy said. She looked at Addy. "You know those Chosen who hurt you? I ripped all of your blood out of them through their eyes."

The statement came as such a shock, Addy couldn't hold back her laugh.

"Are you serious?" she demanded.

Livy nodded. "I'll never let my people hurt you ever again," she promised, her eyes shining with tears as she took Addy's hands in hers.

Addy's breath caught. "*Your* people," she whispered.

Livy's lips parted in surprise, like she hadn't realized what she'd said.

"I'll never let anyone come between us," Livy vowed.

Addy tried to swallow around the growing lump in her throat.

"I'll never let anyone come between us either," she said, even though she found she couldn't look at her sister as she spoke the words.

If Addy gave in to what seemed like an inevitable acceptance of her place among the Forsaken, what would that do to her relationship with Livy?

Nothing good.

"Listen to me," Livy said, her eyes bright with conviction. "I inherited the Celestial's need to protect the Chosen, but I don't have any illusions about their goodness. If there's one thing I've learned through all of this, it's that there are good and bad Chosen, just like there are good and bad Forsaken. At the end of the day, they're just people like any other."

"Always the wise one," Addy said, leaning her head against her twin's shoulder.

"I love you so much," Livy said, wrapping her arms around Addy.

Addy nestled deeper into her sister's embrace. "Love you more."

The screen door banged open with a force that startled them out of their cuddle.

"That ain't what I'm sayin'," Fred's voice said from the hallway.

Even though she couldn't see him, Addy could tell from his tone that he was upset.

"I'm just sayin' I'm not some stupid mortal who—"

"And that's not what *I'm* saying," Nira shouted back. "You're expecting too much. I don't do clingy."

"And I don't do anyone who only wants me for my body," Fred shot back.

Addy gaped at her twin.

Nira let out a high-pitched laugh full of sarcasm. "Don't flatter yourself, Fred. You're not *that* hot."

Fred scoffed. "That wasn't what you were sayin' last night."

"Oh my God," Addy groaned, trying to scrub those words, and all the images they evoked, from her brain.

"He did *not* just say that," Livy whispered, looking as horrified as Addy felt. "He and Nira. They—" She flailed her hands.

Nira, followed by Fred, stalked into the room. They stared at Addy and Livy. Addy and Livy stared back.

"Two hells," Nira muttered.

Fred's face turned tomato-red.

"Let's not talk about it," Addy begged. "I'll throw up everywhere."

Nira planted her fists on her hips. She glared at Addy. "Don't you dare start throwing judgment around. You're sleeping with my leftovers."

Nira turned her back on Addy and pointed a glittery nail at Livy. "And you. I don't even know what to say about your taste in men."

"What's going on?"

Addy's insides warmed at the deep rumble of Tol's voice. He was standing in the open doorway of their room, wearing a pair of low-slung jeans and a V-neck undershirt.

"Nothing," all four of them said at once.

"Where's your prosthesis?" Fred asked.

Tol gave Fred a dark look. "Gone," he said.

"I wasn't tryin' to offend you," Fred huffed. "I was just gonna say I could help—"

"No thank you," Tol interrupted, making it clear his arm wasn't up for discussion.

Fred threw up his hands. "You people need to eat some breakfast. I can't deal with this much crankiness so early in the day."

"Nira?" a familiar, elderly woman's voice called from the doorway. Two women hobbled inside.

"Aunt Marise? Aunt Viola? What are you both doing out of bed? I told you—"

"Marise and Viola are your aunts?" Addy asked, gaping at the other girl.

Marise and Viola were the kind women who had helped dress Addy before her first dinner at the manor. They had made her more beautiful than she'd ever been in her life.

Addy understood now where Nira had gotten her passion for clothes and beauty.

Horror swept in and replaced her surprise. The two women looked like they'd aged a decade since the last time Addy had seen them, and it wasn't like they'd been at the peak of their health then, either.

Addy had no idea how old either of them actually were. From the way they were both always clutching their vials, Addy knew they were much older than they seemed.

Tol had once explained that all immortals eventually stopped ageing, and the vial and chain worked together to infuse the Source needed to keep them alive. The older the immortal, the more Source was needed.

A familiar guilt swept through Addy. Marise and Viola's lives depended on the blood marriage, which had been delayed because of Addy.

"Adelyne, dearest," Marise said, her voice raspy but full of kindness. "It's so good to see you up and about." Her expression darkened. "I hope those good-for-nothing imbeciles who bled you rot in the hells." She cleared her throat. "But now that all that unpleasantness is behind us, you must let us do your hair and makeup the next time there's a celebration."

Nira scowled. "I told you both. No unnecessary physical activity until the blood marriage. You have to conserve your strength."

"Don't you mother us, young lady," Viola said, giving Nira's scowl right back to her.

Knowing that these women were Nira's family made Addy dislike the other girl a little less, albeit grudgingly.

They all jumped at the sound of a gun going off. Everyone raced for the door.

THE CHOSEN UNION

Addy shielded her eyes against the harsh glare of the floodlights. Aunt Meredith shot into the air a second time before lowering her gun.

"That's close enough," Aunt Meredith called to the crowd of mortals who were assembled along the fence that marked the beginning of her property.

Addy just stared. Dozens of people were gathered. Some were shouting obscenities at the Chosen, who were holding their vials in white-knuckled grips. They hadn't Influenced anyone yet, but Addy could tell they were ready to at a moment's notice.

The protestors all wore stickers on their shirts with the words *Alien Hunters*. Some of them were dressed in what looked like *Ghostbuster* Halloween costumes, except they had replaced the anti-ghost armband with one that had a bug-eyed green alien.

"You've gotta be kidding me," Addy muttered.

"This is what happens when you get together equal parts of fear, ignorance, BS, and a whole lotta hot air," Aunt Meredith said.

One of their pamphlets fluttered onto the ground at Addy's feet. She bent to pick it up, examining the writing on the front.

There was a lot of propaganda nonsense, but the Alien Hunters had gotten some things right. Like the fact that the Chosen had long black hair and olive skin, and the Forsaken were pale-skinned, gray-eyed, and had white-blonde hair. Of course, there were regular mortals who fit that physical description, too. And there were some among the immortals, like Addy and the general, who didn't match either description.

Since the mortals couldn't see Haze, these whackos were likely to make a mistake and start attacking unsuspecting mortals who had the misfortune of looking like they belonged with the *aliens*.

"Should we call the cops?" Livy asked.

"Or we could just Influence them," Nira said.

One of the Alien Hunters, catching sight of Nira, turned his *Get Lost, Freaks* sign over. He scribbled *Call Me*, followed by a phone number. Fred growled and cracked his knuckles. Nira gave the man the finger and then turned her back on the entire crowd.

In that moment, Addy's respect for the other girl grew a little more.

Aunt Meredith scoffed. "I may not be able to save the world like you kids, but I can certainly keep a bunch of hotheads off my property."

Off to the side, a much smaller group of mortals faced off against the Alien Hunters. They wore green T-shirts with *Alien Lovers* printed on the front. Some of them wore matching beanies. They held signs that said *No Hate*, *People Aren't Illegal*, and *End Alienism Now*. That last one was complete with a drawing of a little green alien man making the peace sign.

"The more important question is how they found us," Tol said, frowning at the crowd. "If they know we're here, then it won't be long before the Supernal and the rest of the Forsaken know, too."

"Let him come," Addy said, her voice almost a growl.

She hadn't been strong enough to defeat him last time. But that had been back before she'd accepted that she was Forsaken through and through.

The next time she met the Supernal, she was going to submit to the twisted, feral thing inside her. She would draw on its strength until the Supernal understood the true meaning of becoming a monster.

That mental image brought her a dark sense of relief, along with anticipation. She'd never truly unleashed the beast inside her. She didn't know what would happen when she did. All she knew was that, under its control, she would be strong enough to defeat her father.

"Don't worry," Aunt Meredith said, startling Addy out of her black thoughts. "Jaxon has the Londoners watching the property 'round the clock. They've all got walkie talkies, and they let him know any time someone gets within five miles of the farm." She glared at the Alien Hunters before continuing. "Fred has camouflaged tarps to hide the bunker's entrance, Jaxon's people will hide all evidence that this place was ever anything more than a ranch, and the mind-controllers will take care of these dimwit protestors.

"This way, if the Supernal or more of the Forsaken show up, they'll never know we were here."

"You really figured this whole thing out," Addy said, impressed.

Her aunt adjusted her cowboy hat. "Wish I could take credit for it, but all of this was Gerth's planning. That boy is pure genius."

"Besides, what could go wrong when I'm this army's first lieutenant?" a familiar voice asked.

"Mr. Brown?!" Addy whirled around to see Fred's father, grinning as he made his way toward them.

Addy crossed the space between them in two leaps. Even with his braces, he managed to give her a fierce hug.

Everything about Mr. Brown was so comfortable and familiar. When she breathed in his fresh-cut hay smell, she could close her eyes and tell herself everything was going to be alright.

"You look amazing," Addy told him, hardly able to believe it. For the past few years, Mr. Brown's MS had been getting steadily worse.

But the sallow droop of his cheeks had been replaced by a healthy glow. He was still leaning on his braces, but he didn't seem to need them as much as he had the last time she'd seen him.

"Thank you, dearest." Mr. Brown beamed at her. "Nira has been helping me to manage my symptoms. I feel like a new man."

Addy blinked. *Nira was helping a mortal?*

In spite of Nira's earlier comment about Tol being her leftovers, Addy felt her hatred for Evil Beauty Queen crumble a little more.

CHAPTER 17

ADDY

Addy felt the Forsaken before she saw them. She had her garden shears out of her jeans pocket and was striding for them, when Livy stopped her.

"It's okay," Livy said. "They're here because they want to help us."

Addy squinted at the group of warriors, whose weapons flashed as they moved around the cattle pasture. Once she was looking more carefully, Addy realized they weren't fighting with anyone or preparing to attack. They were engaged in some kind of complicated drill.

Addy went over to the fence, where Gerth was leaning over the railing. He was watching the drill with an intense look on his face. Addy followed his gaze to Jaxon and a larger-than-life woman who was taking him to task with a giant mallet.

"Incredible," Addy whispered as she took in their flawless grace.

"You're the same way," Gerth said, glancing at Addy out of the corner of his eye. "With your shears."

It was kind of him to say so, and completely untrue. Addy was more of a brute force kind of girl, hacking away at her enemy until there was nothing left. But watching the way these people fought made her long for their kind of skill.

A pair of fighters who were near the fence caught sight of Addy. They both stopped mid-drill and saluted…*her*.

Within seconds, every one of the Forsaken was standing stock-still, their backs straight and hands frozen in crisp salutes. Every one of them was facing her.

"Uhh," Addy stammered.

"Vol-nah is Russian for *at ease*," Gerth muttered under his breath.

"Vol-nah," she parroted, louder.

The Forsaken let their hands drop, but their eyes continued to linger on her. It occurred to Addy that they were expecting her to say something.

"Our English is passable," the woman who had been practicing with Jaxon said in a heavy accent.

Help me, she mouthed to Jaxon.

"They're being hunted by the Supernal for showing the mortals mercy," Jaxon explained.

"And they came here because...." Addy swallowed.

"Because of you," Jaxon said, holding Addy with his gaze. "They came because they need someone to free them from the Supernal and General Bloodsong, and they...*we*...believe you are that person."

Addy swallowed. She turned her attention on the rest of the group. "If I told you the Supernal is my father, would you still want me to be your leader?"

If the Forsaken warriors were surprised by this revelation, they didn't show it. Their gazes fixed on her. It felt like they were taking her measure and trying to decide whether she was the person they were hoping her to be.

Before she could decide if she wanted to be that person, Addy found herself standing a little straighter and meeting their hard stares.

"You are the only one with the strength to challenge them," the woman who had spoken before said after a long pause.

The others around her nodded in agreement.

"I don't want anything to do with my parents," Addy said in a soft voice.

"Neither do we," the Russian woman replied. "That is why we must find a way to defeat the Supernal and wrest control from the general."

"Tell us what to do, and we will see it done," said a man holding a glowing blue sword.

Addy looked to Jaxon for help, but he seemed to be operating under the same misguided assumption that she had some clue about how to defeat the Supernal.

"This sounds like a job for someone who knows something about battle strategy," Gerth said, coming to her rescue.

He strode onto the field, looking at the warriors as though assessing their strength. The Forsaken gripped their weapons more tightly as he came near. Some of them looked away, probably in case Gerth tried to Influence them. Others stared directly at him with open hostility.

Addy decided to nip this matter in the bud here and now.

"If you want my help, you'll have to accept Gerth's, too," she said.

To her relief, the Forsaken loosened their hold on their weapons, even though their expressions showed no sign of softening.

Gerth was two feet shorter than many of the men and women, and his messy ponytail and baggy clothes were a sharp contrast to their crisp uniforms. Still, Gerth didn't seem in the least bit intimidated.

"Talk to me about the Supernal and what he's planning," Gerth ordered, pulling a notebook out of his back pocket.

First one voice, and then more, began to talk. Some spoke in English and others in Russian. Addy was completely overwhelmed, but Gerth just listened with a thoughtful expression on his face. Jaxon freed the pencil tucked in Gerth's ponytail without missing a beat. He made notes in the notebook Gerth hadn't touched, while Gerth fired questions at the Forsaken in at least three different languages.

Several minutes later, Gerth was cursing to himself as he studied all the notes Jaxon had written down. Finally, he looked up.

"It would seem there's not much we can do at the moment," he said.

"You've got to be kidding me." Addy gave him an incredulous look. "People are dying. The Supernal is getting stronger every day. We have to kill him *now*."

"We can't go rushing into battle with an opponent we have no hope of defeating," Jaxon said quietly.

Addy glared at him.

Gerth nodded at Jaxon in agreement. To Addy, he said, "If there's something I've learned about strategy, it's that circumstances can easily change. We're at a disadvantage today, but who knows what tomorrow will bring. We just need to be patient and wait for an opportunity to present itself."

"A solution isn't going to magically appear out of thin air," Addy argued, growing more frustrated by the second.

"Why not?" Gerth replied. "That's kind of how Jaxon came to us. And because of him, we now have the beginnings of an army." Gerth swept his hand toward the rows of Forsaken soldiers.

Jaxon's cheeks flushed as he and Gerth exchanged a look.

Addy huffed out a frustrated breath. "We can't just sit around and do nothing."

"That's right," Gerth agreed. "So, we keep training. We expand our army. And we wait for an opportunity that will give us the advantage we need." He lifted his chin and gave Addy a fierce look. "And when that happens, we'll bring the bastard down."

✳ ✳ ✳

Addy spent the rest of the day training with Jaxon and the other Forsaken. They didn't go easy on her, even though her arms were still bandaged. She was still irritated that they weren't storming off to battle the Supernal at this very moment, but she couldn't deny the usefulness of more training. And it was fun. Addy was enjoying herself far more than should be possible while waving around deadly weapons.

Nira, who lounged in a beach chair at the edge of their training field, kept shouting at all of the *barbarians* not to pull Addy's stitches out. Even among the iron-willed Forsaken, Addy caught more than a few of their gazes straying toward Nira. Fred sat beside her, twisting wires together with a pair of plyers, while Gerth muttered to himself and scribbled in his notebook.

After Tol finished what looked like a tense conversation with his parents, he joined their small-but-growing group of spectators. There was a wistful expression on his face as he watched her fight. It took Addy another second to understand that Tol wasn't pining after her style of fighting. He was grieving for his own.

A sharp pang went through Addy at the reminder of what Tol had given up for her.

"Can I borrow your sword?" she asked her dueling partner, a man with unfortunately large ears and even more disproportionately-large biceps.

He gave Addy his weapon without hesitation.

She took the sword over to Tol and offered it to him.

Tol gave her, and then the weapon, a skeptical look. "I don't think I'll make a very good swordsman with only one hand."

"Come off it, Tol," Gerth said. "You mean to tell me you can battle all of the gods, but you can't manage a little swordplay?"

Tol gave his best friend a dirty look before reaching for the sword. The moment his hand came into contact with the hilt, the sword flared a brighter blue than it had been before. A vibration began in the weapon's blade, traveling all the way into Tol's hand. Tol didn't have Haze anymore, but an almost-invisible blue shimmer lit up his skin.

"Wow," Tol whispered. He looked at the sword with a new kind of respect.

"Addy's Forsaken blood must be alive and well inside you," Gerth said without looking up from his notebook.

Jaxon, seeing the way the sword reacted to Tol, smiled a little. He said, "You could try a different weapon if you don't like that one." There was a knowing twinkle in his eyes when Tol tightened his grip on the sword.

"Weapons are meant to be used, not cuddled," a cranky Forsaken man informed Tol. "Come practice."

They switched drill partners every five minutes, and the Forsaken weren't quiet about correcting Addy and Tol's every mistake.

"I didn't think you could get any sexier," Addy said, when it was her and Tol's turn to spar. "But seeing you with a sword is making me reevaluate that assumption."

Tol's frustrated expression gave way to a cocky grin. "Plenty more where that came from."

The look he gave her made her whole body grow hot, and it had nothing to do with the sun beating down overhead.

When their insatiable Forsaken task masters finally called for a break, she and Tol sprawled out on the dried grass beside a scrubby cedar tree.

"What's on your mind?" Tol asked, still a little out of breath.

Addy turned toward him, only to find he was studying her.

"They want me to defeat the general and take her place," she said quickly, before she lost her nerve.

Tol's hand tightened around the hilt of his sword.

"Is that what you want?"

A few days ago, Addy would have said *no*. Now, she wasn't so sure. She was reminded of what Livy had said earlier about the Chosen and Forsaken.

There are good and bad Chosen, just like there are good and bad Forsaken. At the end of the day, they're just people like any other.

"I feel more like myself when I'm training with them," Addy admitted. "But I'm afraid if I agree to lead them, then it'll be like surrendering to my evil nature, or something."

"Your evil nature?" Tol raised an eyebrow at her.

"There's something monstrous inside me, Tol," she whispered. "My…mother…is a cold-hearted killer who is willing to sacrifice anything for what she wants, and my father is—"

A murderer and a rapist. Pure evil.

"I love my parents," Tol said quietly, "but I've always feared becoming like them. I almost succumbed to their ambition on Vitaquias."

"But you didn't," Addy reminded him.

"And I think that's the point." Tol tucked a strand of hair behind Addy's ear. "I have those inclinations inside me, but I chose differently, so that makes me different."

"So, are you saying I can be a little murderous, just as long as I'm not too murderous?" Addy asked, nudging Tol with her shoulder.

A smile spread across his face. "I guess I am."

Something blunt hit the side of her head. Addy grabbed a rubber ball off the ground and looked back to the Forsaken woman who had thrown it.

"Enough flirting," she chided. "Break time's over."

"She's a tough one," Tol said picking up his sword and getting to his feet. He winked at Addy before he was absorbed into another drill and she went to duel with Jaxon.

Addy knew how foreign it was for Tol to fight with his body instead of his mind, but he was determined and a fast learner. Addy's heart swelled at the sight of him trading blows with the Forsaken.

Jaxon smacked her shoulder with the flat of his blade.

"Pay attention," he scolded.

Addy stuck her tongue out at him. When Jaxon raised his half-moon blades again, she lowered her shears and held up a hand, breathing hard.

"I have a question," she told him. "Why aren't you like the other Forsaken?"

Jaxon gave her a wary look. "How do you mean?"

"You're not angry like the rest of…us."

It was still difficult to lump herself in with the other Forsaken, but after today, she couldn't deny the rightness she felt in their presence. It was a feeling she'd never experienced in her life on the farm in Nowell or among Tol's people.

Jaxon kept his gaze fixed on the setting sun when he answered.

"I was two years old when our world fell apart, so I barely remember my parents and younger sister, but I heard the story from one of our elders."

Addy started. She had no idea Jaxon had had a sister. Admittedly, she knew next to nothing about him, except that he was Gerth-smart and equally lethal with any weapon he picked up.

"My sister was born the day before the Crossing. She came early, and she was too small. Our physicians were able to keep her breathing, but she couldn't survive on her own. My parents—" he let out a breath. "My parents left her behind. Because she was weak and they assumed she wouldn't survive the Crossing." Jaxon swallowed. "They abandoned her so they could put all of their efforts into getting me, the strong one, out."

Addy felt ill. She was disgusted at herself, because a part of her understood his parents' logic in a cold, removed kind of way.

"Everything that happened on Vitaquias that day was preventable," Jaxon continued. "If it wasn't for greed and violence, we all would have been able to stay there." He lifted a shoulder. "After I became the stone's keeper, I decided I didn't want to be the kind of person who participated in the breaking of a world or the death of an innocent."

Jaxon's words were quiet, and full of a conviction that turned his gray eyes to steel.

"You should be the Forsaken leader," Addy told him.

He turned to look at her, his lip quirking in amusement. "I'm not cut out to be a leader. I belong in an advisory capacity."

Tol, looking hotter than any man had a right to be in his sweat-soaked undershirt, jogged over to them.

"Even if I can defeat the Supernal, I have no idea how to be a leader," Addy admitted, the fear bursting out of her mouth before she could stop it.

"I do." Tol's black velvet voice rolled through her. "I can help you."

"You wouldn't be alone," Jaxon said.

"You'd be okay with this?" Addy asked Tol. "If I became the Forsaken leader?"

"If it's what you want," Tol said, his expression carefully neutral.

This must all be as strange and foreign to him as it was to her. A few days ago, he'd been planning to be the Chosen king with her ruling beside him as his queen. Now, everything was different.

"Why would the Forsaken ever listen to me?" Addy crossed her arms. "I don't know anything about politics, and I can't use a bow and arrows to save my life."

The Forsaken had tried to teach her. Several times.

She was hopeless.

"Our people will follow you because you can offer them something General Bloodsong can't," Jaxon said.

At Addy's questioning look, he clarified, "Your sister is going to be the Chosen queen. If anyone can negotiate peace and a return to our world, it's you."

"And you're part-goddess," Tol added. "That's something else you have over the general."

"It makes me a freak," Addy said with a shudder.

Jaxon's lips curved in the hint of a smile. "In a way, that's something all three of us have in common."

"Being freaks?" Tol narrowed his gaze. "Speak for yourself, mate."

"We've all been alienated from our own people," Jaxon said. "For me, it was when I became the stone's keeper. Addy grew up among the mortals and fell in love with a Chosen, and you," he lifted his chin at Tol. "You abandoned your people for a Forsaken woman."

A muscle flexed in Tol's jaw.

"You didn't abandon your people," Addy said, feeling defensive on Tol's behalf.

"He didn't, but that's how his people will see it," Jaxon said. "All I'm trying to say is that none of us quite fit."

"I disagree," said a new voice.

They all turned to Gerth, who had come up behind Jaxon.

He gave them a fierce look. "All three of you make perfect sense in my world."

"Your world is a pretty twisted place, to be fair," Tol said.

Gerth grinned. "Don't I know it."

CHAPTER 18

ERIKIR

The bunker was complete, and Erikir had to admit it was a work of art. Not that it was pretty to look at...but it was functional. The growing crowd of Chosen, Forsaken, and mortals had somewhere to sleep and a stockpile of supplies. The farmers, led by Fred, were rigging a complicated array of booby traps that would protect those inside the bunker if the coming battle went badly.

Of course, no amount of *Indiana Jones*-style traps could protect them if the Supernal survived, but it was better than nothing.

The farm was an oasis amid the madness. Elsewhere in the mortal world, people were panicking.

All the mortals in Hong Kong had pledged their loyalty to the Supernal. Erikir scrolled through images on his phone of the shrines that had been built and offerings left for the Supernal. Israel and Iran, in a rare show of solidarity, had agreed to fight the aliens together. Other countries were more divided.

As world leaders tried to reach a decision, civilization was crumbling. There was looting, murder, and a general lawlessness that was spreading fear and death even before the Supernal's arrival.

Erikir was reading about a new rash of violence instigated by the Alien Hunters when another headline caught his eye.

English Prime Minister Admits to Being an Alien.

Erikir's blood went cold. His dread rose as he scanned the article.

The English Prime Minister was a good friend of the royal family. The king had appointed him to the role because of his charm that drew mortals to him in spades.

Without discussing the matter with the king and queen, the Prime Minster had decided to out himself as *a visitor from a different world.* He'd given a speech in burned-out Westminster, promising the mortal population that not all of his kind were violent and untrustworthy. He hoped that, by coming forward, he would temper the panic spreading throughout the world.

Predictably, the mortals hadn't been reassured. They were livid.

As Erikir scrolled down in the article, he saw a brief note that the UK contingency of Alien Hunters had made some kind of bargain with English officials. Now, they had the Prime Minister in their custody.

In a shaky video that looked like it had been filmed on a potato, the Alien Hunters announced that they were going to execute the alien at daybreak.

Erikir stopped reading. He ran to the medical tent, where the king and queen were meeting with their guards.

"What's wrong?" Olivia asked as soon as he ducked under the flap of the medical tent.

"Oh, don't bother," Nira told her. "Erikir always looks like that. I'm pretty sure life offends him."

At least she wasn't calling him Weasel *anymore.*

Erikir handed Olivia his phone. He watched her eyes scan back and forth as she read. Her mouth formed into an O.

"They can't," she said in a shrill voice.

"But they're going to," Erikir replied.

"They say they're going to burn him at the stake. This isn't the Salem Witch Trials!"

Erikir had a desperate urge to take her in his arms and comfort her. Instead, he took the phone back and passed it to his uncle.

"What do we do?" Olivia asked.

"That bloody fool," Erikir's uncle fumed as he read the article. He paced to the edge of the tent, turned, and paced back.

THE CHOSEN UNION

Erikir waited.

"Tolumus will take care of it," the king said. "He'll—" The king cut himself off. His gaze snapped up to Erikir's before darting away again.

"You'll have to go as the representative of the royal family," the king told Erikir. "The queen and I are needed here. And Tolumus is…." He scowled. "Unavailable."

Erikir didn't let his surprise register on his face. He didn't know precisely what had happened to Tol on Vitaquias. All he knew was that Tol's Haze was nowhere to be seen, and the king and queen were having a lot of hushed conversations among themselves, which usually ended with Gran telling them to *cool their overheated jets*.

As desperate as Erikir was to find out what had happened, he didn't dare ask.

"I can't spare any of the guards," the king said, turning his back on Erikir to examine a stack of documents Henroix had given him. "So you'll have to find other backup."

* * *

In the end, Olivia had been the only one to volunteer to go with him. There had been a short discussion about whether it was safe for the Fount to be in the thick of danger, but as she'd pointed out, Olivia was powerful enough to deal with whatever the Alien Hunters tried to throw at them.

Gran had insisted they get a few hours' sleep. Then, Addy had portaled Erikir and Olivia to Paris just before the execution was scheduled. They would need to commandeer a ride back to the hideout, since Addy was staying behind at Meredith's and needed to conserve her strength. But getting back wouldn't take more than a cab ride to the airport and some Influencing. Even though Addy had never been to Paris before, seeing the images on TV had been enough for her to create their portal.

They'd arrived a few streets over from the Arc de Triomphe, where the execution was going to be held. After Influencing the mortals who noticed Erikir and Olivia appear out of thin air, they headed for the Arc.

Erikir had been to Paris dozens of times, so he thought he'd been prepared for the crowds that were always milling around this part of the city. What he hadn't accounted for was the general bedlam the city had fallen into over the last few days.

There were so many people it was impossible take a step without having to push through a crush of bodies. The air was thick with tension and barely-repressed hostility.

There hadn't been any Source to spare, so Erikir had to borrow from Olivia's power every time he needed to use Influence. It made him feel like a parasite. The only upside was that it gave him an excuse to hold her hand.

They elbowed and Influenced their way through the crowd until they reached the south side of the Arc, where a raised platform had been constructed.

Erikir's stomach turned over at the sight of the man who was bound and gagged on the platform. The air reeked of gasoline, which was soaked into the Prime Minister's hair and clothes. He was tied to a wooden stake.

"We have to save him," Olivia said, trying to tug Erikir forward.

Erikir held back.

"Come on," she called, her voice barely audible over the voices surrounding them.

"Olivia." He pulled her close enough that she'd be able to hear him. "Where's the Supernal?"

The Alien Hunters were holding this execution in defiance of the Supernal's ultimatum. It was almost dawn, and the Supernal wasn't here.

Erikir took Olivia's hands in both of his.

"You have to find him," he told her in a low, urgent voice.

She shook her head. "It doesn't work that way. I can only sense our own people. The rest of the visions just come when they come."

"You have to try. Please."

Whatever the Supernal was up to, it couldn't be good for them. For all Erikir knew, they were standing in the epicenter of some kind of trap.

All in a flash, it occurred to him how monumentally stupid it had been to bring Olivia here. She was the Fount, his people's one chance of survival. What in the two hells had he been thinking?

"I'm getting you out of here," he decided, drawing her back through the crowd.

She resisted, trying to pull him toward the platform, where Alien Hunters with torches were climbing the steps from either side.

"I'll rescue him," Erikir promised, "but you have to get out of here. It isn't safe."

"Wait." She closed her eyes, and Erikir felt a rush of magic as it rolled off her.

He sensed her mind move far away, searching those strange, dark passages of her magic. Her eyes turned from brown to silver as she fully submitted to the powers of the Celestial.

A few seconds passed. Erikir felt, rather than heard, her intake of breath.

"I found him."

Her voice wasn't entirely her own. It was softer and more penetrating at the same time.

"Where?" Erikir had to shout to be heard over the roar of the crowd that was becoming a mob.

He's—"

Screams erupted as Forsaken sprang out of the crowd. Their Hazes were invisible to the mortals, but the other-worldly blue glow of their weapons wasn't.

Gunfire split the air as the Alien Hunters tried to fight back. Erikir tackled Olivia, pulling her down to the ground and covering her body with his own. The bullets might bounce right off the Forsaken, but they'd rip through him and Olivia.

The Forsaken weren't the only immortals in the crowd. There were Chosen, too…those who didn't live at the manor and thus hadn't evacuated England with the rest of their people. They were fighting against both the Forsaken and the mortals.

Help them, Erikir's brain demanded. These were his people, and their Influence wouldn't shield them from the hail of bullets spraying into the crowd.

But Olivia was still lost in her magic. She had no idea what was going on around her. Erikir had no Source. The only way he'd be able to wield Influence was if Olivia shared her power with him.

"Come back," he begged her. "Olivia, come back!"

He hunched his body around her as another round of gunfire split the air.

"Please," he begged her. "I need you."

Her eyes, open and silver, stared off into a world only she could see.

On some desperate instinct, Erikir pressed his lips to hers.

He was immediately drawn into darkness. The chaos around him slipped away until it was only him and Olivia inside a room strewn with books and loose papers.

The manor's library?

The Supernal and general were flipping through the papers. They were searching for something, yanking books off shelves and then tossing them across the room when they didn't find whatever they were looking for.

Erikir could sense the Supernal's urgency and the general's trepidation. It didn't matter. He needed to bring Olivia back.

Erikir? A soft caress in his mind.

Come back to me, he begged her.

With a startled gasp, the library disappeared. Paris, bullets, and the stench of gasoline surrounded them once again. Erikir looked into eyes that were no longer silver, but brown.

"Come on." He grabbed her hand and yanked her to her feet.

They ran toward the Chosen in the crowd and the Prime Minister on the platform. Erikir felt his veins fill with strength from where his hand was wrapped around Olivia's.

Nearby, a group of mortals was beating and kicking a man to death. He had pale skin and hair, but he wasn't Forsaken. The mortals killed him, anyway.

All around them, mortals were shouting for alien blood. Their faces were filled with fear and hatred. They raised their fists into the sky and spoke in a dozen different languages. Their messages were all the same.

Kill the aliens.

Erikir and Olivia were almost to the platform when a terrible scream rose above all the others. It raised the hair on Erikir's arms. Flames erupted from the platform.

Too late. He was too late.

Smoke billowed from the Prime Minister, who was still shrieking and writhing. The smell of burning flesh filled the air. Erikir gagged.

Olivia yanked him forward toward the platform's steps. He wrapped his arms around her, pulling her back before the flames could latch onto her.

"Let me go!" she shouted at him.

Erikir tightened his hold, bringing her away from the nightmare on the platform.

He had seen both enemies and his own people die. But he'd never witnessed something as horrific as the sight of a man burning alive.

The Prime Minister was his to protect. Erikir felt it in his marrow, a need that went beyond a rational sense of duty. He'd failed one of his own.

It was only Olivia, shaking and crying against him, that kept the black hole in Erikir's heart from destroying him.

"We have to move," he said in a scratchy voice.

There was nothing they could do for the Prime Minister. Mortal police were clashing with the Alien Hunters, and the Chosen and Forsaken were senseless with fury. They were about to get caught in a stampede. Or a massacre.

Olivia said something, but her words were lost in the commotion. When Erikir turned to her, he saw that her Haze had become blinding. Her eyes were molten silver again, and her curls were lifting from a wind that was coming from her own magic.

Before he could utter a word, Erikir was blasted backward, away from Olivia.

He regained his balance in time to see the mortals lifted off their feet. Police, Alien Hunters, and onlookers were swept across the asphalt. The wind only affected the mortals, who slid, rolled, and flew away from the platform. The Hunters' guns rose into the air and crumpled like tin cans.

The mortals shouted and clawed at the air in a vain attempt to slow their progress. They were powerless against the force of Olivia's magic as she continued to drive them away from the plaza. Erikir lost sight of the mortals before the unnatural wind died down.

Within seconds, the only ones remaining near the Arc were the dead bodies on the street and a handful of Chosen and Forsaken. The corpse on the platform was still smoking.

Olivia's silver eyes turned back to brown. She sagged as her magic withdrew. Erikir caught her, holding her against him.

"Nous sommes ici à votre service," one of the Chosen said. He stared at Olivia with reverence as he knelt in front of her. The other Chosen followed, kneeling on the pavement and lowering their heads.

"They're offering you their service," Erikir translated for Olivia.

She gave them a weak smile. "Merci beaucoup," she said in a frightful accent.

Erikir wanted to kiss her.

The Forsaken stared at Olivia with a mixture of confusion and distrust. They held their weapons loosely as they regarded her. No one made a move to attack.

There was a kind of solidarity in all of them having witnessed something so awful. Still, Erikir could sense that their shared experience had a short timeframe that was about to expire.

"We need to get out of here," Erikir said. "It isn't safe."

"Nowhere is safe," one of the Forsaken scoffed.

Erikir met the man's combative stare. The other Forsaken were standing, stiff and wary, as they waited for some indication of what to do.

Erikir looked around at the group.

Olivia was hovering on the verge of unconsciousness, and the Chosen were looking from him to Olivia with a fearful kind of hope in their eyes.

Erikir had to make a decision.

"Come with us," he told the Chosen and Forsaken. "All of you."

At the distrustful looks he got from the Forsaken, and the confused ones he got from his own people, he explained, "We have a place where we can protect you." He turned his attention on the Forsaken. "If you'll agree not to attack any of our people, you can come to our hideout."

He was surprised at himself for extending the offer. He'd seen his people die at the hands of the Forsaken. His own parents were dead because of them.

But there was another part of him that knew they couldn't keep going on this path of hatred and death. It was the same part of him that had tried to bargain with his father's murderer for peace. As he had watched Jaxon, Addy, and Tol training together, he'd thought the future could look different from the past.

"Why should we give them sanctuary?" one of the Chosen demanded. He pointed an accusing finger at Erikir. "You are the king's nephew. You have no authority to offer them safe harbor."

Anger pulsed through Erikir, but he reined it in. He glanced at Olivia, but the conversation was in French, and she had no idea what they were talking about. She was also wavering on her feet from using too much magic in too short a time. She needed food and sleep. Erikir didn't have time to deal with this other nonsense.

"I am here in the king's stead," Erikir said in an even voice. "That means I most certainly do have the authority to do whatever I feel is right."

"Why should we trust you?" one of the Forsaken asked. She ran her hand up and down the curve of her bow, making it clear how little faith she had in whatever promises Erikir gave her.

The mortals' shouts were growing louder as they returned from wherever Olivia had banished them. Part of Erikir wanted to just leave the Forsaken behind. The rest of him knew better.

"The general's daughter is with us," Erikir heard himself say. "More Forsaken are abandoning the general to follow her every day."

A bit of an exaggeration, but it did the trick.

"We have heard about the general's daughter," the same Forsaken woman said. "We will give you our word that we won't attack the Chosen until we've spoken with her."

Good enough, Erikir thought. He turned to the Chosen, who were looking angrier with each second that passed.

"These Forsaken are under the protection of the royal family. Any attack against them will be considered treason."

Erikir was about to say more, when Olivia grabbed his shirt with surprising strength. Her eyes flashed from brown to silver several times in the space of a second.

"The Supernal, he's…still in the manor. He just found whatever he was looking for."

The fear in Olivia's eyes—brown again—sent an icy jolt through Erikir.

"What is it?" he asked. "What was he looking for?"

"A book." She frowned in thought. "It was in a language I couldn't read. It was so old the pages crumbled as soon as the Supernal touched them." She swallowed. "And he set it on fire as soon as he was finished."

There were countless old books in the royal library. And after the chaos with everyone fleeing the manor, it would be impossible to narrow down the specific volume.

A shudder went through Olivia's body. "Whatever they were reading, it had something to do with me."

Erikir started. "What?"

She closed her eyes in concentration. "He told the general their plans had changed. He said—"

Olivia's eyes snapped open. "He said he was going to take my powers for himself."

Rage lashed through Erikir.

"Then, we have to hide you," Erikir said. "Keep you far away where he'll never find you."

Olivia shook her head. "It won't matter." She met Erikir's angry gaze. "The Supernal has a plan to bring me to him."

CHAPTER 19

TOL

They crowded around the television in Meredith's living room, watching in silent horror as the Supernal hovered in mid-air in front of the Eiffel Tower. He was shirtless, and the blue tinge of his Haze reflected in the sunlight.

"W-what is it you'd like to say to the humans of Earth?" a terrified reporter asked, his voice shaking so much the question was barely audible.

The Supernal gave the camera a dazzling smile.

"As you know, the week-long reprieve I've given all of you ends soon." He gestured to the group of mortals cowering behind him.

"Any who wish to avoid the slaughter must swear fealty to me, the one true god of this world. Any who seek to defy me will be killed."

"But—" the reporter began.

"*But*, your lowly human affairs are not what I want to talk about now." The Supernal turned away from the reporter and toward something out of the camera's frame.

There were audible gasps from Tol's parents and friends as the camera shifted and locked on a group of twenty Chosen. They huddled in a makeshift corral, like animals. The general stood watch, her hand loosely wrapped around her spear. Her ruby ring sparkled in the sunlight, a reminder of the fact that she was immune to Influence.

Tol clenched his fist.

"My message is for the Celestial's Fount," the Supernal said, smiling at the camera.

Tol felt Addy's fingers dig into his arm at the mention of Olivia.

"I would like to speak with you," the Supernal said, his gold eyes flashing in the early-morning sun.

"Speak with her," Gerth scoffed. "Kill her, he means."

There was no doubt that was exactly what the Supernal meant.

"The...the Celestial's Fount?" the reporter asked in a tremulous voice. "Is this person another alien?"

The Supernal ignored the reporter.

"I will kill one of your people every hour, on the hour, until you face me."

Tol's breath caught. His father cursed. His mum and Gran were staring at the screen, their faces drained of color.

The Supernal stretched out his arm, palm-up. Blue sparks appeared.

Tol knew what the Supernal was doing even before the reporter's surprised yelp. The unmistakable sound of crackling electricity filled the room. A lightning bolt—smaller than the one that had carved through Tol's chest—materialized in the Supernal's grip.

Keeping his gaze locked on the camera, he crooked the index finger of his left hand at the general.

General Bloodsong, her face devoid of emotion, yanked one of the Chosen out of the corral.

Tol knew the man. His name was Hamovar, and he was the president of the European Parliament. Hamovar had come to the manor several times. Tol was friendly with the man's grandson, who oversaw the Chosen living in New Zealand.

The general shoved Hamovar to his knees on the grass in front of the Supernal.

With his hand that wasn't holding the lightning bolt, the Supernal lifted up an old-fashioned pocket watch. He raised his golden eyebrows. "Look at that. It's noon on the dot."

With deliberate slowness, the Supernal aimed the lightning bolt.

No, Tol thought, desperate.

THE CHOSEN UNION

"Don't," the reporter begged.

The lightning bolt struck Hamovar straight through the heart. Sickness tore through Tol as Hamovar crumpled to a heap on the grass. Tol saw the blackened hole in the Chosen man's chest right before his body dissipated into smoke.

Tol's mother covered her face. Someone else was crying. Tol couldn't breathe.

"One of your people dies every hour, Fount," the Supernal said. "I'll be right here, waiting for you."

Then, as an afterthought, he reached down to where the reporter was rocking and talking to himself. The Supernal wrapped one hand around the reporter's neck and lifted him off the ground. Then, he threw the man.

The reporter sailed through the air. There was a loud bang as he struck the wrought iron of the tower. Then, the screen went black.

"What do we do?" Nira whispered into the silence that followed.

"We get our people out of there," Tol said, his whole body shaking from the rage he could barely contain. "Now."

Tol's father nodded. "We'll get all of our guards ready to go." He glanced at Addy. "Provided you're willing to portal us."

"Of course," Addy replied. "I'll ask any Forsaken who are willing to join us, too."

"Good," the king said. "Everyone meet on the front lawn in ten minutes. We're not losing another one of our people."

"We need to keep Livy far away from him," Addy said, her eyes wide.

"I just heard from Erikir," Gerth said, coming in from the other room. "They're on a plane and on their way back here. Olivia is beside herself over Hamovar's death, but she gets that we can't let her near the Supernal."

Addy let out a relieved sigh. "Good. Because if I had to portal onto a moving airplane, there's a good chance I'd end up just outside it and be stuck thirty-thousand feet in the air."

"Yeah, best to avoid that," Gerth said, giving Addy an amused look.

"Why is the Supernal doing this?" Tol asked. "I mean, why go through this whole game of bringing Olivia to him?"

Gerth's expression turned grim. "Olivia had a vision, and apparently, the Supernal thinks he knows how to steal Olivia's powers for himself."

Several curses filled the room.

The Supernal was next to invincible already. If he added the Celestial's abilities to his own, he'd be unstoppable.

"We'll keep Livy safe here while ya'll deal with this monster," Meredith said, her mouth pressed in a tight line.

Tol turned to Addy, but he saw no fear on her face. Only anger.

"Tolumus, you can supervise the mortals who are stocking the bunker while we're gone," his father said.

Tol choked on air.

"Pardon?"

His father squinted at him. "You aren't coming with us."

"Like hells I'm not," he said.

"There is nothing you can do to help," the king said. "You no longer have your magic."

Tol's heart stuttered. Somewhere between Hamovar's death and their decision to go after the Supernal, he'd forgotten that he wasn't the strongest of his people. He wasn't Chosen at all.

He was useless.

The thought filled his mind until there wasn't room for anything else.

"We need Tol there more than anyone," Addy said, her voice sharp. "He might not be able to Influence, but he still has my blood. That means the Supernal can't hurt him."

Tol hadn't known whether that particular ability had carried over after the gods took away his magic. He'd gotten his answer earlier that morning, when he'd been too slow to block his opponent during their drill. Her blade had cracked on contact with Tol's shoulder without so much as breaking his skin.

Still, there was a difference between being able to block the Supernal's attack and being able to fight.

Addy, he reminded himself. *I gave up my magic for Addy.*

"That's right," Tol said. "I'm the one who's going to keep the Supernal occupied while the rest of you free our people."

Addy gave him a look of such utter confidence that it made him feel anything but useless.

Gods, he loved her.

"Shall we?" Tol said, silently daring his father to order him back to the bunker.

CHAPTER 20

TOL

Tol's mind was consumed with their impending fight with the Supernal. He was utterly unprepared for the mob of Chosen who surrounded him the moment he stepped outside.

"Prince Tolumus, how are you going to save our people?" a scholar asked.

"Can't you just turn the Supernal's brain into porridge?" someone else asked.

Soon, all of the Chosen were shouting at Tol, demanding that he use his infinite power to end the Supernal and save their people.

"And then you'll blood marry the Fount," said Flagillian.

Flagillian was a slightly-less-greasy version of his brother, Migelian. Tol had personally killed Migelian after he had Influenced Addy, back when they'd crossed paths in D.C. It felt like forever ago.

Tol gritted his teeth. He didn't have time for this conversation right now. The Chosen, though, didn't seem to care. They weren't going to back off until he'd done something spectacular. Or told them the truth.

Tol put up his hand to quiet the crowd.

"I no longer have the power you're hoping to see," Tol said. He forced himself to meet their shocked gazes.

Gerth's shoulder brushed against his left side while Addy took his right hand, lacing their fingers together.

Bolstered by their presence, Tol continued. "I gave it up for a future with Adelyne."

He turned to look at her. She smiled at him before squeezing his hand.

"Rest assured that you will have a new king and queen before the month's end," Tol continued. "But—" He forced himself to stand straight. "I am not your future king."

Silence stretched while the Chosen processed his words.

"Weakling prince," Flagillian said into the quiet.

Tol flinched before he could stop himself.

"He fought the gods and bent them to his will, you bloody idiot," Gerth said. "He's already proven his strength a thousand times over."

"You betrayed all of us for that piece of Forsaken arse?" Flagillian demanded. He looked Addy up and down. He licked his lips. "But then, your blood was sweet. Give us another taste, lovey."

Tol's vision went white.

The crowd scattered as two steps brought Tol's sword against Flagillian's throat.

"A quick death is more than you deserve," Tol said, "but I don't have time to linger."

"Tol, it's not worth it," Addy said, tugging his arm down. "We have bigger fish to fry."

"The Supernal's what matters right now," Gerth added, when Tol didn't back down. "We need to go before any more innocents die."

Tol forced in a calming breath. He pointed his sword at Flagillian in both a warning and promise before sheathing it.

"Look at you," Flagillian scoffed, emboldened once there was no longer a blade against his skin. "Must be kind of hard to play at Forsaken when you're a one-armed freak."

Tol froze.

Addy moved. Her arm slashed through the air. Blood sprayed.

Flagillian let out a wet, choking cough. Addy yanked the point of her shears out of his neck and let him slide to the ground.

She ignored the man who was bleeding out at her feet. She glared around at their shocked audience.

"This is what will happen to anyone who insults Tol," she said in a strong voice. "Or anyone who thinks about taking so much as a drop of my blood."

※ ※ ※

"Wait!"

Blue light was already spilling from the stones of Addy's ring when Fred, sweating profusely, sprinted toward them. He was carrying a long box.

"Wait up," Fred called again.

"What bloody now?" Tol asked. Half an hour had already passed. In thirty more minutes, another one of the Chosen was going to die.

"Tol," the farmer gasped, trying to catch his breath. "I need to talk to you."

"Now?" Tol demanded.

"Go on, mate," Gerth said, exchanging a knowing look with Fred. "We can spare a minute."

Addy, that same knowing look in her eyes, nodded. The light withdrew into the stones of her ring.

Scowling at both of them, Tol followed Fred away from the group of people who were waiting for Addy's portal to bring them to Paris.

"What?" he snapped as soon as they were far enough not to be overheard.

"I don't want you to take this the wrong way," Fred said, kneeling over the long box he'd placed on the ground. "It's not a pity thing, it's just that I thought you could use it. And Addy and Gerth agreed."

When Fred lifted off the top of the box, Tol felt his jaw slacken. He was staring down at a prosthetic arm.

Even though his other one had been the top of the line, this one was even sleeker.

"Um," Tol said, because it was the only word he could conjure.

"It's not quite finished, but I can make the last adjustments when you get back." Fred gave the prosthesis a critical look. "There are twenty-six joints, so that should make it easier for you to hold your sword with two hands if you want.

"Gerth dealt with the muscle sensors and electrodes, so those should be good to go." Fred took a breath. "It might take you a little while to adjust to everythin', but anyway," he trailed off and scratched the back of his neck, looking awkward.

Tol felt like such a prat for snapping at Fred when he'd asked about Tol's arm before.

"Thank you," Tol said, finally coming out of his stupor. "Seriously. This is—"

He would never feel the gods' magic in his left arm again, but in that moment, he didn't care. He didn't need that kind of power when he had Addy and Gerth. When he had friends like Fred.

As he and Fred scrutinized the prosthetic arm, Tol realized he no longer felt uncomfortable with others talking about and seeing his missing arm.

The gods had offered to give his arm back, and he'd refused in exchange for something so much more important. The fact that his missing arm was now a choice he'd made, rather than something that had been forced on him, made all the difference. After a lifetime of following a path that had been pre-assigned, it was a relief to control his own fate for once.

"Thank you," Tol said again as he rolled up his sleeve to put on the prosthesis. This one didn't have a harness like his old one. Instead, it hooked into his shoulder. Already, he could tell it wouldn't rub against his skin as much as his old one.

"I got a question," Fred said, shifting from foot to foot.

"Yeah?"

Fred was right. These new finger joints had a lot better mobility than his last prosthesis.

"Nira," Fred said. His gaze darted away when Tol looked at him. "Do you, er, have any advice?"

Tol stared at Fred.

"Are you seriously asking me for dating advice right now?" he asked in disbelief.

"Not dating advice." Fred scowled. "*Nira* advice. She's…difficult."

Tol couldn't help but laugh at that. To say Nira was difficult was like saying Addy was pretty. It didn't begin to scratch the surface.

"It seems like your whole farmer routine is working for her." Tol rubbed at his left shoulder and glanced away from Fred. "She pretends not to care because she doesn't want to be vulnerable. You might need to take things slow…emotionally."

Tol felt a stab of guilt at the reminder of how he had hurt Nira. He hadn't done it intentionally, but he'd done it all the same.

"She's lost a lot of people who matter to her," Tol said carefully. He was walking a line between helping his friends and giving away secrets that weren't his to expose.

"Make sure she knows you aren't just going to disappear on her," he added.

Fred's face was pinched in concentration as he nodded, processing Tol's words.

"Anything else?" Fred asked.

The expression on Fred's face was what Gerth would have referred to as *gaga* eyes. The man was utterly, hopelessly besotted.

Tol's response was drowned out by a loud clanging.

"Code red!" Meredith hollered before Tol could even locate the source of the piercing noise. "Code red!"

Jaxon, a walkie talkie in his hand, jogged across the lawn.

"The general's people," he said without preamble. "Twenty-five jeeps. Eleven kilometers out."

By the time Tol turned back to Fred, the farmer was gone. The London refugees were swarming toward the bunker. They picked up tools, weapons, and food containers spread out on the lawn on their way. A group of Forsaken who had kicked Tol's arse in drills that morning deconstructed the medical tent. The farmers carried the medical supplies stacked on the folding tables, along with the folding tables themselves, down into the bunker.

Tol watched as all evidence of their massive group of people disappeared. The yard appeared empty and completely unremarkable.

"Miles," Meredith barked at Jaxon, sounding like a drill sergeant. "Talk to me in *miles*."

"Six-point-eight," Gerth said. "Approximately."

Following the lead of Gran and Tol's parents, any of the Chosen who had Source to spare were Influencing the crowd of Alien Hunters and Lovers. The mortals silently filed into the bunker behind the others. Fred and his father unrolled a long tarp that covered the bunker and made it look like more of the lawn.

In two minutes flat, everyone was in the bunker except for a small group gathered around Addy and Tol.

Tol's one consolation was that Addy's Haze hadn't turned blue. If the Supernal was here instead of in Paris where he was supposed to be, Addy's Haze would already be reacting.

"What do you want to do?" Gerth asked Tol. "Defending the farm is the priority, but we can't let the Supernal keep executing our people, either."

Gerth was right. Their entire army was on this farm.

"Addy and I will go rescue the Chosen in Paris," Tol said, thinking quickly. "Everyone else should stay here."

Gerth gave him a penetrating look, and for a second, Tol thought he was going to insist on going to Paris with him and Addy.

"You know," Gerth said, rubbing his chin. "I think we may have happened on the opportunity I was waiting for."

At the quizzical looks he got, Gerth explained. "If we can convince these new Forsaken to join us, we'll siphon off more of the Supernal's power. If his army becomes our army, we'll be able to defeat him based on sheer numbers."

"It's certainly worth a try," Tol's father agreed. "I'll drive out to meet them so we can begin parlaying."

Gerth held up a hand. "Why don't you let Jaxon and I meet with them first? It might help smooth the way to have two more neutral parties facilitate the peace talks."

After a brief hesitation, the king nodded.

"Are you sure you'll be alright here?" Addy asked her aunt, worry written into every line of her face.

"Perfectly," her aunt said. She pressed her cowboy hat more firmly on her head. "We have everything under control here. You and Tol just make sure you take care of each other."

While Addy gave her aunt and Fred's father fierce hugs, Tol turned to his parents.

"I love you both," he told them.

They hadn't spoken those words to each other in years, and he caught the look of surprise on his parents' face.

"You've always supported me," he continued, needing to get the words out while he still had time. "I know I've made things difficult these past couple of months. I'm sorry—"

Before he could finish, his mum had swept him into a hug that was tight enough to compress his ribs.

"We love you, Tolumus," she said. "You're our son, no matter what." She gave him one final squeeze and stepped back.

"Your mother is right," the king said, holding out his hand to Tol. "We're proud to call you our son."

Tol bowed his head, overcome by his parents' words. They were words he wasn't sure he deserved, but ones he appreciated nonetheless.

"Hold up." Nira, who was wearing cowgirl boots, squeezed into their group. She pressed a small kit into Addy's hand.

"Splints and bandages," Nira explained at Addy's puzzled look. "This way, if you're clumsy enough to get your left hand broken again, you can tape it up so you'll be able to get back here."

"Thanks, Nira," Addy said, looking like she was trying to hide a smile. "I appreciate it."

Nira sniffed. "Well, Fred would be devastated if you didn't come back, and the poor mortal has such a bleeding heart as it is."

Nira squeaked in protest when Addy wrapped her arms around her and gave her a hug. When Addy let her go, Nira was glaring. It wasn't one of her chilling looks that could stop a person where they stood, though. If Tol didn't know better, he'd think Nira was actually pleased.

"Forsaken are two minutes out," Jaxon announced.

"We better get out of here before they show up," Tol said to Addy. "Or before anyone else tries to hug us." His British stoicism had taken a heavy hit, and he needed time to regenerate before any more emotional displays.

"Remember," Gerth said, giving Tol and Addy a warning look. "You're not going there to fight the Supernal. Your mission is to distract him long enough to get the Chosen out. Then, you get yourselves back here."

"Do you think this is going to work?" Addy asked after they'd hammered out the specifics of their plan. There was a hint of uncertainty in her voice as her ring began to glow.

"It'll work," Tol told her.

It had to.

CHAPTER 21

ADDY

Addy didn't feel too badly when her portal delivered her and Tol directly on top of an unsuspecting Alien Hater. The man *oofed* as she and Tol pancaked him.

"Sorry," Addy told the man, not feeling particularly sorry.

Looking around, Addy saw that the other Alien Hunters and Alien Lovers, who had been facing off, had gone silent. They stared at Addy and Tol, their eyes bugged out and their mouths hanging open.

One of the Hunters said something in French that didn't sound very friendly. Tol gave the man a tight smile and responded...also in French.

Addy loved the way the words sounded in his black velvet voice.

"I'm totally going to have you speak French to me later," Addy informed him.

Tol gave her one of his lazy, sensuous smiles. "Oui, mon amour."

"Peace on earth, or wherever!" an Alien Lover cried in stilted English. And then he threw himself into the crowd of Alien Hunters, bashing people with a police baton.

At least the clashing forces were causing enough of a ruckus that, hopefully, the Supernal wouldn't be paying attention to who else had just arrived. Addy and Tol were on the opposite side of the Eiffel Tower from the corral of Chosen and the horde of mortals groveling before the Supernal.

Addy couldn't see the Supernal, but she felt him. His magic hummed in her veins. It was a sense of familiarity that she didn't want to feel. It was a crying out of her magic to his.

It disgusted her.

A strange tingling began in her bandaged hands, distracting her from her growing nausea. The feeling raced up her arms, her neck, and her back. The lingering pain from her stitches was gone. When Addy peeled back her bandages and inspected her skin, a yelp startled out of her.

The stitches were still in place, but they were holding together perfectly-mended skin. The angry redness was gone, as were the long slashes down her palms and forearms.

Before she could wrap her mind around that unwelcome miracle, she noticed that her Haze was no longer gold. Her skin radiated a shimmery blue...like the Supernal. *Like her father.*

"Addy." Tol spun her around to face him.

She almost couldn't bring herself to meet his gaze. He came from two parents who loved each other and loved him. She came from—

"You're a goddess," Tol said. "*My* goddess. Your parents gave you their strength, but nothing else."

Addy had used to love it when he called her a warrior goddess. Now, it just reminded her of the horrific roots she'd sprung from.

"Do you think I would have fallen in love with a monster?" Tol asked when she stayed silent. "I hate your parents. So do Olivia, Fred, Meredith, and Gerth. And all of them love you."

Addy managed a shaky nod. She wanted to soak in Tol's words until they filled every hollow place inside her. But Tol didn't know how much she repressed her true nature—the dark, angry thing inside her that wanted to maim, fight, and kill. The same beast she would need to unleash to face the Supernal.

Once Tol knew the truth, he might be singing a different tune.

Addy took a deep breath, forcing down her fears and insecurities. She knew what she had to do. She'd deal with the consequences later.

"Ready?" she whispered to Tol.

"I'll see you soon," he replied. He gave her a quick kiss, and then he was gone, sneaking around the tower in the direction of the corral. Addy could see the faint blue outline of the general's spear as she guarded the corral's entrance.

Addy began to creep around the opposite side of the tower, forcing herself to trust in the plan Gerth, Jaxon, and Tol had come up with before they'd parted ways. She couldn't worry about Tol right now if she was going to do what was necessary to take down her father.

And in spite of what she'd promised Gerth, she had every intention of killing her father. This might be a rescue mission for Tol, but she had a half-god monster to slay.

The closer Addy got, the more massive the Supernal became. He loomed over the crowd of mortals, looking even bigger as he hovered a few feet off the ground. His golden skin was tinged with a blue glow, just like Addy's. His hair was thick and wavy, and the sun overhead was pale in comparison to the glowing gold of his reptilian eyes.

There was nothing left of the sock-and-sandal-wearing man who had first stepped out of the helicopter and onto the aircraft carrier.

Addy was determined to make him into that man again.

And then she'd kill him.

She almost faltered when the Supernal's Haze flared brighter, and he turned toward her. His eyes met hers. His jagged, lightning bolt-pupils were both mesmerizing and terrifying.

Addy looked the Supernal up and down. He was wearing some kind of chainmail that looked like it was out of one of the Medieval war movies she and Fred used to watch. The capped sleeves hugged his enormous biceps and cut off above his knees. Addy wondered where on this planet he'd found such an outfit.

"Nice dress," Addy said, pleased to find that her voice didn't waver even a little.

The Supernal didn't seem amused.

"Where is the Fount?" he demanded.

"Detained, I'm afraid," Addy said in a lofty voice, reverting back to her usual sarcasm in lieu of crumbling into a furious, terrified heap. "She sends her regards, though."

The Supernal hissed like some kind of lizard.

Addy could feel the heat of the Supernal's magic radiating off her skin. She felt her own power grow inside her in response. It sickened and invigorated her at the same time. The hungry, angry thing inside her stirred to life.

Addy whipped her garden shears out of her back pocket. Then, she did the one thing she'd sworn to herself she'd never do. She unleashed the coiled cobra…the ravenous beast…the demon.

With a wild scream, she threw herself at the Supernal.

❋ ❋ ❋

TOL

Tol crept around the corral. He got close enough to the fence to touch the nearest Chosen. The woman startled and wheeled around, but Tol hurriedly put a finger to his lips. Her eyes widened at the sight of him. Tol didn't recognize this woman, but it was clear she knew exactly who he was.

He slipped a nearly-empty vial of Source into her hand. It contained the few precious drops of Source the Chosen guards had spared him. Tol only hoped it would be enough.

"Pass this around to the strongest among you," he whispered. "When I give the word, Influence her with everything you've got."

"But—" the woman whispered.

"Be ready," Tol said, his gaze flicking to the general on the other side of the corral.

The Chosen along the fence used their bodies to block Tol from the general's view as he continued to sneak around the makeshift fence. He waited until he was within striking distance before he spoke.

"General Bloodsong."

The general whipped around. Before she could react, Tol called on everything he'd learned from his new Forsaken acquaintances. He struck out.

The motion was fast, and his aim was precise.

Surprise flashed across the general's face before Tol's sword sliced through her wrist. Her right hand, the one with the Supernal's ring on her index finger, landed on the grass with a soft thud.

"Now!" Tol shouted.

Several of the Chosen in the corral turned their gazes on the general at once. One of them threw himself against the fence so his bare arm touched the general's.

Tol waited for her eyes to glaze over. He waited for the spear in her left hand to slip to the ground.

Neither happened.

Even though the Chosen were focusing on her with all of their concentration, it was clear the general wasn't under Influence.

The general gave Tol an amused look. Then, she raised her arm to display her newly-formed right hand. Her index finger was complete with the ruby ring.

"No," Tol stammered.

He looked down at the ground, where the evidence of his would-be triumph still lay. The pale hand, the white of the bone and severed tendons on full display, lay on the grass. All that was missing was the ring. Because it had somehow returned to the general's new hand.

Shite. Tol had thought the Supernal would be too distracted with Addy to pay any attention to the general. Tol had been gambling that if the general was injured instead of killed, it wouldn't set off whatever freaky power enabled the Supernal to bring his people back to life.

Clearly, he'd seriously misjudged. The general's hand had regrown almost as soon as it had been cut off.

"I hope for your sake you've got some other trick up your one-armed sleeve," the general said in a quiet, deadly voice.

She raised her spear.

CHAPTER 22

ADDY

An inhuman scream burst forth from Addy's lungs.
Wrath, murder, and bloodlust boiled deep inside her. For once, she didn't shove the feelings back down. She welcomed them. Instead of consuming her, the emotions fueled her. She felt stronger than she'd ever been. She felt invincible.

Her Haze pulsed a blinding blue as she and the Supernal faced each other.

A knowing smile spread across the Supernal's face. "There you are, my daughter."

"I'm not your—"

The lie died on her tongue. If that was what she needed to become to defeat the Supernal, then so be it.

She lunged.

Addy felt her entire body go weightless. She didn't allow herself to feel awe or fear. There was room only for rage, and she had plenty of that. It wasn't her power that was lifting her into the air, but his. She was somehow drawing from it, solidifying the connection between them as she absorbed his abilities.

As she rose into the air, the Supernal watched her. His gaze was almost wary, like he didn't recognize her.

Addy barely recognized herself.

She stabbed forward with her garden shears. The Supernal flew back away from her, and Addy almost upended herself in her new weightless form. She righted her body in mid-air, letting the invisible ropes of the Supernal's power loop around her and keep her from falling back down to the ground.

"Very well," the Supernal said in a quiet, deadly voice. "Let us fight."

Flames leapt up from the Supernal's palms. The heat wafted over Addy's skin, but instead of burning, it felt…right.

She didn't reject her natural pull toward the Supernal's power. She let the connection between them strengthen. His magic called to hers, and hers answered. She cloaked herself in the power they shared. She embraced it.

Her fingers reached out to him like claws, but instead of locking onto flesh, she caught his fire. She knew it was hotter than any normal fire, and yet, she felt only a pleasant tickling as the flames washed over her skin.

The Supernal's eyes widened in surprise as he stared at her. Addy looked down at herself, only to see that her entire body was wreathed in blue flames.

She was stealing the Supernal's powers for herself.

She was levitating, covered in blue flames, and face-to-face with her father. *Her enemy.*

With a feral scream, she gathered the flames and threw them at the Supernal.

His body rippled as the force struck him. Addy sensed him shudder as the blast of magic encased his skin. He writhed.

A maniacal laugh bubbled up from Addy's throat. She watched as the Supernal's pupils dilated in pain. She waited with baited breath to see the light drain from his eyes.

Instead, the Supernal absorbed the flames, pulling the heat and energy back inside himself. Before Addy could recover, the Supernal retaliated.

There was a crackle of energy. Then, Addy was engulfed in a web of electricity that stretched and scorched as it threatened to tear her apart.

Panting, and with tears streaming down her face, she absorbed the electricity just as the Supernal had done with her flames. She was burning up. Her insides were molten.

THE CHOSEN UNION

They clashed again.

Her fist connected with his skull with a force great enough to break through stone. The Supernal absorbed the hit. He returned with a stab of heat that tore through her.

They were hurting each other, but with the way she was clinging to his magic, she didn't think either of them would be able to kill each other. They were too connected. But if she let go of the Supernal's power, she'd be too weak to do anything to him.

Addy roared in frustration.

Her anger grew fiercer. It blinded her until it was all she could see…all she could feel.

Finally, the beast inside Addy purred. *Free.*

The garden shears, so tiny and insignificant, dropped out of her hand. She made no move to pick them up. Instead, she harnessed the magic she could now sense bubbling just beneath the Supernal's skin. As soon as she gave in to the temptation, she found she could take that magic and wield it herself.

A shocked gasp hissed out of her. A sizzle of electricity coursed through her veins. When she held out her arm, the spidery blue bolts crackled across her skin.

"Finally," the Supernal taunted. "Finally, you understand what you are. *Who* you are."

"Damn right I do."

With an effort, Addy consolidated the bursts of electricity. Then, she hurled them at the Supernal. He dodged her attack, and the mass of electricity hit the Eiffel Tower.

The entire structure flared blue. Smoke rose from the wrought iron bars. The metal began to sag in places, like it was melting.

That gave Addy an idea. If she couldn't use the Supernal's own power against him, then maybe—

She flew to the Eiffel Tower. Using the Supernal's magic, she yanked on one of the iron bars. She felt it start to loosen. It was scalding to the touch, but not impossible to hold. She kept pulling, fueled by her fury and the

Supernal's strength. Her nails cracked and bled as she dug into the molten metal. The wrought iron groaned and warped under the force of her grip.

Addy shouted as another wave of blue flames lit her up. She let the Supernal's attack engulf her as she wrestled with the iron bar. Finally, she felt it come apart from the structure. She grasped the melting metal and lashed out at the Supernal, like she was wielding a giant, metal whip.

The metal wrapped around his body, caging him.

The Supernal bellowed as he strained against the metal. She pulled it tighter around him, feeling a deep satisfaction at the way his skin sizzled everywhere the iron pressed.

Before she could come at him again, the Supernal thrust the cage outward. The metal bars split apart like they were nothing.

The Supernal's laughter shook the air. The Eiffel Tower, which was leaning precariously, wobbled.

"You cannot defeat me," he said.

Doesn't mean I won't try, asshole.

The Supernal flew at her. He was so fast she didn't have time to even bring up her fists. They collided, and then all she saw was a tumbling panorama of blue sky and cityscape.

Addy could feel herself slipping away as they tumbled through the air. The agony was too much. The magic was too much. She couldn't win, and yet, she couldn't lose, either. She was stuck in a battle that could have no end.

Trapped. She was trapped.

"Give up, Daughter," the Supernal huffed, clutching at his chest after her fist delivered another vicious blow.

Daughter. The world rattled around in her mind. It broke through the endless rage that was eating her alive.

Even as the Supernal lashed out at her with more fire…more electricity…that one word struck deeper. She recoiled from it.

She wasn't his daughter. Not really.

Mom, she thought, picturing a woman with brown hair and a shirt dusted with flour. The smell of apple pie hot out of the oven.

Dad. A tuft of graying-brown hair. Smile crinkles at the corner of his eyes. Corn fields and an old tractor and a cow named Jenny.

As soon as the thoughts filled her mind, her magic began to recede. She scrabbled, trying to bring it back.

Addy was thrust to the side. Her shoulder slammed into the mass of wrought iron bars. She cried out as pain shot through her.

She reached out for the Supernal's power, desperate to cloak herself in it before his next attack.

But instead of her desire to kill the Supernal, her mind filled with thoughts of her beloved twin. She thought about Tol, and how he had sacrificed everything for the chance of a life with her.

Addy's back struck the ground with a force that drove all the air from her lungs. Her vision wavered in and out of focus as the Supernal hovered over her.

"Come back," she ordered the beast inside her, desperately clawing at the magic.

It wasn't there. Even before she reached inside herself, she knew it wasn't there.

The Supernal lowered himself to the ground, slowly. Even through her darkening vision, Addy could tell he wasn't tapped out. He hadn't lost the driving hunger that had consumed her before…that had made her strong.

What a time to defeat her inner demon, she thought acidly.

Ironically, the humanity she thought she'd abandoned…the humanity she'd worried she never had…was going to be the death of her. She saw the Supernal's victory in his golden eyes as he struck.

Tol's whole body flashed blue as he appeared out of nowhere, standing over her and facing the Supernal.

The Supernal rained down fire, currents of electricity, and iron beams without mercy. Tol deflected it all.

Addy got to her feet, stiff and weak. She looked around, searching for something…anything…to salvage this loss.

She spotted her garden shears lying on the grass nearby. They were so small. If it hadn't been for the sunlight sparkling off the blades, she might not have noticed them at all.

Another wall of blue flames hit Tol. The fire died as it struck him, but the effort it took to repel the attack brought him to his knees.

"Tol!" Her heart went into her throat at the sight of him, hunched over on the grass.

"Addy, I can't," he said, his voice raspy. "I can't hold—"

Addy dove for her shears. She didn't know why; it wasn't like they could do anything against the Supernal. Maybe she just didn't want to die without a weapon in her hand. *Her* weapon.

"Kill him," the Supernal said, his icy voice booming through the air.

Addy whipped around. A scream caught in her throat at the sight of the general. She was standing behind a kneeling Tol, her spear pointed at his neck.

No. No. No!

She'd forgotten all about the general. She hadn't given so much as a thought to any enemy except for the Supernal.

"Our daughter is about to discover the price for defying us," the Supernal said. His gaze was alight with mirth and expectation.

Tol turned his head toward Addy, ignoring the way the motion made his neck scrape against the general's blade. Blood trickled down into his collar.

"Get out of here," he told her.

Not a chance.

"Don't do this," Addy pleaded with the general, pocketing her shears and holding up her hands to show she was no threat as she went closer. "Let him go."

"Too late for begging, girl," the Supernal sneered. He seemed in no hurry to put an end to her agony…seemed to enjoy watching her beg.

Bastard.

If the general would just loosen her hold on Tol for a second, Addy could get him out. But with the blade against his neck, even her portal wouldn't be fast enough to save him.

"Addy, go," Tol said, his voice still coming out forceful in spite of his helpless situation.

Hell would freeze over before she abandoned Tol. She would sooner die right here at his side than leave without him.

Addy watched in muted horror as the Supernal held out his hand. She felt the burst of his magic, and then a sword made out of blue fire shimmered into existence in his hand. The heat blasting off the weapon made sweat roll down Addy's face and soak through her shirt.

"Kill her Chosen lover," the Supernal ordered the general. "Then, I will destroy our daughter."

The general glanced at Addy. There was desperation in her eyes.

"No—"

The general moved so fast she was a blur. She raised her spear and attacked…the Supernal.

There was a shower of blue sparks as their weapons collided. The general looked so small compared to the Supernal.

Addy's heart was in her throat. She didn't know what she was hoping for, or even what to do. It was like her feet were glued in place.

"You dare to defy me, Lezha?"

The Supernal's voice was like an icicle honed to a deadly point. The general flinched, even though her spear arm remained steady.

"I do not wish to defy you, Lord," the general said, her voice coming out meek compared to the Supernal's. "But this is our daughter."

Acid churned in Addy's stomach as the Supernal stared down at the general. The undisguised lust in his golden eyes was sickening. Addy was assaulted by a tidal wave of pity for the general. Addy wanted to help her, but fear and utter helplessness kept her in place.

She hadn't been able to defeat the Supernal before, when she was stealing his power. She certainly wouldn't be able to do it now that she was spent.

"You raised a weapon against me." The Supernal tilted his head, like he didn't know what to make of the general's defiance.

The Supernal didn't wait for a response. His hand shot out and yanked the general's spear out of her hands. The Supernal turned the general's own weapon on her as he slashed the blade across her skin in two quick strikes.

Two gashes appeared beneath each of the general's eyes before Addy could take in a breath. The wounds wept blood.

Addy screamed.

"Leave, Adelyne," the general ordered, her voice contained.

"Yes," the Supernal said, amused. "Today, we have all learned that you cannot defeat me." He gave Addy a disgusted look. "Your blood is too diluted for you to ever harness the kind of power I wield.

"I could kill you, but I want you to witness the whole of my plan. Only then, after you've begged for death, will I grant it to you."

The Supernal turned his attention back on the general. "But I'm going to punish you now."

Addy stepped forward. She didn't know what she planned to do. All she knew was that she couldn't stomach this torture. She couldn't abandon the general to this nightmare…her personal hell…alone.

The general's posture was meek, defeated. But when she looked up at Addy, her eyes told a different story.

The general's green eyes held a fierce determination that Addy recognized. It was the same expression Addy wore when she had made up her mind and wouldn't be dissuaded.

"Leave," the general said again.

Addy didn't even realize she was still moving toward the general until Tol's arm came around her, holding her back.

"We have to," Tol said in a low, urgent voice.

The Supernal's sword flicked again. This time, a bloody X appeared over the general's lips. The Supernal grabbed the general's shirt and drew her off her feet. He wrapped a hand around her throat. It wasn't in a choking kind of way, but more of a possessive hold. The sight of it made Addy sick.

"Now, Addy," Tol said, his face full of the same revulsion that was filling her.

He didn't want this, either, no matter how deep his hatred for the general ran.

"Come with us if you want to live," Tol called to the mortals. They were all cowering next to the crumpled heap of metal that had once been the Eiffel Tower.

Addy pulled forth the magic in her ring as she sprinted for the Chosen in the corral. Light spilled from the blue stones, and the ropes of the portal began to swirl.

THE CHOSEN UNION

"Hold hands," Tol ordered the Chosen and mortals who had the courage to leave the Supernal behind.

A human chain formed as the rings of the portal widened. As Addy took Tol's hand, her gaze strayed to the general.

How could Addy leave her?

The general had saved Addy…twice now. She was being tortured because she'd chosen to protect Addy.

"I'm sorry," Tol said, his voice barely audible over the rush of wind and magic in Addy's ears. "But there's nothing we can do."

Tol was right, but it didn't stop her stomach from flipping like she was in free fall.

Tol looped his prosthetic arm around her waist and took the hand of the next person in the chain. Then, he stepped into the portal, pulling her with him.

Addy's last view of the world outside the portal was of the general doubling over as blood spurted from a wound in her gut.

CHAPTER 23

ERIKIR

Erikir had never babysat before, but he imagined it would feel similar to what he'd been doing for the last hour on the plane. Except instead of little kids, he was dealing with ages-old enemies.

The Chosen kept trying to Influence the Forsaken, and the Forsaken kept drawing weapons that could bring down the entire plane.

They'd worked together well enough when they'd needed to get to the Paris airport and commandeer a plane. He and Olivia had Influenced the mortals into getting them on an international jet that had been grounded because of everything that had happened in Paris. The rest of their group had used a combination of Influence and threats to get them off the ground as quickly as possible.

But now that the urgency had passed and they had nothing to do but sit around, trouble had started back up.

Erikir had tried banishing the Forsaken to one part of the plane and the Chosen to another—feeling very much like a parent—but everyone was too busy shouting and threatening each other. He didn't think anyone except for Olivia had even heard him.

Olivia could have Influenced everyone into submission, at least until they were on the ground, but the Forsaken had made it clear what would happen if their minds were touched. As soon as they were released, they'd kill every one of the Chosen within reach.

Erikir was tired of the killing. He was tired of the endless cycle of vengeance.

He'd hoped to gain the Forsaken's trust by bringing them back to the bunker. So far, his plan wasn't exactly working out.

"You barbarians killed my grandfather!" one of the Chosen shrieked, reaching for the last few drops in her vial of Source.

The nearest Forsaken drew his machete. "One of yours killed *my* grandmother," he retorted.

Two hells.

Erikir turned to Olivia, who gave him an exasperated look.

Enough of this, Erikir thought.

He got up from his seat and stood in the center of the plane. He snatched the Chosen woman's vial out of her hand, measured out a single, precious drop of Source, and put it in his mouth.

The Forsaken surged forward, weapons in hand.

Erikir backed up a step.

"I, Erikir Magnantius, son of Rikorin and Elshari Magnantius, swear to the gods of Vitaquias that I will never again Influence a Forsaken unless it is in self-defense."

He felt the tendrils of his oath curl around his heart and squeeze.

For a second, as the Forsaken clutched their weapons and gaped at him, he wondered if he'd made a tremendous error. Source-bound oaths were rare, specifically because of the consequences that came with breaking them. If he ever broke his oath, he would die.

What had he been thinking?

Olivia got to her feet and stood next to him. She held out her hand for the vial.

Erikir hesitated. He knew what she meant to do. Unease crept over him at the thought of her making any oath that had power over her life. She waited patiently, her hand outstretched. He could see in her eyes that she'd fight him if he tried to talk her out of it. With no other choice, he handed her the vial.

Olivia took a drop of Source and spoke the words of the oath, swearing on her dead parents. Her Haze brightened and she sucked in a startled breath as the magic bound her to her promise.

"Who's next?" Erikir asked, spinning in a slow circle to stare at their small audience.

There was enough Source between them that everyone on the plane could take the oath.

If only they would.

For several seconds, no one moved. Then, an elderly Chosen woman, whose black eyebrows were a startling contrast to her snow-white hair, got to her feet. Even though she only had a few drops of Source left in her vial, she unstopped it and used her own supply rather than reaching for the vial Erikir offered her.

She made the same oath, to never attack one of the Forsaken.

One by one, the rest of the Chosen took the oath. After they were finished, a heavy silence filled the plane. Erikir felt the weight of the Forsaken's distrust as they decided what to do.

A bald, middle-aged Forsaken man stood up. He laid his throwing knives carefully on the leather seat before accepting the vial of Source from Erikir. Then, with his gray eyes fixed on Erikir's, he swore the oath.

Erikir felt something inside him lighten.

One by one, the other Forsaken took the oath until there was only one who still refused. That man, a giant whose axe looked almost dainty in his enormous hand, retreated to the back of the plane. He scowled and swore in French, but seemed content to sulk by himself.

From all of the arguing that had been going on for the first part of the flight, Erikir knew the man's name was Mikha, and that he had lost three sisters to the Chosen.

Erikir forgot about the Forsaken man when two of his own people returned from the galley with a tray full of mini bottles of champagne.

There were some forced, tight-lipped smiles as the bottles were passed around. Foil crinkled and corks popped. As they all tried to get the fizzy liquid into their mouths before it spilled, the tension started to dissipate.

"I can help with that," one of the Chosen told a Forsaken man, indicating a burn on his forearm.

The Chosen woman rummaged around in the overhead compartments until she found a first aid kit. The Forsaken man watched her warily, but didn't try to stop her as she took out bandages and began to dress his wound.

The airplane went quiet, since no one was trying to kill each other anymore. Erikir sat back down next to Olivia.

"That was amazing," Olivia whispered.

She was smiling at him. It made his heart do a strange hop-step in his chest.

Erikir was still trying to think of a response, when the flight attendant poked her head into the aisle.

"Sir, there's a Master Gerth on the phone to speak with you."

Grateful for an excuse not to stumble over his words in front of Olivia, Erikir went to the phone.

Gerth started talking as soon as Erikir was on the line. Erikir listened as Gerth filled him in on the Chosen prisoners, the Supernal's threat to kill one every hour until Olivia presented herself like a lamb for the slaughter, and how Tol and Addy had gone to free them.

Gerth took a breath and then continued. "The good news is that the Supernal had to give up his promise to execute a Chosen every hour until Olivia comes forward, since all of our people are either at the bunker or in hiding. More good news is that the Supernal sent a few hundred Forsaken to hunt us down, and all of them have now sworn allegiance to Addy."

Erikir couldn't be relieved, not when he could practically feel the tension radiating off Gerth.

"And the bad news?" Erikir asked, massaging his temple.

"The Supernal's on his way to Tokyo to kill all of the mortals."

Erikir swore.

"What can we do?" he asked, hating the helplessness in his own voice.

"Nothing," Gerth replied in a tight voice. "The Supernal has thousands of Forsaken at his command and millions of mortals willing to do whatever he tells them."

Erikir forced himself to loosen his iron grip on the phone before he broke it.

"We can't just abandon all those people," he said.

Anyone who didn't swear to serve the Supernal would be slaughtered.

"Get Olivia back here," Gerth said. "Our last chance is for her to do the blood marriage and see if that makes her strong enough to take the Supernal down. If not, then at least she'll be able to bring all of us back to Vitaquias."

And leave the mortals to deal with the Supernal alone.

Erikir looked over at Olivia, who was smiling as she talked with the Chosen.

"The king and queen want to do the blood marriage at sunset today," Gerth said. "You might want to give her a head's up."

Olivia…blood married today…. Erikir had known it was coming. He just hadn't thought it would be today.

Not yet, a voice in his head begged.

Erikir hung up the phone and cleared his throat. What did it matter if it was today, a week, or a month from now? He still didn't know what had happened with Tol on Vitaquias, but his cousin had obviously cleared everything up with the gods. And that meant Erikir was going to lose Olivia.

"Olivia." Her name came out of him as a croak.

He relayed his conversation with Gerth in a monotone. He felt each word like a nail being driven through his heart. As he spoke, Olivia's face drained of color. She chewed on her bottom lip as she fidgeted with something in her pocket.

"Erikir, there's something I need to tell you. I promised Tol I'd wait, but—"

Tol. That name, coming from her lips, was the final wedge in his chest.

Olivia didn't get to finish whatever she was going to say. The plane hit the runway, and the captain announced that they had arrived back in Texas.

Some part of Erikir was relieved for the interruption. Whatever promises Olivia had made to his cousin, Erikir didn't want to hear them. He busied himself with gathering the nearly-empty vial of Source and the foil wrapping from his champagne so he wouldn't have to look at her. When the door opened, he was the first one off the plane. He'd taken two steps onto the jet bridge when he heard Olivia's gasp.

The plane's engine was loud enough that Erikir shouldn't have been able to hear such a small sound, but he was so attuned to Olivia that he picked out the thread of her voice amid all the other noises.

"Why are you doing this?" she asked.

It wasn't the words themselves, but the timbre of her voice that struck some deep place inside Erikir.

Olivia was afraid.

He spun around and ran back onto the plane, shoving everyone else out of his way.

Mikha, the angry Forsaken man who had refused to take the Source-oath, held the blade of his axe to Olivia's throat.

The other Forsaken and Chosen were begging him to let her go, but he ignored them all.

"Come any closer, and I'll kill her," Mikha said when one of his own people took a step toward them.

Everything except for Olivia blurred out of focus. Nothing else mattered. Erikir took slow, measured steps down the aisle toward her.

"Stay back, Chosen," the warrior warned him. The man kept Olivia in front of him with the blade pressed against her neck.

Fury and terror rolled through Erikir. He went still, even though his every instinct screamed at him to move…to save her…to do *something*.

"Let her go," Erikir said, keeping his voice even so he didn't spook the enormous man threatening Olivia.

"You people killed my entire family," Mikha said. "My mother. Father. Three sisters."

"She hasn't killed any of yours. Ever."

One more step. Another.

Erikir had the vial of Source behind his back. He fiddled with the stopper, loosening it so he would have easy access to Source.

"Liar," the warrior growled. "You're all murderers."

Olivia whimpered as Mikha wrapped his hand around her hair and yanked her head back against his chest.

Erikir was going to kill the barbarian. *Slowly.*

The moment the thought passed through his mind, he felt a tightening around his chest...a reminder of the oath he'd made less than an hour ago. He silently cursed his own foolish optimism.

Peace between the Chosen and Forsaken would count for nothing if Olivia was dead.

"Take me in her place," Erikir said, unable to hide the desperation in his voice. "I've killed your people. Lots of them. It'll be much more satisfying to have me if vengeance is what you're after."

"You'd exchange your life for hers?" Mikha asked.

Erikir could discern nothing from the man's hooded expression.

"Yes," he said. "Let her go, and you can have me."

"No," Olivia gasped.

She started to struggle in the man's arms. A trickle of blood slid down her flawless skin. Erikir clenched his hand around the vial, willing her to go still.

"It is an enormous sacrifice for our kind to offer our life for another," Mikha said, studying Erikir. "Is she your sister?"

Erikir tried to keep a neutral expression, but whatever the Forsaken saw on his face made the other man let out a low, rumbling chuckle. There was no humor in the sound, only cruel mirth.

"I see." Mikha lowered his head so his lips were at Olivia's ear.

Rage boiled through Erikir, but he didn't dare move.

"And do you love him, too?" the Forsaken man taunted, his voice loud enough for Erikir to hear.

"Please don't do this," Olivia choked, her eyes bright with unshed tears.

Erikir had never felt more desperate. More murderous.

He overturned the vial of Source behind his back, letting a single drop pour onto his finger. He felt the tension around his heart as his oath recognized his intentions. He ignored the feeling.

"Answer the question." The Forsaken dug the blade in deeper.

"Yes," Olivia choked. "I love him."

THE CHOSEN UNION

Erikir almost dropped the vial and Source balanced on his finger. He jerked his attention up at Olivia. She was looking right at him.

"How sweet," Mikha crooned. He gave Erikir a carnivorous grin. "I didn't know your kind was capable of love."

Erikir was going to break his oath.

He thought, in that moment, that his mum would have been proud of him.

"You need to get the Fount out of here," a voice hissed at Erikir's back.

It was the Chosen woman with white hair and black eyebrows. Erikir started. He hadn't even realized she was standing directly behind him. But her presence wasn't the surprising part. Erikir had completely forgotten that Olivia was the Fount, and that her death would mean the death of every one of their people. He hadn't even been thinking about that. He'd only been thinking about Olivia, the beautiful woman with the even more beautiful heart.

The woman he loved, and who loved him back.

He swallowed the drop of Source poised on the tip of his finger and willed the Forsaken man to look at him.

Their eyes locked. Mikha's gaze was unfocused, blurry from the effects of Influence. Taking what might be his last breath, Erikir's lips formed the words that would set Olivia free.

"Kill yourself, barbarian."

CHAPTER 24

OLIVIA

Something hot and wet splatted across Olivia's back. Then, the metallic smell of blood that would forever make her think of her family's dead bodies filled her nose. There was a thud as the man who had been holding her hostage crumpled onto the wooden platform.

Don't pass out, she ordered herself.

"Did you do that?" Erikir, his gaze frantic, grabbed her shoulders. "Did you break your oath?"

"N-no," she managed, confused and overwhelmed.

She had tried a subtle manipulation on the man's mind, but it had felt like a hot iron branding her heart the moment she tried. She had been planning to use old-fashioned begging to convince the man to let her go.

She glanced down at where the Forsaken man's blood was trickling down the aisle and soaking into the flat carpet. His body was slumped across two of the seats, his glassy eyes open and unseeing.

Olivia jumped when the man's axe slipped out of his palm.

"How am I still alive?" Erikir muttered, pressing a hand to his heart.

They both looked at the Forsaken man. He had killed himself, but Olivia didn't understand how or why, when he'd been about to kill her.

The Chosen woman standing behind Erikir took a staggering step forward. She sucked in a gasping, wheezing breath. Then, she collapsed.

Erikir caught the woman and gently lowered her to a seat.

Panic overtook Olivia as a strange sensation surged through her. The woman was dying, but Olivia couldn't see any blood or evidence of a wound. There were still a few drops of Source at the bottom of her vial, so why—

"She's the one," Erikir said, kneeling beside the Chosen woman. "She Influenced the Forsaken man."

Emotions passed across Erikir's face. Bewilderment…relief…guilt. "I tried, but she must have gotten to him first."

Olivia's head was throbbing with a pain that was as repulsive as it was becoming familiar. One of her people was dying.

The Chosen were hers to protect, and she had failed one of them. She didn't even know the woman's name.

"Why did you do that?" Olivia asked, holding back tears as she gripped the woman's hand in both of hers.

"You are the Fount," the woman replied, her whisper barely audible even though everyone else on the plane was silent. "You will save our people."

Olivia's throat was too choked with tears for her to reply.

The woman tried to say something else, but no sound came out. Her eyes widened. Her skin turned a mottled purple as her lips formed around a soundless cry. Then, as Olivia held the woman's hand, her body turned to smoke.

"No!" Olivia tried to gather the Chosen woman's dissipating body into her arms.

It did no good. The woman was gone, far beyond Olivia's reach.

The blue smoke hovered in the air for another second before it disappeared.

"She died." Olivia's chest rose and fell with silent, tearless sobs. She hadn't thought she had any tears left in her. "She died for me."

The woman had broken a Source-bound oath…the same oath Olivia had made herself. And she'd broken that oath to save Olivia's life.

Erikir's arms came around her.

"I'm sorry," he said against her hair. "I was going to do it myself, but she Influenced him first. I'm so sorry."

Olivia jerked away and stared at Erikir, uncomprehending.

"You…what?"

"I was going to Influence him," Erikir said slowly, as if she hadn't heard him the first time.

"You would have died."

He gave her a quizzical look. Erikir didn't get it.

"You think your life is worthless," she said, shoving at his chest. "Why?!"

Olivia knew the others on the plane were witnessing all of this, but she didn't care. She was angrier than she'd ever felt. She'd come seconds away from losing him.

The thought was completely different from the vise around her heart she'd felt when the Chosen woman died. This was a feeling like…like….

"I don't think my life's worthless," Erikir said, "but no life is worth as much as yours."

"Because I'm the Fount?" she looked at him through blurred vision.

"Because you're you," Erikir replied.

He seemed as surprised by his own answer as she was.

"Erikir," she began, her voice breaking on his name.

"I know you have obligations," he said, his dark eyes holding hers. "You and Tol—"

Someone cleared his throat.

"We need to get moving," one of the Forsaken said. "The mortals are bound to be asking questions about what this plane is doing here when it wasn't meant to be."

The man was right. Olivia was desperate to tell Erikir everything about Tol giving up his magic, but now wasn't the time. She wasn't even sure how to tell him. And when she did, she certainly didn't want to do it in front of a bunch of strangers.

She didn't look back at the Forsaken man's blood staining the carpet as she followed the others off the plane.

* * *

THE CHOSEN UNION

It was early evening by the time they got back to Aunt Meredith's. On the drive from the airport to the farm, the others had been discussing how to convince all the other Chosen and Forsaken to take the same Source-oath that would end the violence between the two groups.

Despite the conversation's importance, Olivia had been distracted by the stone heating up her pocket. She wanted to tell Erikir, to explain what Tol had done and what she wanted, but she hadn't had the chance.

Since it was already past sunset, that meant she had another twenty-four hours before she'd be blood married. She didn't know why the ceremony needed to take place at sunset, only that a blood marriage couldn't happen at any other time.

Olivia stepped out of the car, stretched, and was thrust backward as Addy barreled into her.

"Squeezing…too hard," Olivia gasped.

When she pulled back and looked at Addy, Olivia's heart lurched.

"What's wrong?"

"The general," Addy said, a shudder going through her. "I—she—and then, we left her. We left her, Livy." Addy's chest rose and fell in quick little breaths. "We just left her with him."

"I'm going to go talk to my aunt and uncle," Erikir told Olivia in a quiet voice, giving Addy a wary look and plenty of room as he skirted around her. Nodding at Erikir, Olivia turned her full attention back on her twin.

She couldn't make heads or tails of what Addy was talking about, but her already-aching heart hurt even more at the sight of her sister's harrowed expression. She wrapped her arms around Addy.

Tol, who Olivia only just noticed was there, explained what had happened.

"It's not that I want to protect the general," Addy said, looking at Olivia with a wild expression in her eyes. "I haven't forgotten what she did to our family."

Neither had Olivia. She would never forget what those warriors had done, on the general's order, for as long as she lived.

"But the Supernal is her worst nightmare, and—"

Addy cut herself off, looking away. Olivia knew her sister well enough to see the emotions at war on Addy's face.

"She's saved my life twice now, maybe more," Addy said. "And I guess I...I feel sorry for her."

Those last words were so quiet Olivia barely heard them.

Olivia stroked Addy's hair in the same way she had when they were kids. She didn't know what she could possibly say to make Addy feel better, so she said the only words that came to her mind.

"I love you so, so much."

Addy gave her a wobbly smile. "Love you more, sis."

Gerth, with Jaxon on his heels, emerged from the bunker. Gerth was grinning and waving his phone in the air.

"You're not going to believe it," Gerth said, a little out of breath. "Tokyo. It...they...." He waved his phone again.

"Judging from the look on your face," Tol said with an amused gleam in his eyes, "I take it the Supernal didn't destroy Tokyo?"

Gerth's smile broadened. "His mortal army turned on him. They were acting like his little acolytes, but when the Supernal ordered them to start killing, they refused."

Olivia was speechless. So were Addy and Tol, apparently, because none of them spoke.

"But," Addy began.

"The Forsaken refused to carry out his orders, too," Jaxon said.

"But didn't the Supernal go insane and kill them all?" Addy asked, looking as startled as Olivia felt.

Gerth shook his head. "He killed a lot of Forsaken and mortals, but it wasn't enough to convince the rest, and so he was stuck. The Supernal wants to be worshipped, and he won't have that if he kills everyone and has no one left to rule."

"So, what happens now?" Tol asked.

Gerth grinned at Addy. "Rumor has it the Forsaken are going off in search of the leader of the alien resistance."

Olivia looked at her twin, who had a deer-in-the-headlights expression on her face.

"Me?" Addy asked. She started to massage the place just beneath her collarbone.

"Yep," Gerth replied. "There's all sorts of speculation about you in the mortal world. They all think you're a *he*, of course, and there have been some fairly amusing artistic renditions of your supposed appearance."

"I've sent some of our people to track them down and bring anyone who wants to fight with us back here," Jaxon said, his voice and expression as serious as Gerth's was jubilant.

Olivia felt like a tremendous weight had been lifted off her shoulders. And yet, she knew Tokyo was a reprieve, not a solution. The Supernal wouldn't give up after what had happened this morning. Still, it did buy them a little more time, which was what they desperately needed.

Olivia felt a fierce pride for the people of Earth. They might not have weapons infused with the Supernal's magic or be able to Influence, but they had a strength of their own.

Erikir, his expression the polar opposite of Gerth's, threw down the flap of the medical tent and stormed back across the lawn.

"Shocker, Erikir's pissed," Addy said under her breath.

"Play nice," Olivia said, jabbing her sister in the side. "You promised."

Addy stuck her tongue out at Olivia.

Olivia felt a little thrill travel through her at the way Erikir's eyes fixed on her and stayed there, as if she was the only one who mattered.

"Our people are refusing," he said as soon as he was within earshot. "They balked as soon as I mentioned letting the Forsaken come back to Vitaquias after the blood marriage." A dark look crossed his face. "They're calling me *barbarian lover*."

"It's better than weasel," Addy said cheerfully.

Erikir ignored her.

"They won't listen to me," he continued.

"What exactly are you talking about?" Tol demanded, using that voice that always made Olivia a little intimidated.

Erikir and Olivia quickly explained what they had done, and what they were hoping the rest of their people would do.

"That's actually a fantastic idea," Gerth said, looking a little bewildered. "I didn't know that much brilliance was possible without my input."

Jaxon shook his head, looking like he was trying to hide a smile. Erikir scowled at him.

"Do you think the Forsaken would agree to swear an oath of peace, if we could get the Chosen on board?" Olivia asked Jaxon.

"I think our people would be willing," Jaxon said. "If they saw the Chosen make the oath first."

"Not going to happen," Erikir said. "I tried. Most of them are saying they'd rather die on Earth than allow the Forsaken back on Vitaquias."

Jaxon turned to Addy.

Addy swallowed. "Then, I guess we have to figure out another way—"

"No," Olivia said, loudly enough that she startled all of them, including herself.

She had already lost the rest of her family. Olivia would do whatever it took to make sure nothing came between her and Addy.

"We'll just have to convince them," she said.

"You might have more luck than I did," Erikir said uncertainly. "But just mentioning peace with the Forsaken had some of them getting their Influence ready."

"Then, we don't give them a choice," Tol said. He looked straight at Olivia. "*You* don't give them a choice."

"I—" Olivia's throat went dry.

She looked at her twin for help.

Addy gave her a look full of sympathy and understanding. "If it was me," Addy said, "I'd wave my shears in their faces until they agreed to do what I wanted, but that's never been your style."

Olivia laughed a little.

No, that definitely wasn't her style.

"A roomful of angry Chosen couldn't be any more intimidating than one of Stacy and Rosie's epic screaming matches," Addy told Olivia.

Olivia couldn't help but smile at the memory of their two younger sisters. Sometimes their mom was the one who ended the fights, usually with the threat of more assignments to keep them occupied, but most of the time Olivia had been the one to make peace.

But those had been her sisters. That was a world Olivia had known. This one…wasn't.

"You've got this," Addy told her, all teasing aside. "And if Livy's special blend of kindness doesn't convince them, I'll be right beside you with these." She held up her garden shears.

"Don't worry," Tol added. "We won't feed you to the wolves alone. Whatever happens, you'll have our support."

Olivia returned his hesitant smile.

She'd always felt a little intimidated by him. Tol was larger than life—the Chosen prince and the man she was originally destined to blood marry. He'd always been polite to her, but in a cold sort of way. Now that the danger of having to be stuck together for eternity had passed, he'd become much friendlier.

"You won't be alone," Erikir said, reaching out for her hand.

When she gave it to him, he raised it to his lips and kissed her knuckles. A little flutter went through her, until she realized that Addy and Tol were looking at Erikir with a combination of suspicion and distaste. Since she really wasn't ready to deal with that particular can of worms, she let out a sigh.

"Come on, then," Olivia said. "Let's go talk to our people."

CHAPTER 25

OLIVIA

Olivia had been expecting a long, drawn-out fight. She'd been girding herself for shouting, threats, and tears. Instead, she found herself seated around Aunt Meredith's kitchen table along with Addy, Tol, his parents, and Getyl. There was a pot of tea in the center of the table. Getyl had insisted they make the tea and pass it around before they began talking, even though it was ninety degrees outside.

The king was the first person to speak.

"My wife and I have been talking, and we feel apologies are in order." He looked at the queen, who gave him a short nod before he continued. "We saw what the Chosen people's greed and ambition caused on Vitaquias, of course, but I didn't comprehend the magnitude of our people's flaws until recently." He looked from Tol to Addy. "That blindness almost caused Adelyne's death, and that is an error of judgement that will continue to haunt us."

Tol shifted closer to Addy and slid his arm around her waist.

"It's okay," Addy told them. "I don't blame you."

Olivia felt her throat tighten at the reminder of what Addy had experienced at the Chosen people's hands. Since her recent encounter with the Supernal, no visible sign of Addy's wounds remained. Still, Olivia knew the scars were there, buried beneath the surface.

"We are to blame," Queen Starser said. Her usual curtness was tinged with regret. "We were unable to manage our own people's fallibilities, and we have all been weakened as a result."

"That is why," King Rolomens continued, "we have agreed that it is time for the next Chosen leader to ascend to the throne."

Olivia almost fell out of her chair when everyone looked at her. Of course, she knew she was the one who was going to take over leadership…eventually…but some part of her still hadn't quite believed it.

"Olivia has the strength to temper our people's flaws," Tol said. "She'll be able to protect our people from themselves."

Olivia didn't think she deserved those words, but they made her feel stronger.

"Then, we'll make the announcement as soon as you're ready," Queen Starser told Olivia.

"In the meantime," the king said, "we'd be happy to introduce you to the most eligible bachelors among our people."

Olivia felt all the blood rush to her cheeks. She felt everyone's attention on her as she looked determinedly down at the floor.

"Don't be dense, Rolomens," Getyl said. "Look at her face. She's already chosen."

Please let me disappear, Olivia thought, staring at the floor hard enough that maybe it really would swallow her up.

"Way to put her on the spot, Gran," Tol said.

"Um," Olivia stammered, "I—"

She was spared from having to embarrass herself further, because Addy grabbed her arm and was hauling her out of the kitchen.

As soon as it was just the two of them, alone in Aunt Meredith's room, Addy turned to face her.

"Do *not* tell me it's Erikir," Addy said, fisting her hands on her hips as she glared at Olivia.

"Addy—"

"Ohmygod." Addy flopped down on the bed. "Are you serious?"

Olivia let out an unsteady breath.

"No." Addy said, shaking her head back and forth so fast she must be dizzy. "No way. No, no, no."

"I haven't said anything," Olivia said, twisting the hem of her shirt over and over.

"You don't have to," Addy accused. "You have *the look*."

"Fine," Olivia said, realizing it was pointless to lie. "I have *the look*."

Addy gaped at her. "Livy, you understand that there's a difference between a little crush and a blood marriage, right?"

"I'm aware," Olivia deadpanned, trying to be patient.

Addy made a disgusted sound. "But Erikir? Really? Have you lost your mind?!"

"Keep your voice down," Olivia begged.

"Why him?" Addy crossed her arms and glared at Olivia. "Even if I could get over the fact that he almost got Tol killed, and I'm not sure I can, he's still…Erikir."

Olivia bristled.

"What would have happened to you if I'd died along with the rest of our family, and you were left alone?" Olivia asked her sister.

Horror washed over Addy's face.

"How could you even say something like that? I can't—" Addy covered her face with her hands.

Olivia hated to put that nightmare image in her sister's head, but she didn't back down.

After another few moments of silence, Addy said, "I would have become bitter and hateful." She let out a dark chuckle. "Probably would have killed a whole lot more people, too."

Olivia snuggled up next to her twin.

"So would I. And that's what happened to Erikir. He lost his parents, and he didn't have a brother or anyone else to turn to like we've had."

"So, you want to blood marry him because you feel sorry for him?"

"No." Olivia shook her head. "I want to blood marry him because…I love him."

Saying those words out loud stirred something inside her, as potent as her magic. It was powerful and terrifying and beautiful.

Addy opened up her mouth to argue, but Olivia held up a hand.

"I love him, Addy."

Addy sighed deeply. "Well, if this is what you really want," she said, squinting at Olivia.

"It is what I want," Olivia assured her sister.

Addy lifted her hands in a helpless gesture. "I can't promise I'm going to be happy about it right away, but I'll...try not to kill him. For your sake."

"I appreciate that." Olivia couldn't hold back a grin.

She stretched out on the bed next to Addy, feeling more at ease now.

"I can't believe everything is actually happening," Olivia said, shaking her head in disbelief.

Addy's uncertain expression transformed to something like awe.

"You're going to be queen, Livy. A freaking queen!" Addy squeezed a pillow to her chest. "My sister is a total badass."

"Yeah, right." Olivia managed a nervous giggle. "If by badass you mean scared out of my mind, then I'm in full agreement."

Addy's face turned serious as she abandoned the pillow and took Olivia's hands in hers.

"Livy, if I become the Forsaken leader, will that mess things up between us?"

"No!" Olivia was horrified at the thought. She squeezed her sister's hands. "*Nothing* will ever come between us."

Addy's brow smoothed out. "Okay, then." She laughed a little. "Who would have thought the daughters of corn farmers would become—" She waved her hand around, like she didn't even have the words for what they'd become.

A knock startled them both. Before either of them could speak, the door opened, and Nira breezed in. Her Aunt Marise and Viola followed.

"I hear you're going to take over the monarchy tonight," Nira announced, plopping a pile of dresses on top of Aunt Meredith's bed. "So, we're going to make you look a little less like a ragdoll."

Olivia tried not to squirm under Nira's appraising stare.

"You're really quite lovely," Marise told Olivia with a kind smile. "You'll have to excuse my niece's flair for the dramatic."

Nira turned her attention on Addy and sighed.

"Red, there is simply nothing I can do to make you look less…." She drew her nail in a circle in Addy's direction and made the same face Baby Lucy had made the first time she tasted a lemon.

Olivia looked at Addy. They both started to giggle.

"What's so funny?" Nira demanded.

That only made them laugh harder.

By the time Aunt Meredith bustled in, carrying a pitcher of lemonade and a stack of solo cups, Olivia was sitting on the bed while Nira did her makeup. Nira's two aunts were going through the pile of dresses as they argued with each other about colors and hem lengths.

It reminded Olivia of all the times she'd sat in her and Addy's bedroom in the farmhouse while Rosie pawed through their clothes, Stacy did makeovers for anyone who would sit still for longer than two minutes, and Addy entertained them all. Nira even had the same bossy attitude as Stacy. She complained about Olivia's imperfections and tilted her head none-too-gently to better apply the appearance-saving makeup.

Instead of feeling homesick, the experience was a comforting reprieve from the saving-the-world madness that had consumed Olivia's thoughts for weeks.

Nira's aunts might be frail, but Viola and Marise were as sharp-witted and opinionated as Aunt Meredith. The three older women chatted non-stop about everything from politics to Aunt Meredith's bewilderment over the Brits' obsession with mushy peas.

Even though Addy and Nira sniped at each other over just about everything, their bickering didn't seem as mean-spirited as it had before.

Olivia couldn't remember the last time she'd had so much fun. At one point, Nira casually mentioned that Fred had asked her to take him shopping for new clothes after they saved the world.

"You know he's just going to ruin those fancy new clothes the first time he fixes a car," Addy warned Nira.

"Hm." Nira tapped her nail to her glossed lips. "Maybe I can convince him to start doing his repairs shirtless."

Addy snorted. "Farmer's tan and motor oil stains. Awesome combo."

Nira sat back on the bed and fanned her face. At the look Addy and Olivia gave her, she scowled at them.

"What? It's not my fault Fred's a sexy teddy bear."

At that, squealing and shrieking ensued.

Tol and Jaxon burst into the room, thinking something was wrong. They left just as fast with their hands raised in surrender as a barrage of pillows chased them back out.

CHAPTER 26

ERIKIR

Erikir didn't usually make a habit of doing what he was told, especially when the order came from Nira. When she'd told him that Olivia needed to talk to him out by the picnic table, he'd gone, because…Olivia.

He'd been waiting for fifteen minutes, and he was beginning to wonder if Nira was just playing a cruel joke on him. He wished he'd brought a book out with him, so at least he'd have that as an excuse for why he kept sitting here like an idiot.

It was eerily quiet in the yard, which was usually filled with people. Everyone was either in the house or down in the bunker dormitories. The mason jar lights over the picnic table had been switched on, and their little shadows danced across the table with the breeze. It wasn't yet fully dark, but stars already peppered the clear Texas sky. It was a setting right out of one of Olivia's books.

Definitely a cruel joke, he decided, getting to his feet.

At that moment, the door to the farmhouse opened, and she stepped out.

Olivia.

She was wearing a pastel blue dress, and her soft curls hung over her bare shoulders. She gave him a shy smile as she crossed the lawn toward him. And Erikir was lost…just lost.

He had never hated his cousin more than he did in this moment. Tol could have the monarchy. He could have his people's love. But the thought of him with Olivia....

"Hey."

Erikir blinked, realizing he probably had a murderous expression on his face.

"You look really pretty," he said. "I mean, not that you aren't always pretty, just, I mean—"

He cut himself off, cursing inwardly. Tol would have said something smooth and with just enough arrogance to make any woman swoon.

"At least I'm not the only one who's nervous," Olivia said with a breathy little laugh.

"Nervous?"

Two more steps brought her close enough that Erikir could see the reflection of his Haze in her eyes.

"I've never even asked a guy out on a date, and now—"

Erikir's heart raced as his mind spun with a thousand impossible hopes.

"What is it?" He tried to take her hand before realizing it was clutched in a fist. He gave her a questioning look.

Olivia's eyes were wide and her breathing shallow. She looked like she was on the verge of panicking.

"Hey." He drew his fingertips down her bare arms, noticing the way she shivered and leaned into his touch. "Whatever's going on, I'll help you."

Instead of saying anything, Olivia opened her fist.

The golden light that sprang forth was so bright it blinded him for a second. Once his vision adjusted, Erikir saw the light was coming from a black stone that was slightly smaller than Olivia's palm.

Erikir could feel magic radiating off the stone. It was a different magic from Olivia's, more volatile. But it seemed to fit with her in a way Erikir couldn't explain. It was like half of a missing puzzle, or something.

"It's Tol's magic," Olivia explained, her gaze fixed on the stone. "He gave all of it up, along with his immortality, so he could be with Addy."

"Sorry," Erikir said, trying to calm his racing pulse. "I think I blacked out for a sec. What did you say?"

When she said what he thought she'd said a second time, Erikir's attention jerked up from the stone to her face.

Tol gave up his magic…the part of him that belonged to the Fount.

"Is that even possible?"

Olivia laughed a little. "Apparently."

"You don't have to blood marry Tol?"

Erikir barely heard his own voice over the rush of blood through his veins.

She shook her head.

Erikir balled his hands into fists because they had begun shaking. His whole body felt like it had been lit from within. Thoughts he'd desperately tried to suppress welled to the surface of his mind.

"Olivia, I—"

"Do you—"

They both started talking at the same time and then cut themselves off.

Shite, he sucked at this. He needed to pull himself together.

Olivia laughed softly. It put him more at ease, which seemed to make her more relaxed.

"I know we haven't known each other for very long," Olivia said. "But whenever I think about this," she glanced down at the stone, "there's only one person I've ever been able to picture sharing it with."

Erikir wasn't breathing.

She looked up at him through her lashes. "You."

The dam inside Erikir that walled off his emotions broke. Ignoring the stone, he wrapped his arms around her. He felt the throb of her heart against his own.

"Olivia," he murmured. "I love you." He kissed her throat, her jaw, her lips. "Gods. I fucking love you."

"I love you, too. With all of my heart." She tangled her hand in his shirt, like she was afraid he might try and pull away.

He never would.

Erikir kissed her. He kissed her the way he'd dreamed of but never had the courage to make a reality. He held nothing back, leaving his chest open and exposed and there for the taking. His mind and heart were hers. He was hers.

When he tried to step back, afraid he would hurt her with how tightly he was holding her, she made a sound of protest and drew him closer.

He couldn't get enough of her. Some part of him knew they were standing in the middle of the yard where anyone might see them. The rest of him didn't bloody care.

When they finally tore themselves apart, they were both gasping. His hands were in her hair. Her lips were kiss-swollen. Her flushed cheeks made her even prettier.

She was perfect.

Olivia held out the glowing stone. Then, she cleared her throat.

"Erikir Magnantius," she said, her expression full of the same hope and desire that were filling him to bursting. "Will you blood marry me?"

"Yes," Erikir breathed. And then, just in case she hadn't heard him, he spoke the word louder. "*Yes*. I want to be your husband more than anything in the worlds."

Olivia's smile was brilliant as she held out her palm, offering him the stone.

Hardly daring to breathe, Erikir raised his hand and put it over hers. He enclosed the stone between their palms.

Heat surged between them. Their Hazes began to grow brighter.

They staggered from the sheer force of the magic pulsing through their joined hands. Erikir felt the rough bark of the oak tree at his back, steadying them.

Their Hazes continued to brighten. Olivia's face disappeared behind a brilliant white glow. His vision flickered out, and then he was inside that mental place where Olivia's magic lived. Except, this time, he wasn't in Olivia's mind. He was in his own, and she was there with him.

He could see her, as clear and real as she was in the physical world. The sensation was strangely wonderful.

Images and feelings passed from Olivia to Erikir. He didn't know how it worked, only that he understood everything without her uttering a word. If their connection was like this now, Erikir couldn't imagine how powerful it would be once they were blood married.

Strong emotions passed back and forth between them. The connection was intensely sexual in a way he hadn't been expecting.

Olivia leaned forward and kissed him. Erikir felt it both in the mental place and in the physical world. It made everything more powerful…more intoxicating.

Magic flowed through them, almost too strong to contain. Liquid heat raced through Erikir's veins as their tongues and bodies tangled. He was burning up, and he'd never felt more alive in his life.

Olivia began to slip away from him.

She was still in his physical arms, but the darkness was yanking their consciousnesses apart.

No, Olivia gasped into his mind. *Not now….*

Olivia tumbled head-first into a vision, dragging Erikir with her. He could feel the way she fought it. Erikir tried to cling to her, to draw her back to the mortal world where their bodies were molded together.

He knew it was useless.

Erikir hovered somewhere overhead, looking down at Olivia. She was standing on the front yard, except her outfit was different and they weren't alone. He saw all of the people from the bunker—the mortal refugees, the Forsaken who had abandoned their cause to join Addy, and his own people. They were all lined up across the lawn like soldiers. Their faces were turned toward something Erikir couldn't see, although he could sense their fear and apprehension.

That's when Erikir saw the Supernal. He loomed over the farmhouse, larger than life.

Erikir saw hundreds…*thousands*…of Forsaken assembled behind the Supernal, their weapons pulsing with blue light.

Then, something happened that shook Olivia so deeply that her reaction reverberated in Erikir's own mind. The Supernal's reptilian eyes locked onto Olivia's.

Olivia tried to back away. Erikir's own heartbeat kicked up as her panic coursed through him.

Erikir was powerless to move. He couldn't even utter a sound. All he could do was watch as the Supernal and Olivia stared at each other.

"There you are, little Fount." The Supernal's voice even sounded snakelike. "I am going to enjoy taking your magic." He smiled. "When I am finished, there will be nothing left of the Chosen except bloodstains and blue smoke."

CHAPTER 27

TOL

The Supernal was coming to the farm. There had been a great debate about whether to flee or stay and fight. In the end, it had been an easy choice. There was nowhere they could go to escape the Supernal, and at least here, they had the homefield advantage.

Since Olivia and Erikir hadn't been certain on the timing of the attack—only that it would come at night—everyone had been scrambling to finish their last-minute preparations. They'd done everything they could to get ready short of having the actual battle.

Now, because Gerth and Jaxon were MIA and Addy was with her sister, Tol found himself alone with their newest batch of Forsaken. Since he was starting to get a handle on how the Forsaken preferred to deal with uncomfortable situations, he was bizarrely leading a drill he'd learned the other day.

It was mostly about footwork, which made his missing arm less of a problem, especially since Fred had taken his prosthesis. Fred had said something about needing to make a few modifications before the *big battle*. Tol had known better than to ask questions.

A nearby argument pulled Tol's attention away from the drill. A group of farmers who were working on one of Fred's booby traps seemed to be in the midst of a disagreement. They were waving their hands and talking in raised voices.

Tol sheathed his sword and went over to see what was up, just as Fred joined them.

"What's the problem?" Fred asked.

One of the farmers gestured at the pile of materials at his feet. "The problem is that we don't got enough bear traps and tripwires to take down an army of thousands."

"Well, what do we have that can be turned into a weapon?" Tol asked, channeling his inner Gerth.

"Aside from cows?" one of the farmers retorted. "Not much."

"Don't forget the cow dung," another farmer added.

Tol scowled as the farmers chuckled. Fred held up his hand.

"Fred?" Tol prompted, when the farmer continued to stare blankly at him.

"I think I've got an idea." Fred's face was pinched in thought as he pointed to a handful of the farmers. "You, you, and you, get as much gasoline as you can find." To another, he said, "I'm gonna need fertilizer. Lots of it." To the rest of the group, he said, "Go to every farm around and get their cow dung. All of it."

"Fred, what the—" Tol began.

"No time to explain," Fred called, jogging for the line of trucks parked on the lawn.

Shaking his head, Tol started back toward the house.

Lifting up the hem of his shirt, he wiped sweat from his face as he listened to the rhythmic and perfectly-synchronized sound of Forsaken blades striking against blades.

Tol felt someone's eyes on him, and he turned.

Addy was standing on the porch and staring at him. Her lips were slightly parted and her eyes were wide.

"What?" he asked.

Addy shook her head, like she was pulling herself out of a trance. "I think you've somehow gotten more attractive."

"Oh really?"

Addy leaped over the porch banister in a single, fluid motion.

That was the one benefit of fighting like the Forsaken instead of the Chosen, Tol thought, as Addy slipped her hands under his shirt to touch his sweat-slicked skin. He would have been more uncomfortable with their proximity when he was in dire need of a shower, but he could tell she was preoccupied with exploring the new shape of him.

He'd noticed how his shoulders had broadened and chest and stomach had definition that hadn't been there before. More importantly, it seemed that Addy had noticed, too.

The screen door slammed, and they split apart. Tol silently cursed Meredith's bad timing.

"Dinner, ya'll!" Meredith called, stomping down the porch steps in her cowboy boots. "We can't expect to win a war on empty stomachs."

Nira's aunts, along with a handful of the Londoners, followed her. They all bore enormous covered trays with delicious-smelling steam curling out the sides.

Tol still hadn't worked out how Meredith managed to feed all of them three meals a day, nearly all of them home-cooked.

Gerth, scowling, slammed the screen door as he came out of the house. He was muttering and swearing to himself in the way he did when he was deep in thought…or deeply agitated. With Gerth, it could go either way.

"What's wrong?" Tol demanded, instantly on his guard.

"He beat me at chess, that's what's wrong." Gerth kicked at a rock on the ground.

If it had been anyone else, Tol would have questioned their sanity. After all, losing a game of chess seemed fairly inconsequential compared to the Supernal's imminent attack. But this was Gerth.

Tol raised an eyebrow at his best mate. "Who's *he?*"

"Jaxon." Gerth's expression turned murderous.

Addy left Tol's side to drape an arm over Gerth's shoulder. She said, "I don't even know how to play chess, and I could tell Jaxon was slaughtering you."

Tol stifled a laugh at the look Gerth gave her.

"I'm impressed," Tol said. It was so rare to see Gerth in a bad mood, Tol felt compelled to take full advantage of the moment. "I can't remember you losing any game ever."

"I hadn't," Gerth snapped. "Dumb Forsaken ruined my eighteen-and-a-half-year winning streak."

Gerth glared at a spot on the ground. Then, seeming to remember something, he raised his head.

"Also, Livy is refusing to leave before the Supernal comes."

"What?" Addy and Tol demanded at the same time.

"I quote." Gerth raised his voice an octave and imitated an American accent. "I'm not going to abandon my family and our people. And that's that."

Tol raked a hand through his hair.

"Think you can convince her?" he asked Addy.

"Oh, I'll convince her," Addy promised. "I'm not letting Livy be anywhere near the Supernal."

"If Olivia and Erikir can blood marry before the Supernal shows up, then I'm pretty sure she'll have the power to defeat him," Gerth said. "Provided we're lucky and get at least one more sunset before the Supernal shows up."

Given the way things had gone for them so far, that seemed like too much to hope for.

"I'll go talk to Livy," Addy said, reaching up to give Tol a quick kiss.

Not feeling hungry, Tol climbed the porch steps and sank down into one of the wicker chairs.

The Forsaken had finally finished their drill and joined everyone else on the lawn. Even though it was dark out, the floodlights made it almost as bright as if it were daytime. Everyone was spread out on the trampled grass with plates of food balanced on their knees.

Tol saw the way the mortals, Forsaken, and Chosen separated themselves, leaving as much as space as possible between them. Furtive, suspicious looks were tossed across the divide.

Only a few people had been willing to take the Source-bound oath so far, so Tol supposed he should be glad no one was being violent.

Still, it was going to take more than pretty words from Olivia and threats from Addy to keep the Chosen and Forsaken from killing each other once they no longer had the Supernal as a common enemy.

He rubbed at his left shoulder, which felt strangely weightless without his new prosthesis attached.

"There you are, Tolumus." Gran, her cane clacking against the wood, made her way up the porch steps.

Tol started to get up, but she gestured for him to stay where he was. Gran settled herself in the chair next to his and adjusted her spectacles on the bridge of her nose.

"Did you know the Americans *ice* their tea?" she asked.

Tol's lip twitched. "So I've heard. Do you like it?"

Gran tilted her head, considering. "It isn't what I was expecting, but I suppose it has its own kind of charm."

Tol looked at her, but his gran was squinting at something across the lawn. When Tol followed her gaze, he saw Addy's curtain of copper hair.

Turning his attention back to Gran, Tol asked, "Is that some kind of a metaphor?"

"I haven't the faintest idea what you're talking about, Tolumus," Gran replied airily.

As you say, Gran.

"Your parents don't think less of you for abdicating, you know," she said in an abrupt change of topic that shattered Tol's good humor.

Tol frowned. "Our family has ruled for hundreds of years, and because of me, our line is ending." He couldn't look at Gran, so he stared at the polished wood slats of the deck.

"The Magnantius line isn't ending."

Gran lifted her cane and pointed it in the direction of the giant oak tree, where Erikir and Olivia were sitting together on a picnic blanket.

"Erikir," Tol said, minding his tone so it didn't come out sounding bitter.

He wasn't quite sure how he felt about Erikir embodying the power that had once belonged to Tol.

"Erikir will be a good king," Gran decided.

Tol felt a strange ache at those words. They were ones that his people had spoken about him.

"Sometimes I resent your grandfather for refusing to blood marry me," Gran said in another change of topic that startled Tol out of his thoughts.

He'd never heard Gran say a single negative word about her husband in his entire life.

Tol didn't know how he was supposed to respond, so he kept quiet as his gaze strayed to Addy. He'd spent his whole life resenting the idea of mentally and physically shackling himself to another. Then, he'd anticipated the blood marriage and the bond it would let him share with Addy. Now, he'd never know that feeling of complete connection…that sense of forever.

"Do you know why your grandfather wouldn't blood marry me?" Gran asked.

"Because he didn't want your life to be tied to his," Tol replied, having heard the answer from his grandfather's own lips.

"Yes." Gran nodded. "But that wasn't the whole of it. While I was entranced by the idea of that unquestionable, eternal connection, your grandfather had a different view. He thought it was more powerful that we weren't blood married, and that we could leave each other at any time."

"Um…."

Gran adjusted her spectacles. "Your grandfather said that every morning when we woke up, we were choosing to be together. When we went to sleep, we were making the same decision. Loving each other wasn't a matter of life or death. It was a choice."

Tol had never thought about it that way before. Gran gave him a knowing look before she continued.

"You and Adelyne have continued to choose each other, when it would have been so much easier to set your feelings aside. That makes me think your love is stronger than it would have been if you'd blood married and your very lives depended on sharing your hearts."

He looked at Gran, who had been his champion and provider of wisdom—whether it was solicited or not—since he was a kid.

His guard must have been down more than he thought, because the next words that came out of his mouth were ones he'd barely allowed himself to think.

"I'm not sure there's a place for me in her world anymore," he said.

"Why? Because you're no longer the Chosen prince?"

"Something like that." Tol gave his gran a rueful grin.

"Rubbish," Gran said. "You still have the same brain and heart you had before. Still have all the makings of a great king." She lifted her chin in the direction of the warriors on the lawn, who were looking a little lost without their weapons in hand. "I'd say it's just what the Forsaken have been missing all these years."

Gran got out of the wicker seat with a groan and started for the house, saying something about needing a glass of iced tea before the Supernal and his ilk descended.

"The Forsaken don't have a king," Tol reminded her.

Gran turned back to him.

"Not yet, they don't."

✶ ✶ ✶

Everything was a mess.

Small arguments were breaking out among the Chosen and Forsaken, even between those who had already sworn Source-oaths not to kill each other. Apparently, that didn't stop them from screaming insults and accusations in at least five different languages. And Gerth was missing.

"No luck?" Addy asked when Tol met her and Erikir at the front of the house.

"Not in the bunker, and no one's seen him," Tol reported.

"He wasn't in the back yard, either," Addy said.

"None of the cars are gone, and none of our lookouts saw him come or go," Erikir said. "He has to be here somewhere."

The house was the only place they hadn't checked, because it was completely dark. It wasn't like Gerth to take a nap when a battle was imminent.

Tol stalked into the house, flipping lights on as he went.

"Gerth, if you're still sulking about that chess game, then we're about to have words," Tol called.

There was no one here. Tol was about to abandon the search when he thought he heard something. He headed for the study, noticing a faint light under the door. The golden light spilling into the hall was definitely Haze.

Tol threw open the door and flipped the light switch.

"Are you seriously dozing off at a time—"

Tol froze.

"S-sorry," Tol managed before stumbling back and slamming the door. He ran into Addy, catching her just before they both went down.

"Tol? What's wrong?" Addy asked.

"I—nothing," he managed.

When Addy reached out a hand for the doorknob, he grabbed her and pulled her back.

"Uh, let's go outside," he said, his mind still reeling.

"Tol, wait."

The bedroom door opened and Gerth appeared, his shirt inside-out and his hair a mess. Jaxon was next. He looking far more put together, although he had missed a couple of buttons on his shirt.

"What were you—" Addy looked from Gerth to Jaxon. "Ohh." Addy's expression transformed from dawning comprehension to delight. "*Thank you*. It's so refreshing to know someone besides me has good taste in a partner."

Gerth was looking at Tol, but Tol couldn't hold his mate's stare. He turned toward Erikir, who was hovering in the hallway behind them. When he met his cousin's glance, a new wave of incredulity lanced through him.

There was no hint of surprise on Erikir's face. He already knew.

"I mean," Addy continued, oblivious to the tension, "my best friend is chasing after Evil Beauty Queen. I'll admit she isn't as evil as I originally thought, but she certainly isn't at the top of my list of approved significant others. And Livy is with—" She waved a hand in Erikir's direction. Her sour expression brightened as she looked from Gerth to Jaxon. "But I like both of you."

"Addy," Gerth said, his voice cracking. "Can I talk to Tol for a minute? Alone?"

Addy looked from Gerth to Tol, noticing their expressions.

"Of course," she faltered.

Erikir seemed only too glad to get away. Jaxon gave Gerth a look that was full of tender concern before following them.

While the others cleared out, Tol searched for a way to put words to everything that was going through his mind.

As soon as the screen door shut, Gerth said, "I'm sorry. I didn't want you to find out like this." He leaned back against the wall. "Hells, I didn't want you to find out at all."

Tol had been planning for something far more eloquent, but what actually came out of his mouth was, "I'm such a bastard."

Gerth's brow furrowed. "What?"

"We've—*I've*—been so preoccupied with my love life for the last eighteen years, I never knew…I never asked…."

His best mate.

Surprise flashed across Gerth's face.

"I wouldn't have told you even if you'd asked," Gerth said carefully. "I wanted to be your Chief Advisor, and our people wouldn't have tolerated me being what I am."

Anger pulsed through Tol. "Our people don't have that right."

"You know it's not that simple," Gerth said in a quiet voice.

Tol didn't have to ask what he meant. For some reason the scholars couldn't work out, Chosen couples were rarely able to conceive more than once in their entire lives. The same problem didn't apply to the Forsaken, which was thus a threat to the long-term survival of the Chosen race.

In the not-so-distant past, the Chosen had exiled anyone who chose not to have children. It was a policy that had been abandoned when Tol's uncle became king, but the stigma against homosexuals hadn't abated.

Tol hated the Chosen for putting Gerth in a position where he'd needed to choose. He hated himself for not being there for his best mate the way Gerth had always been there for him.

Tol didn't know how to even begin apologizing.

THE CHOSEN UNION

Gerth said, "You may not be the Chosen prince anymore, but you're still going to have an important role in everything. I don't want to muck that up."

"You being who you are isn't going to muck up anything," Tol said. "Whatever happens at the end of all of this, there will always be a place for you at my side."

"Nice of you to say," Gerth said with a small smile, "but I don't need to tell you we can't always have it all."

"You wouldn't have any interest in living with the Forsaken, would you?" Tol asked.

Gerth laughed. "They might accept you, since Addy is terrifying and it turns out you're not bad with a sword, but I'm too Chosen to be of any use to them."

An idea began to take shape in Tol's mind. "We could make a new position. Something like intermediary or ambassador between the Chosen and Forsaken. If anyone can figure out how get the two races to work together, and not just not-kill each other, it's you.

"And Jaxon can work with you," Tol added. "So both groups feel like their interests are represented."

"And if Jaxon and I break up?" Gerth asked, raising an eyebrow.

Tol lifted a shoulder. "I'll kill him in a duel." He showed off his new bicep to prove his point.

Gerth laughed. "I'd be more worried if I didn't know Addy would rescue you."

Tol narrowed his gaze. Gerth grinned.

Even though all the tension had gone out of Gerth, Tol was still trying to process what a poor excuse for a friend he'd been.

"Erikir knew and I didn't," Tol said, rubbing his hand across his face.

"Yeah." Gerth smirked. "You'd think someone as smart as me would have remembered to clear his browsing history before lending him my laptop."

Tol felt his jaw go slack.

"You're joking."

Gerth chuckled. "Afraid not. I think it was a very educational experience for Erikir."

Tol couldn't help but laugh at the image that conjured. At the same time, he felt a new respect that his cousin had kept Gerth's secret, even though Erikir hated Gerth almost as much as he hated Tol.

They were in the middle of a back-slapping hug when Addy burst into the house.

"You guys better get outside," she said, breathless. Her hands were gripping her garden shears and her face was drained of color. "The Forsaken…the bad ones…are here."

CHAPTER 28

ADDY

Addy stood at the front of her army as jeeps, tanks, and other insane combat vehicles rolled toward the farmhouse.

There were hundreds of Forsaken, and it wasn't the friendly variety like the ones who stood at Addy's back now. She could sense their intentions through the inherent bond she felt with her own kind. The Forsaken in those tanks were here for one reason: to kill them all.

Addy's one consolation was that she couldn't yet sense the Supernal. Maybe he'd gotten stuck in traffic….

The army vehicles came to a stop on the road, their headlights piercing the darkness.

Addy had thought their group of Chosen, mortals, and the Forsaken who now followed her was impressive when they'd all lined up on the lawn. Now, with the horde of Forsaken and loyal-to-the-Supernal mortals marching down from the road toward the house, Addy began to realize just how far out of her element she'd gotten.

The Forsaken who fought for Addy, or the *Allied Forsaken*, as they'd come to be known around the farm, had armed all of the mortals on their side. But most of the farmers and Londoners clutching machetes, throwing stars, and those creepy ball and chain weapons had no idea how to use them. Some of the mortals looked like they could barely lift their weapons.

Still, not a single one of the farmers or London refugees had wanted to hide in the bunker. They all stood behind Fred and Mr. Brown, who had spent the last few hours setting their booby traps. Addy had understood the purpose of the evil-looking bear traps and wooden stakes the farmers had stuck in the ground, but she hadn't known what they were doing with two tons' worth of dried cow dung. When she'd asked why they were making a mountain of the stuff on the front lawn, Fred had told her it would be a *surprise during the battle.*

Everyone was silent as they watched the line of their enemies, which snaked down the road and out of sight. The blue pinpricks of Forsaken weapons glowed for as far as she could see.

At least Livy and Aunt Meredith had left the farm an hour ago. Addy and Erikir had finally managed to convince Livy that she needed to be far away before the Supernal arrived. Addy still wanted to punch Erikir in the face every time she saw his Haze and remembered he'd stolen Tol's power, but she couldn't deny he'd been the one to convince Livy to leave.

By now, Livy and Aunt Meredith would be on Tol's plane and heading for some remote location that only Gerth and Jaxon knew. Addy didn't even know, just in case the Supernal got the idea to try and torture the information out of her.

The first group of Forsaken reached the driveway. There was a solitary figure out in front, holding a sword that looked like a shorter and fatter version of the one Tol carried.

Addy's garden shears all but quivered in her hand. Power vibrated through her very being. The closer their enemy came, the calmer she grew. She was no longer afraid of releasing the beast inside her, since she no longer feared what she was. She trusted the men and women at her back, and she trusted herself.

She might consider herself the daughter of Sue and Gary Deerborn, but she also had the blood of a god in her veins. She intended to use that strength for all it was worth to fight for the people who deserved it.

There were shouts and the sound of snapping metal as the Forsaken reached the booby traps. Several of them fell, but no one panicked. The Forsaken's perfectly even lines never faltered. They simply kept marching forward.

Addy cursed inwardly.

Addy's heart stuttered when the soldier leading the Forsaken army stepped into the floodlights. There was no other word to describe the person than *grotesque*. The leader's face was a patchwork of bloody wounds. Loose skin hung off, like it had been peeled back to expose the raw undersides. With the cap and military uniform covering the rest of the person's body, Addy couldn't even tell if it was a man or a woman. The soldier barely looked human.

A scream began to build in Addy's mind. Her knees wobbled.

The unrecognizable, mutilated creature was General Lezha Bloodsong. Her mother.

Tol, whose body had gone rigid, pressed his prosthetic hand against her lower back. Addy was breathing so fast her vision was growing spotty. The Supernal had done this to the general for disobeying him. He'd done it to punish her for saving Addy and Tol.

The general looked at Addy through dim, lifeless eyes. All Addy saw in them was defeat.

It made her want to scream her rage at the Supernal. It made her want to fall on him with her shears and cut him over and over again until he begged for mercy.

I'm sorry, she thought, as the rush of her shallow breathing filled her ears. *I didn't want this to happen.*

Addy had wanted to make the general pay for what had happened to her parents and sisters, but she hadn't wanted this. Never this.

Hatred, seething and hotter than the Supernal's blue fire, consumed her.

Without uttering a sound, the general raised her sword in the air. There was a thunderous cry from the Forsaken and mortals at her back. Then, they surged toward Addy's army.

I'm not ready! Addy wanted to shout.

It didn't matter. The battle had begun.

Addy lost sight of the general in the mass of bodies and weapons. Her garden shears whipped through the air. Jaxon's half-moon blades and Tol's sword flashed on either side of her. Blood poured. Bodies fell.

Addy fought like a demon possessed. She felled everyone who came at her. She wielded her shears with one hand and threw weapons discarded by the dead with the other. It wasn't pretty like Jaxon's even, lightning-fast strokes, but it was no less effective.

What Addy's army lacked in numbers, they made up for in determination. She heard Fred's cries of "For America! For humanity!" somewhere behind her as the farmers charged.

Still, nothing could change the fact that they were hundreds up against thousands. A Forsaken standing off to the side of the battle opened his mouth. Glowing blue arrows spewed out, felling a whole line of London refugees before the mortals could even raise their weapons. The air hummed as weapons filled the night sky, zooming from the Forsakens' hands and flying toward their enemies of their own accord. When one of the Forsaken fell, there were ten others to take their place. Addy's army had no replacements.

"Ads!" Fred called from somewhere nearby. "Get our people to retreat."

She yanked her shears out of a Forsaken soldier's neck and turned to him.

"Are you crazy?" she demanded, seeking Fred out amid the crowd.

"Trust me," he insisted.

Addy's instincts demanded that she keep going. Retreating was the last thing she wanted to do. But Fred had told her to trust him....

"Retreat!" she called out.

Tol looked at her like she'd lost her mind, but he helped her drive their people back toward the bunker. Jaxon was ordering the Allied Forsaken to line up between the two armies, creating a human blockade between them. They were holding off the general's people for the moment, but there weren't enough of them to keep the Forsaken at bay for long. The general's forces swarmed around the giant pile of cow dung as they reformed their lines and prepared for another assault.

"Fred, what the," Addy began, but he wasn't listening to her.

Fred, holding a bow and arrow, ran for Jaxon. Addy watched in stunned silence as one of the farmers held out a jug of gasoline. Fred tipped the arrow in the gasoline and then handed it to Jaxon.

As soon as the arrow was nocked, Fred set it on fire. With the smallest of movements, Jaxon released the arrow.

THE CHOSEN UNION

It struck the mountain of cow dung.

Addy shielded her eyes as red and orange flames erupted. Forsaken screamed as the flames leapt onto them and burned them alive. Others ran. Even as far away as she was, the heat of the flames made sweat pour down Addy's face.

For several seconds, she could do nothing except watch as the burning pile of dung wreaked havoc on the Forsaken army.

"That'll teach you to mess with Texas!" Fred shouted.

"Atta boy, Freddo," Gerth said, pumping his fist into the air.

Addy found herself cheering along with the rest of her people.

Then, she gave the order to attack.

She led the charge as they raced into the heavy layer of smoke now blanketing the yard. She didn't look down at the charred corpses as she darted for the ones who were still standing.

She raised her shears in preparation for the first live soldier she encountered. She was about to strike out, when the still-burning pile of cow dung illuminated the Forsaken man's face. Addy froze.

The man's face and arms were covered in third-degree burns. His skin was literally melting off his body in places, and yet, he strode toward her like nothing was wrong.

Addy yelped as she caught movement to the side. One of the corpses, burned so badly he no longer looked human, got to his feet. His scorched hand caught the ball and chain weapon that flew through the air and delivered itself into his hand.

A demonic smile cracked across the man's burned face. Then, he leapt at Addy.

Addy stumbled backward, only to see more of the burned Forsaken getting to their feet. Some of them were charred beyond recognition. All of them should have been dead. And yet, they were alive and moving. They re-formed their lines. And then, they attacked.

CHAPTER 29

ADDY

"Tol, Addy!" a voice called.

Ripping her shears out of a Forsaken soldier's chest, Addy spun to see Erikir. Nira was at his side, Influencing half a dozen Forsaken to clear a path through the battle.

"Olivia contacted me through our mental bond," Erikir said, as soon as he was close enough to be heard over the chaos of fighting. "She has an idea, but I can't concentrate long enough to get it working."

"What do you need?" Tol asked, before turning to slash his sword across another throat.

"Watch my back while we try this," his cousin replied.

Sure, they'd be happy to put everything on pause so Erikir could do…whatever he was going to do.

"Be quick about it," Addy snapped, positioning herself at Erikir's back. Tol took the front, while Gerth, Jaxon, and Nira took up positions around him.

"I'm ready," Erikir muttered, and Addy knew he was somehow mentally communicating with Livy. Before she could wrap her head around the fact that he had a direct telepathic line to her sister, Erikir's Haze grew. It was so intense Addy felt the heat radiating off his body. The Forsaken who were coming toward them stumbled back, shielding their eyes.

"You can't kill an enemy you can't see," Erikir and Livy said in tandem.

THE CHOSEN UNION

The sound of their combined voices filled the yard and seemed weighted with power.

Panicking, Addy looked around, convinced her twin was standing right next to her. But no, there was no sign of Livy anywhere. Somehow, her voice had come out of Erikir's mouth. *Weird.*

If that had been strange, it was nothing compared to what happened next. The Chosen began to wink out of existence. One by one, they just…disappeared.

"Holy hells," Gerth said, his voice tinged with awe. "We're invisible."

When Addy glanced at where Gerth had been two seconds ago, there was no one there. The mortals and Forsaken were still as visible as ever, but all of the Chosen who had been fighting nearby were gone.

Addy reached out a hand and grabbed the air where Nira had been standing.

"Ouch," Nira complained.

Holy shit. Livy made all of the Chosen invisible.

Erikir's Haze was still blazing and his eyes were boiling with molten silver.

"It worked," he said, smiling a little. "You did it, Olivia."

Addy glanced around, still not quite believing what Livy had accomplished when she wasn't even with them. That's when she saw Tol. He was staring at a swath of yard that appeared to be completely empty, but which they all knew was filled with the Chosen. Then, he looked at himself. He was as visible as Addy.

She saw emotion flash across Tol's face before he hardened himself.

Every part of Addy strained toward him, wanting to comfort him, to tell him that she loved him. It was killing her that she couldn't press pause on this battle and tell Tol everything he needed to hear.

The Forsaken continued forward, stumbling like blind people. Any time one of them came near a mortal or Allied Forsaken, their eyes took on that dazed expression Addy knew was the result of Influence.

A wall of invisible Chosen put themselves between the two groups. They shielded the mortals and Allied Forsaken, bringing their enemy down before they could even reach the visible part of their army.

The Forsaken under Influence began to turn their weapons on themselves and each other. Unlike the cow dung fire, the Forsaken soldiers couldn't survive an attack from their own weapons. They fell and didn't get back up again.

It was bloody and terrible. Addy almost couldn't bring herself to watch. To make matters worse, she knew the Chosen were using their last drops of Source against the Forsaken. She saw the proof of this terrible fact before her eyes. Blue smoke rose into the air in places where no one seemed to be standing.

The Chosen were dying to protect the mortals and Allied Forsaken fighting alongside them. Gratitude and horror pulsed through Addy in equal measures. They needed to end this before they lost any more of their people.

Raising her garden shears, Addy charged into the crowd. She, Jaxon, and Tol fought side-by-side. She didn't know if it was because they'd been practicing tirelessly together for the past few days or because they were connected on some deeper level. Whatever the reason, they knew what the others would do before they did it. They spun out of each other's way like they were performers in some kind of graceful, deadly dance. She could fight this way all night without tiring.

Tol flicked his prosthetic hand, and a row of darts spurted out of the fingers. They struck the Forsaken who were surrounding him. The warriors dropped.

"What the—" Addy stopped fighting long enough to stare at him.

Tol spared her a quick grin. "Fred's modifications."

He didn't have time to say more as a warrior came at him. Tol neatly sliced the man's head from his body with one stroke of his sword.

"Could you get any hotter?" Addy asked.

Tol laughed as he let loose another volley of darts. He twisted his left wrist. A spear-like blade, connected on some kind of spring, shot out from his prosthesis. It impaled the soldier who had been creeping up from Tol's back.

The spearhead retracted back into Tol's wrist before the soldier even hit the ground.

"Now you're just showing off," she grumbled.

"We're winning!" Fred shouted.

Addy felt a smile stretch her face as his words were taken up by others. The Allied Forsaken were just as disciplined and focused as ever, but the mortals were jubilant. They wielded their weapons with gusto, even managing to insult their enemy as they did so.

Addy was filled with a righteous pride. She might be a Forsaken by blood, but she was an earthling in spirit. She'd grown up in this world, and she would fight for it with every ounce of her strength. It was the difference between her army and the Supernal's dead-eyed group of mortal converts. Those people were driven by fear. Hers were driven by hope.

Take that, Supernal.

When the general reappeared among her soldiers, slashing at the Chosen cloaked in invisibility, Addy hesitated. For several seconds, they both just stared at each other.

The general moved stiffly, like her injuries went far beyond the exposed skin of her face and throat.

I didn't mean for this to happen, Addy wanted to cry. *Not this.*

Before she could decide what to do, a new horror grabbed hold of her. Addy's pulse sped. Her skin crawled.

Patches of the floodlit lawn had gone dark. It was an unnatural kind of darkness...all-encompassing.

"Tol," she whispered, because her voice had stopped working.

Tol, who was battling two Forsaken at once, didn't hear her.

She saw it, then. It was emerging from the crack that traveled down the center of the yard. It gave her the same spine-tingling feeling that she'd had on Vitaquias when they'd barely escaped it the last time.

The Nyxar.

The inky shadow poured through the crack like smoke, except unlike normal smoke, this sinister force wouldn't simply pass through them.

The Nyxar rose up. Dread filled Addy's every cell.

Darkness rippled and pooled. Then, it began to take shape. It took the form of a reaper, only more massive and terrifying. An awful, rotting smell wafted off the creature. Tentacle-like arms reached out as its shadowed face loomed over them.

Chosen began to pop back into existence as their invisibility disappeared. Something about the Nyxar must have destroyed whatever Livy had done to make them invisible. Now, they were as exposed as everyone else.

Horror filled the yard as the Nyxar descended on them all.

Addy and the general were consumed with trying to organize their people, all of whom were panicking. The general was herding the Forsaken away from the Nyxar and deeper into the ranks of Addy's soldiers. Addy lost sight of the general as she tried to get her own forces to retreat. She shouted until she was hoarse, but her people were senseless with fear. Everyone was running, and in their terror, many of their soldiers were running right into the Nyxar.

It attacked Forsaken, Chosen, and mortals indiscriminately. People screamed as the shadowy arms pierced their bodies. There was no blood. Instead, darkness spread through the victims' bodies. Black, spidery veins appeared anywhere there was bare skin. The victims gasped and choked. Their faces twisted into expressions of pure terror. Then, the Nyxar retracted its shadow arms, dragging its victims closer to its body. The people were absorbed into the shadowy folds of its cloak and never emerged.

The two armies intermingled until there was no longer a divide between them. It was simply them against the Nyxar. And they were losing.

Mortals, Forsaken, and Chosen were drawn into the undulating black shadow, their cries cutting off as their bodies disappeared. With each life the Nyxar absorbed, it grew larger and more solid.

Fear turned the sweat on Addy's back to ice. The creature's shadowy cloak absorbed more victims into its depths.

"Addy." Tol, his bloody sword gripped in his hand, gestured at the mass of people who were in the clutches of panic. "Bunker."

Would it protect them from the Nyxar? Addy wasn't sure. All she knew was that, if they didn't do something fast, there would be no one left to battle for Earth.

"Retreat!" she tried to yell, but the petrified cries filling the yard drowned her out. Only the people surrounding her heard the order.

"Get to the bunker!" Tol ordered, his voice carrying farther. "Move—"

A tendril of darkness, shaped like a hand with claws, shot out from the Nyxar's core. It wrapped around Tol's ankle.

Addy screamed.

Source. Somehow, amid her hysteria, she remembered how they'd fought the creature last time.

"Hit it with Source!" she shrieked, digging the point of her shears into her palm and racing toward the blackness.

Jaxon reached the shadow first. He slashed out with his half-moon blades. Addy expected his weapon to cut through the shadow the way it would slice through smoke, but an inky blackness began to pour from the Nyxar everywhere his blades touched.

"Our weapons are forged with Source," Jaxon called to any of the Forsaken who were in hearing distance.

The Forsaken looked from Jaxon to each other.

"Kill the Nyxar!" one of them shouted.

That was all it took. The Forsaken who had been coming to kill Addy a few seconds ago turned their weapons on the shadow. They stabbed and hacked and drove the terror back.

The Forsaken and Chosen took up positions around the Nyxar. The shadow was so bloated that there was enough room for hundreds of soldiers to fight it without brushing elbows. The creature was massive.

Tol struggled and hacked at the darkness with his sword. It writhed but didn't release him.

A hollow whistling sound filled the air. It had a shattering glass quality that set Addy's teeth on edge. Holes began to appear in the Nyxar's shadowy cloak.

It didn't matter. Nothing mattered except Tol, who was being pulled deeper into the shadow. Addy kept slashing at her skin, drawing out her Source-filled blood and using it to push the Nyxar back.

It wasn't enough.

The creature was strengthened from all the lives it had stolen. It blotted out a huge chunk of the sky, covering the stars and draping everything in a blackness that was denser than anything she'd ever seen. The Nyxar was even stronger than it had been on Vitaquias.

Another tentacle shot out, knocking Tol's sword from his hand before twisting around his neck. It lifted him off the ground. Tol wrestled with the shadow arm as he fought to breathe.

"Livy," Addy cried, even though her sister was far away.

Livy had helped her drive away the Nyxar last time. Addy needed her twin. She needed—

"Addy, take that side," a familiar male voice called. "I've got this one."

Erikir, his eyes an unnatural silvery-brown, raised his hands in the air. Addy saw that they were gold, like all of his Haze had gathered itself on his palms.

He shoved outward, and wherever his palms touched the Nyxar, the blackness disappeared. The Nyxar continued to make that screeching sound as more holes appeared in its cloak.

Addy let herself be absorbed into the writhing mass of shadows. She pressed her bloody hands against any part of the Nyxar she could reach.

The shadow froze and burned her at the same time, but she didn't care. She saw the Nyxar release Tol as she and Erikir continued to throw every ounce of their power at the creature.

She paused long enough to make sure Tol was alright. He was coughing and gasping, but he was alive.

Addy renewed her attack, fighting her way straight through the Nyxar's cloak. She toppled out of the hellish darkness as relief and exhaustion overcame her. She would have hit the ground, but Erikir caught her.

Addy was aware of the Chosen and Forsaken surrounding the Nyxar, fighting it from all sides. But she forgot about the shadow creature as Tol got to his feet.

"You okay?" he asked, his voice scratchy.

With a strangled cry, Addy threw herself into Tol's arms.

The shattering glass sound reached a fever pitch. Addy clapped her hands over her ears, but it did nothing to stop the sound. She ground her teeth as the sound got louder and louder. She felt a wetness on her palms. When she drew them away from her ears, they were covered with blood.

The Nyxar's shriek was unbearable. People were writhing on the ground, their hands clamped over their bleeding ears.

Just at the moment when Addy thought she would lose her mind completely, the screech cut off. The Nyxar burst apart. Flecks of shadow sprayed into the air like ash.

The sky opened back up, revealing stars where there had been only blackness before. As Addy looked up, wetness began to speckle her face.

At first, she thought it was raining. But as the liquid touched her cracked lips, her Haze flared.

It wasn't rain, she realized. It was Source.

Source was pouring out of the destroyed Nyxar.

All around her, people were crying out the discovery she had just made. Chosen and Forsaken held up their empty vials and tipped their open mouths to catch the precious liquid. Dull Hazes were brightening back to full strength. Vials that had been empty or nearly-empty for eighteen years were filled to the brim.

The sight was enough to bring tears to Addy's eyes.

The gentle patter of Source hitting the ground came to a slow stop. The awed sounds of the Forsaken and Chosen trailed off.

A strange quiet had taken hold of the battlefield now that the Nyxar was gone. Addy looked around.

Hazes were bright, but everyone was sagging in exhaustion. She and Tol weren't the only ones who were leaning on each other for support. All around her, Addy saw the others holding each other up. Burned Forsaken and bleeding Chosen watched each other warily, but no one lifted a hand against each other.

Forsaken let their weapons drop to the ground. The Chosen replaced the chains around their necks and tucked their full vials of Source beneath their shirts. They kept their gazes averted from the Forsaken's, making it clear they weren't about to Influence anyone.

Addy wondered....

"We can stop this," she told the Forsaken, who were staring at her with the same uncertainty she felt. "We don't have to kill each other."

When no one came at her with a blade or laughed in her face, she continued with more boldness.

"We don't have to be on opposite sides. We can all go back to Vitaquias together. No more killing. Just…living."

Addy cringed. *Really smooth.*

Incredibly, everyone was still listening to her. She looked at Tol, who nodded at her in encouragement.

Addy continued, "I'm the Supernal and general's daughter. I'm also the future Chosen queen's sister.

"If you stop fighting and join with us, you can return to your home. If you choose me as your leader, I'll give you something you'll never have if you stay here with the Supernal." She paused for dramatic effect, letting her gaze rove over the crowd. "Your freedom."

Addy forced herself not to let her shock show at the expressions crossing her opponents' faces. They were considering her offer.

"Fools," the general snarled in a raspy voice. She cut through the crowd of Forsaken to face Addy. "The Chosen will never see you as equals. You will become their slaves."

"You won't," Erikir's strong voice replied. "I am the future Chosen king, and I give you my word right now that any who agree to peace with my people will live among us as equals."

"You cannot defeat the Supernal," the general said. "The only way to survive is by joining him. If you don't, you'll just be another tally in his massacre."

It was difficult to tell from the general's ruined face, but Addy thought she saw fear in the woman's eyes.

"The Supernal isn't here," Addy said. "But we are, and we're giving you our word that you'll live an eternity of peace on Vitaquias if you put down your weapons."

"Not to mention," Gerth added. "We've got the power of the Celestial on our side. When our future queen blood marries at sunset tomorrow, she'll have her full strength. She'll be able to defeat the Supernal."

For several seconds, no one moved. No one spoke. Addy held her breath.

And then one of the Forsaken stepped across the invisible divide between the two armies. He knelt on one knee before Addy and stared up at her. In a clear voice, he said, "I will follow you for a chance to return to Vitaquias, my general."

Before Addy could come up with an appropriate response, more of the Forsaken were doing the same. Some held back, but the majority were pledging their loyalty to Addy. They put down their weapons as Erikir reiterated his promise that they would be welcomed back to Vitaquias as equals. He repeated the vow in at least four different languages. Addy got the feeling his words were far more eloquent than the ones she'd used.

Addy wouldn't go so far as to say she liked or trusted Erikir, but she was beginning to feel something like respect for him. There was a determined, brave expression on his face.

"Addy."

She jerked her head up at the tone in Tol's voice.

"Your Haze."

Addy looked down at herself, and her heart stopped beating. Her Haze wasn't its usual gold color. It was blue…blue like the Forsakens' weapons. Like the Supernal's Haze.

She had been so intent on all of the Forsaken swearing fealty to her that she hadn't noticed the prickle traveling across her skin. It was a familiar sense that was both unwelcome and alluring.

She met Tol's wide-eyed stare with her own. There was only one reason her Haze would react this way.

The Supernal was here.

CHAPTER 30

TOL

There was a sound like thunder, only it was too loud to be thunder. Blue lightning cracked overhead. And then the Supernal descended from the sky, his blue Haze shrouding him.

Enough, Tol wanted to yell to the gods. Hadn't the gods put all of them through enough, already?

The Supernal hit the ground in front of them with a soft thud. Tol moved closer to Addy so he'd be able to shield her if the Supernal attacked.

The Supernal scanned the battlefield, an amused twinkle in his golden eyes. His inhuman eyes caught on General Bloodsong, who seemed utterly unsurprised by the Supernal's appearance.

She'd known he was coming.

Tol didn't know what game they were playing, but it was obvious the Supernal's dramatic appearance hadn't been random. They'd planned this…whatever *this* was.

"Look at you, Daughter," the Supernal said.

Addy flinched and tightened her grip on her shears. Tol moved closer, using his physical presence to let her know he wasn't going to let this monster do anything to her.

"Leader of an army of weaklings," the Supernal said, his upper lip curling in disgust. "Mortals, Chosen," he spat the words. His reptilian eyes focused on the Forsaken still kneeling before Addy. "Betrayers."

The word came out as a snakelike hiss.

THE CHOSEN UNION

"She has offered us freedom," Jaxon said, his voice as calm and unafraid as ever. His gray eyes showed no hint of fear as he stared up at the Supernal.

"Freedom." The Supernal drew out the syllables, like the word was unfamiliar to him. "Let me show you what your freedom has earned you."

The Supernal raised his hands, and Tol couldn't stop himself from flinching as a blue lightning bolt split the air. It was accompanied by a clap of thunder that left Tol's eardrums pulsating.

A heavy silence fell. Jaxon's half-moon blades slid out of his hands. Then, without a sound, Jaxon collapsed.

"Jaxon? Jaxon!" Gerth fell to the ground beside the other man. He pressed his fingers to Jaxon's pulse. With an anguished cry that cut through Tol like a blade, Gerth started CPR.

Tol knew it would do no good. So did Gerth. The wild look on his face told Tol the awful truth. Tol took a step toward Gerth when Addy's gasp made him pull back.

Tol tore his gaze off Gerth and looked around. He sucked in a breath.

All of the Forsaken who had been kneeling in front of Addy were collapsing. They hit the ground and didn't move again.

Tol reached for a Forsaken woman who had been fighting beside him for the last hour. He caught her just as she collapsed. Tol felt the boneless, unresisting way her body sagged against him. He felt the warmth drain from her skin even before he'd gently lowered her to the ground. Her body was stiff, like she'd been gone for hours rather than seconds.

Tol stood up, trying to get air into his lungs.

All of the Allied Forsaken were down. Every single one of the Forsaken who had pledged themselves to Addy was sprawled out on the ground. None of them turned into blue smoke, but it was obvious they were gone. The garish glow of the floodlights illuminated each of their still faces.

It was too horrible…too vast…for Tol to wrap his mind around what the Supernal had done.

Without any blood or wounds to explain their deathly pallor, Tol could almost convince himself they weren't really dead. Except he'd felt that woman's body grow cold. He could see the way Gerth had stopped trying to revive Jaxon, and was now holding the lifeless man against his chest.

The Forsaken who stood behind the Supernal and general were still on their feet, looking as healthy and lethal as they had before the Supernal showed up. Whatever the Supernal had done, it only affected the ones who were loyal to Addy.

Gerth let Jaxon's limp body sag back to the ground. Then, with a broken cry, he threw himself at the Supernal.

Tol reacted just fast enough to catch Gerth and drag him back before he got himself killed.

"Bring him back!" Gerth yelled at the Supernal, flailing in Tol's grip.

"What did you do, you bastard?!" Addy demanded.

The Supernal stared down at them. "The Forsaken belong to me." He looked almost bored. "And soon, the rest of you will, too."

A choked sound escaped Tol's throat as he finally understood. The Supernal and general had planned all of this. They had planned for the Forsaken army to show up, for them to battle, and for Tol's people to think they had a chance.

Within seconds of arriving, the Supernal had wiped away that illusion.

The Supernal had given them a taste of hope, and then ripped it away only after they'd fought so hard for it.

Addy's scream of rage made it apparent she'd come to the same conclusion.

"One day," Gerth groaned. "One gods-damned day more, and Livy would have been blood married. She would have been strong enough to kill him."

The Supernal's gaze focused on Gerth. Tol tensed, readying himself for whatever horror the Supernal was about to rain down on them.

"Perhaps. Perhaps not." There was a vicious twinkle in the Supernal's eye. "But imagine how strong that godly power would be if it was combined with my own."

Gerth inhaled sharply, which only seemed to heighten the Supernal's sense of triumph.

"That's right," the Supernal continued. "Once I take the Celestial's magic for myself, I will be as powerful as the gods themselves."

"Great plan," Addy said, her voice tight with fury. "Too bad Livy's far away from here."

The Supernal's knowing smile made the hairs on Tol's arm stand on end.

"I wouldn't be so sure of that," General Bloodsong said, her voice scratchy from untold trauma done to her vocal cords.

The Supernal raised both of his hands into the air. A strained expression crossed his face as his eyes turned to pure gold. A warning prickle traveled down Tol's spine as he sensed the Supernal's magic flare.

Addy grabbed Tol's arm as her own Haze brightened in response to whatever the Supernal was doing.

Tol's sense of foreboding only grew when the sound of an engine filled the otherwise-silent night.

The Supernal tilted his face up at the sky just as the blinking lights of a plane appeared in the distance. The Supernal drew his fingers together, and the plane began to descend in unison with the motion.

Tol shook his head. It wasn't possible.

The sound of the engine grew louder. The small plane came into view.

Tol thought he was going to be sick.

"No," Addy whispered. "It can't be."

But it was. It was his family's plane, which was carrying Olivia and Meredith. And it was flying straight for them.

Terrified cries tore through the yard as people sprinted for the bunker. Tol and Addy stayed frozen in place as the plane descended. It lurched to the side. Addy screamed.

The plane passed just overhead, the thrum of the engine drowning out every other sound. When the plane touched down, the ground underfoot lurched.

Tol was thrust to his knees but was back up in a second. He was about to run for the plane, when he felt the bite of cold steel at his neck. He turned just enough to see the two Forsaken, one on either side of him, with their naked blades resting against his skin. A third Forsaken ripped Tol's sword from his hand and tossed it out of reach. Three more Forsaken surrounded Addy.

A roar built in Tol's throat, but he could do nothing except watch as Gerth, Erikir, and Nira were surrounded by a wall of Forsaken soldiers who blocked them from moving.

The ground shuddered again as the plane spun and skidded across the field on its belly. Thick, black smoke trailed in its wake. A chemical burning smell made Tol's nose burn.

Addy and Erikir were oblivious to the blood that poured from their wounds as the Forsaken yanked them back.

"Addy, stop," Tol begged, but she was as senseless as Erikir. They both had a wild look in their eyes.

Tol had never seen that much emotion from his cousin, and it rattled him almost as much as the sight of Addy's blood.

From where he was standing, Tol could just see the general and a group of her Forsaken guards wrenching the plane's door free. They pulled two people free from the wreck.

Meredith, looking stunned and supported by a Forsaken on either side, stumbled forward on her own feet. The general was carrying Olivia.

"Don't worry," the Supernal said above the sounds of Addy and Erikir's frantic shouts. "I won't let her die until I've absorbed her powers."

Addy shrieked and fought against her captors, but they held her in place.

Tol was desperate to go to Addy. He needed to get Olivia away from the general. But the Forsaken at his back made it clear that if he tried anything, he'd be dead before he took a step.

He was powerless to do anything except stand there as the Forsaken brought Olivia and Meredith before the Supernal.

The Supernal looked drained, although not as much as he should, all things considered. It had never occurred to Tol that the Supernal might be strong enough to pull a plane right out of the sky.

At the sight of the general, standing before the Supernal with an unconscious Olivia in her arms, Tol's entire body went numb. As though she could feel everyone's attention on her, Olivia's eyes cracked open. She glanced around, looking dazed and lost, until her gaze landed on the Supernal. She started to struggle, but the general held her with a tight grip.

"Here is the Fount, My Lord," General Bloodsong said, holding Olivia out like some kind of offering.

"You *bitch*!" Addy screamed at the general.

"I told you, Adelyne," the general said. There was a deadened expression in her green eyes, which no longer reminded Tol of Addy's. "This is the only way to survive. And that is what the Forsaken do. We survive."

Fred, who was surrounded by the other farmers, strode forward. "You won't get away with this," he said.

"Go ahead and stop us," the Supernal replied benevolently. "It doesn't matter to me if you want to spend yourselves on my servants' blades."

The Supernal crossed his arms and shifted his weight. It was like he was getting more comfortable as he waited for the opposition to make their last stand.

There were fewer than a hundred Chosen and mortals against the thousands of fresh and hardened Forsaken. They didn't stand a chance.

Fred's uncertain gaze moved from the general to the Supernal.

Tol's fury was replaced with a growing sense of helplessness. If the Supernal could take the Celestial's powers for himself, then he truly would be invincible.

Everything they had worked for…all of their hopes….

One of the Forsaken holding Addy yelped and staggered back. Tol barely processed the bite mark on his forearm as Addy spun. She cracked her elbow against the second soldier's temple while she kneed her third captor in the groin. Then, she ran.

"Get 'em!" Fred yelled. His group of farmers swarmed around Addy. The used their weapons to part the crowd of Forsaken for her as much as they could.

Tol knew this was going to turn into a bloodbath. He twisted away from the Forsaken whose blade was closest to his neck. His moves were far less graceful than Addy's. He stumbled, almost losing his balance entirely.

The Forsaken hadn't been expecting him to trip over his own feet, and it gave him a precious few seconds of lead time. He grasped a knife tucked into one of his captor's boots and slashed the soldier's thigh.

Tol rolled away from his other captors' grasping hands. He launched himself to his feet and sprinted after Addy.

Addy made like she was going for the general. The rest of the Forsaken converged around their leader, protecting her. At the last moment, Addy swerved.

Tol tried to go after her, but there were dozens of farmers and Forsaken standing between them. He shoved and slashed his way through the crowd as he fought to get to her.

Just before she reached the Supernal, Addy turned back. She locked gazes with Tol, like she'd known exactly where he would be.

I love you, she mouthed.

Tol saw the determination in her eyes. Icy terror surged through his veins.

A few moments earlier, he'd thought he had nothing left to lose. Now, he saw the truth. There was always more to lose.

Addy's ring was glowing. Tendrils of light spilled out of the stones and whipped into a lasso of magical energy. The Supernal's attention jerked down to Addy.

"What are you—" The Supernal moved, but Addy grabbed hold of his arm.

Tol lunged, finally understanding what she was about to do.

"Addy, no. Addy!"

Tol's hand closed around empty air.

Addy and the Supernal were gone.

CHAPTER 31

OLIVIA

"Addy!" Olivia screamed.

It was too late.

Tol roared. It was a broken, wild animal sound.

"No!" the general cried. "Where did they go? Where did she take him?"

The general dropped Olivia, only to dig the point of a knife into her skin, drawing blood. "Where did she take the Supernal?" the general demanded.

Olivia felt a moment of panic. She couldn't Influence the general because of the ring and Olivia's Source-bound oath. But that didn't mean she had to be useless, either. She'd been doing enough of that lately.

Olivia might not have her sister's Forsaken strength, but she had grown up on a farm carrying bags of corn seed and doing a hundred other chores. Her petite frame held a strength no one expected. Taking a page out of her sister's book, she elbowed the general in the ribs.

She spun away from the shocked general.

"Get the bad alien!" Fred hollered, before pouncing.

The other farmers were right behind him. They tackled the general, like it was football instead of a fight for their lives.

The Chosen swarmed around Olivia, Erikir, and Tol, forming a protective shield.

"Where did she go?" Tol's harsh demand pulled Olivia out of her fog. "Where did Addy go?!"

I don't know! she wanted to cry.

"Think, Olivia." Tol grabbed her arms and forced her to face him.

"I—"

Addy could be anywhere.

But Olivia knew her sister. Addy wouldn't have taken the Supernal anywhere on Earth where other people could get hurt.

"She wouldn't risk any mortals getting caught up in their fight," she said out loud.

Addy didn't intend to kill the Supernal…she couldn't. She was only trying to get him somewhere far away until Olivia could blood marry and then kill him herself.

"She'd need to take him someplace where he couldn't just leave and come right back here," Tol said, his face blanching in understanding.

There was only one place that fit those unique requirements…only one place from which the Supernal couldn't escape no matter what happened to Addy.

"Vitaquias," she and Tol said at the same time.

Tol took her arm and started shoving his way through the crowd, toward the site of the portal. She sensed Erikir nearby, even though she couldn't see him through the crush of bodies surrounding them.

"Hurry!" Tol shouted at her.

The farmers and Chosen were clashing with the general's forces, but Olivia could see how grossly outnumbered their side was. They wouldn't be able to hold off the Forsaken for long.

By the time they reached the crack down the center of the lawn, Olivia's hands were shaking so badly she barely managed to slice the tip of her finger on Tol's blade.

Olivia let her blood drip into the crack in the ground.

"No," she told Erikir, when he stepped closer to her. "You have to stay here."

"You can't go," Erikir said, his voice tight with panic. "It's too dangerous."

She gave Erikir's hand a squeeze, and then she let go. She caught sight of Fred and Aunt Meredith herding what was left of the mortals and Chosen into the bunker. Then, Olivia turned her attention on the portal.

"Let's go," she told Tol.

"Erikir's right." Tol wavered, caught between his desperation to get to Addy and his fear of what could happen to Olivia if she came with him. "If the Supernal kills you before the blood marriage, there's no hope left for anyone."

That argument had worked on Olivia the day before. She'd hated the idea of running, even though she knew it was to save herself for a more important role to come.

Olivia met Tol's hard stare with one of her own. "Hiding from the Supernal didn't work so well the last time."

She was done with running and hiding. And she definitely wasn't going to leave Addy and Tol to battle the Supernal alone. From what Tol was saying—and not saying—it was obvious he didn't expect either himself or Addy to be coming back from Vitaquias.

Olivia felt Erikir's frustration and fear in her mind, just like he sensed her determination. She tried to tell him everything she wanted to say with a touch of her mind into his.

Go, she begged Erikir.

He was furious, but he knew nothing was going to change her mind. He also knew that someone had to stay behind to lead the Chosen. She waited until Erikir had gotten all the way to the bunker before she turned her attention back to Tol.

She let her blood drip into the crack in the earth.

She felt Tol grab hold of her. Just before her view of the farm was swallowed up by the portal's darkness, a second hand wrapped around Olivia's arm. Then, the three of them were sucked into the spinning vortex.

CHAPTER 32

ADDY

Addy and the Supernal were tangled together. It was a good thing, because his back hit the ground first, shielding her from a spray of ice and shattered stone. It hadn't been this cold the last time she was on Vitaquias, but she knew from Tol that the world had been degenerating since her last visit.

The air smelled like Nowell always had right before a blizzard hit. *Felt like it, too.*

As though it wanted to confirm her forecast, the sky opened up. Fat flakes of snow fell, coating the ground and making it impossible to see more than a few feet in any direction.

She scrambled to her feet, wrapping her arms around herself in an effort to get a hold of her uncontrollable shivering. She was wearing jeans and a T-shirt, and she was on a planet where it must be zero degrees…before the wind chill factor.

She could hear her mom's voice in her head, warning about frostbite, and her dad's listing the many benefits of long underwear. She could almost hear her younger sister Stacy's voice saying, *If you die in long underwear, I'll be too humiliated to identify the body.*

In spite of everything, Addy couldn't help but smile. Her good mood vanished the second she remembered where she was, and who she was with.

Addy didn't want to look, but she forced herself to turn toward the polluted lake of Source, which had been the landmark she'd chosen to portal to. It had been one of two places she remembered well enough to portal to directly, and the other option was the castle ruins where Walidir lived. Unwilling to put Tol's grandfather at risk for the sake of her plan, she'd brought the Supernal to the location she feared most.

The place where all of her drowning nightmares originated from.

The murky liquid lapped at her sneakers, taunting her. Addy felt her breathing go shallow before she leashed her fear.

She was done with being manipulated and threatened by the ones who had brought her into being. She rolled her shoulders and tightened her grip on her shears. Then, she faced the Supernal.

The Supernal towered over her, seemingly unaffected by the nausea that crippled most people who emerged from Addy's portal. His face was angled toward the dark clouds above.

"So long," the Supernal said, his face still upturned. "I've been gone for so, so long." He looked around at the deadened landscape with an expression close to reverence.

"Enjoy the view while you can," Addy said, her teeth chattering together. "You won't be here for long."

The Supernal glanced down at her, and the look he gave her almost made her cower.

Almost.

Addy wasn't suicidal; she had a plan. She might not be strong enough to kill the Supernal, but because of the blood and magic they shared, she could keep him busy. Livy and Erikir would blood marry at sunset the next day, and then Livy would be strong enough to kill the Supernal. All Addy had to do was hang on for the next twelve hours or so.

No sweat.

Seriously, who needed Gerth when Addy was turning out to be a real mastermind?

"Sorry to mess up your plans to take over Earth," Addy said, not feeling sorry at all.

The Supernal looked down at her. Addy didn't think she was imagining how the blue of his Haze was even brighter here than it had been on Earth. A shiver went through her that had nothing to do with the cold.

Had she underestimated him? Was he somehow even more powerful here than he'd been on Earth?

"You stupid girl," the Supernal said in a quiet voice that had all sorts of warnings firing in her brain. "My aspirations were never so small." He looked at her the way someone might look at a mosquito.

She was an irritation…an inconvenience, but not a threat.

Addy tightened her hand on her shears, more to give herself courage than because she expected them to be of any use against the creature towering before her.

"It was always my intention to take over Earth and then claim Vitaquias for my own. What you've done won't change anything. It will simply delay me."

His gaze rested on Addy's ring. "That is a useful ability," he told her. "Even I am not yet strong enough to create portals."

Saying those words made the Supernal's face contort like he'd just swallowed something sour.

He continued, "The reason why you can generate such power from the Celestial's ring is because her magic combined with the strength in your blood. It is a lesser version of what will happen to me when I take the Celestial's powers for myself."

"My sister is going to kill you before you claim anything," Addy said.

"Your *sister* is still a mortal," the Supernal spat. "There is nothing she can do to me."

"She won't be mortal for much longer," Addy said, crouching down into an attack pose.

If she didn't start moving, she was going to freeze to death. Or be talked to death.

She wasn't sure which would be worse.

She leapt at the Supernal. She was fast, but he was faster. He backhanded her, and Addy went sprawling back. She bit into her lower lip as she struck the frozen ground. The metallic taste of blood filled her mouth.

She felt the foul liquid from the Source lake seep into her hair. The Supernal put his oversized, bare foot next to her shoulder, making it clear that one swift kick would send her sprawling into the contaminated Source.

Addy's lungs began to seize. The flakes of snow that melted on her face felt like the drops of Source. Phantom liquid filled her throat, choking her. She couldn't breathe.

She pulled frantically at the magic in her ring, thinking that she would portal farther away from the Source lake. The Supernal, seeing what she was doing, shifted his foot until it rested on her left hand.

"Try it," he said, his voice the honed edge of a blade. His golden eyes flashed and his Haze sparked. "We'll see which of us is faster."

Her Haze answered, growing as bright as her father's.

She hated it. She hated the reminder that she was like him…*of* him.

You aren't him, she told herself, repeating the words in her head. And she wasn't the helpless infant her mother had submerged in a lake of Source until she nearly drowned.

She was Forsaken, like Jaxon and the others she'd begun befriending and who had fought side-by-side with her and Tol. She was also Addy Deerborn, whose parents raised her to know right from wrong.

"I'm not going to kill you," the Supernal said. "Not yet, anyway. You are useful for motivating my general."

"Monster," she hissed, trying to roll away from him.

He moved with her, keeping her pinned while making it clear that, whatever move she tried, he was faster. Stronger.

Addy had another vision of herself as a mosquito, except this time, she imagined herself squished under the Supernal's oversized foot.

He could kill her, she realized. Something about being here was making him stronger, while she was still the same as she'd been on Earth. Addy felt a tear leak from her eye. It froze partway down her cheek.

This wasn't supposed to happen. She was supposed to be the one in charge. The Supernal was the one who had been outsmarted. And yet, as she stared up at the Supernal—who was even more massive from her vantage on the ground—she knew she's been wrong.

So, so wrong.

"Leave my future granddaughter alone, Supernal," a voice called.

The Supernal spun around, freeing Addy enough for her to sit up.

Panic consumed her sense of defeat as Walidir appeared through the falling snow. He shook his head, spraying the white flakes that had accumulated on his long beard.

"No," Addy said, her voice tight with anxiety. "You weren't supposed to be here."

He was supposed to be in the castle, where he'd be safe....

"Help is on the way, dear girl," Walidir told her before turning his fierce expression on the Supernal.

"Chosen," the Supernal snarled, as though there were no filthier word. "You will become smoke along with the rest of your kind. There is nothing you can do to threaten me."

"Are you so certain?" Walidir rolled up his frayed sleeves, displaying his wrinkled skin, and planted his feet before the Supernal.

"No, Walidir." Addy scrambled forward, trying to block Walidir with her own body. She refused to let Tol's grandfather die on her watch. She wouldn't let the Supernal hurt anyone else she cared about.

A whispery sense at Addy's back had her spinning around. Even though she couldn't see anyone, she felt the barely-there presence.

The Celestial.

Her ghostly form was emerging from the ruined Source lake. She was barely visible through the falling snow, but Addy could feel her more than see her. The Supernal sensed her, too.

"You," he said. His rage was more terrifying to witness than anything else Addy had seen from the Supernal thus far. He howled as he threw himself at the Celestial, Walidir and Addy forgotten.

The Supernal shot into the air, tangling with the invisible Celestial.

"That isn't good," Walidir said, staring up. The Supernal was now so high in the clouds he was no longer visible through the snow storm.

"Can he kill her?" Addy asked, more relieved to have the Supernal gone than she was worried about the Celestial.

What harm could he do to a ghost?

Walidir's response was torn away as a fierce wind picked up. The snow was still falling, but it separated, like a current of warmth was cutting through the center of the storm. A fierce, golden light emerged.

Addy shielded her face as her hair lashed across her cheeks.

"They're here," Walidir said, bouncing on his worn boots in impatience.

Addy didn't have room for anything but apprehension as the golden light solidified into a person, flanked by two others. As the three figures came closer, her worst fears were confirmed. Addy's heart stopped beating.

"No," she gasped.

CHAPTER 33

TOL

Tol forgot about the snow and frigid air when he caught sight of Addy. A layer of snow had gathered on her copper hair as she stood beside the Source lake, her bloody hand clutching her shears. Even though he knew what had happened to her at this place, she didn't look afraid. She looked fierce.

Her green eyes widened in shock at the sight of him.

"What are you doing?" she demanded. "You're not supposed to be here!"

Of course, he was. Addy was here.

Olivia scrambled to her feet, wrapping her arms around herself and shivering with so much force she looked like she was convulsing.

And...*Gran?*

For a second, Tol stared stupidly at his grandmother.

"How did you get here?" he asked. It was a ridiculous question. He shook his head. Blinked. When Gran was still there, panic took over.

"We have to get you out of here," he told her. "Addy can—"

Gran wasn't paying any attention to him. Tol's seven-hundred-year-old grandmother was running. She didn't even have her cane.

Gods, she was going to crack her head on the ice....

"Walidir!"

Only then did Tol notice his grandfather. He darted out from behind Addy and sprinted—actually sprinted. He and Gran collided.

THE CHOSEN UNION

They were both sobbing.

"Getyl, my beautiful Getyl," Walidir said, his frail shoulders shaking as he gathered Gran into his arms.

"Walidir, my love," Gran cried. "Oh, Walidir."

They held each other like they would never let go. Tol felt a strange burning in his throat as he watched Gran wipe tears off his grandfather's face.

"I told you," Walidir choked, reaching up to touch Gran's hair. "I told you we'd be together again, didn't I?"

"You always were too intelligent for your own good," Gran scolded. She was laughing and crying at the same time as she cupped her husband's cheeks in trembling hands.

Tol looked away from his grandparents, his eyes drawn straight to Addy. Tears glistened on her cheeks. She had one bloody hand pressed to her heart as she met his gaze.

He glanced back at his grandparents and did a double-take. They looked…different. In the eighteen-and-a-half years he'd known Gran, she'd looked the same. Same white hair pulled back in a wispy bun, same thick-lensed spectacles perched on the bridge of her nose that made her look a bit like an owl, same wrinkled skin and arthritic pinky she held aloft when she drank tea.

The woman in Walidir's arms wasn't that person. She had thick black hair that cascaded down her back in glossy waves. Her skin was bronze and unwrinkled. Her spectacles dangled on their chain around her neck, displaying brown eyes that didn't have the cloudy appearance of age. And her Haze was bright…really bright.

So was Walidir's. When the couple broke apart from another kiss, he saw Walidir had been transformed, too. He looked like a shorter, slimmer version of Tol's father. The resemblance was so stark Tol had to look twice, just to make sure his father hadn't somehow hitched a ride onto Vitaquias along with Gran. Only the eyes were different. Walidir's were kinder and full of mirth, whereas the king's were serious and heavy with all of the responsibility he carried.

"What happened to them?" Olivia asked in a soft voice.

"I...don't know."

In spite of the weirdness of it all, Tol couldn't help but laugh as Walidir lifted Gran off her feet and spun her around.

"Don't throw out your back, Walidir," Gran told him, but she was laughing, too.

"How is this possible?" Tol asked when they finally separated.

There was a twinkle in his grandparents' eyes that was familiar, but also brighter than anything he'd seen on their faces before.

"Love, Tolumus," his grandfather said, his smile broadening.

"We were always more powerful together than we ever were apart," Gran added, glancing up at Walidir with the same kind of adoration that filled Addy's expression when she looked at Tol.

"Don't look so shocked, Tolumus," Gran said in the stern voice she used whenever someone was being especially dense. "Do you think it was pure chance that you were born the most powerful of our people?"

"I—" Tol stuttered. He'd never considered why he was so powerful. It was just a fact of life.

"You certainly didn't get it from your parents, gods love them," Walidir said, grinning at Gran.

They shared a knowing look, like they were having an entire conversation without speaking a word.

Apparently, that was all the time they were getting for a heartwarming reunion. A warning prickle shot across Tol's jagged scar moments before a flash of blue light streaked across the sky.

Addy's Haze flickered from gold to blue. She brightened until she looked like she was herself a Forsaken weapon. She looked down at herself and then at Tol. The shame he saw in her eyes stabbed right through him.

"Look out!" Addy yelled.

The Supernal hit the center of the Source lake with so much force he made a crater. Tol grabbed Olivia and pulled her out of the way of the dirt that was being sucked into the gelatinous mass of ruined Source. Addy crouched like she was a tigress ready to spring.

"The Celestial's here," Olivia managed through her chattering teeth.

THE CHOSEN UNION

The Supernal rose to his feet as the dark liquid beaded on his skin and slid away like oil. He reached down into the crater he'd made and pulled at something beneath the liquid. The Celestial emerged from the puddle of Source.

Her ghostly form staggered out of the lake and collapsed on the crater's edge. Her image wavered in and out like a failing hologram.

"She—she's dying," Olivia said, her voice filled with raw pain.

The Supernal had his hands raised upward. Lightning filled the sky as his magic grew too powerful to contain. It was like someone was raising a lever of power, and it had reached the *danger: will explode* stage. The ground trembled beneath their feet.

When the Supernal spoke, his voice echoed all around them, as though it was coming from everywhere at once.

"You thought to take my strength so you would be the only of our kind."

They all looked at the Celestial. Tol saw raw emotion flicker over her ghostly face.

"I do not deny it." The Celestial's whisper was so faint it was barely audible. "I was arrogant and shared the greed of my Chosen." When she spoke again, her voice was even fainter. "I justified my actions because you were trying to take more than was your due as the Supernal. But instead of using my power to help both of our people, I used it to deprive you of your magic.

"I am to blame for the imbalance that caused the destruction of our world."

Tol had heard the Celestial say as much before, but he'd had little sympathy for her then. Now, he found himself pitying her. With the Celestial's ghostly form lying on the ground, she looked like the weakest and most helpless of them all.

The Supernal laughed. "Your Fount is weak. I will take her power, and then I will destroy what is left of your people. I will have dominion over two worlds, and more power than you could have ever dreamed of. I will be invulnerable."

Olivia shuddered next to Tol. He put his arm over her shoulders, worried she might actually freeze before the Supernal could make good on his threats.

The Supernal shot into the sky.

"He's going to kill her," Olivia cried.

Tol felt it, too. He just had no idea what to do about it.

What could they do?

Olivia wasn't yet at her full strength, Addy couldn't harm the Supernal, and Tol was—

Magic-less, for one. Mortal, for another. He'd managed to reclaim his sword before they entered the portal, but he didn't think it would be much use against the Supernal.

A piercing roar filled the air. Then, the Supernal was hurtling back down. He looked like a shooting comet as he plummeted through the dark clouds.

The Supernal was hells-bent on the Celestial, who was still lying on the crater's edge as she flickered in and out of sight.

"Move!" Tol shouted to her.

The Supernal was going to crush the Celestial. As a ghost, the Celestial should be resistant to such an attack. She was a ghost, after all. But Tol saw the way the Supernal's fists glowed. He knew the being wasn't about to deal an ordinary blow.

They were about to watch the Celestial be destroyed.

Olivia turned her face into Tol's shoulder. He couldn't hear anything except for the whistling of the Supernal's body as he shot through the air. But he felt the wetness of Olivia's tears.

Tol winced, anticipating the Supernal striking the ground and ending what little remained of the Celestial's essence. The impact never came.

A shockwave of energy made the ground tremble underfoot. The Supernal had struct some kind of invisible barrier several meters above the ground. The Supernal bellowed in rage.

Tol had been so absorbed with the Supernal, who was now hovering in mid-air and reaching toward the Celestial with claw-like fingers, that he hadn't noticed his grandparents. They were standing on both sides of the Celestial, their hands joined and raised to the sky.

Tol could almost see the shimmer of magic radiating from Gran and Walidir. Heat and power wafted off his grandparents' intertwined hands.

Tol let go of Olivia and ran for them. He had almost reached them when his body struck something. Hard. He ricocheted off the invisible wall and barely managed to stay on his feet.

It had been like trying to walk through a solid bubble. The space surrounding the crater contained the Celestial and Tol's grandparents…and kept everyone else out.

Tol could see veins standing out on the Supernal's neck as he fought whatever his grandparents were doing. At the same time, the Celestial stopped flickering. Her shape took on more definition. She began to look less like a ghost and more like something solid. The white outline of her body turned to ebony skin. The smoky wisps of hair became frizzy black curls. Her ghost-pale eyes transformed to molten silver.

As his grandparents' silent struggle continued, Tol saw them start to change. The youth they'd so recently gained began to fade. They didn't look as old as they had before they aged in reverse, but somewhere in-between.

Horror struck Tol at the realization that whatever they were doing was killing them.

"Give up," the Supernal snarled.

His voice sounded faraway now. Weaker.

"Never," Walidir replied, his voice thin and reedy. "You're going to pay for your arrogance."

"And this time, it'll be permanent," Gran added, breathing hard from the strain of her magic.

Tol needed to help them. Whatever they were doing to weaken the Supernal and strengthen the Celestial, it was draining them. He could see the exhaustion in every new wrinkle on their faces.

"Gran!" he shouted, shoving at the barrier with all of his strength. "Let me in!"

"Listen to me very carefully, Tolumus," Gran said.

Her voice sounded like she was standing right next to him, even though she was on the other side of an invisible bubble with blizzard-level winds swirling between them.

"The Supernal will be weak for several seconds after we are gone."

After we are.... What?!

"No, Gran—" Tol started, but she was still speaking.

"The Celestial must survive. She will communicate with the gods on your behalf and guide the new king and queen."

"Let me help you," Tol begged, but Gran didn't even seem to hear him.

"You never knew your grandfather and I when we were together, but our combined strength is vast. We'll hold the Supernal until you escape."

"I'm not leaving without you." Tol planted his feet.

"Tolumus," Gran said, her voice sounding wafer-thin and missing all of its usual spunk. "You and Erikir have been the greatest blessing in a life full of blessings. You have both found your true loves, and you'll both be powerful leaders."

Tol's lungs felt like they were lined with broken glass. He pushed against the bubble separating him from his grandparents. He shoved his whole body against the barrier, trying to break through. Addy beat at it with her fists. Olivia tore at it with her mind.

The barrier held fast.

"You will make this world all that it once was and so much more," Walidir said. "We are proud to have a legacy of family and love. We couldn't ask for more."

The Supernal howled again, making the ground tremble.

"They're tearing the Supernal apart," Addy said excitedly. "Look."

She was right. Holes began to appear all along the Supernal's bare face and chest. Clear, liquid Source leaked from the wounds. The Supernal screamed.

Tol, Addy, and Olivia were thrown to the ground, scrambling away from the crater as it expanded and more earth was pulled down into its depths.

Gran and Walidir both had their eyes squeezed shut in concentration. Tol could feel the magic flowing off them. The Celestial became a little more alive. And his grandparents....

Their physical bodies seemed to become translucent.

"No, Gran!" Tol beat on the invisible shield. He left bloody streaks on the transparent surface. He didn't even feel the pain. All that matter was getting to them…making them stop this madness before….

"We will love you for eternity."

The words came as a combined whisper from both of his grandparents.

One of the girls—Olivia, Tol thought—cried out. Tol was utterly helpless to do anything except watch as his grandparents' bodies began to dissipate.

Wisps of blue smoke curled around and through them.

"Gran! Gran!!"

The barrier fell away, and Tol crashed through. He ignored the Supernal, who was writhing in the air, and the Celestial who was getting to her feet. He reached for his grandparents and found—nothing.

They were gone. They'd become two clouds of shimmery blue smoke, which coalesced and wound together in a hypnotic dance. Then, a cold gust pulled the smoke away.

They left behind a whisper of their undying love for their family and each other. Then, that was gone, too.

Tol sunk to his knees, barely noticing as the ground rumbled beneath him. He felt Addy at his side, heard her voice. Her words blurred into a meaningless drone in the background.

Gran was gone. His grandfather was gone.

Tol started to shake. His teeth chattered with so much force he thought his jaw might crack, but he couldn't make himself stop.

He felt Addy's hand on his shoulder, warm and strong. Her touch grounded him, even though he was blinded by rage and grief.

The Supernal shrieked and tore at his own flesh.

"Attack!" the Celestial whisper-shouted. "Don't just stand there. Take him down. They died to weaken him. Do not let their sacrifice be in vain!"

The Celestial's words touched something inside Tol. He looked up at the godly being. All he could think was that her new corporeal form had come at the expense of his grandparents' lives.

The Celestial wasn't looking at him, though. All of her attention was on Olivia.

"This is your only chance," the Celestial told her. "You won't get another."

CHAPTER 34

ERIKIR

The smell of smoke hung heavy on the air. The giant pile of cow crap had burned down, and now its smoky remains were curling through the air and making Erikir's eyes burn.

The general stood in the center of a group of farmers, all of whom had a Forsaken blade jabbing into a different part of her. The two armies stood on opposite sides of an invisible divide. Now that Olivia, Addy, and the Supernal were gone, no one seemed quite certain about what to do.

Before Erikir could reach any kind of decision, he felt a whisper in his mind.

Olivia.

He let his gaze go unfocused, not caring what happened to his physical body as long as his mind was with her.

He found Olivia standing next to the remains of the Source lake. He could feel the way the ground shuddered. Something was very wrong.

You have to get away from there, he thought, all of his fear pouring through the bond between them. *Now.*

Olivia's arms were wrapped around herself, and she was crying.

I'm so sorry, she told him. She glanced up, at where Tol and Addy were locked in a tight embrace.

Erikir's pulse began to speed up.

Are you hurt? he demanded, looking her up and down as he searched for injuries.

She shook her head. *Your grandparents.*

Then, before he could process her words, she showed him.

Erikir saw everything as clearly as if he had been standing right beside her. He saw his grandparents fight the Supernal. He saw them save the Celestial. And then, he watched them die.

A scream built in Erikir's mind. It was the cruelest kind of torture, to see everything with perfect clarity and yet be unable to do anything to stop it.

Erikir watched helplessly as his grandparents' essence was pulled from their bodies. He felt the gods welcoming the blue smoke that was all that remained of two people who had existed for almost a thousand years.

His grief threatened to crush him. If it wasn't for the loving caress that Olivia sent through their bond, he'd—

Olivia turned, and Erikir caught sight of the Supernal through her eyes. The being crashed into the ground beside Olivia. Dirt and snow burst upward. Then, Erikir's connection to Olivia winked out.

Olivia? "Olivia!"

He scrabbled at blackness, clinging to a connection he had no control over. He let loose a string of curses that would have appalled Gran. But Gran wasn't here. She was...she was....

"Come on, mate," Gerth said, his voice heavy with his own sorrows. "We need you here."

Erikir opened his eyes, disoriented for several seconds.

He looked around for his aunt and uncle. The thought of having to tell them what had happened to Gran and Walidir was almost more than he could bear.

"They're helping Nira with the dying," Gerth said, knowing who Erikir was looking for even though he hadn't said anything.

Sometimes, Gerth's ability to read people was scarily accurate.

Gerth gave Erikir a smile that didn't reach his eyes. "I guess as the only Magnantius who's on Earth and otherwise unoccupied, it's up to you to give the orders."

For several seconds, Erikir's mind went blank.

"Might want to start there," Gerth said, jerking his thumb off to the side.

Erikir followed the motion to a group of Chosen and Forsaken who were tensing in preparation of an attack.

"Enough." The word came out of Erikir with so much force that the Chosen froze with drops of Source halfway to their lips. They looked at him with expressions somewhere between puzzled and resentful.

"Enough," he said again. "Put down your vials. Release your Influence."

"You must be joking," one of the Chosen said. He gestured at the Forsaken. "They'll kill us as soon as we let our guard down."

The Erikir from months ago would have agreed wholeheartedly. The old Erikir had been so single-mindedly focused on saving the Chosen, he hadn't thought about anything or anyone else. That blindness had almost gotten Tol killed. It had been the reason why he'd almost lost Olivia.

He wouldn't make that same mistake again.

The Chosen man's nostrils flared. "You aren't our king," he accused. The others surrounding him nodded in agreement.

Erikir was used to retreating back into some dark corner. He was used to letting Tol and his parents capture the love and loyalty of their people.

Erikir might not be the beloved prince their people had always believed would save them, but he was a Magnantius. He was Getyl and Walidir's grandson. He was the previous king and queen's son. Royal blood flowed through his veins. And now, he possessed the power and strength that was the Fount's perfect match.

Erikir met the gazes of every one of the Chosen. "I may not be king yet, but I am your new queen's chosen one."

Saying those words made a rush of power course through him. His Haze flared brighter—something none of his people could ignore. A few of them faltered, stepping back from the intensity of his Haze.

They looked at him with a new respect, and maybe even a little fear.

He wished Olivia was with him now. He might know everything there was to read about Chosen politics, but Olivia was the one with her finger on the pulse of their people's emotions. She would know what to say to convince all of them.

Even though she wasn't in Erikir's head right then, he could almost hear her speaking the words.

"We are going to restore Vitaquias," he said, "but it is up to all of us to create a world that is worth living in."

He had captured the attention of every one of the Chosen and Forsaken standing in the yard. It emboldened him.

"If we carry on the way we've always done, then we can't expect to have a future that's any different from our past."

He read skepticism on his people's faces, but he pushed on.

"Your future queen's sister is Forsaken. Many of our so-called enemies sacrificed everything because they were fighting by our side." He gestured at the dead Forsaken surrounding them. "We owe them more."

Some of his people's expressions began to soften.

"Is there a single one among you who can recall a time when our people weren't at war?"

Erikir paused, letting the weighted silence answer his question.

"I want my children to know a world without war and violence. And that begins here. Today."

He went to stand in front of the thousands of Forsaken. They didn't raise their weapons, but their merciless gray eyes followed his every movement.

"I made a Source-bound oath not to attack any of the Forsaken, except in self-defense." He forced his voice to carry so that everyone would be able to hear him. "Whether the rest of you make the same promise is up to you, but the fighting stops today."

At that moment, there was a commotion. The general, despite being surrounded, had evaded the farmers. She yanked a knife away from one of them, sliced it across the man's throat, and bolted.

She made it two steps before two of her own people grabbed her.

The Forsaken gathered around the general. One of them snatched the knife out of her hand, while the others trained their weapons on her.

Erikir shook his head in disbelief. The Forsaken weren't protecting her. They were restraining her.

Because of him, he realized. Because of his words, his promise, and the oath he'd made.

When Erikir strode up to them, the Forsaken parted to give him a clear path to the general. In the harsh glare of the floodlights, her scarred face was even more terrible to behold.

He looked at the woman who had murdered his own father and so many other Chosen. Erikir had spent years fantasizing about killing her. Now, finally, he had his chance.

So, why was he hesitating?

Olivia had taught him the value of mercy. Erikir would never forgive the general...Olivia hadn't rubbed off on him *that* much...but he understood now that his personal hatred was nothing compared to what they all stood to gain.

Taking a deep breath, he faced the general.

"I look forward to peace between our people on Vitaquias," he said.

At the mention of returning home, many of the Forsaken leaned closer. Some of them even sheathed their weapons.

"No." The venom in the general's voice had everyone tensing. The air grew warm from all of the Hazes flaring.

"The Chosen are liars," the general said. "They drained the Source and then were the first to escape our dying world."

Some of the Forsaken's expressions clouded over in uncertainty.

Erikir tried not to wince at the ugly truth of those words. Unease pulsed through him as he felt the budding optimism of a few moments ago transform into suspicion and aggression.

"Unless you want to end up like them," the general swept a scarred hand around at the ground, where the Forsaken who had fought alongside the Chosen lay. "I suggest you put this imposter prince's empty promises out of your minds and raise your weapons *against the Chosen*."

Damn, he needed Olivia. She would know what to say to salvage this conversation.

"Don't stop now," Gerth said out of the corner of his mouth. "They're still on the fence. Make them listen."

Erikir forced himself to stare back at the general.

"I'm telling all of you the truth," he said. "Agree to peace, and you'll return home with us. As equals."

The general took several steps forward, and then stopped. Her mutilated face registered shock when her people didn't follow.

"The Chosen king is right," a Forsaken woman with a blade in each hand said.

Erikir almost looked around to see who she was talking about, before he realized the woman was staring at him.

"I don't want my children to know the bloodshed of our past," she continued.

With everyone watching, she let her blades drop out of her hands. They hit the ground with a dull thunk.

"Then, no one can protect you from the Supernal," the general said. The softness in her voice was more terrifying than a shout.

The general raised her knife, and a small contingency of the Forsaken broke away from the others to follow her. Erikir tensed.

General Bloodsong swept her gaze over her people. Then, she pointed her knife in the direction of the bunker, where most of the mortals had barricaded themselves.

"When the Supernal returns, his first act will be to slaughter the weakling mortals who refused to worship him," the general said as she strode toward the bunker. "He will be pleased to discover we have already taken care of the nuisance for him."

Two hells.

The general and several-dozen Forsaken who were following her were going to kill the mortals. Erikir was frozen in place. His oath wouldn't let him do anything to stop them, since they weren't threatening Erikir's life.

"I ain't lettin' you kill anyone else," Fred said, his voice carrying across the space that separated them. He stood on top of the bunker's entrance. His father and Meredith flanked him. They all held Forsaken weapons, and yet, Erikir knew that wouldn't help them against the Forsaken general.

"If Addy was here, she'd stop you herself," Fred continued, unintimidated by the general and warriors at her back. "Since she ain't, we're gonna do it for her."

Meredith threw the knife in her hand. It spun through the air, heading straight for the general.

THE CHOSEN UNION

The general raised her hand. In an almost casual motion, she caught the knife's hilt. She stared at the blade as something between a smile and a grimace pulled at her scarred lips. Then, she let the weapon fly.

The knife moved too fast for Erikir's eyes to track. He'd barely registered the knife hitting its target before Nira's piercing scream cut through the air. It was soon joined by another—Fred's father.

Fred wavered for a moment. He stared down at the knife's hilt protruding from his stomach. Then, he collapsed.

"Get the general under control," Erikir ordered the Chosen guards. "Now!"

Erikir waited until the general and her Forsaken followers were restrained and being led away. Then, he ran for the fallen mortal.

Nira, Meredith, and Fred's father were already on the ground beside Fred.

"Get my kit!" Nira screeched. "Tourniquets, clean towels, disinfectant. Move!"

While people scattered to obey Nira, Erikir knelt beside Fred. He felt the wetness of blood soak through his pants.

"Just a scratch." Fred coughed, and blood bubbled out between his lips. He reached a hand out toward Nira, but it fell back to the ground like it was made out of lead. "Don't worry."

"Hold his arms," Nira ordered. Her usual clarity and focus during a medical emergency were rapidly devolving into hysteria.

Erikir knelt on the ground, locking down Fred's right wrist while a sobbing Meredith held his left. Fred's father was hunched beside his son. He was weeping and saying, "You'll be alright, my boy. You'll be alright."

Nira pushed up Fred's shirt, exposing the wound.

Acid filled Erikir's throat. The dark fabric had hidden the blood, which was everywhere. The wound wasn't large, but Erikir didn't need to be a doctor to know it was deep. Too deep.

Erikir wasn't squeamish, but he'd never seen a wound bleed so much and so fast. He felt dizzy just from looking at it. Nira's hands and forearms were stained red as she soaked towel after towel with Fred's blood.

Erikir kept hold of Fred's wrist, even though the mortal had stopped struggling. Fred's eyes fluttered open as Nira shouted at him.

"Don't do this to me," she ordered Fred. "Stay with me, damnit!"

"Like…my outfit?" Fred asked, his unfocused gaze resting on Nira's face.

Nira let out a choked laugh as she looked at Fred's polo and jeans, both of which were soaked through with blood. She smoothed back Fred's sweaty hair.

"It's better than overalls."

"Son, please," Fred's father begged, his voice full of so much misery Erikir couldn't draw in a breath. "Please. *Please.*"

Fred rolled his head to better see Nira. "When I'm better, can I take you out?" he asked.

"Idiot mortal," she choked. "If you get better, I'll muck out a cow's stall in a bikini."

A lopsided smile crossed Fred's face. "Cows here don't live in stalls," he murmured.

Then, his eyes closed. His head fell back against the ground. His heaving chest went still.

"My son," the older farmer sobbed. "Oh, my son."

Nira's scream of pain split the air.

CHAPTER 35

OLIVIA

The Supernal might have been weakened, but his magic was regenerating fast. It was taking all of Olivia, Addy, and Tol's combined strength just to keep the Supernal from killing them.

Every time the Supernal got close to Olivia, Addy attacked him like a wild beast. Tol shielded Addy from the jets of blue fire and bolts of lightning the Supernal kept sending her way. And Olivia chipped away at the Supernal's mind.

It wasn't enough.

"The sooner you give up, the sooner your pain will be at an end," the Supernal said.

"Dream on," Addy replied, even though she was out of breath and her clothes were torn and bloody.

Help us, Olivia silently begged the Celestial.

The Celestial shook her head. Her newly-solid body leaked Source and smoked faintly from a blast of the Supernal's lightning. Even though she didn't speak, Olivia heard the Celestial's voice in her head.

I am powerless. This fight is up to you.

Addy couldn't open a poral because it would require too much energy and draw her attention away from the fight for too long. Without Addy, Tol, and Olivia working together, the Supernal would overpower them.

As the three of them grew weaker and more exhausted, the Supernal grew stronger.

Already, the holes Tol and Erikir's grandparents had carved through the Supernal's magic were healing. Once that process was complete, even the three of them together wouldn't be a match for the Supernal.

Olivia was so, so tired.

"Mom and Dad would be so proud of you," Addy said, her voice raw.

Olivia's chest expanded.

"*Us*," she corrected.

Olivia forced a brave smile on her face. Whatever happened next, they'd end it the way they'd started.

Together.

Some deep, ingrained need to survive and protect her sister had Olivia fighting again, clawing at the Supernal's mind with magic fingers. It wasn't enough. It would never be enough.

Before her frustration could consume her entirely, Olivia thought of her parents.

Whenever she had been discouraged by a seemingly impossible physics assignment, her mom would say, "Don't forget, Sweet Livy. There's more than one way to cook an egg."

Olivia would approach the problem from a different angle or try a different formula, and then, lo and behold, she'd find the solution.

But there was no other angle or different formula when it came to this problem…was there? They needed to kill the Supernal, but in order to do that, they needed to overpower him.

There's more than one way to cook an egg.

They'd been trying to kill the Supernal to destroy his power, but maybe….

The Supernal wanted to steal her power for himself. What if she could do the same to him, first?

Excitement began to build in Olivia's mind before a crushing realization set in. She didn't know how to steal someone else's magic.

Before she slumped to the ground in a pile of defeat, a vision tickled at the back of her mind. It was the one she'd shared with Erikir in Paris, when they'd witnessed the Supernal in the Chosen library. He'd been searching desperately for the book that held the answer to how he would steal her power.

Olivia had sensed the Supernal's triumph when he found the right volume. She'd watched him pour over the pages that held the information he needed.

The book had been written in a language Olivia couldn't read, and with everything else that had been happening at the time, she hadn't given the vision another thought.

If she could just know what the Supernal learned from that book….

While Addy and Tol picked up her slack, faltering under the Supernal's barrage of blue fire, her brain raced with possibilities. Maybe, if she could re-visit the vision and take mental snapshots of the book's pages and send them to Erikir, he could translate them. It hadn't occurred to her to ask him before. She hadn't thought that vision might hold the answer to defeating the Supernal.

Olivia didn't have time to berate herself over ignoring something so crucial.

She closed her eyes. The vision crystallized, and she found she was able to see the pages the Supernal had been reading. The meaningless symbols she hadn't understood before rearranged themselves into words that made sense.

It wasn't her magic. The translation came from a corner of her mind, from a magic that wasn't hers but was inextricably linked with her own.

Erikir, she realized.

They hadn't completed the blood marriage, but the day she'd given him the stone with Tol's magic had fused their power. Now, that bond gave her access to some of Erikir's magic, which included an ability to read this language.

Her eyes snapped open as a shout from the other side of the Source lake drew her attention. Addy dove away from a jet of blue fire. Tol threw himself on top of her, his body taking the brunt of the attack. The sickly smell of burned flesh filled the air.

They were dying. Both of them.

Even Tol's shields against the Supernal were shattering. His shirt had caught fire, and Olivia could see a patch of charred skin across his back. Tol blocked another wave of blue fire. He absorbed the fire, pushed it back, and then collapsed on the ground. Addy's scream filled the air.

Olivia fell to her knees beside them, the icy ground biting into her skin.

"I can't," Addy said, looking up at Olivia through green eyes that burned with hatred and defeat. "I can't kill him."

"Can you keep him busy for me?" Olivia asked. "Just for a few more minutes?"

"I—I can try," Addy said. "What are you going to do?"

"No time to explain." She didn't even know if it would work.

Tol got to his feet, wincing as the icy wind cut across his burned back.

"Tol," Addy began, her voice breaking.

"My shield will last a little longer," he told her, his expression full of a love that made Olivia think of Erikir.

To Olivia, Tol said, "We'll hold him off as long as we can. Do what you need to do."

Olivia drew back, letting Tol and Addy protect her from whatever the Supernal might throw at them. With a war cry that spoke of last chances, Addy leapt at the Supernal.

Olivia let her mind slip away to a place where she felt nothing except for her magic. It was Erikir's knowledge that helped her understand what she needed to do, but in the end, the magic she called on was all hers.

The words on the page transformed to images. She saw the Celestial's victory against the Supernal two-thousand years ago. She saw the way the Celestial had woven the strands of her power together.

Olivia turned her magic into claws that pulled free from her own mind. She wasn't gentle and stealthy as the Celestial had been. There wasn't time to be. Of course, she didn't need stealth. The Supernal wasn't even paying attention to Olivia. Until her mental claws latched onto his mind.

The Supernal roared. His blue fire winked out as he raised both of his hands to dig at his skull. Addy didn't give him time to recover. She jumped onto his back, stabbing her shears into his neck over and over again. As she weakened his physical body, Olivia tore at his mind.

Her magic found the fiery center of his power. The Supernal's scream would have been enough to turn her blood to ice if she'd give it a chance. She didn't.

She tore, yanked, and gathered his power. Her attack was as merciless as Addy's.

She sensed the precise instant when the Supernal realized what Olivia was doing. She felt his fear…his desperation.

Olivia gave his power a final, vicious pull.

Her hands, which were stretched up to the sky, began to glow. A searing heat engulfed each of her palms.

Twin globes of golden light pulsed in her hands, brimming with the Supernal's magic. The balls of magic looked almost like beating hearts. They thrummed in her hands.

The power was too great, and too repulsive, for Olivia to keep hold of it for long. Already, her hands were shrieking in pain. She couldn't see her skin through the glowing gold, but she could imagine her flesh melting away under the sheer strength of the magic.

The Celestial used a Vitaquias-forged stone as a conduit, the book had said. *It absorbed and contained the magic.*

But Olivia didn't have a stone, or any other vessel to funnel the magic into. She couldn't simply release it into the air, otherwise it would shoot right back to the Supernal. She glanced down at the ground, squinting through the blinding brightness of the power gathered in her hands.

All she saw were chunks of ice and dirt. There was nothing that could be used to contain this much magic.

Get rid of it before it kills you! she ordered herself.

Olivia could sense the power eating through her own magic. If she held onto this power for much longer, it would destroy her.

She remembered her mother teaching her about the supernovae during one of their science lessons. She remembered the brightly colored images of the stars exploding in space.

That was going to be her.

She needed a vessel. Something…anything….

"How do you like someone carving up *your* face?" Addy shouted.

Olivia couldn't see anything beyond the golden brightness clutched in her hands, but she knew her sister was close by.

An insane thought entered Olivia's mind.

There wasn't time for her to ask questions or permission. She just hoped she wasn't making a mistake that would cost two worlds their future.

She gathered up the power in her hands, and threw it...at Addy.

CHAPTER 36

ADDY

Addy looked down at the Supernal. He was rolling around on the ground as he clutched his skull and babbled. Addy wasn't sure if she was supposed to have sympathy for this godly creature that had been reduced to a pitiful heap. She didn't.

She was the daughter of two of the most vicious people on any world, after all. She could allow herself a little perverse savagery. Just this once.

Addy fell on the Supernal, driving her shears into him over and over again. She watched the Source flow out of the wounds. She watched his beautiful face turn as grotesque and deformed as he had made the general's.

Addy didn't know if the Supernal could be killed or not, but that wouldn't stop her from trying.

That was when she felt it.

A brick wall of power and seething magic struck her full-on. She went sprawling, not even feeling when her back smashed into the icy ground. Heat flared in her heart and mind. It was so hot, so all-consuming, she couldn't move.

The magic seeped into her every pore. It filled her up until she had no room left, and then it continued to saturate her.

She knew she was screaming as it tore through her…devoured her…but she couldn't make herself stop. She couldn't make the magic stop.

She felt Tol's arms around her. If it hadn't been for him, she probably would have knocked herself out with the force of her convulsions.

Addy was burning up from the inside out. She heard Livy and Tol's voices, but their words were meaningless. All she understood was the rush of power through her veins.

Her back bowed. And then light exploded from her. It wasn't blue, but gold. Brighter than any Haze. It was the most beautiful and terrible thing she'd ever seen.

Some part of her recognized and craved this magic. The rest of her feared the moment when it became too much for her to bear…when it destroyed her.

"Look at me." The order came as a harsh growl.

Tol's prosthesis, frigid from the icy air, helped cool the fever raging within.

"You're a goddess," he told her, his voice sounding far away. "You can bear his magic."

That was when she understood. Somehow, she had absorbed the Supernal's magic.

Livy had done it. Her kick-ass sister had defeated the Supernal by dragging his magic right out of his body. And now, that magic was inside Addy.

The burning inside her was getting more tolerable. It still felt like her bones were melting and her blood had turned to lava, but she could see through the brightness surrounding her. Her senses were strangely heightened. She could see the individual flakes of snow, with their delicate patterns, as they fell out of the sky. She could smell the putrid stink of the lake of Source. She tasted blood and Source on her tongue. She felt the gods' silent, watchful presence.

As she struggled to her feet, part of her was sure her whole body would combust. It didn't. She leaned heavily on Tol and Livy, but she managed to stand without imploding.

Addy's eyes fixed on the Supernal. He was lying in a heap on the ground, but he wasn't dead. His one golden eye—the one she hadn't had time to stab with her shears—glared at her.

She took one wobbling step toward him. Then another. She shrugged off Tol and Livy, wanting to do this all on her own.

THE CHOSEN UNION

She crouched beside the Supernal.

She didn't know where her garden shears had gone, but she didn't need them. She pressed her hands to the Supernal's chest.

A rush of power sped through her. Her touch burned through flesh and bone. Addy didn't stop until her fingertips brushed the Supernal's pulsing, very human, heart.

His cries had become completely unrecognizable. She had no pity for this…creature. He had raped her mother. He had killed countless mortals. He had been intent on stealing Livy's powers and enslaving everyone Addy loved.

She held the Supernal's beating heart in her hand. She closed her fist around the organ.

Addy didn't just make it stop beating. She incinerated his heart. All the Source was squeezed out. Finally, the brittle organ crumbled in her fist. She opened her fingers, letting the dust dissipate onto the wind.

She heard a sound like rocks breaking apart. She looked down at the Supernal's body, at the hole she'd burned straight into his chest.

His golden skin turned gray. Cracks shivered down the Supernal's face and bare arms. He looked more like a stone statue than the living, breathing creature he'd been.

Then, with a puff of blue smoke, his body disappeared. The wind swept in, carrying the smoke away.

The Supernal was gone.

Addy turned back to look at Tol and Livy. They were watching her, their expressions full of awe.

"Your eyes," Livy breathed. "They're pure gold."

Addy's own heart stuttered at that. "Like the Supernal's," she said, hating the ring of those words.

"No." Tol took her face in his hands, studying her eyes. "Yours are beautiful." He smiled. "Just like the rest of you."

"You did it," Livy said, shaking her head in amazement. "You killed the Supernal." There were tears on her cheeks.

"*We* did it," Addy corrected.

The Supernal was gone, but his magic lived. Inside of her.

Part of Addy was already getting used to the feeling of power surging through her veins. But she couldn't ignore the way Livy flinched every time she got too close, like Addy was a live flame. If Addy was being honest with herself, she was just as reluctant to get near Livy's magic.

Would she ever be able to hug her sister again?

The thought sent an ache through her very being.

"Come on," Tol said, putting her garden shears into her hand. "Let's go back and see what mayhem the others cooked up in our absence." He lowered his voice and spoke against her ear. "And after that, I'm going to make love to a real, live goddess."

Addy shivered at the promise in his black velvet voice. She was more than a little tempted to tell Livy they'd meet her back at the farmhouse, but their fight wasn't over yet.

Sighing, she awakened the magic in her ring. She wrapped her arms around Tol and Livy, and then she let the portal take them.

※ ※ ※

They spilled out onto Aunt Meredith's front lawn. Dawn was just beginning to break, and Addy blinked as the brightness from the rising Texas sun seared into her eyes.

It took her only a few seconds to take in the scene around them. The general and a row of other Forsaken were on their knees, their bodies trussed up with so much finality there was no chance of them going anywhere.

Addy's new magic pulsed at the sight of them. It was more than the pull she'd always felt toward the Forsaken. This was more of a need to protect. To guard. To save.

"Oh Tolumus, thank the gods."

Tol's parents converged on him, demanding to know what had happened to his back, which was red and blistered from the burns he had taken to protect Addy.

"Erikir!" Livy ran to him and threw herself into his arms. He didn't miss a beat, gathering her to him and fusing his mouth to hers. Addy's shy, sweet sister wrapped her legs around Erikir's waist and kissed him right back.

Addy found herself smiling in spite of herself. Erikir might be an ass, but it was obvious he loved Livy more than life itself. And if he ever did anything to hurt Livy, Addy would turn his heart into pulp.

Addy made a mental note to give Erikir that friendly warning later.

Erikir put Livy down and said something in her ear that transformed her joy to a look of horror. Both of them looked at Addy.

Addy was about to demand what was going on, when something more important caught her attention. With everything that had happened, she'd completely forgotten about Jaxon and the rest of the Allied Forsaken. Nothing had changed since the last time she'd seen them. They lay on the ground, dead.

But the magic inside Addy rebelled at the idea. It told her she now had the power to reverse whatever the Supernal had done to them. She'd seen him do it before, although she had no idea how he'd done it.

Addy looked down at Jaxon, his limp hand clutched in both of Gerth's.

And then, with a surge of the new energy inside her, Addy knew what to do. She closed her eyes, letting the magic boil and grow until it was a raging mass inside her. She gave herself over to the instinct guiding her and released the magic.

It flowed out of her in a wave of invisible heat. Her magic rippled through the air before settling all around the dead Forsaken. Addy felt all of them—their still hearts, their congealed blood, their cold skin.

Her power curled around their organs, sparking them back to life. Her ears filled with a rushing wind sound as her magic filled the emptiness of all those bodies.

Her senses, perfectly attuned to all of the men and women on the ground, flared in recognition.

Alive. Her people were alive.

Addy staggered. Not from exhaustion, but from the overwhelming sense of all of her people coming back to life at once. She had an intense urge to shout at the top of her lungs for the sheer joy of it.

Her people were alive.

She heard their first ragged breaths. She felt the rush of their blood. She opened her eyes and saw their limbs stir.

She looked down at Jaxon as he stirred. He curled his hand around Gerth's.

Gerth made a small sound as he stared down at Jaxon. Gerth lowered his head, resting it gently against Jaxon's chest. Jaxon, looking dazed, ran a hand over Gerth's wild tangle of hair.

It was such a quietly beautiful gesture. It was just so…them.

Jaxon looked up at her.

"I never doubted you were the one meant to lead us." He lifted himself off the ground, only to go down on one knee before her. "I am yours to command, General Deerborn."

Addy's mouth opened and closed, but no sound emerged. Movement drew her attention away from Jaxon.

She sucked in a breath at the sight of the other Forsaken. Every one of them was kneeling, murmuring the words *General Deerborn* and lowering their heads in reverence.

"I—thank you," Addy stammered, not knowing what else to say. The magic she'd shared with them, and which linked her even more strongly to them than she'd been before, was making her feel lightheaded.

Amid her people's quiet reverence, one sound caught her attention. It was the sound of tears splattering onto the ground.

It was such a quiet sound, Addy knew the only reason she could hear it was because of her magic.

She turned her attention in the direction of the sound and froze. The general, her wrists bound and her head bowed in defeat, was crying. Addy could see the tears coursing down her mangled skin, and she had a sudden, desperate urge to go to the woman.

The general lifted her gaze to meet Addy's. Addy saw regret in her mother's eyes, but she also saw something of that fierceness the Supernal had almost beaten out of her.

They stared at each other for a long moment. Addy felt something like understanding pass between them. They'd each made their choices, and now they'd both accept the consequences that came with them.

Addy didn't know what she was going to do with her mother, but she knew one thing. Just because she had been born from her parents, it didn't mean she would become them. Even as the Supernal's power flowed through her veins, she felt no desire for world domination. Darkness still lived inside her…it always would…but it was a very different thing from her father's evil.

And unlike either the general or the Supernal, Addy had people who would drag her out of any black holes she found herself in.

She had Tol and Livy. She had Aunt Meredith and Fred—

Where were they?

She spun around in a circle. When she didn't catch sight of them, she headed for the house, figuring they were inside with Aunt Meredith. She opened the screen door and caught sight of Tol and Nira, locked in a fierce hug. Addy blinked. Blinked again.

What. The. Hell.

It took her a second to rein in her fury before she realized that Nira was crying. Tol met Addy's gaze over the top of Nira's head. Addy knew Tol's every expression, and this one made her heart stop beating. It was sorrow and an apology all in one.

"What?" Addy demanded. "What happened?"

It wasn't the right question. She knew from Tol's sorrow and Nira's tear-stained face that the right question wasn't *What* but *Who*. A horrible feeling spread through her gut.

"Addy." Tol swallowed. "I'm so sorry." He let go of Nira and reached for her, but at that moment, Addy caught sight of the view he'd been blocking. She froze.

It was the same feeling she'd had months ago when she'd come home and found her family's blood smeared across the porch. She'd run through the house, screaming the names of her parents and sisters before she'd found their lifeless bodies.

Just as it had been then with her family, blood was everywhere. Aunt Meredith and Mr. Brown clung to each other as they sobbed. And there on the floor, unmoving, was Fred.

"No." The word whispered out of her.

Addy stared down at her best friend in the entire world.

She was hyperventilating, and yet she couldn't get any air into her lungs. She fell to her knees. Fred's blood soaked through her jeans.

Addy grasped for her magic, trying to bring him back the same way she'd brought the Forsaken back.

But Fred wasn't Forsaken.

A howl of rage burst out of Addy.

She wouldn't accept this. Fred had been in her life almost as long as Livy. He wasn't just her best friend. He was family. He couldn't die.

She wouldn't let him.

"Addy?" Aunt Meredith asked in a tremulous voice.

Addy couldn't make any words come out. So instead of answering, she wrapped her arms around Fred. She ignored the sticky wetness of his blood as it soaked through her shirt.

She barely thought about what she was doing as she called up the magic in her ring. Her mind was already fixed on the conversation…the fight…she was about to have.

"Addy? Addy!"

The voices calling for her cut off as she and Fred were drawn into the portal. She kept her arms locked around Fred, refusing to let the terrible winds yank him loose from her.

When they hit the cold ground, Addy made sure her body landed first, protecting Fred.

He was so still. His skin had gone cold.

Addy let him down gently before getting to her feet.

"Celestial!" She screamed the name into the wind. When she didn't immediately feel the being's presence, she used her magic to project her voice louder. She felt the soundwaves ripple through the air, traveling out in every direction.

Addy startled when the Celestial appeared in front of her. There was still a bloody gash across the Celestial's temple, but she was awake and as solid as Addy.

"He is almost gone," the Celestial said in her whispery voice.

"Yeah," Addy agreed, "and you're going to bring him back to life."

"I never had that kind of power," the Celestial said.

"We both know there are exceptions to every rule," Addy said. "You proved it when you gave your magic to Livy eighteen years ago. You let Tol give all of his power to Erikir. Now, you're going to help me save Fred."

Addy gave the Celestial a fierce look, making it clear the other woman wouldn't be rid of her until Addy got what she'd come for.

"Life and death are part of the balance," the Celestial said. A mournful expression filled her eyes. "If I had understood the necessity of balance sooner, much heartache would have been spared."

"I'm not interested in your philosophical musings," Addy snapped.

Fred didn't have time to spare.

"You and your adopted sister taught me what is possible when the Forsaken and Chosen work together," the Celestial said, tilting her head in thought. "Perhaps…."

"Name your price," Addy said.

The Celestial did. Her terms were as steep as Addy had expected.

"Done," Addy agreed. "But I have conditions."

CHAPTER 37

TOL

Tol paced in the yard. He ground his teeth. And paced some more.

Where the hells had Addy taken Fred?

He went back into the house, wincing a little as the screen door banged shut behind him. Meredith, Nira, and Fred's father didn't even seem to notice the sound. They were all sitting at the kitchen table and staring at the bloody marks on the floor.

Where was Addy?

Tol turned on his heel. He needed to find Olivia. Maybe she had some clue about where Addy had taken Fred.

He was reaching for the door handle when blue sparks appeared in mid-air. Addy's copper hair, and then the rest of her, fell through the portal. Fred was next.

"Ads, what the heck?" Fred asked, rubbing his head.

A heavy relief lifted off Tol.

Fred wasn't dead…not even close.

"You're okay," Addy said, her voice muffled as she threw her arms around Fred.

Then, Meredith and Fred's father were surrounding them, hugging and crying and shouting questions that seemed to require no answer.

Nira, who was standing with her back against the table, stared at Fred in disbelief. She made a small noise.

The others let go of Fred as Nira ran to him. Instead of hugging him the way the others had, she closed her hands into fists and hit his chest.

"You stupid, stupid mortal," Nira raged.

Fred just stood there, looking bewildered.

"I hate you," Nira shrieked. "You—you left me."

She hit him again. Then, she reached up to wrap her arms around his neck and pulled his face down to hers.

When they finally separated, Fred's eyes were glazed over, and he had a ridiculous, loopy smile on his face. Then, they were back at it again.

Tol stopped paying attention to anyone else in the room except Addy. The moment her aunt released her from a tight embrace, Tol caught sight of her eyes. They weren't gold the way they'd been when she left. They were green.

Tol wasn't sure what that meant, but he knew it must have something to do with the fact that Fred was alive and well again. As glad as Tol was to see the farmer up and moving, he couldn't shake the feeling of dread that had seized hold of him.

He stared at Addy, trying to read the expression on her face.

"Wait a second." Fred stopped kissing Nira but didn't let go of her. He narrowed his eyes at Addy.

"What did you do, Ads?" The alarm emerging on his face was an echo of Tol's panic.

"I just yelled at the Celestial until she brought you back," Addy said, giving Fred an easy smile.

Fred wasn't buying it. Neither was Tol.

"What did you do?" Fred asked again.

Tol didn't trust himself to speak, so he stayed silent and tense as he waited for Addy to drop the bomb he knew was coming.

"Oh, didn't I mention?" She gave Fred's arm a pat. She avoided Tol's gaze, which she must know was burning a hole into her back. "You're immortal now. Congrats."

Tol's breath caught.

"W-what?" Fred stammered. "Why?"

"Because you're my best friend," Addy replied.

"You're immortal?" Nira asked Fred. She turned to Addy. "He's immortal?"

"Courtesy of the Celestial," Addy said. "And I asked. He can live on Vitaquias. So can both of you," she added to her aunt and Fred's father, who were staring slack-jawed between Addy and Fred.

Tol had had enough.

"Everyone. Get. Out."

He didn't have to ask twice. He might not be a prince anymore, but he still had the bearings and demeanor of a future king.

Tol didn't take his eyes off Addy as the room cleared.

"We're not finished with this conversation," Fred said, pointing a finger at Addy as Meredith and Nira herded him out.

The screen door shut, and they were alone.

"What did you do?" Tol's chest rose and fell with the emotions he was barely containing.

"Tol, listen—"

"What did you do?!"

Addy crossed her arms. "Calm down, and I'll tell you."

"Calm down? *Calm down?!*"

Tol's heart was trying to pound itself out of his chest. He understood how these things worked by now. He knew there was no way the Celestial would bring Fred back from certain death unless Addy had done something irrevocably horrible.

Addy crossed her arms and glared back at him. With an enormous force of will, he reined in his temper.

"Only a powerful sacrifice could bring back a life," Addy said, her voice even and calm. "So, I gave up the Supernal's magic. I transferred it to the Celestial."

Tol couldn't breathe.

"I still have my Forsaken abilities, but the Supernal's magic is gone," Addy continued. "The Celestial realized she caused the Forsaken to become…well, forsaken. So, the magic I gave her will let her take over the role as the Forsaken's go-between with the gods." Addy took a breath. "She'll protect the Forsaken, while Livy will fill that role for the Chosen."

It was a lot to take in, and yet, Tol could tell the most important detail had been left out. He could see from the way Addy kept shifting from foot to foot that she was working up to something. Tol clenched his jaw until it ached.

Addy crossed the room until they were nearly toe-to-toe. Tentatively, like she thought he might reject her, she put her hands on his waist and met his stare. When she spoke, her words were soft.

"I gave my immortality to Fred. I'm mortal now."

Tol staggered back, away from her.

"How could you?" he whispered, and then, louder. "How could you?"

Immortality was a priceless gift. How could she just give hers away?

Because she's Addy, you idiot. She would do anything for the people she cared about, no matter what it meant for her.

The thought of Addy's life having an end point…of her fire extinguishing….

Tol couldn't bear it.

"You would have done the same thing for Gerth," Addy argued, defensively. "You *did* do it for me."

"That's not the point." Tol shoved his hand through his hair as he began to pace. "You have responsibilities. You're going to lead the Forsaken. What happens to them when you—"

He couldn't finish that thought. He couldn't say the word.

"Who knows?" Addy lifted a shoulder. "Maybe Gerth and Jaxon will take over. Or anyone else who's a capable leader. The Celestial will watch over them, and I'm not irreplaceable."

"Beg to differ," Tol shot back.

He didn't know how to deal with the awful truth Addy had thrust at him, so he reverted to anger.

Addy reached up and put a hand on Tol's cheek. Even though he was prepared to rage at her, he couldn't stop his body from betraying him as he leaned into her touch.

"You talk about sacrificing my immortality," she said, her voice quieter now. "But it wasn't a sacrifice."

She looked at him, her eyes searching his.

"Do you remember what you said to me the night you told me you'd given up your immortality?" she asked. Without waiting for an answer, she said, "You told me I was the strongest person you'd ever met, and that I could survive anything."

Tol nodded, his throat too thick for him to speak.

Addy continued, "The truth is, I don't want to survive without you. After I gave up my immortality, all I felt was relief, because it meant I wouldn't have to spend an eternity without you."

Tol's chest was threatening to crack open.

"My immortality went to a good cause," Addy said. "It makes me happy to know that Fred will live forever. He'll be there for Livy when I can't be anymore, and—"

Tol kissed her. He put all the thoughts he didn't have words for into touch.

Addy melted against him, making a soft sound that sent a fire racing through him. He lifted her off the ground as their kisses turned feverish.

He gripped her thighs, pressing closer until not even air separated them. Even with everything they'd been through, Addy's piña colada smell wafted off her hair, intoxicating him.

"No matter how long we live," he told her between gasping, heated kisses, "I'll love you for eternity."

A sharp rap at the window startled them both back into reality.

"Ad-dy," Gerth called. "You need to address your people." And even though there was no way he could see them through the curtain, Gerth added, "You two can snog yourselves into oblivion later."

Too late, Tol thought, his mind in a complete fog.

Addy looked at Tol, her chest rising and falling against his own. As much as he wanted nothing more than to lose himself in her, they didn't have nearly enough privacy in this house for what he had in mind. They both heaved a dramatic sigh as Tol lowered her to the ground.

"Come on," Tol said, winding their fingers together. "The sooner we get this stuff over with, the sooner I can take you on our first date."

"What makes you so sure I'll agree to go out with you?" she teased.

"I'm not asking," he replied, letting go of her hand to wrap a possessive arm around her waist.

"Bossy." She stuck her tongue out at him.

"You have no idea."

They both sobered when they were out on the lawn. Sheets had been used to cover the dead who hadn't evanesced. Tol could see the lumpy forms of their limbs and patches of blood through the thin fabric. Flies buzzed around the covered bodies, and Tol knew that if they didn't deal with the corpses soon, they'd quickly rot in the Texas heat.

There were also the Forsaken, including the general, who were tied up and awaiting Addy's sentencing. As her first act as the new Forsaken leader, everyone would be looking to see how she handled her authority.

Addy climbed up on the picnic table, surveying the crowd of Forsaken who had gathered to hear what she had to say.

"Okay people, here's the deal," Addy said.

It was such an Addy thing to say, Tol couldn't help but smile. He watched as she captured the attention of every Forsaken just by being herself.

"I killed the Supernal and gave his powers to the Celestial."

There were murmurs in the crowd, but Addy didn't give them time to turn into anything more.

"The Celestial has agreed to care for the Forsaken on Vitaquias."

Addy paused for only a second before continuing.

"My sister is about to become the Chosen queen, and if you want me to be your leader, then you'll have to get along with her people.

"If you're not cool with that, then you can go hang out with them." She jerked her thumb in the direction of the bound and gagged Forsaken still kneeling at the edge of the crowd. "So, what'll it be?"

In answer, the gathered Forsaken army of thousands saluted Addy.

"And because we all know I'm not qualified for this job," Addy added, "I'd like to introduce you to my official, knowing-their-shit advisors." She gestured Gerth and Jaxon over.

"He's a Chosen," one of the Forsaken said, eyeing Gerth.

Tol tensed.

"He is," Addy agreed. "And while we're on the subject, there's someone else you need to meet."

Her gaze cut straight to Tol. She held out her hand, making it clear she wanted him to join her on the picnic table. He did.

"If you want me," Addy said, "You're also getting the man I'm going to spend the rest of my life with."

Tol didn't let the surprise show on his face when the Forsaken turned and offered him the same snappy salute they'd given Addy.

CHAPTER 38

ADDY

Addy strode toward the group of Forsaken on their knees. They tilted back their heads to give her challenging stares. She paced across to the far side of the line where the general was tied up.

Addy suppressed a shudder at the sight of those hideous wounds, some of which were red and swollen from infection.

There was no sign of the tears Addy had seen in the general's eyes before. Now, there was only a cold kind of acceptance.

"Listen very carefully," Addy said, speaking loudly enough that their audience could hear her every word. "I'm giving you one chance to swear an oath to keep peace with the Chosen. If you make the vow, you'll live."

She didn't add in the part about what would happen if the general refused.

"I will not submit to Chosen rule," the general replied, her voice raspy but no less powerful.

"You'd be submitting to my rule," Addy corrected, looking away from the ruin of her mother's face before pity took hold.

She reminded herself of the sight of Fred, covered in blood and corpse-still, and hardened herself.

"They will betray us," the general said. "They will steal our free will."

The general got to her feet. Even with the way she was tied up, there was a deadly grace to her movements. Addy couldn't help the small flare of respect she felt for the general's iron will. Even defeated and mutilated, she still stood tall and held her head high. It was just as Addy would have wanted to go down if she was about to meet her death.

Addy swallowed.

"So, that's your final decision?"

The general lifted her gaze to the Allied Forsaken who were standing at attention, waiting for any order Addy might give.

"Do you think she'll protect you from the Chosen people's insatiable greed?" the general called in a strong voice. "Who would you rather answer to—a proven leader, or this mortal-raised girl?"

The Forsaken moved their heads back and forth between the general and Addy, like they were watching some kind of deadly tennis match.

Addy knew the general expected her to falter. Months ago, she might have. That wasn't the case anymore.

"I am mortal-raised and proud," Addy replied. She spoke for the crowd, but her stare was pinned on the general. "I may not know much about being a leader, but I'm the reason why you're free from the Supernal, and why you have the chance of a peaceful eternity on Vitaquias."

Addy spun her garden shears around her finger. She could feel the eyes of every single person on her, waiting to see what she would do. She had no choice. She was the Forsaken leader now, and the general had loudly and openly challenged her.

More than that, this was the moment she'd been waiting for ever since she discovered the general had ordered the deaths of Addy's family.

Mom and Dad. Stacy, Rosie, Lucy.

They were gone, and it was the general's fault. Now, finally, Addy had her chance for revenge.

The general didn't flinch as Addy raised her arm.

A hand on her shoulder stopped her just before she struck. Tol's spicy, masculine scent surrounded her, comforting and enticing at the same time.

"You don't have to do this," he said in a low voice only she could hear.

She did, though. *Didn't she?*

"She killed my family," Addy said. She remembered the way each member of her family had looked, sprawled out on the kitchen floor and soaking in pools of their own blood. Nausea roiled in her gut at the memory.

Tol turned her around to face him, giving the general a look that dared her to so much as move a muscle. "I know what you're thinking," he said. "But there are other ways to make sure she never poses a threat to us again."

"I have to kill her," Addy whispered, hearing the uncertainty and hesitation in her own voice.

Tol leaned closer. "From everything you've told me about Sue and Gary, I don't think they would want you to do this."

"Tol's right," Livy's soft voice said from her other side.

Addy turned to her twin…the soon-to-be Chosen queen.

"Mom and Dad wouldn't have wanted you to kill for them," Livy said. "Neither would Stacy, Rosie, and Lucy. Not like this."

Addy let out a breath. "Then, what do I do?"

"We have the bunker," Tol said. "We can lock the general and her followers up there. Then, the Celestial can hold them prisoner on Vitaquias until they agree to swear to peace."

It was an anti-climactic ending for an enemy Addy had waited months to destroy. But as she stared at her mother's scarred face, Addy realized she'd lost her appetite for vengeance. She looked around at the faces of the people she'd come to love with all of her heart—family new and old. Tol, Livy, Aunt Meredith, Fred, Jaxon….

The Deerborns were a memory she would always hold close to her heart. But these people, the family surrounding her now…this was her future.

Addy let out a slow breath and tucked her garden shears back in her pocket.

"Lock the general and her followers in the bunker," she told the steely-eyed Forsaken who were awaiting her orders. "Give them food and water, but don't engage them in any way." To the general, she said, "I'm going to let the Celestial decide what to do with you once we're all on Vitaquias."

Addy tried not to act like it was a big deal when several Forsaken jumped to carry out her order. She'd have to be careful, or this could go to her head.

"Just a moment," Nira announced. She stalked up to the general. When she began untying the ropes around the general's wrists, Addy and her Forsaken guards tensed.

Nira gave the general her signature ice queen smile. "I heard about how your hand grew back after Paris." She leaned closer, like she was confiding in the general. "But I don't think that little trick will work now that the Supernal's gone, will it?"

"Nira," both Addy and Tol said, moving closer.

"Oh, don't get your knickers in a twist." Nira scowled. "I'm not going to cut off her hand.

Nira took the general's scarred hand in her own dainty one. She squinted at the general's fingers.

"You need a manicure," Nira informed the general. Then, in a move almost as fast as any Forsaken attack, Nira drew a scalpel from inside her sleeve and cut off the general's index finger.

For several seconds, they all just stared at the blood spurting from the wound, and the finger now resting on Nira's palm. The general's lips had gone white, but she didn't make a sound.

Nira pulled the ring off from the detached finger. She scrutinized the giant ruby in the center, and then tossed the ring to Fred.

"What—" Fred began, reflexively catching the ring.

"Who knows," Nira said with a haughty flick of her hair. "Maybe you'll find a good use for this at some point."

"But it's all bloody," Fred complained.

Nira gave Fred a dirty look, which transformed into a little smile when Fred slipped the ring into his pocket.

Nira tossed the finger away with a disgusted look, and then met the general's hate-filled glare with one of her own.

"That was for trying to kill my man," Nira told the general.

"Nira," Tol said in a warning voice.

"Alright, alright." Nira rolled her eyes. "I'll bandage her up." She cocked her head and gave the general a sickly-sweet smile. "Eventually."

"Maybe I should have killed her, after all," Addy said, as the guards led the general away. "Everyone's going to think they can walk all over me now." She heaved a resigned sigh.

"I'm not so sure about that," Jaxon replied. His face was wan, but that was the only indication that he'd been dead only a short while ago. He looked strong enough to fight a hundred more enemies. Addy had a sudden urge to hug him, but since the big guy didn't really seem like the hugging type, she settled for patting him on his muscled arm.

"You showed mercy," Jaxon continued. "It's not what the Forsaken expect from their leader. You've shown everyone that you're carving your own path."

"Well played, General Deerborn," Gerth told Addy with an approving nod.

Addy felt something shift inside her, and for a few seconds, she was left completely unbalanced. Then, she figured out what was missing. The cobra...the ugly beast that lived coiled up inside her, waiting for its chance to spring and devour...was gone.

"My rage disappeared," she said to no one in particular, her voice full of wonder. "That awful, scary thing inside me."

"Told you," Jaxon said, his lips tugging up into a knowing smile. "Now that you've accepted who and what you are, you no longer have the two sides of your nature warring for control."

"He thinks he knows everything," Gerth grumbled.

Addy laughed.

"We're going to have to stop calling ourselves Forsaken," Addy said thoughtfully. "And I don't think *Allied Forsaken* is going to cut it, either."

"Big Bad Scary Warriors?" Gerth suggested.

"*Sexy* Scary Warriors," Tol corrected, smoothing back Addy's hair and pressing a kiss to her neck.

CHAPTER 39

OLIVIA

Olivia stared at Addy in horror. The words coming out of her twin's mouth were almost beyond comprehension.

"You what?" Aunt Meredith demanded, slamming her glass of sweet tea down on the kitchen table.

Olivia and Meredith sat across from Addy and gaped at her.

"I did it for Fred," Addy said. "He would have died otherwise."

Olivia hadn't had much time to think about immortality, or the fact that she would gain it as soon as she blood married Erikir. But now that she'd just learned that Addy had given hers up, it was all she could think about.

The sheer vastness of immortality, and what it would mean to have it when her twin didn't, hit Olivia. Tears sprang to her eyes.

"Fred would have done the same for any of us," Addy said.

It was true. It just didn't make Olivia feel better about what Addy had done.

"It's going to be okay," Addy said when Olivia still couldn't form her lips around a reasonable response. She reached over and squeezed Olivia's hand.

Instead of letting her tears fall, Olivia crushed her sister into a hug.

"Thank you for understanding," Addy said.

Olivia wasn't sure she did. Eternity was too big for her to wrap her mind around. Eventually, she'd have to come to terms with the meaning of a life without her sister. Right now, though, she just wanted to appreciate the fact that they were all alive and together.

"Aunt Meredith, please say something," Addy said.

Aunt Meredith's hands shook as she reached for a napkin on the table. She blew her nose loudly, crumpled up the napkin in her fist, and then looked from Addy to Olivia.

"Do you have any idea how dang proud I am to be your aunt?" she asked, sniffling. "I know your parents are smiling down on ya'll right now."

She reached for another napkin as more tears spilled down her cheeks.

"Will you come with us?" Olivia asked. "To Vitaquias?"

She couldn't bear the thought of leaving their aunt behind.

"You think I'm going to give up a chance to go to a new world and wrangle some alien cattle?" Aunt Meredith pffed. "Besides, where you girls go, I go."

The screen door creaked open. The three of them straightened on instinct as Tol's parents came into the kitchen.

Olivia searched their faces, trying to decide whether she should offer them her condolences about Getyl and Walidir.

One look at the pristine, regal, and perfectly-put-together couple, and Olivia shrunk in her seat a little. Her nerves went into a flutter when she saw Erikir come into the room behind them.

There was a tentative look on his face. Anxiety...*his* anxiety...shot through her mind.

"What's wrong?" Olivia asked, immediately on her guard.

"We have an urgent matter to discuss with you," Tol's mother told Olivia in that curt, no-nonsense way that made her feel like a little girl in trouble.

"We'll make ourselves scarce," Aunt Meredith said, getting up from the table.

Addy bugged her eyes out at Olivia, mouthed *good luck*, and hurried after their aunt.

Tol's parents took the seats Addy and Aunt Meredith had vacated. Erikir stayed standing. His nervousness was building in Olivia's mind, and she had to sit on her hands to keep from fidgeting.

"The blood marriage is set for today at sunset," Rolomens said. "All the preparations have been made."

Olivia jerked to attention.

"Today?" she squeaked.

She'd known it was going to happen soon, of course, but she'd thought with the king's parents and all the other Chosen they'd lost during the battle, there would be a delay.

"There's no sense in waiting any longer," Starser said with crisp brusqueness, like she wasn't talking about the most life-changing event that would ever happen to Olivia. "And our people are well and truly out of Source. Unless you want all of our elders to expire, you will complete the ritual today."

"Oh. Of course," Olivia stammered.

"Tradition calls for a red gown for you," the queen continued while Olivia's mind spun. "Viola and Marise have prepared the gown and will be by soon to make any last-minute alterations."

Olivia's mouth opened and closed, but no sound came out.

"Excellent," Rolomens said, pushing back from the table. He glanced at Olivia's ragged appearance and frowned. "You may wish to…wash up before the ceremony."

Rolomens and Starser breezed out of the room, discussing corpse removal and flower arrangements. It was so bizarre that Olivia had to pinch herself to make sure she wasn't dreaming.

A hysterical laugh bubbled out of Olivia. She slapped a hand over her mouth.

"We can wait if you want," Erikir said. "We can tell them we need a few more days."

Olivia immediately sobered.

"Is that what you want?" she asked.

"Hells no." Erikir's reply came immediately. "I want to marry you before you come to your senses and change your mind."

Olivia got up and wrapped her arms around Erikir's waist. He held her back, pressing her to his chest and burying his face in her hair.

THE CHOSEN UNION

"I'm choosing this because I love you with all of my heart," she told him. "I'm never going to change my mind about wanting to be with you."

The pulse of feeling that went through their shared bond was strong enough to take her breath away. When she looked up at Erikir, he caught her mouth in a kiss.

Olivia felt herself falling in love all over again.

CHAPTER 40

ERIKIR

Erikir had expected to feel nervous, but as he stood in front of the mirror and tied his bow tie, he felt only a calm sense of rightness. He craved this bond with Olivia…craved the closeness it would bring between them.

His only regret was that his grandparents wouldn't bear witness to any of it. A flash of pain went through him, which he quickly suppressed. He didn't want Olivia to feel anything from him except his love and anticipation.

There was a knock at the door.

"Come in," he called, pulling on his jacket.

Tol and Gerth came into the bedroom. They were both dressed in tuxedos, except their shirts were white instead of the deep, rich red of Erikir's.

"Looking smart," Gerth said, appraising Erikir.

Gerth sprawled out on the bed, oblivious to the way his shirt came untucked and his bow tie seemed to be hanging onto his neck by nothing more than a prayer.

"Sunset on Vitaquias is in half an hour," Tol said, standing stiffly by the door. "Just thought you'd want to know."

Erikir cleared his throat.

"I never thanked you for giving me your magic," Erikir told his cousin.

When Tol raised an eyebrow, Erikir hurried to clarify, "I know you didn't do it for me, but I wanted to say thank you, anyway."

"Yeah." Tol rubbed the back of his neck, looking as uncomfortable as Erikir felt. "You're welcome."

Gerth sniffled and wiped a fake tear from his eye. "That was so beautiful, gentlemen."

Scowling, Tol grabbed a crochet pillow off the dresser and threw it at Gerth's head at the same time Erikir said, "Piss off, Gerth."

Erikir exchanged a stilted grin with his cousin.

"Shall we?" Gerth said, motioning toward the door.

Erikir looked at Tol. He knew how much his cousin had wanted it to be him and Addy going through this very ritual.

"If you don't want to stick around for this," Erikir told him, "I won't be offended."

"It's all good." Tol gave him a shrug. "It turns out you were right after all. Well, at least about me not being the right man to be king of the Chosen." He frowned. "You definitely weren't right about thinking I needed to die."

"You're never going to let me forget that, are you?" Erikir asked, crossing his arms.

"Nope." There was no animosity in Tol's expression, only amusement.

An easy silence that they'd never had before filled the room.

"Although," Tol raised a finger. "I did want to ask if you minded if Addy and I don't stay for dinner."

Erikir doubted he'd even notice who came and went tonight. He knew he'd have eyes only for Olivia.

Tol added, "I'm taking Addy on our first date."

Erikir laughed at that. When he thought of a couple going on their first date, Tol and Addy were the last people who came to mind.

"I hope after everything you two have gone through, you're taking her somewhere nice," Erikir said.

Tol grinned. "I've got it covered."

"And what he means by that," Gerth added, "is that Nira and I helped him set the whole thing up."

"Semantics." Tol waved a dismissive hand.

* * *

The front yard was empty. There were no people, no medical tent, and no evidence of the army that had been living here for the last week. The bunker doors had been left open, and no sounds came from within. There wasn't so much as a soda can left out on the lawn. Aside from Erikir, Tol, and Gerth, the property was abandoned.

"Ready?" Tol asked.

Erikir looked at the vial that contained a single drop of blood. *Olivia's blood.*

Addy and Olivia had been helping to transport people and supplies to and from Vitaquias all day. They were both on the other world now. Erikir had been banished to the farmhouse so he wouldn't catch sight of Olivia. Nira had said it was bad luck to see a bride before the wedding, even if it was a blood marriage. Erikir had argued the point, but there was no changing Nira's mind once she'd made it up.

Tol overturned the drop of blood on the crack in the earth. The wind kicked up, stirring Erikir's hair.

Erikir glanced back at the farmhouse once, knowing it would be his last view of this world. Then, he let the portal take him.

What could have been seconds or hours later, the three of them spilled out of the portal. It was an effort to make sure he didn't fall on his arse and ruin his clothes before Olivia even saw him. Somehow, he managed to stay on his feet.

He braced himself for the icy rain and biting wind that had raged the last time he was on Vitaquias, but neither came. The air was colder than it had been in Texas, but it wasn't unpleasant.

"The Celestial is holding off the storms," Gerth explained, sensing the direction of Erikir's thoughts.

Erikir glanced up at the sky, which was a deep purple. Black clouds sped across like they were agitated. The setting sun threw off harsh reds and oranges.

The three of them were quiet as they made the walk from the portal to the castle ruins. If Tol and Gerth hadn't been with him, Erikir probably would have sprinted the entire way up the cliff path.

His heart was beating like he'd just run a marathon, and the magic he'd absorbed from Tol was its own storm inside him.

He knew he wouldn't settle until he saw Olivia.

As they approached the castle ruins, Erikir saw that a halo of gold surrounded it like a bubble. He didn't have to ask where it had come from. He could feel Olivia's magic as he walked through the shimmering light.

Erikir came into the castle ruins and stopped.

"Holy—"

"Pretty cool, huh?" Gerth clapped him on the back.

Pretty cool didn't begin to cover it. The rubble had been completely transformed.

High-topped cocktail tables ringed the flat marble floor, which had been cleared of all the broken stone. Huge arrangements of red roses and red orchids took up most of the surface area. The black tablecloths and chairs made the red of the flowers stand out even more.

Erikir's eyes were drawn to the stone pedestal. A dagger and the two vials of Source that had been saved for this day rested on top.

A long table held champagne flutes and crystal glasses filled with a red cocktail. All of the drinks were garnished with a slice of blood orange.

The Chosen were easy to pick out. They all wore white, as was the custom for a blood marriage. Their expressions were full of a disbelieving kind of hope.

The Forsaken were in full military attire, their uniforms pressed and starched to within an inch of their lives. The three honorary mortals—Fred, Fred's father, and Meredith—were dressed up like they were going to prom or a mortal wedding. The only color that no one else was wearing was red.

Erikir swallowed, forcing himself to breathe as everyone's eyes settled on him.

"You got this, Cuz," Tol said, slapping his back before disappearing into the crowd, probably to find Addy.

The sun was steadily lowering on the horizon.

Where was Olivia?

Erikir saw Addy, wearing a short black dress, come through the Haze bubble. Nira was behind her. And then—

Erikir forgot how to breathe.

Olivia's red gown billowed around her. The top part was a delicate lace that melded to her perfect curves. Capped sleeves cut off just below her slender shoulders. The bottom part of the dress was satin. It flowed around her like water. There was so much material it trailed behind her, but the gown didn't overwhelm her. Her Haze made her skin glow gold. Her hair was down, with her silky curls spilling over her shoulders.

Her gaze immediately found his. She looked at him, her eyes widening at the sight of him. He heard her voice in his head.

So handsome.

He felt his cheeks warm.

Gorgeous, he thought back to her.

A smile lit her face, and he knew she'd heard his thought.

The crowd parted as they made their way to each other. Erikir took her hands in his. He'd wondered if she would be trembling from nerves, but her grip was steady.

He didn't get too close to her because he was afraid he'd step on her dress, but he put a hand on her lower back. He was pleasantly surprised to find that her back was bare. He loved the feeling of her skin beneath his fingers…wanted more of it.

"Everyone's staring at us," Olivia whispered, her anxiety sparking to life in his mind.

"Keep your eyes on me," he told her. "Forget anyone else even exists."

Olivia let out a soft laugh. "With you looking like that, it shouldn't be too hard."

He brought her hand to his lips as they walked to the stone pedestal. Everyone else made a ring around them as they prepared to witness the ritual.

Erikir's aunt and uncle stood at the pedestal, along with other important elders.

THE CHOSEN UNION

"Still time to change your mind," Erikir whispered to Olivia as everyone else took their places.

"Not a chance." She gave him a smile that splintered his heart into a thousand pieces.

Aunt Starser took Olivia's shoulders and steered her to the opposite side of the pedestal. Erikir had to stop himself from reaching out for her.

The king turned his attention to the crowd of people surrounding them.

Erikir didn't hear any of the king's words. He was completely absorbed by the enormity of what they were about to do.

He still couldn't believe they were about to save their entire race.

He was aware of the elders moving around them and chanting in the ancient language of Vitaquias. The king picked up the dagger and one of the vials of Source. He looked at Olivia when he spoke, but his voice carried throughout the crowd.

"Do you, Olivia Deerborn, willingly enter into this blood marriage with Erikir Magnantius, to be bound in body and spirit, for all of eternity?"

Olivia looked at Erikir. She spoke her answer clearly and without a hint of hesitation.

"I so swear," she said, repeating the age-old language that had been used in blood marriages throughout the millennia. "This is my chosen union."

Warmth flooded through Erikir. He let out an unsteady breath, feeling a little lightheaded.

This was really happening. She was really and truly his....

"Do you, Erikir Magnantius, willingly enter into this blood marriage with Olivia Deerborn, to be bound in body and spirit, for all of eternity?" the king asked.

"I so swear." To Olivia, he mouthed, *With all of my heart*. "This is my chosen union."

The king offered Olivia the open vial of Source and told her to drink.

Olivia's eyes met Erikir's over the top of the vial as she tipped it back and swallowed. Her Haze flared to life. The king took her arm and lifted the dagger.

Olivia held his gaze as the king sliced a line across her forearm.

Erikir twitched, needing to go to her. Someone put a hand on his shoulder, holding him in place. Erikir clenched his jaw as he watched blood slide down her flawless skin. It caught in the stone bowl that two elders held against her skin.

Erikir seethed. Olivia was his to protect. Nothing else in all the worlds mattered more than her.

"She'll be healed shortly after the ritual is complete," Aunt Starser said in a quiet voice.

Erikir barely managed to wait until his uncle had finished speaking the ancient words. He snatched the vial of Source off the pedestal and drank it down in one swig. Erikir didn't wait for his Haze to grow or for the king to speak the words of the ritual. He took the dagger and slashed it down his own arm. He didn't even feel the cut.

He held his arm over the stone basin, letting his blood pool there.

The basins were exchanged, and Erikir found himself holding the one that was full of Olivia's blood. He met her eyes over the stone rim. Then, he lifted the bowl to his lips.

Erikir drank, just as the sun dipped below the horizon. The bite of iron on his tongue transformed to the taste of watery nothing as the Source in Olivia's blood overcame everything else.

Erikir had expected it to feel like when he'd put his hand over the stone and absorbed Tol's powers. He'd been ready for the feeling of strength flooding his body as their magic combined.

It didn't feel anything like what he'd expected. This had nothing to do with their magical strength. This was a merging of their spirits. He'd thought Olivia already lived in his mind and heart, but he realized it had been a bare whisper of what he felt now.

She was all around him, in him. His every thought and emotion mingled with hers. He didn't get flashes of her thoughts; he knew them all. They flowed into his mind in a deluge, so fast and with such ferocity that he couldn't distinguish them from his own.

They were still the people they'd been before, but now they were entangled in each other until one couldn't be separated from the other.

THE CHOSEN UNION

He strode around the pedestal and took her into his arms. The red satin of Olivia's dress swished around his legs. Erikir no longer cared about tearing the fabric or even the fact that his arm was bleeding all over it. He drew Olivia to him, tasting blood and Source on her lips as they kissed.

I love you.

He had no idea if the thought was hers or his. It didn't matter. They were one entity now.

I love you.

Erikir didn't want to let go of Olivia, but there was a growing heat in the air around them that was impossible to ignore. He released her, only to find that their Hazes were growing. Golden light spilled out from them. Magic churned inside both of them, demanding release.

"All hail the Chosen king and queen," Rolomens said, raising Erikir's still-bleeding arm in one hand and Olivia's in the other.

"Forever live King Erikir!" the Chosen called out. "Forever live Queen Olivia!"

At that moment, Erikir heard a voice in his mind that was neither his nor Olivia's. The Celestial appeared before them, her silver eyes a storm.

"With this chosen union, immortality is returned to your people," she said in a voice that was clear as bells and strong as iron. "With this blood marriage, you have earned the power to restore Vitaquias.

"Forever live King Erikir and Queen Olivia."

With those words, their magic erupted.

CHAPTER 41

OLIVIA

Glowing orbs of power rested in each of Olivia's hands. Unlike the Supernal's power, which would have torn her apart, this magic was stable. The globes were hot, but not unbearably so. It looked like she held twin suns in her palms. She sensed every tendril of magic. More importantly, she had full control over them.

Erikir stood at her back, wrapping his arms around her and giving her something solid to lean against. Without fully understanding what she was doing, Olivia separated one strand of magic from the rest and set it loose.

The gold beam of light shot forward, swirling around the kneeling and speechless Chosen.

Olivia blinked through the golden light pulsing at the edges of her vision. Before her eyes, the Chosen people aged in reverse.

People who had been on the brink of death, hobbling around on canes, took on the appearance of twenty- and thirty-year-olds in the peak of health. Joyous shouts filled the air. Nira was hugging her aunts, who were almost unrecognizable. Marise and Viola had shed the elderly, weakened appearance they'd had before.

All around them, the Chosen people's physical bodies were returning to the way they'd been before their world was destroyed.

Gran and Walidir would have loved to be here for this.

The somber thought flowed from Erikir's mind into Olivia's.

THE CHOSEN UNION

Olivia felt Erikir's rush of loss cut through her own heart as he looked at the people around them. Images of his grandparents entered her mind.

"Iseth et esleywn loraifil meiyn," she murmured.

Honor the dead with the richness of life.

Erikir nodded, brushing her hair aside to press a kiss against her neck.

She wanted to say more, but she couldn't ignore the well of magic that was now bubbling and frothing within her.

The satin train of her dress whipped around both of them as she led Erikir to the edge of the castle ruins. She looked down at the murky Source lake below and out at the dead landscape.

So much darkness, she thought with despair.

Let's change that, Erikir's voice replied in her head.

Olivia took Erikir's hand, leading him down the cliff path and to the edge of the muddy Source lake. She could sense the rest of the Chosen and Forsaken following them, but she couldn't see anything beyond the brightness of her and Erikir's Hazes.

As the muddy water lapped at her dress, Olivia released more of her magic. The golden beams flew through the air and straight down to the bottom of the pool of oily muck.

Olivia could feel the cleansing power sweep in and purge the toxins from the lake. She felt a slow heat build in her head as pure Source began to seep through the obsidian stones lining the bottom of the empty lake.

In the distance, Olivia heard awed exclamations and cries of joy. People were shouting her name. Somewhere, the gods were watching her work with a deep sense of approval.

Instead of feeling exhausted from the effort, Olivia's energy expanded. As the Source rose, she and Erikir grew stronger. Their Hazes flared brighter. She sent out more of her magic.

Swirling ribbons of golden light shot through the air like comets. Rather than burning out, each strand of magic grew brighter.

Dozens…hundreds…thousands of golden ribbons of light filled the air. They cut through the fog, melting away ice and mud. They left a trail of life where there had been nothing but death. Burned husks of trees filled out and sprouted leaves. The smell of rot and decay in the air turned to one of freshness and growth. It was a smell that reminded Olivia of home.

She used the love and nostalgia she felt for Deerborn Family Farm to guide her magic. Closing her eyes, she sent her power deep underground, where it coaxed frozen and shriveled roots back to life. She directed her magic up to the castle ruins on the cliff, too. There, her magic wove in and out of the spirits of the most powerful Chosen who had ever touched this world. Those people were gone, but their essence lingered. Olivia and Erikir's magic drew on the whispers of a power so old and beautiful she couldn't have begun to describe it.

Olivia felt the castle reassembling itself in her bones. She felt the shift of rock and the happiness of sun-drenched afternoons.

She felt power and magic and history. More than any of that, she felt love. She felt the way Erikir's heart pulsed with it. She felt his devotion to their people and his love for her.

As Erikir wound his arms tighter around her, his lips murmured promises in a language so beautiful it made her heart ache. His words somehow fed the magic inside her. As he spoke, her magic reacted. The world around them expanded and contracted, as though it was itself a living, breathing thing.

With every inhalation, part of the world was renewed. With each exhale, poison and rot were expelled.

Olivia had no idea how long she and Erikir clung to each other, knitting back the fabric of their world with the combined forces of their minds. They kept going until every strand of magic had left Olivia's hands.

Her magic wasn't gone; it was alive all around them. She could feel it pulsing in the ground and sweeping through the air. She felt it in the newly-remade stones of the castle and in the charming cluster of houses nestled together in a grassy valley.

Even though she had seen her magic changing the world in her mind, nothing could have prepared her for the sight that greeted her when she opened her eyes.

She gasped.

"This is a dream," she whispered.

THE CHOSEN UNION

Erikir held her against him as they both stared around in wonder. "Then I hope I never, ever wake up."

It was difficult to tell if it was day or night. The sky was a cobalt blue, but there were shots of pink and gold through the clouds that illuminated the new world around them. The castle glittered on the clifftop, its white stone façade clean and whole and new.

Trees, their bows heavy with flowers and fruit, surrounded them. Curved bridges, with vines growing along the wooden slats, rose over bubbling streams. Homes with golden lights filling their windows made a serpentine trail on either side of a cobbled road that stretched far out of view. In the distance, Olivia could see endless forests and snow-capped mountains. A blue-green sea with foamy waves was just visible in the distance. The smell of fresh-cut grass and new blossoms perfumed the air.

"Okay Liv," Fred's voice said from somewhere nearby. "I've seen some seriously cool stuff in the last few months, but this takes the cake."

Olivia turned to see an open-mouthed Fred, standing beside an open-mouthed Gerth. Jaxon and the rest of their Forsaken guards remained as serious and watchful as ever, but there was a softness in their gray eyes as they took in the world around them.

Addy and Tol came to stand beside her and Erikir. Addy slung her arm across Olivia's shoulders as they stared up at the castle. Addy pointed.

"Dibs on that turret way at the top."

Olivia craned her neck, looking behind them.

"What is it?" Erikir asked.

"I think I'm losing my mind," she said, still staring through the crowd of Chosen and Forsaken. "I could swear I heard the Cluckers."

As if on cue, Aunt Meredith, her signature cowboy hat in place, appeared. She was carrying a cage with five squawking chickens.

Olivia laughed in delight when Mr. Brown appeared, leading Jenny, the Deerborns' cow.

"How?" Olivia asked her aunt.

Aunt Meredith winked at them. "I have my ways."

Olivia reached out to stroke Jenny's velvet-soft nose.

Erikir grinned at Olivia. "You can take the girl off the farm, but you can't take the farm out of the girl."

He pointed at something in the distance. Olivia and Addy both laughed at the sight of what was unmistakably a field of corn, the silken gold of their tassels shifting lazily in the salty breeze.

"What's left for the rest of us to do?" Fred asked as they all stared out at the sprawling paradise.

"Plenty," Gerth replied. "The skeleton is complete, but we can't survive on beauty alone. We're going to need to actually be able to produce everything we need to survive. I'm guessing the Celestial's magic didn't account for things like furniture and plumbing. That part is going to be up to all of us."

"Now you're talkin' my language," Fred said, mollified. He patted the tool belt strapped around his waist. "Let's get to work."

* * *

ERIKIR

Several hours later, Erikir and Olivia found themselves standing on the castle's highest balcony. They were surrounded by Tol, Addy, and Erikir's aunt and uncle. All of the Chosen and Forsaken stood on the lawn before them, their faces tilted up toward them. Given that the general had been turned over to the Celestial for judgment, Addy and Tol had already been appointed as the Forsaken leaders.

Erikir was now filled with a rush of anticipation and nerves as his aunt and uncle officially abdicated the throne. It was all ceremonial at this point, but the Chosen had expected a formal announcement. So, here they were.

As Erikir's uncle placed the king's crown on his head, and his aunt gave Olivia the queen's, cheers erupted from down below.

"Forever live King Erikir!" the Chosen shouted. "Forever live Queen Olivia!"

THE CHOSEN UNION

Erikir turned to look at Olivia. The gold of her crown sparkled as it caught the light from her Haze. She looked every bit the queen who had rescued their race and restored their world.

Her brown eyes softened as she read his thoughts.

She took his hand. A breeze swirled around them, carrying with it the scent of the sea.

A thought whispered through Erikir's mind. He didn't know if it had come from him, Olivia, or some spirit on the wind. Whatever its source, the truth of those words nestled against his heart.

Home, the voice whispered. *You are home.*

They looked out over the balcony. Together, they faced their people and a future that held the promise of forever.

CHAPTER 42

ADDY

Everyone began to head toward the new switchback path that led up the cliff for the blood marriage feast.

"Not us," Tol said into her ear when she started to follow Livy and Erikir.

When Addy raised an eyebrow in question, Tol explained, "I'm taking you on our first date."

"Speaking of first dates," Fred said, elbowing Nira. "I seem to recall you saying you'd go out with me if I lived."

"I don't remember that," Nira replied haughtily. "You must be confused."

"No, no." Fred held up a hand. "You said somethin' about wearin' a bikini."

Nira gave him a freezing look. "You were in hypovolemic shock. You must have been hallucinating."

Fred gave her a broad grin. "We could take it easy for starters. Go for a hike, or somethin'."

Nira gave him a horrified look. "*As if.*"

The two of them wandered off, still arguing.

Gerth clapped his hands together and announced, "Addy and Tol, your chariot awaits."

Addy looked in the direction he was pointing. A surprised laugh escaped her. There, in a new river bordered by flowering trees, a gondola-style boat was waiting for them.

Tol turned to Addy and offered her his hand. "Will you do me the great pleasure of joining me?"

Addy laughed. "You're kidding, right?" She glanced at the boat and then back at him.

"Not in the least." Tol waited with confident patience for Addy to take his outstretched hand.

It took only another second before she threaded her fingers through his.

"You know I could have just portaled us to wherever we're going, right?" Addy asked.

"No way." Tol gave her a wink that made her weak at the knees. "This is our first date, and I'm doing it right."

"You sure it's okay if we leave?" Addy asked Livy.

"Of course." Livy kissed her on the cheek. "Have a good first date."

"Wonder if he's any good at kissing," Addy mused, tapping her chin and squinting at Tol in consideration.

"Let's find out, shall we?" Tol grabbed her, dipped her over his arm, and lowered his mouth to hers.

Whoops and catcalls erupted from their friends. Tol didn't let Addy recover before he lifted her into his arms and carried her down the hill toward the river.

He put her down on the bank, where they both pulled off their shoes to feel the pure white sand beneath their feet. Tol turned toward the boat, but Addy held him back.

She clasped his hand as realization crashed over her.

"Tol, we did it."

His brow furrowed in confusion. "Defeated the Supernal and saved our people, you mean?"

She shook her head.

"We found a way to be together."

Tol's expression softened as he pulled her against him.

She laughed a little. "All it took was trading in our immortality and almost annihilating two worlds."

Addy reached up to nuzzle the side of his neck. She breathed in his spicy, masculine smell.

"A small price to pay," he murmured against her cheek, "for a lifetime with you."

She drew back to look into his dark eyes. He tucked her hair behind her ear as they stared at each other. Then, Tol kissed her.

He wrapped both of his arms around her until they were close enough to feel each other's heartbeats.

"I love you," she gasped, overwhelmed by the rush of sensation. "My Tol."

He looked down at her.

"Adelyne Deerborn." His voice was rough and his eyes so full of love it stole her breath away. "This is my chosen union."

She almost choked on her emotion at the way he said those words. She felt their echo in her bones as she reached up to twine her hands around his neck.

"Tolumus Magnantius," she said, "this is my chosen union."

They sealed their promise not with blood, but with a kiss.

THE END

* * *

Because reviews are so important for a book to be successful, please consider leaving a brief review on your favorite retailer if you enjoyed *The Chosen Union*. Many thanks!

※ ※ ※

Sign up for Stephanie Fazio's e-Newsletter to learn about upcoming books at:
https://StephanieFazio.com/subscribe/

Acknowledgements

This series was so much fun to write, and I'm sad that it's over (for now, at least)! Thank you to all of the amazing people on my team who helped bring this series together.

To my editor, Ellen Schaeffer. Thank you for your attention to detail and wonderful suggestions!

To Keith Tarrier, for making such incredibly beautiful covers. Thank you also to Bob Brodsky, Rhoda Schneider, and the rest of my ARC team. Your advice, support, and encouragement are invaluable.

To Mom and Dad, for your endless support and advice. Thanks for always believing in me.

Thanks to Two Steps From Hell and Thomas Bergersen for your fantastic music. This book would never have been finished without you.

To my incredible readers. Thanks for making what I do matter!

And to Andrew. For being my Chosen one.

About the Author:

Stephanie Fazio is a fantasy author. She grew up in Syracuse, New York, and prior to writing full time, she worked in the fields of journalism, secondary education, and higher education. She has an undergraduate degree in English from Colgate University and a Master's degree in Reading, Writing, and Literacy from the University of Pennsylvania. Stephanie lives in Austin with her husband and crazy rescue dog. When she isn't writing, she's getting lost in parks, hosting taco nights, or ironically and miserably losing at word games, but having fun while she does it.

Connect with Stephanie Fazio:

Visit her Website: https://www.StephanieFazio.com
Sign up for her newsletter: https://StephanieFazio.com/subscribe/

Stephanie Fazio's New Series

Book 1, *Opal Smoke*
AVAILABLE JUNE 2020!

StephanieFazio.com

Discover other books by Stephanie Fazio

Bisecter Series

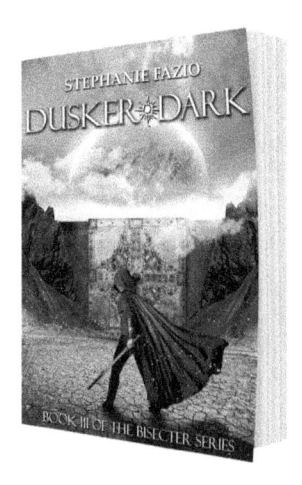

StephanieFazio.com